ABSOLUTE
KNOWLEDGE

DREW CORDELL

To Liz, thank you for your unwavering love and support.

Acknowledgements

Thank you to my fellow authors (Jenna Whittaker, P.J. Benney, and Matt Reese) for all the helpful insight and constructive criticism of my work during the beta reading phase. Without your help, Absolute Knowledge wouldn't be what it is today. I'm also very thankful for my Kickstarter supporters that helped bring this book to life. Thanks to you, I have the opportunity to share this story with the world.

Paragon Thinkers
Andy and Susan Cordell, Elizabeth Howard, Mandy Mowery, Susan Mowery, and Remi Nadeau.

Print Ultra backers
Jeff Armstrong, Chad Bowden, Wayne and Roberta Cordell, Kylee Davidson, Michael and Brian Goubeaux, Patty LeBlanc, Patrick Mamer, Chris W. Miller, Zen Phony, Beverly Sanders, Jenna Ward, Joshua Williams, and Charles and Mary Yates.

How many thoughts do humans have each day? If you're not a Prolific, the answer is fifty to seventy-five thousand. How many of those thoughts have value? All of them.

1
THOUGHTS

"Jacob Ashton," the woman in the suit called out at the front of the lobby. I gained my feet and gave her a nervous smile which she returned with cold disinterest. She was tall and slender, and her graying hair was pulled back in a neat bun. "If you'll please follow me to the back."

I walked across the grime-coated linoleum flooring as I followed the assistant to the exam room located behind a reinforced steel door. There were others in the lobby, waiting for their exams. Some of them, mostly the young like myself, had that nervous spark of hope, while the veterans sat with something that more or less resembled a disheartened sense of duty. The other people waiting in the lobby faded away as I walked. My heart pounded in my chest as I prepared for my three-year evaluation, the evaluation which could decide my future for the rest of my life.

"Any health problems we should know?" she asked in a flat voice.

"No, ma'am."

"Very well, if you'll have a seat in the chair we will get started," she said as she pointed to a cushioned red chair.

The woman's heels clacked against the surface of the floor, and I took a seat in the chair. I breathed deeply and tried to collect myself, though I knew the jittery nerves wouldn't affect my performance.

I heard that this wasn't going to be like a typical thought collection session, but rather a system presenting challenges for my brain to solve, problems I wouldn't remember when waking up.

The restraints on the chair latched around my arms and legs, and I tried to keep my breathing calm.

"Just relax please, Jacob," the woman said as she rubbed an icy alcohol wipe on my forearm, the strong scent flooding my nose and bringing about more anxiety.

"Will this hurt?" I asked, already knowing the answer.

The woman gave a sigh, indicating she'd responded to the same question many times. "Yes, it will, but only for a second."

She slid a long IV needle into a large vein in my arm, and I winced. There was a cold sting as the fluids trickled into me.

"Your session will take about four hours, and you'll be paid for your time regardless of whether we select you for a unique Government position," she said as she put the headgear with the neuro pads on my head.

"Breathe deeply for me, Jacob," the woman said as she injected a blue fluid into the IV bag that hung above the chair. The color trickled down the tubing and connected with my arm. I breathed in several deep breaths as I felt my head spin and vision go white.

I awoke with the impossible feeling of weightlessness and weighing a ton. Worse, balancing my head proved difficult and my limbs felt like rubber. The IV tube was coiled and replaced back in its position on the bag, and my arm was bandaged, but the chair still bound my arms. The woman walked over and flashed a small light into my eyes, her voice sounded distant and faded in and out as I tried to focus on the light.

"How did I do?" I asked.

"The system is still evaluating your performance. There were a few... anomalies," she said, apparently choosing the word with care.

"Is everything okay?"

"Yes. We just need to see if something malfunctioned in the system. Nothing to be concerned about. If anything, it will be good news for you. Do you remember anything from the test?"

The strange thing was that I was actively processing information in my head during the session. I remembered the problems I was solving. They made little sense in a logical way, but I remembered the strange, distinct geometric shapes and patterns of light and color.

"Lights, shapes, and colors," I responded as I fought to remember the distant events through the haze.

"Probably a dream or the side effects of the IV serum," she answered. "You're free to go now, Jacob. We will contact you if you are of interest to us." She unfastened the restraints, and I started back toward the lobby.

"Please collect your payment and vouchers from the desk."

I returned to the reception desk and waited behind a few other Thinkers before it was my turn. As I walked up to the desk, a re-purposed Enforcer robot confirmed my identity with a retina scan before handing me a summary sheet of the session, and a week's worth of drinking water and food vouchers.

Name: Jacob Ashton
Age: 16
Test: Tri-Annual Aptitude Evaluation
Session Length: 04:00:00
Thoughts: NA
Thought Originality: NA
Aptitude Assessment: NA
Base Value: 600 Credits
Originality Bonus: NA
Tax: 192 Credits
Total Payment: 408 Credits

I exited the Government building and walked forward on the dark street. A tattered bandana wrapped around my face shielded me from the wretched smog that stagnated down in the Slums of New York, the synthetic cloth providing suitable protection for short excursions. It had been worse so I couldn't complain. I wanted to get the hell out of the Slums, like everyone else. A partially corroded vent on the filthy asphalt groaned then shot a blast of scalding steam up toward me. My old sneakers protected my feet as I jumped off with drowsy reflexes. Despite knowing these streets quite well, one could never predict the sporadic pattern of the vile vents coming from below the ground, and the aftereffects of my session still weighed me down.

New York was built skyward; the history lessons I had learned taught me that there was once only one level. Now, New York consisted of four levels if you count the Undercity which housed most of the utility plants and farms.

Neon signs illuminated the hazy air and advertised their goods and services. On each sign hung a camera that looked onto the street. I kept my hood over my head as I walked through the Slums—I found it better to go unnoticed.

For the past three years, I had been on my own. I had my own flat, paid my own bills, and worked my own hours. There weren't many employment options, so I did what most others did, I worked as a Thinker. In other words, I sat in a chair for four hours every day with electrodes and neuro collectors attached to my head. Working as a Thinker was the best way to earn a living within the confines of the law.

The Thought Collectors stored all thoughts as data for the Collective Thought. Absolute Knowledge was the end goal, the goal considered to be perfection. The Government promised that everyone would be well off, never having to work again once they completed the project.

As I walked, I looked at the faded posters as I always did, the relics of a grand purpose.

'Your thoughts are valuable!'
'Only you can help us achieve Absolute Knowledge!'
'You are special!'

The faded red ink looked dull compared to the bright colors on the posters. Children sat reading books on verdant green grass, others were climbing trees. There weren't any trees in the Slums anymore. One of my neighbors, Mr. Barton, used to have a tree in his house, a ficus he had called it. It must have cost him a considerable sum of money, but he said it was well worth it. Mr. Barton swore it made the air in his flat fresher, but I couldn't tell. The air filters took care of most of the smog anyway.

After I paid my bills, and I had eaten, I would put all of my remaining money toward educational lessons to improve my thought output and quality. The Government promised more pay for those who purchased an education. Education was the key to Absolute Knowledge they said. The digital lessons weren't cheap, and Mr. Barton used to berate me for spending everything extra on them.

"You won't earn more. Believe me, I used to spend everything on education, trying to get out of the Slums. The payments never increased. Once you are born in the Slums, you don't leave the Slums," Mr. Barton had told me.

I walked to the nearest grocery store, a large building denoted by neon green lights and an increased presence of Enforcers. All the grocery stores had large gates and were lined with Government issue linoleum flooring. I grabbed a plastic cart from one of the stands at the entrance, the dull green material having faded long ago. Despite the hour and assuming it was before curfew, the grocery stores were almost always crowded. City run stores were split into two sections, vouchers, and credits. The voucher section contained basic and cheap goods such as bread, canned soups, and frozen meat. The credit section was much more expansive, but the prices were high—something I wanted to avoid to get out of the Slums.

Many people were browsing the closely watched aisles of goods, congregating and discussing the rumors of the streets. An Enforcer walked up to a group of young men that stood huddled around in a tight cluster, unmoving for several minutes. Most of the Enforcers in the Slums were the older models deployed in the riots that took place when I was around four years old. They were bulky things with heavy, geometric plate armor, hydraulic servos, and large energy rifles that were welded to their arm. They were painted matte black, and the Enforcers that worked outside were often coated in a layer of rust. They had a single lens system on their heads that gave them vision.

The Enforcer gave a gruff beep, indicating that the group of men needed to stop loitering then took a series of aggressive steps forward until they moved. The people in the group complained and protested their innocence as they continued to shop.

Not wanting to attract trouble, I grabbed the necessities; a loaf of bread, a few cans of soup and vegetables, and one luxury item: a pack of mint chewing gum. The pack of gum wouldn't be covered by my vouchers, but also wouldn't cost me too much. Chewing gum was a far cheaper vice than smoking cigarettes, something many people in the Slums did. I approached the automated console and bagged my groceries in a brown paper bag and inserted the voucher and twelve credits for the pack of gum. The light above the exit gate turned green, and I was free to go. The Enforcers guarding the door scanned my bag as I exited the store.

I popped a piece of the mint gum into my mouth and chewed slowly after walking out of the store, the tingling sensation flooding into my mouth. I raised the frayed bandana back over my face and moved at a brisk pace, heading home. The artificial lights of the ceiling faded, and the smaller streetlights crackled to life, their light pale and dull. I looked at the scratched up mechanical watch on my wrist, it was already 8 PM.

The door of my flat scanned my retina and opened with a click. I walked in and closed the door as fast as possible, preserving my fresh air. I put my drinking water jug under the Government owned water pump. The machine quickly consumed my water voucher and dispensed one gallon of drinking water.

Some people in the Slums filtered their own water so they could trade their water vouchers for other things, but the salt water from the tap wasn't safe for drinking, and I didn't trust their filtration process. That was a good way to get sick or worse.

I would wait awhile to eat. Not only did I want to savor the piece of gum for as long as possible, but I also was still feeling sick from my testing session.

A sharp spike of pain jolted through my head, and I collapsed to the cold floor of my flat. Geometric patterns flashed in my vision as I closed my eyes. The image of my surroundings had burned into my eyes, and I still saw everything when they were closed. Colors danced around the gray flooring and sent waves of pain jolting through my head. I tried to scream but couldn't. I heard my TV power on and opened my eyes to see a flickering screen. There were words on it, blurred by my distorted vision and the splitting pain reverberating in my skull, a single sentence.

'You've got my attention now, Jacob.'

2
BREAK

After a few minutes, everything stopped, and I felt fine again. I didn't understand what the hell had just happened, but it terrified me that memories of the aptitude testing lingered when everyone I knew said I shouldn't remember a thing. I regained my feet and shrugged the event off thinking it might just be a side effect of the strange IV fluid. My TV was off, and it was probable that I had imagined the words on the screen.

Deciding it couldn't hurt, I started getting out the supplies to make a cup of tea when I was finished with the soup. After I had microwaved the mug of drinking water, I added the tea pouch to the water and stirred. Mr. Barton told me they used to sell many different teas from other countries in a wide variety of flavors and colorful packaging. I didn't know if I believed it or not—

everything was made in New York; the only country in a vast and empty world.

I sat down on my bed and turned on the TV; disappointed to see regular programming. News channels reported on the progress of Absolute Knowledge, promoting visits to local Collection Parlors. There were two movies on as well, also focused on the importance of Absolute Knowledge.

I finished the cup of tea and turned off the TV—there was no need to use electricity on things I had already seen. I grabbed a worn-down textbook from the shelf. 'Calculus,' it said on the cover. The math on the inside was above my knowledge level, but I liked to read it anyway. The book was interesting enough to keep me occupied while I waited for curfew and for my door to lock.

Enforcers were notoriously ruthless at night, and they weren't the only danger, so I never stayed out past curfew. I set the book down on my desk and climbed into bed, knowing I should try to sleep. I hoped I would see Mary Dunn tomorrow, the cute girl that lived a few flats down from me. She was also sixteen and had long brown hair, and beautiful blue eyes. The excitement of the day and thoughts of Mary made sleep difficult, but it came eventually.

The alarm clock next to my bed buzzed and woke me from a deep slumber. 8 AM. I grabbed a small plastic cup from the kitchen and put a splash of drinking water in it, enough to brush my teeth with. I walked into the bathroom and dug through the cardboard box marked 'Hygiene.' As long as I completed at least one session a week, I got a box full of hygiene stuff for free. Otherwise, I'd have to buy it from the store.

Brushing my teeth, I looked into the mirror. I wasn't too skinny and had developed some muscle by doing some routines in my flat. My father would be shocked at how much I looked like him. I had his deep green eyes, defined jaw line, and medium-length brown hair. After appraising my appearance, I applied a generous coat of deodorant.

I walked over to Mr. Barton's flat. He saw me coming and opened the door expecting me for our morning tradition.

Edgar Barton was in his thirties and rather tall and well-built compared to others his age. He was holding an old paperback novel, and kept his thumb pressed on the page as he let me in.

"Morning Mr. Barton," I said.

"Good morning Jake, I put the coffee on."

That was one of the many things I loved about being friends with Edgar Barton, he always shared his coffee.

Mr. Barton closed the door behind him and sat down at the table, returning to his book. 'A Tale of Two Cities,' it said on the worn spine. Most of his books were contraband and illegal. I stopped asking to read them a couple years ago. Mr. Barton had told me I couldn't read them because I was a Thinker. He said that if I read them, I would be sent to the Sculptors. He was a teacher, teaching some of the digital educational classes for a monthly paycheck. It wasn't enough to get him out of the Slums, but it was sufficient to keep him from having to visit a Collection Parlor.

"How was your aptitude test?" he asked me as he continued to read the frayed book.

"I don't know. The operator told me there were anomalies and that they'd get in touch with me when they figured them out."

He looked up from the text and raised an eyebrow, "do you remember anything from your test?"

"Some shapes and patterns, they mean nothing to me, but I saw them again last night when I got home to my flat."

"I'm sure it was just the side effects of the IV," he said as he dismissed the idea. "Keep me updated if you hear anything else." He looked back down and continued reading his book.

"Good book?"

"Mmhmm."

"What's it about?"

That caught his attention, and he once again looked up and shook his head.

"Must be about two cities," I said. He knew I had no intention to find out—he had scared that idea out of me long ago. I always wondered what was in those books, though—the ancient manuscripts from a different time.

Edgar set down the book and poured two large mugs of coffee. He brought them to the table and handed me one. Some people put cream and sugar in their coffee, but that was an expensive practice that neither of us cared for. Edgar and I drank it black—it was better that way.

"What do you have going on today?" he asked me as he took a scalding sip of coffee.

"I'll probably do another session, then hopefully spend some time with Mary." I cursed myself for mentioning it. Edgar liked to capitalize on every opportunity he could to mess with me, such is the way with friends.

"Mary you say?" he asked, a sly smile forming on his face. I could tell that I was in for it.

"Yeah," I conceded. "You know how I feel about her."

I sipped at my coffee and looked down. I was eager to change the subject. Both Edgar and I knew how much of a crush I had on Mary.

"Just tell her how you feel, you're never going to get anywhere if you don't say anything," he said.

"I promise I'll mess something up. I'll be awkward or say something wrong then Mary will never want to talk to me again," I was eager to change the subject, but couldn't leave his suggestion unanswered.

"Hmmm. You do have a tendency to act awkward," he considered, flashing me a grin. "I'll make things easy and tell her how you feel for you!" he proclaimed with a dark smile.

"Anyway, I've been reading that Calculus book you lent me. It's a lot more complex than the algebraic ones. Could you help me learn derivatives sometime?" I asked, desperate to escape the hole I dug.

"Sure, Jake," he said with a laugh as he backed off about Mary.

"I want to get out of the Slums and live in a high-rise apartment in the Mids or Upper Level one day."

"Well, come up with a Paragon Thought, and you'd be set for life."

"If only," I replied. There were only twelve Paragon Thoughts in over one hundred years, probably all discovered by the Prolific.

"Or just steal an airship and fly up to the Mids yourself."

"Even if I knew where to find an airship, I wouldn't be able to fly it. And the only ones I've ever seen were Enforcer Dropships. You and I both know that people that get taken away on those don't come back," I said.

He grinned. "Maybe they are just getting a free ride to the Upper Level. Living it up in a high-rise apartment."

I returned the smile. "Maybe so."

"Well, it looks like your only choice is to create a Paragon Thought then."

"Yeah, maybe one day. I bet you have one in your head, Mr. Barton."

"Actually, my mind is filled with poison. If the Government found out what I knew, well... Let's just say no amount of sculpting could repair my mind. I know too much I'm not supposed to. Too much that should be known by a... Sorry, I shouldn't press my views or criminal activity on you."

It was so strange. Mr. Barton was one of the worst criminals known to society, yet he was also one of my best friends. He stayed inside reading books and drinking coffee while actual criminals wandered the streets selling illegal drugs, stealing, and worse yet, in the eyes of the law, he was considered treasonous. Was there something wrong with this? I was thinking about it more than I should have.

Snapping out of my thoughts, I finished drinking my coffee. "I'll see you later Mr. Barton, I'm going to try to meet up with Mary."

"Good luck, kid," he said with a smile. "Just tell her how you feel. The definition of insanity is doing the same thing over and over and expecting different results."

"I'm not insane, I'm just playing it safe."

"Playing it safe and three years of bottling up feelings are two very different things. Anyway, I wish you the best of luck Mr. Ashton."

"You do have a point, I promise I'm working on it," I said.

I thanked him for the coffee and walked outside. The air burned, and it would only get worse. If I were lucky, I'd be able to hang out with Mary inside. I ran across the street to her flat and knocked. She opened the door and motioned for me to come inside. I hustled in, and she sealed the door behind me. Aside from a few cosmetic differences, our flats were identical—all the flats in this district were. I turned to Mary and smiled as I pulled off my bandana.

"Hey, Jake," she said with that smile that sent my heart racing.

"Hey, how's it going?"

"The usual." Mary started walking over to the couch then jolted back, as if remembering something.

"Hey, I made something for you. Come to the table," she said, jumping in excitement.

She skipped to the table, and we sat down. Mary grabbed a manila envelope and passed it to me. I looked over at her, and she was smiling, which only made me more anxious.

I opened the worn envelope and pulled out the folded paper. This wasn't cheap fibrous paper, this was white paper, the type the upper class used. The cost of the paper alone made me even more anxious, and I looked up at her with concern.

"Mary... This paper is expensive."

"Look, Jake. You've been a great friend, and I wanted to make something for you. It's a gift. And I got a good deal on the paper. Bought it off of one of those traveling merchants. Go on! Open it up."

With hesitation, I unfolded the paper and opened a drawing of me. It was incredibly realistic. Mary had rendered me using charcoal and various colored pencils, the most precious and expensive of her art supplies. She had even signed her name with real ink in her beautiful ornamented form, and there was a small heart next to her signature which I knew I would spend hours trying to interpret.

"Mary... I don't know what to say. This is incredible," I said as I looked up at her, blushing.

"You like it?" she asked, her voice timid.

"I love it. I'll hang it above my bed," I said.

She leaned in to hug me and my heart kicked rapidly. When she pulled back, I'm sure my face was red.

"I forgot to ask you! How was your aptitude testing?"

"Still waiting to hear, they think there was some equipment malfunction," I replied. I didn't want her to think I was crazy for seeing shapes and a message on my TV. I refolded the paper with care and returned it to the envelope.

"What's the plan for today?" she asked.

"I was going to do a session since I'm close to buying my next education lesson. What about you?"

"I was just going to draw, maybe go shopping later. How do you afford all these lessons?"

"I never use the pill."

"Jake... that must be excruciating. I've seen people get messed up from that."

"I've been doing it for three years, the extra pay is worth it. I get a lot more credits without the pill," I said, surprised I hadn't told her before. The tiny pill cost about a fifth of the earnings from a typical session.

"I'm glad we don't go to Collection together; I couldn't stand to see you in that kind of pain," she said with a frown.

"It's only temporary, once the connection is established it's painless."

She shrugged. "I guess, but I wouldn't be willing to go through that."

I pulled out the pack of mint gum from my pocket, pulling out a piece and offering it to Mary.

"You sure, Jake?"

"Of course, I am."

She took the piece and chewed. I popped a piece into my mouth, embracing the flavor of the *Gods*. My mind was filled with incorrect terms. The Collectors didn't care about incorrect thought. Few incorrect thoughts were treasonous, and the thoughts that were treasonous were only a liability if the Thinker knew what they meant. I only knew one treasonous word: *Democracy*, and I was very thankful that I didn't know what the word meant. A boy in my class a few years ago had spoken it, and after that, he had simply disappeared. Rumors went around that the Sculptors got him. There was a very real temptation to bring up the word with Mr. Barton, but I thought better of it.

"This is where the rest of my credits go," I said, laughing.

"At least you don't smoke. As if we need more noxious fumes down here. I'm just glad the filters take care of the smog."

Mary and I continued to talk for a while, and I watched her start a new sketch. She usually didn't like it when I looked over her shoulder when she was drawing, but she didn't seem to mind as much, apparently growing more comfortable around me.

"How about a game of Shift?" I asked.

Mary smiled then reached behind her tin of pencils and pulled out the ragged deck of Crown playing cards. It was by luck that Mary had come by a physical deck of playing cards, and by even more luck she had been able to purchase it for so cheap. The traveling merchant that sold it to her tried to sell it for five hundred credits, a fair price for the condition and rarity of the item. Mary had looked through the deck and counted only fifty-three cards. One was missing, which reduced the value to two hundred credits—a day's worth of thinking, but not out of reach for someone in the Slums. While the cards were somewhat frayed on the edges, the plastic coating on the cards gave them a satisfying amount of slip when held, a drastic improvement over a homemade cardboard set, plus they were a collector's item, likely at least one hundred years old.

We had eagerly been looking for another four of hearts to replace the lost card but settled on using one of the two jokers as a substitute. Unfortunately, the merchant didn't have or know any rules for games to play with the deck and that wasn't knowledge available to the public through the New York Internet System available in every residence. Because of this, we had made up our own game, one we played on a regular basis.

Shift was fun—and much better than the limited gaming options offered on our personal computers. To make things even better, we would throw in friendly wagers, placing a bet of a credit per hand. Mary was a lot better than me at cards, and I lost more money than I ever won, but spending time with her more than made up for the loss.

"I'll deal," she said.

I gave her a suspicious look. There were no doubts about the fairness of her dealing, I just liked to blame her for stacking the deck when dealt a garbage hand.

"Fair enough, but I'm watching you," I said with a smile.

She returned the smile and dealt each of us seven cards. Mary laid down a three of diamonds and passed the turn. I smirked and laid down my three of clubs and took her three. The vision of victory was within reach. She pouted and drew an extra card. She managed to win with a strong combo and took my credit with satisfaction, outplaying my moment of greatness.

"You're lucky we play with such a low buy-in, you'd be broke otherwise," she said. It was a playful jab, but I had to take the bait.

"It's one loss, let's play another. Five credits." My pride was at stake now. I lost three more hands in a row, ask to deal, then lost two more.

Mary tried not to laugh and eventually failed after my ninth consecutive loss, but I found it impossible to be angry at her.

"Well, it looks like I'm going shopping with you and you're buying us lunch with your new fortune," I said.

"Agreed," she said, happy with the arrangement.

Mary pulled on a light jacket and zipped it up. After tying an orange bandana around her mouth, she was ready to go. I put my bandana on and pulled my hood over my head. The next moment we were out on the streets moving toward the shopping center.

Although it was early in the morning, the smog from the Undercity was already thickening in the air. The large lights at the top of the Slums illuminated the otherwise dark street. People were walking around, and the streets were bustling with activity. It was hard to believe that some people lived outside at all times. The Slums were crowded, but anyone with a decent stream of thought should have been able to afford a standard flat and utilities. People that lived outside distinguished themselves with a thick cough and pale skin that had a slight yellow hue as if stained by the air.

Mary and I continued along the road, and it wasn't long before we came up to a large man wearing a huge backpack with various goods tied to the back. He was dressed in a light jacket and wore an electronic respirator mouthpiece. The emblem on his jacket identified him as a merchant from the Scavenger Guild, the largest legal organization of traveling merchants.

Traveling merchants didn't wander the Mids or Upper Level of New York, they were exclusive to the Slums and searched far and wide for new wares to peddle across the large districts. Supposedly, they had people combing through the garbage from the upper levels to find valuables to resell to the public.

I could see Mary's eyes light up as she saw him. We approached, and he waved at us.

"Care to browse my wares?" he asked in a distorted voice through the mouthpiece.

"Please," Mary said.

Carefully, the man unfolded a small square of blue tarp and set it down on the concrete curb. He took off his pack and placed it on the worn surface. He grabbed a small cylinder from one of the outside pockets and motioned us closer. We both stepped forward, and he placed it on the ground, pressing a large button on the top.

The canister made a sharp hissing sound and formed a thin barrier of energy between the three of us and the outside air. A second later the canister emitted a spray of gas and purged the smog from the air inside the bubble. We removed our bandanas, and he removed the respirator.

"I don't like my customers having to breathe smog while they browse my goods and I'm not going to breathe it myself," he grimaced. "What can I interest you in this morning?"

"Just browsing, what have you got?" Mary asked.

"Really depends on what you're looking for. I've got a lot of utility gadgets, some clothing, some books, collectibles, spices, trinkets, you name it."

"What do you have book wise?" This brought about an eye roll from Mary. She always joked about how much time I spent buried in books. After making the comparison that she spent just as much time with her artwork, she concluded that it was fair, but asserted that the difference was that she was creating something new, while I was merely absorbing something old.

He pulled out an assortment of books from his pack and handed them to me. Most were just standard literature available in the bookstore south of my flat, but there was one title that stuck out from the rest: 'An Essay Concerning Human Understanding,' The print on the cover was barely visible, and the author's name was missing. The pages of the book were mottled and yellow, but the ink of the text was dark enough. I flipped through it quickly and looked up at the man. Perhaps Mr. Barton would find it as interesting as I did.

"Have you read this yet?" I asked.

"Haven't had time. This book is meant for you, though. I'll give it to you for free if you buy something else," he said as he dug in his pack for more things for Mary. Merchants weren't known to give anything away for free, it was bizarre, but I decided to take him up on the offer anyway.

Mary ended up buying a blue rubber ball, a candle that smelled like vanilla, and a steel ruler with visible markings. I purchased a circular magnet, and a length of parachute cord and took the free book. Overall, it cost me seventy-three credits—not a bad deal at all. I took my extra bandana from my pack and wrapped up the book before putting it in the bottom of my bag. Mary put her belongings in her backpack, and we both thanked the merchant and replaced our bandanas on our faces before he turned off the canister.

There was no planning to shop with a traveling merchant, they came and went unexpectedly, but I'd found it was always worth browsing their wares if there was the opportunity. Mary and I continued toward the shopping center and entered the open door of the building. There was a thin barrier of energy that maintained a pressure gradient which kept the clean air in and the bad air out.

"What are you looking for?" I asked her.

"Just more tea, maybe another packet of paper for art, that sort of thing."

I nodded and followed her around. A group of Enforcers were questioning an elderly man wearing a battered coat—he was clinging to a can of soup. Mary and I moved closer to listen.

"I just need one can to get through the day, they won't let me do Collection this week," he said.

"Merchandise is not to leave the store without full payment," an Enforcer retorted.

"How am I supposed to pay if I can't work?" he demanded, tears in his eyes.

"Not our problem. Relinquish the canned good, citizen."

If he couldn't work as a Thinker, that meant he was already an Exile or in danger of becoming one. If a citizen's thoughts weren't beneficial toward the project, then they couldn't work. After that, it was only a matter of time until they succumbed to death from starvation or exposure to the outside elements once they had been evicted. With limited resources, few people volunteered to take the Exiles into their homes, and they were more or less always doomed.

"I have to eat," the man said, his voice weak. Tears rolled down his haggard face.

It broke my heart, and I swore I'd always work to improve my thinking so this would never happen to me. I couldn't always help the Exiles, but I could help this man.

"Excuse me," I said to the group of Enforcers and the man. They all turned to me as I walked over.

I pulled a twenty credit piece out of my wallet.

"I'll pay for his soup, a loaf of bread, and some drinking water," I said, handing the credit chip to the man.

His eyes welled up in tears again. "*Bless* you, son," he said, grabbing my arm with both hands and shaking it, giving me a gracious smile.

An Enforcer gave him a shove on the chest and he staggered back, almost losing his footing. "Watch your language and don't loiter. Don't even think about stepping into the credit section of the store," the Enforcer said to him.

The man gave a weak nod to the Enforcer then walked over to pick up some bread and water before getting in line to pay.

"That's nice what you did there. I hate seeing Exiles, it's heartbreaking," Mary said as we walked away.

"I can't always help, but I like to when I can. That man was in for a beating if I hadn't stepped in."

"Yeah, that wouldn't have been good. You're sweet, Jake."

I smiled at her and grabbed a few things of my own as she added a box of tea to her basket. I hadn't done it to impress her, and I knew she would have done the same if I hadn't stepped forward.

After paying, we exited the store with plans to grab some lunch. While Mary was putting on her backpack, a hooded man sprinted past and snagged the bag, taking it and pulling it close to his chest while maintaining his quick momentum. Mary stood motionless and stunned.

"Stay here!" I yelled at her as I took off after him, my sneakers struggling for purchase on the slick pavement.

The man was quick, but so was I. We barreled down the street at breakneck speed, diving to the left and right to avoid the people which jumped back in surprise and yelled after us. I looked back to see three large robots chasing us with their lights flashing. This was now Government business.

I kept up my high speed, trying to limit my breathing. Even with the bandana, I was taking in large quantities of toxic air due to my physical exertion. As I continued to chase the man, I could no longer limit myself and took large, full breaths. I'd be damned if I let him take Mary's belongings.

I was gaining on the man now. He looked back for a split second, lost momentum, and flinched when I dove forward and tackled him to the ground. Without a second of hesitation, I reached back and punched him square in the face. The hit drove him to the ground, and I was able to reclaim Mary's pack. He was gaunt, and the yellow tint of his skin identified him as an Exile. The man wore an expression that was a combination of shock, anger, and fear.

"Do not move, citizens!" a metallic voice commanded from behind me. I lowered the pack to the ground and raised my arms in the air. The Enforcers were here. I looked back and felt a strong blow on the side of my neck—the hooded man had dared to punch me in the presence of Enforcers. Taken by surprise, I fell to the ground hard and raised my hands to protect my head.

Almost instantly an Enforcer was standing over the man and lifted him to his feet with an iron grasp. A flood of relief washed over me until I was lifted the same way, feeling an enormous force squeezing my wrist. Startled, I tried to explain the situation but was cut off by the third Enforcer. My bandana was torn from my face and my identity was confirmed.

"Citizens Jacob Ashton and Lewis Gale, you are both charged and found guilty of one count of public disturbance, one count of theft, and one count of public violence."

"He sto…" I started to defend myself but was cut off by the unwavering Enforcer.

"For punishment for your crimes, you will each lose functionality of the hand used to strike the other citizen. The break of the wrist will be clean, and medication for pain will not be provided."

The Enforcer holding the hooded man pulled his arm to the side and chopped down on his wrist with incredible swiftness. There was a wretched snapping sound as the man's wrist broke with cruel precision. The man's hand flopped down at a terrible angle, and he cried out in pain. The Enforcer released him, and he fell to his knees holding his arm close to his chest, tears cascading down his face. Panic was beginning to take over my body, but it was no use struggling against the hydraulic pumps which gave the Enforcers unmatchable strength.

"The break was clean," the Enforcer reported to the one in charge after scanning the man's wrist.

"He stole from me! I did nothing wrong!" I yelled at the calculating lead Enforcer. It was no use. There was no reasoning with the Enforcers, they were ruthless robots run by millions of lines of code. The Enforcer that was holding me pulled my arm to the side, and I fought back tears. Panic had all but blanketed me into a state of disbelief, was this really about to happen?

There was an incredible crackling that I felt deep within my arm. Pain splintered up my arm and through my body in waves, and I looked over to see my hand flopped over backward, the skin around my broken wrist already turning to a sickly purple. Still in shock, I stared at my wrist dumbfounded. What had I done wrong? Suddenly, the grip on me released and the three Enforcers were standing over us. They scanned my wrist.

"Sir, this break wasn't clean, I'm seeing compound fractures," the Enforcer said.

"No matter, we're done here," the leader said to the other.

"The consequences of your crimes are completed," the lead Enforcer said. The flashing lights on the Enforcers turned off, and they walked away.

Mary ran up to the scene and raised her hands to her mouth when she saw my wrist. It must have looked horrible. Looking up at her, I felt the full force of the pain and vomited all over the street. After that everything went dark.

3
FRIENDS

My eyes slowly peeled open, and I was unsure where I was. It looked like my flat, but then again, so did every flat in the district. Thick goop blurred my vision, and I tried to raise my arm to wipe my eyes and was surprised to feel a sharp pain. Grimacing, I lowered that arm and rubbed my eyes with my left hand. I was in Mr. Barton's flat, there was no doubt of that now. I heard the coffee pot bubbling and could smell Mr. Barton's signature brew, the unique dark coffee with accents of orange and chocolate. I turned my head and saw Mary sitting on a chair looking at me with worried eyes. She got up and ran into the kitchen when she saw me stir.

"He's awake!" she shouted.

Mr. Barton walked over and was standing in front of me.

"Jake, how are you feeling?"

"Terrible," I said in a groggy voice.

"That I don't doubt. Your wrist has a compound fracture," he said as he appraised me.

"They said the break would be clean," I croaked.

"I'm afraid it isn't," he said.

I grumbled under my breath and looked down at my wrist. It was wrapped in heavy medical cloth—not the cheap stuff. Mary stood to the side of him looking at me nervously, and I could see tears pooling in her eyes. Still, I didn't understand how she had managed to get me here, I weighed at least fifty pounds more than her.

"I'm so sorry Jake," she said, her voice wavering as the tears spilled down her cheeks.

I gave her a weak smile, "it's not your fault, I wasn't going to let someone steal your things."

She smiled back half-heartedly, and I could see that she was suppressing more tears of guilt.

The light on the front door glowed red.

"How long have I been asleep?"

"It's been over ten hours. I gave you some medicine for the pain, and I imagine you'll be needing another dose soon. I'm going to put dinner on for the three of us, then you can have more medicine," Mr. Barton said.

"How did you get medicine? I can't afford it," I said, but he was already back in the kitchen. Mary was still staring at me.

"Did you get your stuff back?" I asked, turning to Mary.

"Yes, I'm just so sorry. You did nothing wrong."

I nodded and closed my eyes, drifting back into sleep despite the aching pain that was throbbing through my arm.

When I awoke again, Mr. Barton was handing me a large tray with a bowl of steaming potato soup, and a large slice of bread with melted cheese. The three of us ate in silence, and I could only hope that Mr. Barton didn't disclose my undying crush for Mary when she had brought me here. I was content with the way things had been going and was so thankful for the time and memories I had with her that I was unable or unwilling to convince myself to take things further for fear of losing the person dearest to me. I knew what it was like to lose everything, and I never wanted to go through that again.

The food took away the edge of hunger. Mr. Barton brought over another ladle of potato soup and a thick slice of bread for me, which I gladly accepted. We enjoyed the meal, but it was evident that both Mary and Mr. Barton were concerned with my health.

After dinner, Mr. Barton brought over three steaming mugs of coffee and passed them out. Mary took her mug and eyed the drink with caution.

"I've never had coffee before," she said, swirling the contents of the mug in slow circular motions.

Mr. Barton and I looked at her in shock then smiled.

"It's the best drink available, and Mr. Barton happens to be a coffee brew master," I said, mustering the energy for social conversation now that my stomach was comfortably full.

We drank the coffee in peace, enjoying each other's company and the refreshing beverages.

"Thanks for the coffee, Mr. Barton," I said.

He nodded and gave me another dose of the liquid medicine, sending me into a deep, dreamless sleep.

4
DELUSIONS

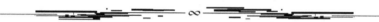

During the night my sleep turned feverish, and my dreams stormed with delusion. I awoke in a cold sweat only to see the light above the door still glowed red. Sweat had beaded on the surface of my skin, and I suppressed a deep shiver. Shaking, I pulled on the large comforter that sat at the foot of the couch and tried to get warm. My body felt like it was covered in ice. I thought it best to let Edgar and Mary sleep. In my delusion, I shifted onto my side only to put my full weight on my wrist. I fainted from the pain and slipped into the coldest and longest night of my life.

When I woke up again, I had sweat through my clothes and could feel the heat of my body building up and burning. I threw the large blanket off and tried to get out of my shirt.

"Help," I croaked. It wasn't much at all; it was a weak and desperate attempt to wake Mary or Mr. Barton, but it was enough.

Mr. Barton turned on the light and gasped when he saw me. Acting quickly, he gave me a cocktail of pills, had me sit up and stay awake, and made me strip down to my boxers and sit without a blanket. He had instructed Mary to remain in the other room—even in my delusional state, I didn't want her to see me like this. Powerful shivering took over my body, and my teeth clattered together like bricks.

"What's wrong with me?" I managed.

Mr. Barton walked over and unwrapped my bandage.

"Look away, I don't want you seeing this," he instructed.

I did as he said and felt cold air rush over my wrist.

"Mother of God," he murmured.

Unable to resist, I looked over and was horrified at the sight. My wrist was puffed out to three times its normal size and was purple in color. Besides that, thick yellow pus with streaks of blood leaked from pustules that had formed. The purple discoloration continued down my hand and up my forearm. The sight made me sick.

"Jake, your arm is infected. I'll get you some medicine in the morning that will make you better."

"I ca... I can't afford anything."

"Don't worry about that, I can get it," he said with grim determination.

Mr. Barton brought over a large basin of water and a washcloth. He cleaned my arm as gently as possible. After cleaning it, he re-wrapped my arm in fresh medical cloth and gave me a couple more pills with a glass of water. I drifted back into a sleep peppered with delusion and discomfort.

When I awoke again, Mary was approaching with a bowl of oatmeal.

"I'm not hungry," I croaked.

"Mr. Barton says you have to eat it," she said her voice firm.

Not daring to fight her, I grumbled then accepted the bowl and got a few spoons of it down when Mr. Barton re-emerged with an unlabeled orange pill bottle.

"This medicine will help you, Jake," he said as he uncapped the lid. He placed one blue pill in my bowl of oatmeal which I ate with some difficulty. Though my fever was down, I still felt weak and exhausted despite sleeping for almost twenty-four hours straight.

Things remained the same for the next three days. Throbbing pain, fever, and irrational thought plagued me. Mary and Mr. Barton took turns watching me, and the medicine Mr. Barton had acquired for me slowly staved back the infection in my arm, taking the swelling down and returning my arm's coloration to something closer to normal.

Out of guilt or loyalty, Mary stayed over at Mr. Barton's flat at night, unwilling to leave me by myself. Mr. Barton told me that he could tell that Mary really cared for me, which brought a smile to my face.

After he was satisfied that the infection was gone, Mr. Barton created a cast with thin slivers of steel and medical cloth. He coated the fabric in a thick wax-like material, and it set into a cast that was about the same as the expensive ones sold at the hospital. Though Mr. Barton wouldn't hear of me repaying the cost of the medicine, I was sure I owed him over four units for the cost of my recovery. Without the medication, I would have lost the arm or my life. It was such a humbling experience to have people in my life like Mary and Mr. Barton, they had saved me in my time of need, and that wasn't something I would be forgetting anytime soon.

5
CATCH-22

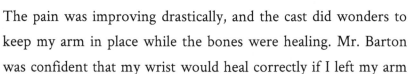

The pain was improving drastically, and the cast did wonders to keep my arm in place while the bones were healing. Mr. Barton was confident that my wrist would heal correctly if I left my arm in the cast for a couple of months. After a remarkable recovery, I had returned to living in my flat.

The sight of the Enforcers patrolling the streets now made my stomach drop and brought back the lingering fear of another severe injury. They had snapped my wrist like a toothpick, without emotion, as if it was as simple of a task as walking.

Deciding that it was best to catch up on my sleep and relax, I sat on my couch and grabbed the book I had purchased from the merchant instead of watching TV. I sealed the room to my flat behind me and put on a kettle of tea, struggling to use my fingers in the bulky cast.

I was relieved that the strain of my running had not caused the frayed spine of the book to fall apart, had that happened the pages could have been seriously damaged. The cover looked like it had sustained heavy wear in its lifetime, but the cardboard had served its purpose in protecting the manuscript. The paper didn't look synthetic, but it was also so mottled that if it were real paper, it wouldn't be worth much. The page with the year of print said 1991, it had to be a typo. Books that old didn't exist.

History taught us that there had been a great flood in 2039 that had wiped out New York completely. Survivors rebuilt the country into what it was today, but almost everything, including all books printed before 2039, had been destroyed or sucked into the toxic Atlantic Ocean. The book in my hands suggested one of three things: the print date was a typo and it was supposed to read 2091, the book was as old as it claimed to be and had somehow survived the Great Flood of 2039, or there was never a Great Flood of 2039. The third thought was dangerous—worse than incorrect. That was the kind of thinking that got someone sent to the Sculptors.

A wave of fear rippled through my mind as the realization that the book was potentially treasonous dawned on me. I could have had Edgar test it before I read it, but I had paid for the book and didn't have anything else to do if I decided not to read it. I felt something else as well, a deep thirst for knowledge. Perhaps the book could help me improve my thought output and lead to my own Paragon Thought. Unless the book included history and dates that precluded 2039, I would assume it to just be a simple typo. Deciding to learn the book's secrets, I turned the page and started reading.

"An Inquiry into the understanding, pleasant and useful. Since it is the understanding that sets man above the rest of sensible beings, and gives him all the advantage and dominion which he has over them; it is certainly a subject, even for its nobleness, worth our labour to inquire into. The understanding, like the eye, whilst it makes us see and perceive all other things, takes no notice of itself; and it requires art and pains to set it at a distance and make it its own object. But whatever be the difficulties that lie in the way of this inquiry; whatever it be that keeps us so much in the dark to ourselves; sure I am that all the light we can let in upon our minds, all the acquaintance we can make with our own understandings, will not only be very pleasant, but bring us great advantage, in directing our thoughts in the search of other things."

I paused after the first paragraph. This was no ordinary book; the first paragraph alone told me more about Absolute Knowledge than anything I had ever known. While it made no mention of Absolute Knowledge itself, it was clearly a book about the project, perhaps even in its earliest stages of development.

I continued for a few pages.

"Our business here is not to know all things, but those which concern our conduct. If we can find out those measures, whereby a rational creature, put in that state in which man is in this world, may and ought to govern his opinions, and actions depending thereon, we need not to be troubled that some other things escape our knowledge."

Something was wrong with this book. Panic shot through my body like venom and my heart pounded in my chest. My mind was telling me to stop reading before it was too late. This book was a book of treason. Still, was there truth to this? I had only read through a couple of pages, was it too late to turn back? Was the damage already done? I knew I should stop reading, but I wanted nothing more than to see if there was any truth to the words. Pressing on, I was intent on finishing what I had started. I could destroy the evidence when I was done.

Three hours later I had finished the book with more questions than answers, hungry for more—but full of fear. It was impossible to tell when the book was actually written based on the text, but it was peppered with incorrect words. A long length of the book talked about *God* in relation to man. *God* was referenced as a person. Mr. Barton made frequent references to *God* or *Gods,* and I simply understood it to be another incorrect word in his expansive criminal vocabulary.

When I closed the cover of the book and slid it under my couch, I noticed that my hands were shaking. I knew I needed to go to Mr. Barton for help, for advice. I dreaded it knowing that he wouldn't take it well. He would know that I knew better than to keep reading after spotting a single incorrect word.

Despite my fears, I stayed awake and re-read the entire book to get a better understanding. It was satisfying to get such an interesting perspective on ideas. The author's writing was rather difficult to break down and understand at certain points because I was unfamiliar with many of the terms mentioned in the book. It was also the first time I had ever seen thoughts compared to infinity. Before reading the book, I only thought infinity to exist within the confines of mathematics. Infinity was a complex idea, and after reading the book about what it had to do with thoughts, both simple and complex, I didn't understand anything more about it than before I read it. If the author's words were truth, I now knew more about the formation of ideas than ever before, and perhaps I would be able to increase my thought output.

Even if I could increase my thought output, it wouldn't make a shred of difference if I was sent off to the Sculptors for knowing and understanding treasonous words. No matter how I looked at it, I knew that I needed to consult Mr. Barton. Teaching classes for a living was out of the question, and I didn't want to sink to the level of becoming a criminal. Until I got this sorted out, I wouldn't be able to visit a Collection Parlor, wouldn't have an income, and wouldn't have any vouchers for drinking water or to purchase basic food. In other words, I was screwed. Cursing, I realized that seeking Mr. Barton's help was my only option. I wouldn't dare put the financial burden on Mary and rely on her kind nature. It felt terrible to need Mr. Barton's help and put him in another problematic situation right after he had saved my life and incurred huge expenses that I wouldn't be able to repay any time soon.

I walked into the kitchen of my flat and opened one of the drawers which held my vouchers and spending credits. Roughly twelve hundred credits, three water vouchers, and two food vouchers. Assuming that I needed to drink a minimum of half a gallon of water a day, I had roughly six days to live without the help of anyone else and without breaking into my credit reserves. Education was out of the question now; the next lesson would have to wait while I tried to find out how I was going to survive. I opened one of the lower cabinets in the kitchen and pulled out the large steel safe that I had purchased from a traveling caravan the previous year. After dialing the combination into the safe, the door popped open revealing a small brown paper bag filled with all of my credit savings I had been putting aside throughout the years. In total, it was just over three units, enough to keep me holed up in my flat for a couple months.

I would be able to purchase food and water vouchers on the streets from individuals with my credits at a better rate than purchasing food and water for credits directly from the Government. At best, I could manage three months without going to a Collection Parlor, or resorting to becoming an entrepreneurial criminal. Surely Mr. Barton could help me come up with a solution within three months. One thing I was certain of was that I wouldn't take anything else from him other than advice, and that I would work to repay him for taking care of me in my time of need.

Content with my plan, I replaced the brown sack in the safe and put my remaining vouchers and spending credits back in the drawer. The fear that I had ruined my life in a few hours' time was slowly fading and I went to sleep with mixed feelings and jumbled dreams.

In the morning, I ate a quick breakfast and packed the book in my backpack along with a few of the texts that Mr. Barton had lent me. Today was the day I would tell Mr. Barton of what I had done, and hope for the best. If anyone could help me, it was him.

I pulled the bandana over my face and exited my flat into the dark streets of the Slums. Though I was tempted to visit Mary, I knew it wasn't a good idea—I had too much on my mind and didn't want to involve her in my mistakes or put her in any danger. The Sculptors like many other things, had always just seemed like stories invented to keep people off the streets and working to further Absolute Knowledge, but they were entirely different now that I actually had reason to fear them. It was as if they had become a very real, tangible thing—and I had given them a reason to take me away.

I walked over to Mr. Barton's flat and knocked on the heavy steel door. My heart was already pumping in my chest. My biggest fear was not that my life was in danger, it was that I'd lose Mr. Barton as a friend. Mr. Barton opened the door and quickly motioned me inside.

After taking off my bandana, it was clear that he could see something was wrong with me.

"Are you okay, Jake?" he asked.

"I don't know honestly. I uh... I bought a book from a traveling merchant and don't think I was supposed to read it."

Mr. Barton's expression went blank. "Do you have the book with you?"

I nodded and pulled the book out of my backpack. His expression changed instantly; first, it was shock, then anger.

"Where did you get this?" he hissed with venom in his voice.

"I told you, a traveling merchant," I managed, my voice sounded weak, and my legs were shaking.

"How much of it did you read?" he asked in the same tone, a mix of fear and anger.

"All of it."

"The sculptors will kill you for this. I assure you that they're very real."

Tears welled up in my eyes as I felt my strength and courage fade.

"What can I do?" I said, looking down and avoiding eye contact.

Mr. Barton sighed and rubbed his face with his hands. He was silent. The only noise suppressing the deafening silence was the burbling of the coffeemaker.

"I suppose I'll need to teach you a few things," he said, sighing again. He looked defeated. "I'm not going to let you die because you know a bit of truth."

A grave silence filled the room as the coffee machine completed its brew cycle.

"What you managed to read is one of the most treasonous pieces of literature you could have possibly found, a book worth about thirty units on the black market. The author's name is John Locke, a British Philosopher."

I didn't know what British or Philosopher meant, but knew that the book was worth about five months of income as a Thinker, an unthinkable sum of money.

"Was the book actually written before 2039?" I asked.

"It was written almost five hundred years ago. In another country," he replied. "This copy is still extremely rare; I'm surprised it survived so long."

"Is there truth to the book?" I asked.

"Yes, more truth than anything you have ever read. Almost everything you know is a lie. All the history and literature you have read is a lie. The only truth you know is the laws of English, mathematics, and science."

I was taken aback by this. More questions filled my mind, the hunger for truth was sharp and frantic. Before I could ask anything, Mr. Barton was already talking again.

"It's time we start your first lesson, Jake."

I nodded. We'd probably be going over new books or New York's real history. I frowned when Mr. Barton pulled out a Collector canister and set it on the table.

"We're going to see how poisoned your mind is from reading Mr. Locke's work."

I nodded and sat still while he attached the electrodes and neuro collectors to my head.

"Do you have a trash bin I can use?" I asked, worried about the vertigo from the connection.

"You won't need it. Collectors were refined long ago. The pill they give you does nothing. It's another way for the Government to reduce what they pay for thoughts. When you choose to take the pill at a Collection Parlor, the Collector doesn't send a harsh jolt of electricity to targeted areas of your brain." I was baffled. Mr. Barton flipped the switch on the Collector and the light that indicated a secure connection turned green. There was no nausea and no sensation of my brain being ripped in half.

"Now, what you're going to do is not think about An Essay Concerning Human Understanding," he said simply.

As soon as he said the name of the book, another light started blinking red.

"You thought about An Essay Concerning Human Understanding. If this were real, the Government would know what's in your head, and you'd be dead within an hour after they scour your brain for everything you know with horrible torture."

This made me mad. "How the hell would I not think of it when you say it?" I shouted, the lights on the Collector continued to blink red.

Mr. Barton pointed at the blinking lights with anger in his eyes. "Every time that light flashes, the Government knows you know something that you shouldn't. Every time that light blinks, the Government will wipe you off the face of the Earth without leaving evidence that you ever existed. Your flat will be cleaned, someone new will move in, and you'll simply disappear forever. You will be nothing but an insignificant memory to those that cared about you. Even those you consider among your best friends won't question your death or go looking into it, they know better than that. When that light blinks, you will cease to exist. Not even Mary will go looking into your death."

That last attack sent anger flooding through my veins.

"How can I not think about something when you say the name of it? It's impossible. And Mary would go looking into it, just like I would for her," I seethed.

"You're referring to a Catch-22, and I assure you this isn't one."

"A what?" the anger I felt was growing into hot fury.

"It's an expression coined by Mr. Joseph Heller in 1961. A Catch-22 is a situation that is impossible to escape. In his novel, he presents the idea in the example of fighter pilots in World War Two. While I know you don't know what World War Two or a fighter pilot is, just know that they were people with an extremely dangerous job in an extremely dangerous period of history. To try to get out of doing their jobs, these individuals would go to a doctor to request a mental evaluation for insanity in the hopes that they would be found insane and incapable to do their assigned jobs. Unfortunately for the pilots, by seeking a psychiatric evaluation in the first place, they had demonstrated their own sanity and could therefore not be declared insane."

It didn't make any sense. "That's just as impossible of a situation as not thinking of something when you hear it," I responded.

"How could the pilots have gotten out of their jobs?"

"They couldn't have. You just said it was a Catch-22."

"Was there something different they could have done to avoid their jobs and the infinite loop of impossibility they faced?"

"I suppose they could have had their friends ask for them to have their evaluations done," I responded as I tried to fight down the frustration that was creeping up again, threatening to take control of my actions.

"Well, yes, but that probably wouldn't work either. If their friends also wanted to get out of the job, which I assure you they did, then by requesting that their friends have an evaluation for insanity, they had to be sane enough to recognize insanity and therefore couldn't get out of the jobs themselves. If they asked someone insane to ask for them, then the insane person which would still be flying as I mentioned before, couldn't be taken at their word and wouldn't be able to recognize insanity, but if they could recognize insanity then they wouldn't be insane and both individuals would still have to fly. In the end, everyone did their jobs and no one could be deemed too insane to fly."

That was too much for me. "So there was no way for them to avoid flying?"

"No. That's why it's called a Catch-22, it was an impossible situation to escape."

I slammed my fist on the table and glared at Mr. Barton, about ready to either walk out or hit him.

"So how is my situation different from theirs?" I asked, my voice low and cool, anger and frustration boiling my mind.

"Because I can help you break the infinite cycle. An Essay Concerning Human Understanding."

The light on the Collector didn't blink red.

6
UNLOCKED

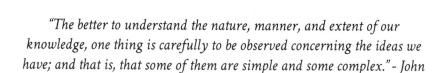

"The better to understand the nature, manner, and extent of our knowledge, one thing is carefully to be observed concerning the ideas we have; and that is, that some of them are simple and some complex." - John Locke.

"Do you know what you just did, Jake?"

I shook my head. My anger calmed as I realized it had just been an exercise designed to draw out my anger and make me lose clear thought. For the most part, Mr. Barton hadn't meant what he said.

"You were able to avoid thinking about something specific despite hearing something about it. The way you did it that time was by concentrating all of your thought on something else. You were trying to think of something to prove me wrong and your concentration was fueled by your frustration."

It made sense, but after talking about it again, my thoughts automatically drifted back to the book I had read and the light began to blink red again.

"Thoughts are layers and projections of external stimuli and past experience, and they are created by reflecting on our past and personal knowledge pool, and by combining any number of simple thoughts. By learning to layer our thoughts and hide critical knowledge beneath harmless thoughts, we can protect ourselves and our knowledge from those that would seek to take our lives away from us."

"How can I learn to do that?" I asked. It seemed reasonable on paper, but it didn't seem like an easy ability to learn.

"Let's start with something basic. This is a simple layering exercise that will create a basic layered link in your thoughts."

Mr. Barton went to the kitchen and brought over a bag of coffee beans. He set the bag in front of him and continued.

"When you smell the coffee beans, I want you to think about tea. While this is a very watered down layering technique, it will help you as we progress." He pulled out an old datapad and typed 'tea' in one of the parameters. As he opened the coffee bag, the light on the Collector started blinking red. He closed the bag and modified the parameter again.

"Good. Now I want you to think about tea and not think about An Essay Concerning Human Understanding."

I nodded, and he adjusted the parameters on the datapad.

Mr. Barton opened the bag of coffee beans, and the light began blinking red. We continued this for almost an hour without success. I was frustrated but continued because I had already seen slight success in layering my thoughts with the whole Catch-22 argument. He typed something else into the datapad and sighed after a couple of minutes as the light continued to flash.

"Do you know what I typed?" he asked.

I shook my head.

"Mary. You're thinking about her almost nonstop. I need you to concentrate."

I let out a frustrated groan. "It's hard not think about her, I'm worried I'll never see her again," I admitted.

"That's a very real danger if you don't focus."

I nodded and tried to concentrate on the task at hand, but it was hopeless.

Mr. Barton raised his hand, and I stopped concentrating. He turned off the Collector and took off the headgear. "That's enough for today, we aren't going to get anywhere further with this."

"Am I going to learn any history today?" I asked, frustrated with the complexity of the layering exercises.

"No."

"Why?" I was shocked at his swift and emotionless response.

"Because you aren't going to learn anything new until you can properly conceal what you already know. We do, however, need to talk about your living arrangements and expenses."

I winced. "I've got enough savings to live three months without visiting a Collection Parlor."

"Jake, you've got three options, I don't care which you choose. Take your time and think on it and go with what's best for you. Option one: you train with me until you are able to effectively bury what you have learned about An Essay Concerning Human Understanding. When you are able to do so, you will never read another book purchased from a merchant without first consulting me. You will continue your life on the surface of New York, but you won't be able to work as a Thinker.

"Option two: You train and study under me for an undetermined time period. When I am confident that you are ready, you will be free to apply your skills in any way you'd like.

"Option three: Everything will be the same as option two, but you'd have the option to work with my organization and make something more of your life and learn the truth."

"What will I do if I can't work as a Thinker?"

"That's up to you. I'm teaching you to protect yourself if you absolutely need it, but it's not worth the risk to put your protected mind in danger every day."

"What's your organization?" I asked, my head swimming with thoughts.

"That I cannot tell you until you are ready. Until I know that you can layer your mind indefinitely, they will only be referred to as my employers." Mr. Barton frowned. "We'll refer to them as my colleagues. Our relationship is more complicated than that of an agent and principal."

Think it over and let me know tomorrow. Until then, no Collection Parlors, and don't even think about telling anyone else about our conversation—not even Mary."

This was a big decision. I had always sought to improve my knowledge, I hungered to learn more and hone my mind, but I didn't consider myself a criminal. If I accepted Mr. Barton's offer of teaching me, I'd be considered worse than the drug dealers, worse than the thieves—I'd be considered the worst sort of criminal there was. I already knew enough to be killed on the spot, would devoting my life to learning the truth put me in any more danger than I was already in?

My fate as a criminal was sealed when I read An Essay Concerning Human Understanding. I then felt a wave of uncertainty come over me. Could I turn back and erase my mistakes? Could I return to being a regular citizen free from treasonous thoughts? I looked down at the cast that covered my wrist and was angry. For the first time in my life, I was angry at the Government. Why should I be punished for helping a friend and stopping a thief? Why should the truth be kept from me? Who were they to say I couldn't know what had actually happened in the past? Who were they to decide what books I couldn't read, and what words I couldn't know? I wanted more, I craved the truth, I craved the knowledge that Mr. Barton could offer.

I had nothing left other than Mary and Mr. Barton, and a future with Mary without help would be impossible now. This was the only logical decision. There was no point waiting until tomorrow to decide.

"I would like to start with option two. If I am seeking to learn more or make use of my skills within your organization, I would like the opportunity to switch from option two to option three at that time."

"I think that is a great option for someone of your intelligence. I need you to know that this is a life of danger, you will be a criminal, and if you're caught, you will be killed by the Government. It might be scary, but you'll be serving a greater purpose and fighting for something bigger than yourself. You can make a difference in the world."

I nodded intently.

"Let's talk about your expenses. In exchange for your copy of An Essay Concerning Human Understanding, you will be absolved from your debt of the medical expenses I incurred from your wrist injury. In addition, I will pay you two units per week for the duration of which you are studying under me until you have been paid a sum of twenty-six units. At that point, you will be presented with new opportunities for income or, should you be deemed ready, the ability to return to live your normal life on the surface, without being able to visit Collection Parlors, of course."

"You've got a deal," I responded, thankful to rid myself of the debt.

"We will continue for a while then. We need to keep working on your layering before we progress to other matters. Needless to say, anything you learn from me and everything we discuss is private. You can't tell anyone. If you do, our agreement will be void, and you will never see me again. You also need to know that telling someone else what we discuss could lead to both of your deaths."

"I understand completely, sir," I replied.

"Good, but drop the sir, you make me feel older than I already am. Now, you are undoubtedly executing some degree of layering right now at all times. Simply put, layering is the ability to create mental barriers which separate individual ideas and thoughts from your conscious and subconscious. Our subconscious is what makes layering so difficult. It influences our thoughts and feelings without our direct control. What I'm going to teach you is how to actively control your subconscious mind. When we are able to control our brains completely, there is very little that we cannot accomplish."

I was baffled. How could I control something automatic while retaining control over the active part of my brain? "Can this actually be learned?" I asked.

"When you didn't think of An Essay Concerning Human Understanding when I mentioned the name, you exhibited brief control over your subconscious mind. You were thinking so intently that you put regions of your brain that are usually passive to active use. While distractions are a great way to introduce the concept, they won't get you far. I'm going to teach you to unlock your brain, and you must forgive how I'm going to start."

I gave him a quizzical look.

"I want you to think about your parents."

I wasn't expecting that, and it hit me hard. The amount of memories of my parents that I had buried and left undisturbed was staggering. I hadn't thought about them or the accident in months with anything other than a passing thought. The sudden surge of emotion was powerful, and I suppressed tears that were attempting to well in my eyes.

"I know that it's something you don't like to talk about and something that you likely don't think of often anymore. If you'll forgive the personal nature of my question, how long has it been since you've actively thought of them?"

"Months," I muttered.

He nodded, his face solemn. "I truly am sorry that this is the best example, but it can't be beat in helping you understand. You use part of your subconscious actively every waking minute of your life suppressing thoughts and reflections of your parents and ignoring external stimuli that would trigger such memories. You've trained your subconscious mind to reject stimuli and therefore create a mental barrier which layers your thoughts and memories from your active, conscious mind, it's incredible."

"It makes sense, but how do I learn to do something like that? Isn't my subconscious mind doing that passively and without my direct doing?"

"Yes and no. You've accepted the fact that thinking of your parents and memories of them ultimately lead you to pain. In response, your brain has layered those memories and protects them to a certain degree from external stimuli. The barrier you've created with your layering isn't strong enough to allow you to not think about them when you hear a direct mention, but it is strong enough to create a barrier which prevents you from thinking about them when faced with stimuli that doesn't directly relate to them. Seeing children with their parents, walking past places you visited with them as a young boy, things of that nature you are able to tune out. On the other hand, I'm sure you have trouble with familiar smells all the time. Even I struggle with smells sometimes."

"Why can I tune out some visual stimuli, but not certain smells?"

"Smells trigger brain response on the area of our brain that is mostly emotional in nature, powerful aromatic stimuli can overcome even the most shielded of minds. Layering and creating a single barrier won't be enough, in the end, you'll have to be able to break down thoughts and memories into smaller components and store them in multiple parts of your brain behind multiple barriers. We won't be working on this for a long time, for now, we will focus on simple barriers and one level of layering. I don't expect your layering to be strong, I just want to see that you are developing the foundation needed to learn what I have to teach."

"Before we get started, can you show me that you can actually perform layering and prevent yourself from thinking thoughts?" I asked.

Mr. Barton smiled. "Of course, Jake. I don't expect you to take what I say at face value without first seeing what you can accomplish through my training." He picked up the headgear and attached it to his head before flipping the switch on the Collector. Mr. Barton handed me the datapad and pointed to the parameter field.

"Enter anything you'd like there and then tell me. If I think it, then the light will blink red."

I typed 'coffee' into the parameter field. If Mr. Barton said he could ignore any stimuli, then I wanted to test him with the aroma. "Alright, don't think about coffee." The light didn't blink. "What's the secret to your brew? How many scoops of ground coffee per cup of water? Is there a special way you grind the coffee beans?" The light didn't blink. I reached beside him and grabbed the closed bag of coffee and held it up to his eyes. He looked directly at the bag and gave a slight smile. The light still didn't blink. I pulled open the bag and wafted air to Mr. Barton, the sweet aroma of the coffee beans flooding the room. Somehow the light still hadn't flashed.

"Eat a coffee bean," I said.

Mr. Barton shrugged and popped a bean in his mouth. He crunched audibly and yet the light still hadn't flashed red. "Alright, I believe you," I managed, clearly impressed with his abilities.

"Once your brain is unlocked, you'll be amazed at what it can do. Let's get back to work," he said, tossing another coffee bean into his mouth.

7

MIND GAMES

Mr. Barton trained me for six hours a day for a month straight. I found myself spending more time with him than without him. Mary had begun to join us for dinner at his flat almost every evening. While we couldn't talk about what I was learning to do, it was great to share a meal with them.

Mr. Barton liked to cook, and we enjoyed helping him when possible. The tasks he gave Mary and I were usually pretty simple, but it was nice to see how basic ingredients could be combined to form something greater than the sum of their parts. Mary had a natural affinity for cooking that extended well beyond my ability. When Mr. Barton noticed, he began allocating more advanced tasks to her which could jeopardize the overall quality of the meal if they were performed incorrectly. I was never offered the opportunity for such tasks, and it didn't bother me.

Though Mr. Barton and I had only practiced layering, I was already able to create simple barriers for any thought that were relatively durable. I expected either advanced lessons in layering or to finally learn some new history soon.

"Jake?" Mary asked, waving an arm in front of my face.

"Huh?" I snapped out of my thoughts.

"Can you pass me the pepper?"

"Sure." I handed her the small canister of pepper, and she sprinkled some into the simmering pot of soup before turning to Mr. Barton. He stood expressionless, watching her closely. Mary added a little more pepper, and he flashed her a grin, pleased with the increased pepper content.

The aroma of the homemade soup flooded the flat, and I couldn't believe how hungry I was. After the soup simmered for another half hour, we sat down to eat. Mr. Barton brought out a large loaf of wheat bread and broke it for us, passing out large chunks to Mary and I before placing one on his plate. The soup was perfect; I was always amazed with Mary's and Mr. Barton's cooking. When I had finished my third bowl of soup, I used the crust from the bread to mop up the remaining broth in my bowl.

"So Mary, any chance you have any of your artwork with you? Jake has told me a lot about your talent over the past year," Edgar said. I felt my heart drop, unsure of where he was going.

She blushed and gave me a quick and nervous smile. "Uh, yeah," she said. Mary walked over to her backpack and pulled out a crudely bound sketchbook filled with pulp paper made with chemicals that smelled like beef and brought it over to Mr. Barton. He flipped through the pages appreciatively.

"These are quite good," he said with approval. "But I'm afraid Jake did you an injustice in his description of the artwork by calling your work wonderful. These are even better than wonderful," he said with a smile. Everything on the inside of me tensed, and I felt Mary's gaze on me as I ate, her eyes dancing with thought as she considered what he'd told her. I looked over and gave her a nervous smile, trying not to blush.

She broke into a broad smile before turning back to Mr. Barton. "Thank you."

After we finished our meal, Mary left early so that she could stop by a store before curfew. I decided to stay and talk with Mr. Barton more before I retired to my flat for the night.

"Jake, I picked something up for you the other day. I got a great deal on it, so don't worry about paying me back." He pulled out a small leather-bound sketchbook and flipped through the pages, revealing white archival grade paper. "I figured you can give it to Mary as a gift," he said.

I couldn't help but blush. "If you're sure I can't buy it from you... This looks quite valuable," I said as I flipped through the small treasure.

"Only paid ten credits for it. My treat," he said with a wink.

I pocketed the book.

"I'd like you to get here a bit early tomorrow, we've got a big lesson to work on. You've learned the layering needed to progress to subdivided operating."

"Yes, sir," I responded automatically. Mr. Barton frowned at this.

"Jake, please just call me Edgar. No more sir, and only Mr. Barton in formal occasions. I would also appreciate you relaying that information to Mary. You two make me feel a lot older than I'd like to feel," he said.

"Alright Mr.- Edgar," I managed.

I grabbed my backpack and shook Edgar's hand before returning to my flat. I had spent little time in my own flat over the past couple of weeks. I was surprised at how bored I was on my own time now, I could practice creating barriers with my mind and layering my thoughts, but I had no way of telling if my subconscious mind was betraying me without the indicator of the Collector. I decided against practicing alone for fear of developing the wrong intuition. I settled on brewing a cup of tea and sitting in front of my computer console. I might as well practice some mathematics and chemistry. I steered clear of the free history and literature lessons available through my flat's computer system. I was close to getting my certification in intermediate chemistry. It would cost five units to take the certification test, but I decided it wasn't worth the extra mental strain during my time as a student under Edgar.

If things didn't work out with Edgar's colleagues, perhaps I would pursue a career in reactor maintenance in the Undercity. With my knowledge of chemistry, I could probably get the job and also get free advanced chemistry lessons. Without employment in a Government position that dealt with chemistry, certain classes were off limits to the civilian population. Focusing, I managed to learn some new mathematical concepts over the next few hours. It surprised me to find that it was becoming easier to learn.

After finishing my tea and brushing my teeth, I decided to get some rest. I set my alarm for 6 AM and fell into a restful sleep.

Trudging out of bed, I took care of my hygiene needs and walked over to Edgar's. There was no need to prepare a breakfast as Edgar always enjoyed cooking it for the two of us. Edgar rushed me inside, trying to keep as much of the smog out as possible.

"Thanks for coming early, Jake. I've got something critical to teach you today." Edgar motioned for me to sit down at the table and brought over two large plates. There were eggs, a rasher of bacon, and a hefty serving of potatoes cooked in a skillet with oil. I had only had bacon a couple of times in my life, it was a luxury, and I expected the food was worth about eight hundred credits. After setting the plates down, Edgar brought over two large mugs of his signature brew.

"What's the occasion?" I hadn't had a meal of this sort of luxury since my twelfth birthday. I cursed under my breath as the smell of the bacon broke through the barrier protecting the memories of my parents.

"Breakfast is the most important meal of the day, and I need you at your best for today's lesson. Also, keep working on that barrier. I saw from the expression on your face that the aroma triggered a memory and broke your layering."

I nodded. There was no sense in trying to hide it. Trying to deny it wouldn't help me improve my mind or protect me from the Government.

We took our time eating the meal. I was surprised that even the coffee was different, it tasted like vanilla and had sugar and cream in it.

"Edgar, this food is fantastic," I said with genuine thanks.

"My colleagues wanted to treat us to a nice meal for the copy of An Essay Concerning Human Understanding. They were thrilled to have a copy in such good condition added to their archives."

I would learn more of his colleagues and organization as I progressed in my studies—or so he'd told me. After we had finished eating, Edgar took the dishes to the sink and returned to the table. He attached the neuro gear to my head and readied the tablet.

"I'm going to teach you how to subdivide your mind now. This will be difficult at first, but you will know when you accomplish it. We won't be working with the Collector today. What you're going to do is create a barrier in your conscious mind. I want you to imagine you have a small box to hide. You are in a vast and empty building, its layout is completely unknown to you, and you are standing at the front door. With your conscious mind, I want you to walk in and hide the box somewhere. Let me know when you've hidden the box."

"Who came up with this idea?" I asked, the exercise seemed childish.

"It's an old Buddhist meditation exercise. But that doesn't matter, just do what I'm telling you," he said.

I closed my eyes and focused, I began generating the building in my mind and proceeded through the empty rooms. Some of the rooms were empty and clean while others were completely trashed and filled with graffiti. I found a perfect place to hide the box and set it underneath a small desk so that it was hidden from plain sight. "I hid the box," I said without breaking my concentration.

"Good, now I want you to create a barrier with your subconscious mind and start looking for the box."

I concentrated and created a second barrier with my subconscious mind and experienced something unlike anything I ever had. It felt like there was a stream of electricity moving through my brain, and it caused the hair on my skin to rise. I was in control of two separate versions of myself, each without knowledge that the other was in existence. I moved the subconscious part of my mind through the rooms, and it truly was the first time that version of me had ever seen the rooms. My conscious mind continued to move, listening for the seeker and moving to stay away and hopefully draw the other version of me away from finding the box that I had hidden. I rounded a corner and ran into myself, losing all concentration and jumping upright from my seated position back in Edgar's flat.

"Drink some water," he said. His voice seemed to be muffled despite the fact that he was sitting right in front of me. "You're alright, just breathe and drink some water."

I picked up the glass with a shaky grip and took a deep drink. I set the glass down carefully and looked at him, struggling to focus and collect my thoughts in any coherent order.

"Wha... What just happened?" I managed.

"You just had a collision. I didn't expect your first collision to happen for at least a month."

"Collision?"

"You had separated your mind into two independent subdivisions that were more or less unaware of the other's existence. When the two subdivisions of your mind ran into one another inside the building, both parts became fully aware of one another, and both barriers that you had created were destroyed in a fraction of a second, hence the shock and side effects that are affecting you right now. I'm very proud of you."

I struggled to take in the information and nodded. I remembered turning the same corner from two different sides and running into myself twice. After that, everything went blank before I was pulled back into Edgar's flat.

"It felt like I was really there. I could tell you almost everything about that building. What it looked like, what it smelled like, the exact layout of it."

"You created a durable barrier then sustained it while you formed another barrier with your subconscious mind. The result was an almost total immersion within your thoughts in the two subdivisions of your mind."

The thoughts that surged through my head were beginning to become clearer. "So I held two separate but equal versions of my mind that were competing against one another?"

"Yes. Your conscious mind hid the box from your subconscious mind. The box was actually a key to the barrier you had formed over your conscious mind and your subconscious mind was working to find the key while your conscious mind worked to distract your subconscious. It's quite mentally taxing, but it does get easier over time."

"How am I able to do this at all?"

He grinned. "It's an unintended side effect of long-term exposure to Collectors. They rewire our minds and mutate our neural networks over time."

"Okay, but what do you mean the box was a key?"

"When you create multiple barriers, you distribute little pieces of information that can unlock other barriers—it's a safety mechanism. They aren't obvious things that anyone would think of, but you can use them to escape your mind if you get stuck and don't want to cause a collision."

"How many subdivisions can you divide your mind into?" I asked with wonder.

"I can manage four for a decent amount of time but can hold five for a short duration. Collisions get a lot worse with more subdivisions. For example, if I've broken my mind into four pieces and two of them collide, hopefully, I can hold the barriers of the other two parts that didn't collide while the two parts that collided restore their barriers. If three parts run into each other, it's incredibly hard to sustain, and if all four collide, it's a hard crash. One collision between four parts often cause the individual to pass out."

"I can't even imagine a third subdivision. I'm exhausted from two."

"Well, I didn't even expect you to make subdivisions that were more than ten percent separate. Your compartments were at least ninety percent independent from one another which is truly incredible for your first time breaking your mind into more than one piece. Controlling your subconscious and using it with your conscious mind is one thing, but separating them from one another and using them independently is much more challenging. Let's go again. This time I want you to hide the box with your subconscious and seek it with your conscious mind."

Mr. Barton put the neuro pads back on my head and readied his tablet. "When you're ready, Jake."

I focused and took control of my subconscious mind and tried to pull it apart from my conscious mind. It was more difficult, and I struggled to keep active thoughts from my conscious mind from leaking in. The barrier was not as strong, but I still had control over my subconscious mind while my conscious mind sat inactive and unaware of what I was doing with the part of my mind that was now protected with the barrier. Something shifted in my head and a sensation of falling washed over me.

It was different this time. The building was darker, there wasn't as much light, and something felt off. There was a dull buzzing sound, low and ominous that seemed to grow louder as I progressed through the rooms. I knew where I was going because it was the same building I had created in the previous exercise. The rooms were messier now, most of them destroyed and littered with broken furniture and concrete. The windows that were in some of the rooms were pitch black, and dense black fog leaked in and fell to the floor in a swirling pool from the cracks in the glass.

My movements were becoming more sluggish, and a feeling of dread was growing inside of me, I didn't want to be here. When I tried to break the barrier, I felt it resist my efforts, trapping me inside. Reluctantly, I continued through the rooms holding the box in my hands, the key to escape, as Mr. Barton had called it. Deep cramps in my legs slowed my movement further. Most of the rooms I went through were now empty, there was nowhere to hide my box. I continued through growing wearier. I heard a giggle echo through the rooms, and it was impossible to tell where it came from. The buzzing sound was growing louder, and the light in the rooms was being pulled in strange looking streams into the black fog that lingered on the edges of the walls.

The walls were turning from gray to a crimson red. Blood red. It kept getting darker as I progressed further into the building of emptiness. I tried to move faster, to get away from the maze of frightening rooms. Deciding I wanted no part of this any longer, I turned around, but the room I had just come from was now consumed by the void-like black fog, and I had no intention of finding out whether the fog could hurt me. Having no other options, I trudged forward through the maze, through one more room.

As I cleared the door in front of me, I was suddenly in the Slums. I saw my parents across the street standing and looking at me. They started walking toward me with warm smiles. I turned my head and screamed when I saw a large construction truck barreling down the street and swerving wildly, the truck I knew all too well. There was nothing I could do other than try to change the past.

I screamed at them. I tried to run, but my rubber legs were faltering. My parents showed no signs of fear, it was as if they couldn't hear my screaming. They continued walking toward me, stepping down from the curb, waving and smiling at me as the truck closed in. The box in my arms was getting heavier, pulling my arms down and holding me back. I tried to drop it but couldn't, it seemed to be glued to my arm. I continued to scream then watched with disbelief as my parents disintegrated in front of me as the truck struck them and flung them into the distant shadows. Their bodies flew through the air like rag dolls, mangled and broken. They were swallowed whole by the thick walls of black fog that were locking me inside the projection.

The black fog from the walls was creeping forward along the streets now, it was getting closer. I could hear it now, a great rumbling sound and saw it approaching with great speed. The walls that bound my projection were caving in. The buildings that were touched by the fog began to crumble and turned to dust on contact. I started trying to run away from the approaching fog but could no longer move. The fog swept over my legs and I screamed. It climbed and consumed my body, and everything faded to a deep nothingness.

8

ESCAPE

I became aware of the fact that I was sitting in a cushioned chair. It didn't feel like I had been sleeping, it just seemed like I had been out of focus—daydreaming almost. The disturbing thing was that I couldn't remember where I was, or how I got there. I was sitting in a long hallway with many rooms on either side. The laminate tile floor was well cleaned, and the air smelled of strong disinfectants. It looked like a hospital, but there was no one in the hallway, and only a few of the old fluorescent lights were lit, giving the entire scene a sinister look. The hall didn't look complete—as if details were missing. It was close enough to what I remembered to make me think it was a real hospital and believe it was possible that I was actually here, but there were small inconsistencies that made me despise the place of lies, the projection of my mind. The best way to describe the inconsistencies was that they were glitches in my mind like something hadn't materialized properly. Some objects were blurry in appearance, while others were crystal clear. A few shadows cast from the lights also weren't correct. I noticed my cast was missing as well.

The numbers on the empty doorways to the rooms were there, but the patient clipboards were blurry, and I was unable to read the names on them, it was as if someone had smeared the marker boards with an alcohol-soaked rag.

I was surprised to find that my legs worked efficiently and remembered how they had felt when I was trying to run from the black fog that consumed me. Something was off, though—my legs moved how I told them to, but I couldn't feel them like I had been able to before. I turned around and saw that the hallway wasn't complete, at a certain point, the same black fog from before was hiding whatever was on the other side. I was still trapped. How long had I been here?

"Hello!" I cried out, trying to wake myself from the horrible dream-like trance I was stuck in.

The words had no feeling even though I was using my diaphragm. What had gone wrong? Why couldn't I break out of my thoughts and return to the real world? Was I even still awake? Still alive? I realized that I had to be awake still, as my thoughts were still coherent, and I was still in control of my mind, but the lack of feeling anything was very concerning. I couldn't feel the air being pulled into my lungs, couldn't feel what my hands were touching, all I could do was see, hear and smell. What was this strange place?

The hands on my watch weren't moving. I unscrewed the crown of the watch and wound it. I returned the crown to the set position and saw that it still wasn't moving. The clock on the wall was also frozen. This was a place without time. There was no way to tell how long every second of time that I spent here transferred to the world I knew.

Shrugging off the disturbing thoughts of losing a significant amount of time in reality while trapped in my mind, I decided to try to find the way out or cause a collision. Unlike the previous exercise I had done, I wasn't aware of any other copies of myself in this strange place. I continued forward in the hallway toward a single door on the end. I hadn't realized how quiet it actually was here. There was no noise other than the light contact of my shoes on the tile of the hall. Even the lights that flickered overhead were silent. All the rooms along the length of the hallway didn't have any doors and were filled with the void. The light from the hallways didn't even seem to light a single inch of the room, it was simply destroyed on contact.

I continued forward until I could read the sign on the only door in the hallway: Wesley Ashton. Hesitating, I grabbed the steel handle and almost yelled out in surprise when an icy shock cascaded through my wrist. Gritting my teeth, I turned the knob and slowly pushed the door open. After the door was open, I could no longer feel anything; the cold that had shot through my arm was replaced with a lack of any particular temperature. I was in the hospital room my father had been taken to after the accident. It was the hospital room where I had watched him die. As the door fully opened, I could see that I was already in the room, sitting close and watching my father—except it wasn't actually me.

The best way to describe it was that I was an outsider looking in on a moment in time with perfect clarity. Neither the version of me that was sitting with my father nor my father himself looked up to watch me as I walked in.

"Jake... You have to get out of the Slums, there's no life worth living down here." He started coughing, wiping away a streak of blood with his shirt. "If any of us can make it out, it's you. I need you to be strong," he said.

Younger Jake was in tears, nodding as one only can when they know they are about to lose the last of their family. He was holding his father's hand loosely, aware of how cold it felt, how close to death his father really was. His mother had been killed at the scene, yet he had somehow clung to the idea that his father was going to make it, he just had to. He had realized in that moment that his childhood was over and things would forever change.

"I've left you our savings so that you can start your life and have somewhere to live. You're old enough to start working."

Younger Jake nodded, tears cascading down his face. I continued to watch the scene from the doorway, only realizing I was crying when tears blurred my vision. I was trapped in a memory of pain and sorrow.

Just as I remembered, a doctor came in and told me that I had to leave the room for a little while. As soon as younger Jake had left the room, the doctor walked up to my father. He had whispered something, I couldn't hear what he had said, so I slowly walked closer, hoping that they wouldn't realize I was there.

"I'm going to give you something else for the pain so that you can spend more time with your son." The doctor prepared a solution in a syringe and added it to the IV bag that hung over my father. Mr. Barton walked into the room slowly and made his way over to my dad. I had no memory of my dad ever knowing or seeing Mr. Barton. After the doctor gave my father the medicine, he nodded at Mr. Barton and walked back out of the room, fading into a black mist and disintegrating from the scene.

"Wesley, I'm so sorry this happened."

My father looked at him and said something I couldn't make out. Deciding to risk it, I crept closer to the bed to get to where I could hear.

"I need you to watch over my son, and when the time is right, I need you to take him into the Guild."

"You know I will. If he's anything like you, he will make an excellent Archivist."

Archivist? Was this guild working for the Government to establish Absolute Knowledge? I stopped myself from letting a stream of questions surge through my brain. I was never here, this couldn't be a memory because I wasn't in the room. It was some sort of dream, some irrational chain of thoughts deep within my subconscious. It had to just be another illusion that my mind was creating to trap me. I needed to escape.

I saw a door on the other side of the room, where an LED exit sign hung visibly over the frame. Had the door been there the whole time? I couldn't tell. I looked back into the hallway that I had come from and was surprised to see that the black fog had crept up to the door I was standing in. I moved forward and closed the door, hopefully shielding myself from the fog that had already consumed me once. It seemed like my mind was passively pushing me forward through the world my mind had created. What terrified me was the fact that I didn't know if it was pushing me deeper into increasingly complex layers of thoughts and behind deeper barriers of entrapment or if I was subconsciously trying to free myself from the prison I had created.

Mr. Barton was already gone from the scene; he must have disappeared when I closed the door. My father was now asleep. I crept forward toward the exit door, trying to be as quiet as possible. Just as I had cleared the bed, my father's hand lashed out and grabbed my wrist. I felt a shock leech the heat from my arm again, but it was much deeper this time. The cold threatened to freeze my bones. I tried to scream out, but the cold was filling my lungs now. He looked at me with terrible lifeless eyes devoid of all color. His skin had turned a sickly blue, and he looked like he had been dead and frozen for days. Thick purple veins bulged from his papery blue skin in the hand that constricted my wrist like a vise grip.

"You shouldn't be here!" he screamed in a ghastly voice with no fragment of recognition. His eyes looked past me, perhaps even through me.

I tried to pry away but felt the cold continue to flood through my body. Dark purple marks were spreading on my arm where the skeletal hand grasped with impossible strength. I felt myself shivering, unable to break free of the frozen grip.

"You're not real," I murmured, attempting to suppress my hysteria.

"Hah," the terrible voice said in a gritty tone. "There's an interesting thought." The cold, lifeless eyes continued to look through me. "You know of treasonous things. You will be killed and erased just like your mother and I."

My thoughts froze in my mind; I was unable to control my body.

"You will join us soon enough," the thing before me said. It was in rapid decay; the frozen, fetid skin of my father fell off in thick sheets revealing a smoldering, black skeleton below. I screamed like I never have before, fear shackling my body, freezing it in place. I felt like I was on the brink of hysteria like my brain was about to split.

There was a flash of darkness that covered my vision, and I felt the ground shift below me. I was standing just past my father and saw that he was still sleeping in the bed and still alive. I looked at my arm and saw that the dark purple marks were gone and I once again felt nothing. While I had felt the greatest cold of my life seconds ago, I once again had no sense of temperature or feeling. I moved as quickly as possible to the door and yanked open the handle, walking into a room of light. A flood of whiteness washed over me, and a great booming sound rung in my ears as the ground began to shake.

A second later I was back in Edgar's flat, lying on the couch. I could feel my heart pounding rapidly in my chest. I could feel the breath entering and leaving my body. I could feel my movements as I made them and was fairly confident that I had returned to the physical world. A sliver of panic jolted through me as I thought about the possibility of becoming trapped in a deeper layer of my own mind.

I quickly shook the thought out of my head and looked at my surroundings. The lighting was exactly correct, there was no black fog made entirely out of nothing, and I once again felt like my normal self. With the lighting the way it was in the Slums, I had no idea how long I had been gone from a state of physical consciousness. My watch said 9:15, there was no way to tell if it was morning or evening, but at least it worked. The fact that it was still running meant that I had been unconscious for less than two days. I knew that it lasted for a little under forty-eight hours with a full wind. I searched desperately for any inconsistencies that would give away the fact that I'd slipped deeper into my mind, but there were none.

Edgar walked over and saw that I was awake. "You're back," he said without expression. "We've got a lot to talk about, Jake."

9
NANOTECH

I was struggling to keep my composure, the horror of what I had seen was sending electricity through my veins. My body felt cold and clammy despite being wrapped up in a blanket. Edgar was sitting in front of me, observing me carefully as if he wasn't sure I was sane. I reached up and wiped a thin layer of sweat from my head and continued to look around the room. At least I felt something—the lack of feeling when trapped in my mind had been terrifying.

"Don't talk until you're ready. You are alright, you are safe."

I managed a nod and sat still for several minutes—though they felt like hours—taking care to keep my breathing steady and trying to recollect myself and gain mental composure.

"I'm alright now," I said. Edgar carefully removed the neuro-connectors from my head.

"Tell me what you saw, Jake. I need to try to get an idea of what happened."

I told him a detailed account of everything I had experienced. The simple act of retelling it to Edgar brought back the emotional pain and fear that I had felt when trapped. When I got to the part about him talking with my father, I studied his face carefully to see if there was any indication of surprise. There wasn't. I fought through the story, pausing at moments when I thought I would break down again.

"Hmm. It sounds like you had at least five subdivisions of your mind, maybe six or seven. Your session data is off the charts."

I shook my head. "There was only one version of me from the start."

"I think you created multiple subdivisions and your mind wasn't ready for it. When you created too many for your mind to handle, your brain created one more barrier and trapped your active mind under that so you would perceive only one use of your brain. I can't explain what you saw, nor what it means. I do know that you must have been trapped very deep to lose the ability to feel. I am not sure if you were having collisions or just created an incredibly strong barrier in which you subconsciously forced yourself to unlock to bring yourself out of the projection gently."

"Did you know my father?" I blurted.

"No, I didn't know your father, Jake. I only know what you've told me about him—which isn't much."

"Sorry," I murmured.

"What's good is that you had the ability to think rationally. Projections such as what you experienced can harm the mind, and things that are illusions can be perceived as truth and memory if the layering is strong enough."

"Was I not supposed to be able to create more than two subdivisions in my projection?"

"No. And I certainly didn't think you'd make five plus, instantly. I can't do that and I've been training for years. I'd like to take you to talk with someone, Jake. I need to show him the results from your session."

"Who?"

"One of my colleagues in the organization that I'm with. He is an expert on subdividing the mind and mental projections, and can evaluate exactly what you did."

"Where is he?" I asked.

"We'll be going to the Undercity," Edgar said.

"Your organization is down in the Undercity?" I asked, trying to read his expression.

"Oh yes, it's much nicer than it is up in the Slums."

I stared with disbelief.

"Once you're in the Guild Hall," he amended. "If you agree then we will leave now. I'd like to be back by dinner time."

"Yeah, let's go," I said.

Edgar walked over to his closet and pulled out a black leather jacket, it looked expensive and not the sort of thing that could be purchased from any of the local shops in our district. He crouched down and pulled out a small black briefcase from which he pulled out a holstered handgun. Any sort of weapon more dangerous than a butter knife was illegal to possess. I hadn't ever seen any type of firearm aside from the rifles the heavy Enforcers carried when diffusing illegal activities. Edgar must have seen the look of shock on my face because he smirked as he secured the weapon to the inside of his jacket and added a couple of strange looking magazines to an inside pocket. After replacing the briefcase, he pulled out two respirator mouthpieces and handed one to me. "Don't put it on until we're in the Undercity, it'll draw too much attention."

"What about your jacket? It's leather," I said.

He smiled and raised his arm. The forearm of the jacket had a built-in screen with several small buttons. He hit a couple of them and the jacket pixelated in a blur of motion in front of me. A second later, it looked as though he were wearing a simple green hoodie.

"Is that... Nexweave?" I managed.

"Yes, and it's very expensive. Are you ready to go?"

I nodded and pulled the bandana over my face. Edgar hit another button, and a matching face shield materialized on his face.

I couldn't believe he had a Nexweave jacket. Nanotech-enabled Nexweave clothing was extremely illegal due to the technology itself and the ability to allow its user to impersonate anyone or hide in any situation. The cloth itself was hyper-magnetic and made of metallic fibers that were sensitive to different voltages. When combined with Nanotech, which consisted of billions of microscopic robots that could alter the cloth or protect the wearer from harm, it was some of the most potent and expensive apparel one could own. Nexweave clothing could stop a knife, bullet, or directed energy blast, and it weighed close to nothing. Most had assumed it only existed in the Upper Level; others, like myself, doubted its existence at all, chalking it up as another rumor.

We moved through the streets at a brisk pace as I followed close behind Edgar. We turned down an empty alleyway, and Edgar knocked on a rusted steel door on the end. A shady looking man in a ragged hoodie opened the door and motioned us inside. The building looked as if it had been abandoned for many years, the air inside was dusty and dry, and random bits of debris littered the grimy floor. Edgar led me to a large steel hatch at the end of the room. "Put on your respirator."

We put on our respirators, and he lifted the hatch. A blast of yellow steam emerged from the vent as the pressure inside released. A fan above us on the ceiling of the building activated rapidly and expelled the gas into the outside air. I followed Edgar down the steel ladder rungs that protruded from the rough concrete walling of the hole. We reached the bottom, and I found that we were in a long concrete passageway with huge metal pipes on either side. Portions of the pipes were spewing hisses of steam, and large turn valves were sticking out every twenty feet or so. I didn't feel comfortable at all down here. Clouds of discolored steam obscured light and could allow someone to hide alongside the dark walls, unnoticeable until they were just a couple of feet away.

"Don't touch the pipes, they aren't insulated and will give you a nasty burn," Edgar warned.

I could actually breathe with the respirator, which surprised me—I never thought that the air down in the Undercity was breathable. The parts of the Undercity that we traveled through had many sub-climates which were separated by steel doors and hatches. Some portions were unreasonably hot and humid due to steam leaks in large pipes that were partially corroded. Other lengths were cold and dry, void of the colossal steam pipes.

We continued through the tunnels, taking many turns and going through many steel doors, none of which were locked. Edgar pointed out various hazards as we proceeded: Metallic stairs coated in slick oil that was dripping from an overhead pipe, a puddle of some sort of acid that would eat through the soles of my shoes, and a section of low hanging pipes that weren't visible when approaching them. I could see how easy it would be to get lost or killed down here.

The lighting in most of the tunnels was poor at best, and it didn't look like anyone had taken the effort to replace the failed lighting units for a very long time. There were all sorts of bugs crawling along the walls, which Edgar didn't seem to mind at all, but I gave them wide berth.

We approached a large clearing and saw three men smoking cigarettes, their faces unprotected from the poisonous air. When they saw us, they started approaching in a slow manner, dropping their cigarettes and stamping them out. I could see that they were armed now: one held a long knife, and the other two had short lengths of iron pipe, holding them as makeshift bludgeons.

"Look what we've got ere', boys," the man with the knife said in a thick accent.

I positioned myself behind Edgar for safety. I wouldn't be much good in a fight with my broken wrist, not that I knew how to fight at all.

"We'll be passing through here without your hindrance," Edgar said simply.

The man with the knife laughed. "We shouldn' hinder their path, boys," he shouted, and the others joined in laughing.

My heart was beating rapidly now, these were the type of people that should be avoided at all costs, and down here there was barely anywhere to run. If I got separated from Edgar, I knew that I'd have a very hard time finding my way out.

The man with the knife brandished the weapon and slashed it with manic motion in the air in front of us before grinning again. "We'll be takin' your belongins' and you can be on your way."

Edgar hit a button on his wrist, and the light jacket returned to the appearance of the oiled leather jacket. The men backed up slightly at this.

"Do you think he's with the Government?" one of the men asked the leader.

"No, it's jist' a trick, get em!" the man beckoned. I could see the knife shaking in his hand, unsure if it was from fear or from breathing in too much of the bad air.

One of the men beside the leader lunged out at Edgar with an overhead blow, swinging the thick iron pipe in a wide arc. I was surprised to see that Edgar quickly sidestepped the swing. After dodging, Edgar lowered his posture and punched the man in the rib cage with incredible force. The man doubled over and fell to the ground while the other man came in swinging the pipe sluggishly. Edgar caught the man's wrist during the clumsy swing and kicked him in the gut. The man held his ground, but missed another swing and received a well-aimed punch to the nose that sent him sprawling. I heard the distinct sound of bone cracking and saw the man reach up to his nose to try to stop the bleeding as he crawled away from Edgar.

Edgar pulled out the handgun with a swift, fluid motion and held it steady on the leader. Surprisingly, the leader's expression didn't change.

"I'll bet on my knife oer' your cutter torch any day."

Edgar shifted the gun to the left and pulled the trigger. A great flash of purple light emerged from the barrel, and I could see a glowing orange crater on the wall to the left where the blast had hit several feet away.

The man with the knife shifted the blade and held it with his palm to show that he was backing off. The others followed, and they retreated into one of the tunnels, cursing along the way.

"Sorry about that, Jake. I assure you that it's much nicer once we reach the Guild Hall."

"Where'd you learn to fight like that?" I asked, in awe of his skill.

"My colleagues taught me when I was about your age. The Nanotech helps significantly." He raised his hand and I could see that it was coated in a glove that looked like carbon fiber.

"What kind of gun is that?" I asked.

"Directed energy weapon. HexTox gas."

"HexTox gas?"

"Hexathoxian gas, HexTox for short. It's used in reactor cooling to transfer a lot of heat very quickly. It heats and cools at a very fast rate. It's ideal for short-range weapons and packs quite a punch. Anyway, we've got to get moving," Edgar said as he re-holstered the gun. He hit another button, and his jacket took the appearance of a different leather jacket. It was red and black, and I could see a strange insignia on the shoulder. The Nanotech shifted again, and the jacket bulked up. It now had armored pauldrons and thick pieces of reinforced leather on the front and back. I wanted a jacket like his.

"It's time you meet my colleagues, Jake," Edgar said.

10

AS IRON SHARPENS IRON

We continued through the narrowing tunnels for some time, descending several flights of rusted stairs. It was getting colder and drier as we descended, the tunnels void of pipes. There was no way to tell exactly how expansive the Undercity was, but it wasn't something I wanted to learn by myself.

"Now Jake, when we reach the Guild Hall, and I introduce you to my colleague, you will address him as sir, and you will not hold back in your vocabulary. Incorrect words up above are correct down here, and they hold particular value amongst us," Edgar said as we continued forward.

"What do I do if he says something that I don't know the meaning of?"

Edgar took a moment to consider this. "You may ask him what the word means, but do not stop him frequently, try to infer the meaning if possible. You won't be expected to have a refined vocabulary as an outsider of the Guild. Just be respectful and listen to what he has to say to you, you might learn a lot. I'm going to leave you with Master Aarlen while I speak with the others about teaching you and possible recruitment in the future."

"What if they don't like me, will I be free to leave?" I tried to keep the nerves out of my voice. This hardly seemed like something that one could walk away from.

"Of course you'll be free to leave. We aren't in the business of killing civilians. Don't worry about that, just try to learn as much as possible from Master Aarlen while you have the opportunity, I expect that he will be able to provide you with great guidance."

"Thanks, Edgar."

We turned the corner, and Edgar moved in front of me and pulled back a small lever on the side of a steel panel in the concrete walling. There was a dull click, and the panel slid back revealing a passageway behind it. When we moved past the doorway, Edgar pulled another lever, and the panel slid back into place, closing us in utter darkness.

All of a sudden, a light from Edgar's jacket illuminated the dark passageway in front of us. We walked further down and approached a small mechanical lift which dropped us down a long distance at a speed that made my stomach drop. At the last possible second, the elevator slowed to a standstill, and we were level with a massive steel blast door with mostly faded fallout shelter icons. Two men in the same jacket as Edgar stood guarding either side, short rifles of some sort hanging from slings rested in their hands. We approached, and the doors opened automatically. I was not prepared for what was inside.

My impression of the outside was that it was going to be some run-down emergency shelter from another age. It was anything but that. The first thing I noticed was how huge the complex really was. We were standing at the bottom of a colossal room that was filled with red carpeting instead of laminate tile or steel flooring. Warm amber light bulbs lit several tables off to the left where people sat enjoying a meal with one another. A man moved from behind the bar carrying strange mugs to the patrons. The right side of the complex was devoted to huge, towering bookshelves filled to the brim with books of all colors.

Toward the back of the giant room, there were several doors that looked to be made of wood lining the building, and plenty of tables where people sat reading books and working on datapads. There was a second story as well, overlooking the massive main hall with balconies along all the walls. I could see some more bookshelves on the second level of the facility and more tables as well. The entire room was impossibly large. I kept looking around, trying to absorb my surrounding and the elegance of this place.

"Follow me, I'll take you to Master Aarlen," Edgar said.

I got several curious looks as we walked to the right toward the bookshelves. The people here were many different ages, and some were dressed differently than others, wearing nice dressy clothes instead of the rugged leather jacket that Edgar was wearing. The books smelled slightly dusty, but it was a welcome smell, a smell of knowledge. It occurred to me that there were probably more books here than I could ever read in my lifetime, thousands and thousands of volumes filled with knowledge. Huge ladders on rolling tracks ascended the bookshelves which looked about twenty feet tall. I struggled to keep my eyes forward and not slow down, I wanted nothing more than to browse the shelves and find something new to read, something new to learn.

We continued to the end of the shelves and approached a wooden door. I couldn't even remember the last time I had seen anything made of wood, the rare material made from trees which were extinct in the Slums. What trees had been planted around the districts were run down by cars, hacked down by makeshift axes and sold during the shortage of wood that had started well before I was born. Now wood of any kind was a precious commodity, hence the reason real paper was so expensive.

As we were approaching, a girl around my age stepped forward from the side. She was wearing the same jacket as Edgar but had a black headset over her hair. She was slightly shorter than me but looked very athletic—much more so than I was. She moved in front of the door.

"Hi, Edgar. Who is this?"

"Hello, Caeldra. This is Jake, I would like for him to meet Master Aarlen. He might be the next great Unbound."

"Hmm, doesn't look like much," she said in a soft voice as she appraised me with critical ice blue eyes. "Especially with a broken arm. Master Aarlen is eating his lunch, but I will let him know he has a visitor."

The girl pressed a few buttons on an old looking datapad.

"Thank you. I think that you and Jake have a common disdain of Enforcers, Caeldra," Edgar said with a smirk.

She shifted slightly and I could see a thin scar that ran down the side of her cheek. It wasn't ugly and was quite faded. She was beautiful with her slicked back blonde hair and light complexion. The scar was the only blemish on an otherwise flawless face.

"I see. Well, Jake, this is a good place to be if you don't care to live under the rule of the Government or participate in their Absolute Knowledge bullshit."

I almost winced but caught myself. Speaking badly of the Government got people sent to the Sculptors. Things were different here.

"I'm afraid I must meet with the Council. Caeldra, I will leave Jake in your capable hands while I attend to other matters. I trust that you will keep him occupied while you wait for Master Aarlen to finish his lunch," Edgar said.

"Certainly," she said with a slight grin.

Edgar walked away and left us alone. I turned to Caeldra and smiled nervously, and had no idea what to say.

"Unbound, huh?"

"I don't even know what that means," I confessed.

"That figures. Master Aarlen is the only Unbound in the Champions of Liberty."

More questions rushed into my head. "That's the name of your guild, the Champions of Liberty?"

"Yes and the Unbound are those with an enhanced ability to layer and create projections of incredible depth and immersion. I suppose you've done something to impress Justicar Barton."

"Justicar?" The word was unknown to me.

Caeldra sighed. "He's one of the Council members. We've adopted the word Justicar, based on the Latin term justiarius or justice in English as a title for the Council members. If you've got a Justicar backing you, then you've got a good chance of guild admission."

Her answer filled me with more questions than answers. I didn't know what Latin or Justice meant, they were new words to me.

"And Master Aarlen, is he in the Council?"

Thankfully, she remained patient with me. "No, Master Aarlen is responsible for expanding and maintaining our knowledge pool. He is in charge of the library, and the electronic knowledge base."

"The Guild is collecting knowledge like the Government?" I asked, regretting the question the second it slipped my mouth.

"You'd best mind your tongue. We collect truth to preserve through the ages, books and tomes of ancient times past, things we can't afford to lose," she said, her voice sharp.

"I apologize; I didn't mean the question the way I'm sure it came across."

She nodded, "it's alright, just don't say anything like that when you speak with Master Aarlen. He won't appreciate it or have the patience for such things."

"I understand. Thank you, Caeldra."

"You've got a whole life to catch up on if you're admitted to the Guild. I hope you're ready to work hard. Do you know how to fight?" she asked.

"No, I've never learned. I generally just avoid dangerous situations."

"How'd the Enforcers get you?"

"A thief stole a friend's belonging and took off. I took off after him and managed to catch him. We caught the attention of Enforcers, and they decided that we were both guilty for crimes against the Government. One broken wrist each."

"Trying to impress a girl?"

"More or less," I conceded.

She smiled and nodded in approval then raised her hand to her ear. "Yes sir, I'll send him in." Caeldra looked at me, "mind your manners and treat him with respect," she said in a serious tone.

I nodded and thanked her before stepping forward and opening the door. The office was rather small but contained a large wooden desk that had neat stacks of books on either side. Most of the surface was a large holoprojector that was currently turned off. Behind the desk sat an elderly man with thick brown glasses that was wearing a crisp, gray button-up shirt and brown slacks. He was considerably well dressed compared to the rugged appearance of most of the Guild members in their leather. He had a sharp looking nose and many wrinkles on his face that exposed his age. Caeldra closed the door after I walked in.

"Ah, Jake I presume? I'm Master Aarlen."

"Yes sir," I said, careful to be polite and respectful.

"Please have a seat, Jake. I'm very excited to speak with you. Edgar has told me a little bit about what you've done with your mind. He also mentioned that you were the one that found this copy of An Essay Concerning Human Understanding," he said as he pulled the book from under the desk. "I was quite pleased to find the complete set of essays in print form, we had a digital file of most of the work, but we were missing a few pages that were lost due to corrupted data."

"Mr. Barton has been very kind and has helped me through a lot over the years. After teaching me layering and mental projections, he wanted me to speak with you due to what happened to me. I was hoping that you could give me guidance."

"As iron sharpens iron, so one person sharpens another," he said with a smile.

"Sir?"

"Proverbs 27:17. It's a verse from an ancient book, I'm sure you don't know what I'm talking about and that's quite alright. Think of it like this; you've come to me for guidance with your layering and projecting, I am quite experienced with both and can probably help you. In doing so, I would likely gain something in return, be it a new friend or new information, perhaps I'll even learn to do something new. In our conversation, we are able to both improve on some level. Now, tell me exactly what you've done."

I told him everything that had happened to me in my projection of my mind. He sat and listened with appreciation as I told it, remaining quiet until I had finished.

"You most likely had six divisions of your mind. As it was the first time that you had divided your mind in such a way, I'm quite surprised you were able to manage what you did. The fact that you managed to create them instantly is even more incredible." He paused and folded his hands across the desk.

"Let me tell you what happened and why things were the way they appeared. As you create more divisions of your mind, you delve deeper and deeper into what I like to call your sleeping mind. On a daily basis, we suppress thoughts and ideas, burying them deeper and deeper, creating natural layering that protects us. We hide our fears, painful memories, and nightmares deeper and deeper down.

"As far as I and all the Unbound before me have learned, there is no hard limit to how many subdivisions we can create. I can consistently produce thirteen, the late Master Robert, my mentor, was able to create sixteen before he passed. It varies by individual, but who is to say there is a hard limit? The Unbound are individuals that are able to unlock the potential of the brain to do amazing things. Based on your experience and the data Edgar sent me, I think you've got the potential to become the next great Unbound."

"What do the Unbound do in the Champions of Liberty?"

Master Aarlen smiled. "The brain is more powerful than any computer, no matter how fast it is. Computers will always be limited by the sum of their components, the brain is not. Think about it, the brain is a dense block of neurons that can communicate with each other in endless varieties. The Unbound are able to use projections and subdividing to create encryption codes that are virtually unsolvable. By breaking portions of the code down and spreading them throughout multiple layers of our mind, much like what you did when Edgar had you hide the box, we are able to protect and preserve our data in a way that the Government will never hope to understand.

"Even if the Government found our Knowledge base, it would take lifetimes for a quantum computer to break down the work that has been done by the Unbound over the last hundred years.

The Unbound protect and preserve information through the ages to pass on to future generations. We defend the truth, and in doing so, the truth protects us. Nothing is more absolute than the laws of mathematics which will always hold the test of time, they were there in the beginning, and they will be there in the end."

"I don't know what to say, Master Aarlen. You think I could become an Unbound?"

"Yes, and I'd like you to train with me. I've already discussed this with Edgar, and he is discussing your recruitment into the Guild with the Council, something in which I have no say. Would you like to learn from me?"

"Does it ever get better? More subdivisions, I mean."

He frowned. "No, it gets worse. As you progress in your studies, it will get worse, but you will learn to better control your mind and internally manage your mental strain. We as Unbound work to develop layered encryptions over time, it is not a fast process. If I am permitted to teach you by the council, you will learn to break free of your subdivisions instantly. Things can get quite dangerous as you delve deeper into your mind. Sometimes you need to break free quickly and escape something awful." He frowned and rubbed his eyes with his hands after removing his glasses. "I'm sorry Jake, I don't mean to scare you away. We find truth to be the most valuable trait and method of approach to situations in the Guild."

"I'd like to train with you if I am permitted, Master Aarlen."

This was a man that could teach me great things, a man that could give me new skills to live the best life possible.

A smile appeared on his face. "Splendid, I hope the Council will admit you. You must excuse me, Jake, I've got another appointment which I must keep. It has been a pleasure meeting you and I expect great things from you."

"Thank you for everything, Master Aarlen," I said as I exited the room. Caeldra was still standing outside, and she motioned another man wearing the Guild's leather jacket inside as I exited.

"So?"

"He wants me to become his student," I said with a smile.

"Wow, I'll be seeing a lot more of you if you're admitted to the Guild then."

"Should I wait here for Edgar?"

"Yes, you shouldn't go wandering around since you aren't part of the Guild. It wouldn't sit well with the Council."

Just as I started nodding, I saw Edgar walking toward us.

"How did your meeting with Master Aarlen go?" he asked me.

"It went quite well."

He nodded. "Jake, the Champions of Liberty would like to admit you as a member of the organization, but there's a slight problem."

11
SKETCHBOOK

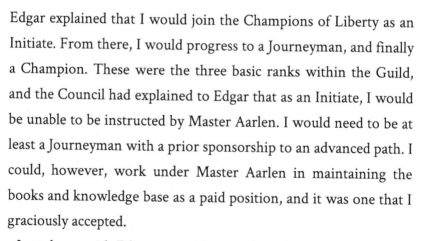

Edgar explained that I would join the Champions of Liberty as an Initiate. From there, I would progress to a Journeyman, and finally a Champion. These were the three basic ranks within the Guild, and the Council had explained to Edgar that as an Initiate, I would be unable to be instructed by Master Aarlen. I would need to be at least a Journeyman with a prior sponsorship to an advanced path. I could, however, work under Master Aarlen in maintaining the books and knowledge base as a paid position, and it was one that I graciously accepted.

I sat down with Edgar at a table near the pub, and he ordered us each a short mug of a dark beer. I watched with fascination as the bartender poured the mugs and used a wooden knife to slice off the extra foam on top. The beer was strangely delicious. It was a strong flavor and tasted of wheat.

"Now Jake, I know you were expecting to learn from Master Aarlen, but working under him for the time being while you seek sponsorship elsewhere will help you make some money and get acquainted with how things work down here. As an Archivist, Master Aarlen will provide you with an enormous reading list to continue your education. I'm afraid I won't be teaching you anymore either. We need to focus on finding you a sponsor that is at least a Journeyman in rank. You need to consider what it is that you'd like to be doing in the Guild if becoming an Unbound doesn't work out."

"What options do I have, and what do you recommend?"

"There are several paths to choose. There are Runners which are paid quite well in the Guild, and it's the path I started with. You mostly complete odd errands and various tasks, but will also learn to fight if you need to. You can become a Tradesman and work to improve our commerce and working relations with other organizations. Or you can join our military and train to be a soldier or guard, though life as a soldier is pretty dull right now. Those are the options for official sponsorships that could land you an apprenticeship under Master Aarlen in the future. You can be whatever you want to so long as it doesn't interfere with the code of conduct, something you'll have to read thoroughly before we leave today."

"Did you enjoy being a Runner?"

"Very much so. But you do need to know that it's dangerous. If that's the path you choose, I know the perfect sponsor."

"Would I be able to change my path if it didn't suit me? And will I still be able to live my normal life on the surface?"

"If it doesn't suit you, then you are welcome to change your path. You would be able to live your normal life, and you're actually required to live on the surface as a Runner. We like to have eyes and ears in the Slums wherever possible."

It wasn't a hard decision. I wasn't ready to give up my life with Mary and it seemed like becoming a Runner would be my best shot at maintaining as normal of a life as I could.

"I'd like to become a Runner for my advanced path and work as an Archivist under Master Aarlen on my off time."

He smiled, "an excellent choice. I will alert your potential sponsor. Let's go read The Code today before we leave so that you'll be ready to be sworn in tomorrow."

We walked back over to the library and sat down at a large desk. Edgar brought over a small book and slid it in front of me. "Read it cover to cover and ask me if you have any questions."

It was a small book of only thirteen pages; the code of conduct for members of the Guild. The basic idea was that I would swear to always act in the interest of providing for and protecting the Guild, safeguard and preserve the lives of civilians, and work to establish and preserve liberty and political freedom. Everything seemed reasonable, despite being the most treasonous thing against the Government that I had ever read, and I was anxious to join and begin my education. I wanted nothing more than to hone my brain and learn more truth. I was hoping to train under Master Aarlen and didn't care if I had to be a Runner for a while to get there.

"I don't have any questions; it all seems pretty straight forward."

"Great. Let's start heading back to the surface, Mary will be expecting us for dinner soon."

Edgar and I exited the Guild Hall and took the lift back up to the narrow tunnel. "What does Caeldra do?" I asked him as we proceeded down the dark path.

"She's a Runner."

It was starting to make sense. Caeldra obviously worked under Master Aarlen.

"Is she training under Master Aarlen?"

"Yes, but in data technology, she's not attempting to become an Unbound. She is also the head Archivist—best one we've got by far. She'll make an ideal sponsor for you as she can help you improve as a Runner and Archivist."

I remembered my memory from the projection I had been trapped in and the conversation between my father and Edgar regarding me becoming an Archivist and decided to chalk it up to coincidence. Still, how could I have known that position extended to the Champions of Liberty having known nothing about the Guild up until this point of my life?

"I see. Thank you," I responded.

We proceeded the rest of the way up through the Undercity in silence. Once we returned to the surface, I went back to my flat to freshen up before dinner at Edgar's. The day's travels had left me smelling like sweat and sulfur. I expected that Mary would be by later and decided a shower was in order. I hoped there would be a good time to give her the small sketchbook.

I returned to Edgar's flat and was rushed in as usual. Edgar already had his apron on and was chopping some vegetables for the dinner.

"Is there anything I can help with?"

"Not yet, you and Mary can start on the soup once she gets here," he said as he diced an onion.

"Why do you chose to live in the Slums instead of the Guild Hall? I don't see the appeal in living in a standard issue flat when you can live so much better."

"Well, that's a tough question. It started as a requirement. I was a Runner for fifteen years and was required to live on the surface. When I was elected Justicar, I never made the move despite the residency requirement being lifted. Living in the Slums gives me perspective, it allows me to see the true value in what I do, what I choose to fight for."

"Why do you teach Government sponsored classes if you hate the Government so much?"

"It was a requirement. I needed a job on the surface—something legal. I had to find something to do that would make it appear to the Government that I was a normal citizen. With my scores, I was able to become a teacher. I made much more as a Runner, but again, it's all about blending in and it's something I don't mind doing. You'll note that I only teach subjects of truth. As far as I know, no one has ever returned to work as a Thinker after joining the Guild. You don't have it yet, but you'll be required to carry around a small glass vial of cyanide for if you're caught, and the Government is going to interrogate you."

"As in the chemical compound that is extremely lethal?" I asked.

"Yes, unfortunately so. It's mixed with some other chemicals to make it as painless as possible. Sometimes it's necessary to preserve the greater good. It will also give you a way out if you're stuck dying somewhere," Edgar said, his voice grim.

I hadn't even thought about something like that. It was a scary thought.

"But don't worry about that, it's only meant to prevent a slow and painful death if your fate is sealed. It's more of an insurance policy, really," he said.

There was a knock on the door.

"We can continue this conversation on the way through the Undercity tomorrow morning. Let's enjoy a nice treason-free dinner with Mary."

I let Mary in quickly and smiled. She pulled off the bandana and light jacket. She was wearing her orange dress, the fanciest thing she owned by far. It was by no means fine clothing, but it made her look as beautiful as ever.

"What's the occasion?" I asked.

"Oh, I just want to dress up from time to time," she said as she twirled around in a circle, showcasing the dress.

"Beautiful as always," I said with a grin.

Mary blushed and looked at me with her big eyes the way she always did when I said something sweet. That look always made my heart race and my thoughts grow frantic, but I loved it.

"Ah, Mary. It's great to see you. You and Jake can get started on the soup if you want, I'm almost done prepping the ingredients. Just be sure to keep Chef Ashton away from the intricate workings of the meal," he said.

Mary laughed, and the two of us entered the kitchen. Under orders from Edgar, we washed our hands in the sink with some drinking water and soap before getting started on the soup. I picked up the large steel soup pot from under one of the cabinets and filled it halfway with drinking water before setting it on the stove to boil. Mary and Edgar far surpassed my cooking abilities, so I was more or less always assigned to do the menial tasks such as lifting a pot, measuring out some water, fetching measuring spoons, etc. I was never trusted with dispensing spices, cutting vegetables, or doing any of the actual food chemistry that turned simple ingredients into delicious meals.

"Chef Mary, I will trust the creation of the soup to you and give you access to my extended spice rack," Edgar said with a grin as he reached up into the cabinet and pulled down a wooden box filled to the brim with glass spice bottles. Some of the bottles were wrapped in cloth ribbon.

Mary's eyes lit up. "Where did you get all of these!" she exclaimed as she shifted through the box.

"They were a gift from a friend, I don't use them often, but would really enjoy a fine soup this evening. I trust you will find them useful in spicing things up if you'll pardon the pun."

She began opening the bottles and smelling the contents inside. There were all sorts of different looking herbs, seeds, and spice concoctions, all of which were unlabeled.

"It seems I have forgotten to purchase some bread. You two keep cooking, I'll run to the store." Edgar brought over the tray of diced vegetables and set it on the counter. When Mary turned away, he made a strange gesture in the air, drawing a rectangle with his fingers. I suddenly understood. He was giving me a chance to give the gift to Mary. Alone.

Edgar stepped out and headed off in the direction of the store. He was wearing the same light jacket as before; I was pretty sure it was the Nexweave.

"Jake, can you pass me the vegetables please?"

"Sure," I responded as I handed her the tray. My heart was already pounding in my chest, how was I going to do this? Would it be awkward? What if she didn't like the gift?

I pushed the fears out of my head and decided to try a real-world application of the small amount of layering training I had received. I focused and pushed the fear of rejection under a segment of my mind which I sealed under a barrier. I was overcome with an instant sensation of calmness. When Mary wasn't looking, I smiled at the minor success I had just experienced. My fear of timing and uncertainty of when to give the gift to her was replaced by knowledge that I should do it once everything was simmering on the burner when there wasn't anything to do but talk while we waited. For the next twenty minutes, I assisted Mary with menial cooking tasks and waited until we were done with the cooking. I was very thankful that Edgar wasn't back yet in case I embarrassed myself. I suspected that he was giving me ample time to give her the gift, knowing that I'd try to delay it as long as possible. He was such a great friend.

When the work was done, and a marvelous aroma radiated from the kitchen, I was almost as excited to eat the soup as I was to give Mary the sketchbook.

"Mary, I picked up something for you the other day. I saw it and couldn't pass it up, I knew it would make a perfect gift for you," I said looking in her eyes. She looked excited and nervous at the same time, shifting slightly from foot to foot. She probably felt the same way I had when she gave me the amazing drawing.

"Jake! You know you don't have to buy me anything," she said, appraising me.

I reached into my pocket and cupped the small sketchbook with both hands, concealing it from her as I brought up my hands. I uncupped them and handed her the sketchbook. Her face went pale for a second, and I heard her take in a sharp breath of air and hold it as she looked over the gift. She fingered the stitched leather surface and flipped through the pristine white paper pages.

"Jake... This is too much; it must have cost a fortune."

"It didn't, and I knew that it was meant for you. You need something where you can put your treasured ideas and store them to last."

"Thank you, Jake. This is the best gift anyone has ever given me. It's perfect," she was elated now and lunged forward to scoop me up in a hug. I felt my barrier start to waver as I was pulled into the close embrace, but it held firm.

She pulled back slightly then kissed me on the cheek, and I could feel myself starting to blush when we heard a knock on the door. Edgar was back. Mary turned to the door and started toward it, then turned back to me and gave me a kiss on the lips. Her soft lips radiated heat as they came into contact with mine. It was perfect, and I was stunned, but before I could say anything she had already let Edgar back inside the flat. When she had kissed me, my barrier that was protecting a portion of my mind had shattered, but the nervous thoughts behind it had already been replaced with a mixture of joy and disbelief.

Edgar walked back into the kitchen and gave me a questioning look, which I responded with a wide grin. He nodded in subtle approval. After he had passed, Mary gave me a sincere smile and another hug before returning to check on the soup. It felt like the best day of my life. Mary, the girl of my dreams, had kissed me, we were about to eat a meal that would rival the luxury breakfast Edgar had prepared for me, and I was about to join a secret organization of treasonous criminals—in a good way. Things were moving fast and for the first time in my life, I felt like I had a greater calling—I felt like I could be something incredible.

The three of us sat down and ate a perfect meal, enjoying each other's company and sharing a great bond of friendship. No amount of layering could keep me from looping the kiss over and over in my mind, recollecting the way her lips had felt on mine, the soft, comforting sensation. After dinner, I walked Mary back to her flat and went inside knowing that I couldn't stay long, it was approaching curfew.

Mary was blushing hard when we were inside the entrance of her flat. "Jake, I'm sorry for kissing you. I was just really excited about the gift and I…"

I cut her off. "Don't be, it was perfect." I didn't know where the words were coming from, I only hoped I wouldn't mess things up now. "I really like you, Mary. More than as a friend. I…" This time she cut me off, with a kiss.

After, we both stood there in perfect silence, each of us contemplating just how much we meant to each other. "I should get going, curfew is approaching."

She nodded and smiled. "I'll see you tomorrow, Jake."

I left and started back, grinning like an idiot under my bandana facemask. As I was approaching my flat, I saw a hooded figure walking toward me rapidly. I increased my speed and noticed that the figure had done the same and was now gaining on me. I broke into a run toward my flat and attempted to use the retina scanner on my door when I was grabbed from the doorway by powerful arms. I tried to scream, but my mouth was already covered with frigid metal.

12
INITIATE

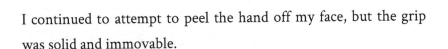

I continued to attempt to peel the hand off my face, but the grip was solid and immovable.

"Shhhhh!" a metallic voice hissed. "I'm a friend."

I relaxed slightly as the hand retreated from my face. I had no idea who it was—the identity of the voice was hidden by the voice modulator of a thick respirator mask. "I've put something in your pocket for you to consider. Have a nice evening."

I saw a brief jolt of motion on the figure as pieces of something shifted shape and location, it looked like Nanotech. As quickly as they had appeared, the person had walked off casually away from me. I decided it best not to pursue them. Anyone that was that size that could lift me with such ease shouldn't be messed with, especially since I had no clue how to fight and my wrist was still healing in the cast.

Still trembling, I made my way inside my flat and locked the door behind me, my fingers fumbling on the lock. I reached into my pocket and pulled out a folded block of pulp paper. There were two pieces of paper. The first was some sort of receipt for claiming Asset 47CZ-K8b, and the other was a note from the mystery assailant:

Take the requisition scrip to the Guild Quartermaster once you're admitted.
    —Your Guardian

It was such a strange encounter; I was just glad that I hadn't been injured. Had someone in the Guild given this to me? Was it a trap? I knew that it wasn't Edgar or Caeldra, the figure that had grabbed me was huge, much taller and bigger than either of them. Aside from a brief glance as I was leaving Mary's flat, I hadn't seen the person at all. He was wearing what had looked to be a dark gray jacket with a large hood and metal respirator mask. I felt metal when the person wrapped their hand over my face, but it could have been a glove.

I decided that I would take the scrip to the Quartermaster after I was admitted, as the note told me to. I would have to ask Caeldra where they were located. I also decided that it would be best to keep the encounter secret from Edgar, as I didn't want to do anything that would keep me from being admitted into the Champions of Liberty. If things got more serious, or I perceived that I was in danger I would seek help from Edgar, but not tonight. I tucked the scrip into my backpack in a secure place then got ready to sleep. It would be another early morning.

Unfortunately, my sleep was filled with nightmares of my parents—terrible dreams that kept continuing from where they had left off after each time I had woken up. Needless to say, I was in a foul mood when it was time to wake up in the morning, and I desperately hoped there would be coffee.

After a simple breakfast, I pulled on my clothes and zipped up my jacket. 6 AM, my watch read. I groaned and pulled on my backpack and face mask before exiting my flat. It was starting to get colder now, and I would have to break out my heavy jacket and gloves soon to stay warm. I had no idea how winter would affect the temperatures of the Undercity, it seemed to have countless micro-climates with an endless variety of humidity and temperature.

I walked over to Edgar's flat, taking a long glance over at Mary's. It looked like she was still asleep, and all the lights were out. I knocked on the door, and Edgar walked out, fully geared.

"We've got to get going right away," he said.

I had really been hoping for some morning coffee to wake me up and give me some energy, and my disappointment was probably clear to Edgar. But I was thankful that I had decided to eat some breakfast before heading over. I followed him back to the same building where the same suspicious looking man let us inside. After putting on the respirators, we descended the hatch and entered into the tunneling of the Undercity.

"You lead," Edgar told me.

"What? How am I supposed to know where to go?" I demanded.

"Do your best. As a Runner, you'll need to learn quickly. Caeldra isn't going to put up with you if you don't learn fast."

I frowned and continued down the tunnel. It was such a long way to get to the Guild Hall that I knew I'd never make it. I relaxed slightly as I was walking and felt my mind sharpen. It felt like a projection, but I was completely conscious. The memory of the previous day's travels played in my mind. I held the concentration and knew which turns to take, which ladders to descend, and before I knew it, we had arrived at the lift that would carry us down several hundred feet to the gates of the Guild Hall. Edgar smiled.

"Nice job, Jake. Now, when we enter the Council Hall, you will be asked a few questions by the Council. Each member will introduce themselves to you, and you will call them Justicar or Councilor, followed by their names."

I nodded, and Edgar flipped the lever on the lift, shooting us down through darkness at gut-wrenching speed.

We slowed to a stop outside of the gates and were once again admitted. As we walked in, Caeldra emerged from the side and walked along side me.

"Try not to mess this up, I was starting to like you," she said with a smirk.

"I don't plan on messing it up," I responded.

"Good, because I really don't want to kill you."

I felt the color drain from my face. Was I going to be killed if I failed? Would I be allowed to leave?

"Caeldra," Edgar said, his voice flat.

"Sorry. I'm just messing with you, Jake. You'll be fine. Besides, we don't kill people that aren't admitted," Caeldra said with a smile.

It calmed me, but the butterflies in my stomach continued. I was nervous about this, more nervous than I had been when I was about to give the sketchbook to Mary. I feared that if I sealed my nerves behind a barrier, then I would be at risk of appearing bored or uninterested in joining. Would my nerves make me too jittery or nervous to be admitted? Unlike the Government test, nerves could make a difference here.

"We're here. Remember what I told you, Jake. Since I've already given you my support, you will meet with the other five Council members."

We were outside a dark wooden door, there weren't any windows so that I could see what waited inside.

"You'll do great," Caeldra said as she leaned in and gave me a kiss on the cheek before whispering in my ear. "Don't mind Alex."

I stood there shocked for a moment, unsure why she had kissed me, my face felt hot. Composing myself, I took a deep breath before opening the door and stepping inside.

There was a small desk in front of me with an empty chair. In front of the desk was a large half circle desk where six people in loose black robes sat. The room was bigger than it appeared from the outside with a high arching ceiling and floor that was lower than the entrance, a short series of stairs leading down from the doorway I was standing in. There were three men and two women that sat before me, eyeing me with ranged emotion as I walked in.

"Please have a seat, Mr. Ashton. My name is Chloe Schaff," one of the women who looked to be in her forties said to me. Her bright blonde hair contrasted the darkness of the robe.

"Thank you, Justicar," I responded as I took the seat. My hands had grown clammy, and I was doing my best to hide my nerves. I scooted the chair up closer to the desk on the carpet and folded my hands on top of the desk surface to keep them from fidgeting.

"I'm going to ask you a few questions myself, and then any of the other Council members will be able to do the same. When we have concluded, we will meet briefly and make our decision. Now, onto my first question. Was there a Great Flood of 2039?"

"No," I responded. Justicar Chloe's expression didn't change, and she proceeded to the next question.

"Have you ever directly defied the Government in a treasonous way?"

"Yes. I read a book that I wasn't supposed to."

"The title by John Locke?"

"Yes."

"Master Aarlen informed us that the full book had been recovered. I'm guessing that was you?"

"Yes, ma'am."

"What do The Champions of Liberty stand for?"

I hesitated. "Freedom of the people and preservation of truth throughout the ages."

"What do you wish to do if you are admitted into the Guild?"

"Train as a Runner then seek apprenticeship under Master Aarlen to become an Unbound."

"That's all the questions I have for you, Mr. Ashton," Justicar Chloe concluded.

"Mr. Ashton. My name is Alex Price. I question if you are ready for admittance into our organization. It seems you have only recently learned some bit of truth," said one of the men in front of me. He had dark brown hair which was combed over and plastered with gel, his eyes dark and fierce. I waited for him to continue and he didn't. What he had said wasn't a question, but I decided to address it anyway.

"I'm confident in my ability to quickly learn and become a valuable asset to the Champions of Liberty," I said hoping that I sounded more confident than I felt.

"I'm not sure I believe that," Alex said in a flat tone, boredom clear in his expression.

"Master Aarlen believes that I have potential to bec—"

"Master Aarlen doesn't have any say in this matter," he responded, cutting me off.

I didn't know what to say.

"What skills other than your mind games would you bring to this organization?" Alex asked, impatience creeping into his tone as if he had much better things to do then speak to me.

"As I stated earlier, I wish to train to become a Runner."

I saw him eye my cast. "Is your arm expected to heal soon? You won't be much use to us if you can't use that arm."

"Justicar Barton thinks it will be fully healed in a couple of weeks."

"That's all from me," he said in an annoyed tone as he waved his hand dismissively.

I breathed out a quiet sigh of relief and hoped none of the others would be so harsh.

"Mr. Ashton, my name is Clark," said the man on the end, he looked much friendlier than Alex and appeared to be in his thirties. He wore a look of amused bewilderment. "My only question is: what happened to your arm?"

"I got into an encounter with some Enforcers. I didn't do anything wrong, I was just trying to catch a thief."

He nodded, satisfied with the answer.

After answering a few questions from Rachel Hensley and Tomas Escobar, I was free to leave. I thanked them for their consideration and exited the room to where Edgar and Caeldra were waiting. Caeldra had taken off her jacket and was wearing a dark gray tank top.

"Sorry about the kiss," Caeldra said. "It's best to not think too much when talking to them, as pre-planning your answers can hurt you. I didn't mean anything by it other than to give you a mild distraction."

I nodded unsure of what to say to that.

"How did it go?" Edgar asked.

"I honestly don't know. Alex seems to hate me."

"He's always in a foul mood. Don't take it personally," Caeldra responded. Edgar gave a brief smile, I supposed it wouldn't be proper for him to say negative things about fellow Council members.

"I've got to go discuss with the Council. I'll leave you two together."

Caeldra looked at me again with her sharp blue eyes. "Just you and me again. Edgar told me that you want to be a Runner. If that's the case, then I'd be happy to be your sponsor. It's not easy, though, so you have to commit if you want me to teach you, I value my time and don't want it wasted."

"I understand that. I want to learn, and will do whatever it takes."

"Good," she ran a hand through her shoulder-length blonde hair and pulled it back under the headband she was wearing, once again revealing the thin scar on her cheek. She was beautiful. Had I not been crushing over Mary for such a long time, I would have no doubt been more awkward around her. Caeldra had a lean, toned frame. She looked very fast and agile, no doubt the result of her occupation. I knew that she could teach me a lot about the Undercity and about knowledge that was unknown to me. I wanted to be admitted into the Guild more than ever to become something more and work toward a greater purpose.

"You honestly sound like the perfect sponsor for me, and I'm very thankful for your time," I said.

"Yeah, we'll see how you feel when we start your training. We will discuss your financial situation after you are admitted. We will need to get you geared and you're going to need a loan."

"I've got almost ten units right now, and Edgar is going to pay me two a week for the next ten weeks."

"That'll help, but it won't get you everything."

I remembered the scrip in my pocket and wanted to know what it could be redeemed for. "Caeldra... Someone approached me on the streets last night, they gave me a scrip to use at the Quartermaster."

She eyed me suspiciously. "Were they wearing a guild jacket?"

"No, some sort of heavy gray coat and a full metal face respirator. Sound like someone you know?"

She frowned. "No, it doesn't. Let's go see what it is. The Council might take a couple of hours to decide anyway."

I followed Caeldra through the Guild Hall to one of the back corners where we descended several stories deeper into the Undercity into a large opening that was very different from the main floor. This level was entirely made of dark metal and was illuminated by white LED lights, it was much more similar to that of a building on the surface of New York. There were people dressed in armored camouflage uniforms walking around and eyeing my street clothes with suspicion. This must've been where all the weapons and military operations were staged. People were working down here as well, smelting metal in large forges, operating printers that were manufacturing gun parts. It was a bustle of illegal activity.

Caeldra led me to the far side of the large open room, and we approached a man wearing a brown apron that sat behind a desk with a large computer console. He looked up at us as we walked over.

"Hello Caeldra, who is this?" he asked as he eyed me suspiciously. I really stuck out in my street clothes, everyone else on this level was in uniform or guild leather.

"This is Jake, he's a new Initiate," she responded.

I kept my composure, not wanting to discredit her lie.

"He was given a scrip from a mysterious stranger on the surface and would like to redeem it if it's valid."

I reached into my pocket and pulled out the scrip that entitled me to Asset 47CZ-K8b and handed it to him. He looked it over and then looked back at the two of us.

"This is quite old. Let me check the system to see if we still have it." He typed something in looked it over with appraising eyes. "It's still here. Sending a request to have it brought up."

A few minutes later, two men emerged pulling a cart with a large metal footlocker on it. "Asset 47CZ-K8b," one of them said.

They brought over the footlocker and set it in front of me. My heart froze when I read the faded writing on the box:

Asset 47CZ-K8b, Property of Wesley Ashton.

13
WINDFALL

I staggered back when I read the label on the crate but somehow managed to catch my footing. Caeldra observed me and grabbed my arm to support me from falling.

"What's wrong?" she asked, worried.

"That's my father's name. Wesley Ashton was my father and Edgar told me that he didn't know him."

"Well, it's possible another guild member acquired the box from your father and had it stored, let's not jump to conclusions. We can discuss this with Edgar when there is more time. You can either open it up now or wait until you hear from the Council."

"I'll open it now," I said.

I reached down and fumbled the two latches on the crate and opened it. Inside was a menacing looking gun that rested on top of a leather jacket and backpack.

"Guild leathers, a Runner's pack and a C-15. Wow. Well, this will help you reduce your costs for supplies if you are admitted. The bag and jacket are a little old, but they'll do the trick."

I pulled out the jacket, careful not to jostle the gun too much, and tried it on. The inside was still soft, while the exterior leather looked slightly cracked. It was a perfect fit.

"That jacket needs some oil, but it's still in excellent condition," Caeldra commented.

I picked up the backpack and examined it. It was made of some sort of synthetic material and only had one strap. A sealed envelope rested inside the backpack. I picked up the envelope and carefully slid it into the pocket of the jacket I was wearing. I didn't care to hold the C-15 as Caeldra had called it because I had no experience with guns and didn't want to put anyone in danger. It was a short and stocky looking rifle that held a massive tank of some sort of gas under a metal cage.

"That rifle won't be ideal for your occupation, but it will fetch a nice price from the Armory and will help you purchase the gear you'll be needing."

"Why isn't that a good gun for a Runner?"

"Too bulky, too heavy, too big. You want a compact firearm that will be ideal for close to medium range only, you also want it to be quiet. Take a look," Caeldra said as she pulled her handgun from her hip holster and flipped it in her hand so the back of the gun was facing me. The gun seemed to be made out of a light metal alloy which had been painted black and neon pink in an exotic pattern.

I took the gun from her and examined it in my hands awkwardly. It had a decent weight to it but felt very nimble.

"Press the button on the side to open the targeting sight."

I pressed the side button, and a digital hologram sight digitized from the top of the gun. The digital sight seemed like it would make aiming easier. I nodded and handed the weapon back to her. After returning it to its holster, she turned back toward me.

"It's a CZR-7. Single or burst fire with a hybrid receiver that accepts CO_2 or Hexathoxian. Best weapon a Runner could ask for, and also way cheaper than C-19—which is the much newer version of that rifle you've got there. The C-15 does have its merits, though."

"You do realize I have no idea what you're talking about, right?"

She blushed. "Yeah, but you'd better start taking notes. Anyway, I'll store this stuff for you right now, and we'll get you back up to wait for the Council's decision."

Caeldra closed the footlocker with all of my stuff in it and handed it back to the man behind the counter.

"Keep it safe for me please," she said to the Quartermaster. The small man signaled one of the workers to grab the case, and it was moved behind the counter.

"Again, don't bring this up with Edgar until we hear from the council and be respectful when you do. You need to give him the benefit of the doubt that he didn't lie to you. He's gone out of his way to help you, much more so than you probably know."

"I understand. It's just odd."

"I hear you, Jake. Let's get you back up to wait for the Council's decision."

Caeldra led me back up to the main level, and after several flights of stairs, I felt winded and short of breath. Caeldra seemed completely unfazed by the trip. She led me back through the hall where we stood and waited outside the Council Hall. I didn't really feel like talking, and Caeldra didn't press me; she could probably tell that I was upset. After about fifteen minutes, Justicar Chloe Schaff opened the doors and motioned me inside. It was impossible for me to discern any clues from her calm demeanor. I sat in the desk and looked at the Council members before me. Edgar was also impossible to read though I suspected that he was required to be professional on official Guild business.

Justicar Schaff addressed me and started the session.

"Jake, it is with great pleasure that we offer you admittance to the Champions of Liberty and invite you to become an Initiate under an accepting sponsor. Once you find a sponsor in your chosen path of specialty, you will be eligible to earn salary as well as promotions. Until you find a sponsor, you will be assigned to the barracks for general training. You will speak to the Admittance Counselor to get everything in order. For the record, all but one of the members of the Council voted for your admittance. If you would like to proceed and join us, then we will swear you in right now."

I nodded. "I'm ready to swear in." I saw Edgar give me a proud smile as I said the words, I didn't react and tried not to look at him or think about what was troubling me.

A man in a suit walked over and handed me a sheet of paper with my oath to read to the Council.

"Please place your right hand over your heart and recite your oath," Justicar Schaff said to me.

I placed my hand over my heart and began reading aloud.

"I pledge my honor, life, and faith in The Champions of Liberty. I vow to serve the Guild and serve the people in all of my actions and to preserve the truth until my death. I will seek to better myself and others through the unalienable rights given to me as a human being, the rights that the Government has taken from me. I understand and accept the dangers of being in this organization and pledge never to betray this guild or any of its members. Above all, I swear to preserve the concept of liberty throughout time."

"Jacob Ashton, it is with great honor and privilege that we accept you into our ranks. You are dismissed to speak with the Admittance Counselor," Edgar said to me.

I nodded my head and took my leave. Caeldra was grinning at me when I exited the room. She pulled me into a hug and slapped my back a little too hard. "I'll take care of your paperwork, I'll be sponsoring you. Let's go get you geared, and we will start your training."

Caeldra guided me back toward the stairs we had descended before.

"I'll cover your gear, and you can pay me back with your earnings. It isn't going to be cheap, but you need it all for the job you're going to be doing. Without the right gear, you're likely to lose your life," Caeldra said to me.

"Alright. Will there be an interest expense?"

"No, I don't plan on gouging my student. You'll earn one-quarter of your wages until your debt has been paid. Leroy will get you fitted for everything once we get down there. You'll have a couple of choices to make with some of the pieces available to you, so he'll give you some gear to try out over the next few days to decide what's best for you."

"Got it. Thank you, Caeldra. I really appreciate you taking the time to help me out, I'm looking forward to learning from you."

"Again, we'll see about that when we start your training," she said with a smirk.

After descending all the stairs, Caeldra led me over to a counter close to the Quartermaster where a tall man with dark skin in his twenties stood. He had a thin beard and short cut brown hair. He was cleaning some sort of rifle on the counter and had various parts and tools scattered across the workspace.

"Who is this?" he asked Caeldra in a warm voice.

"My new apprentice, Jake," she replied.

He wiped his hand on a small rag and extended it toward me. "The name's Leroy," he said with a smile.

"My pleasure," I replied as I shook his hand.

"I'd imagine you are here for some gear. Let's get your measurements," he said.

"I'll be right back, Leroy. Jake has a mystery benefactor who has provided him with some equipment. He's got something to trade in as well," Caeldra said as she walked over to the Quartermaster.

Leroy nodded and walked over and began measuring me with a tape ruler. After a couple of minutes, Caeldra returned with my footlocker and placed it on the counter. After opening it, she pulled the short rifle out, and I could see Leroy's eyes light up.

"A C-15? Very nice. We'll take good care of you for that, Jake," Leroy said as he took the rifle from Caeldra.

Leroy examined the gun in his hands and adjusted a small knob on the gas tank. He aimed the gun at the floor and pulled the trigger. The weapon hissed to life, and small bolts of energy began to slam into the concrete ground producing small scorch marks.

"Excellent condition. I'll give you fifteen units against your gear."

I was stunned and looked toward Caeldra who gave me a slight nod. I had no clue how much everything would cost, but fifteen units was a lot of money—a small fortune actually.

"He's got a working jacket and backpack in here as well so he won't need those," Caeldra told him.

"Alright, let me grab some stuff from the back, and we'll get you set with your kit," Leroy said as he walked into a back room. After a few minutes, he emerged carrying a large cardboard box loaded to the brim. Leroy handed me the cargo pants and running boots first.

"Military grade synthetic material. It will adapt with your Artemis link to keep your temperature regulated."

I almost asked what an Artemis was, but waited, as it would probably be addressed. Next, Leroy passed me a black harness with a hip holster and large looking carabiner attached to the front of some sort of mechanical gadget.

"This is your harness. The hook will be essential for moving quickly between levels on your routes. It's designed to be comfortable."

"Go ahead and put on your jacket, Jake," Leroy said to me.

After doing as he asked, Leroy attached what looked to be a metal plate to the front of the jacket.

"This is your Nanotech module. It will protect you from energy blasts as well as kinetic forces and can be morphed into a variety of tools or weapons that include mechanical parts. Of course, you will be limited on what you can create in terms of mechanical devices due to the nature of Nanotech. This module will link with your system. Now for the most important part."

"Can I change the appearance of my jacket?" I asked.

"No, Nexweave isn't available anymore, and we can't manufacture it. I'm guessing you saw Justicar Barton's jacket. Cool, huh?" he asked.

"Yeah, it's awesome," I replied.

Leroy pulled out a thick looking wristband which included a large screen. I pulled up my sleeve as he slipped it on my right arm, the one without the cast.

"You'll feel a slight pinch," he told me.

I winced as his words proved true, then the screen lit up and displayed my heart rate, and several other stats as well as a small map with my location. I felt my jacket shift and looked down to see the Nanotech patch dissolve into the leather.

"Pull down your sleeve then think that you want to see the display," Leroy told me.

I did as he said and when I willed the screen to appear, it did— only it looked as though the display had been delicately sewn into the leather jacket itself.

"You're now connected to Artemis, our most powerful asset. Caeldra will teach you to use it, but Artemis will keep you alive and give you access to any information available to us."

Leroy then attached a flashlight to the shoulder of my jacket and slid a large sealed pack of medical supplies, food, and water to me. He passed me a strange looking earpiece and small black box.

"The earpiece will allow you to communicate with anyone else as well as receive audio information from Artemis. Just think what you want to do, and Artemis will take care of the rest. The small box will be your contact lenses. They also connect with your system and will augment your vision. Now, let's get you a weapon."

Leroy opened three cases in front of me. I recognized one of the pistols as the same one Caeldra carried, but the other two were different.

"We've got the CZR-7, which is what Caeldra uses, the CZ-7, and the C8 here. You'll have to decide which one is best for you. The CZR-7 is specifically created for Runners, the CZ-7 is the standard sidearm for the Guild, and the C8 is designed to have more power at closer ranges at the cost of accuracy and ammo consumption."

"Your choice, Jake, but the CZR-7 is more versatile than the others," Caeldra told me.

I picked up all three weapons and liked the feel of the CZR-7 the most. The CZ-7 felt a bit heavier than the CZR-7, and the C8 felt clumsy.

"Can I change this out if I don't like it?" I asked as I realized the weapons might perform differently than they felt just by weight and balance.

"Yeah, we'll get you taken care of. That's a fine choice," Leroy told me with a grin as he passed me three extra magazines and a large CO_2 tank.

Finally, he passed me a small bracelet which held the glass pill containing the poison concoction Edgar had mentioned. "That will be thirty-two units in total," he told us.

I gawked at the price of the equipment. "Is that the cost before or after my trade-in?" I asked as I tried to keep the fear out of my voice.

"That's with your trade in. This equipment is worth the cost, though," Leroy said.

Caeldra paid Leroy, and we both thanked him. He wished me the best on my training as we departed. Caeldra led me further down to the locker rooms and gave me a key with the number 731 written on it.

"Get changed and store your footlocker. You'll need everything else."

I nodded and walked into the room. Thick clouds of steam and a strong but pleasant scent flowed through the tiled room. Several other people were walking around the locker room, and I could hear the hiss of water from the showers that were in the back. A naked woman walked past me, and I did my best not to stare at the strange sight. Reading through the steam proved difficult, but I eventually found my locker.

I decided to return the unopened letter to the footlocker so that I wouldn't lose it in training. After storing all of my old clothes and changing into my new ones, I slung the backpack over my shoulder and walked out. Caeldra grinned when she saw me.

"You don't look so green now. Let's get your bag packed," she said.

Caeldra showed me where to put all of my supplies as well as how Artemis could keep track of what I had on hand. After packing everything, we walked over to a thick steel door that was marked with a spray-painted skull. Caeldra placed her hand on a scanner, and the door clicked open. It was pitch black down the narrow corridor, and I couldn't see anything past a few feet. She motioned me to take the lead and walked behind me as I slowly moved forward.

"Hey Jake?" she asked.

"Yeah?"

"Your training starts now," she said as she gave me a hard shove on the back.

I stumbled forward and suddenly felt myself falling into a pit of darkness.

14

DARKNESS

I felt a cold rush as I rapidly fell. My breath was pushed out of my lungs as I unsuccessfully tried to scream. The air started to whistle in my ears then howled as I accelerated. I hit something soft that gave way under the impact and seemed to crunch. I groaned and rolled onto my back, trying to pull myself out of the deep pit my impact had created across the surface of the landing pad. I grunted and focused on breathing as I tried to stretch out the tension in my shaking body, still unable to see a thing.

It was much hotter down here, the air was thick with unpleasant moisture and the smell of rot. I was thankful that I hadn't landed on my bad wrist.

"I'll assume you've landed now," a familiar voice called through my earpiece.

There was no way of telling where I was in the darkness.

"What the hell! Caeldra, where am I?" I yelled.

"We like to call it the Gauntlet, and you'll have to choose whether you make it out. I don't think you'll have long before the residents of those parts realize you are there, especially if you yell like that. Use Artemis, and you'll get out alive."

My heart was pounding in my chest and the fear of the residents Caeldra had mentioned caused my thoughts to become manic.

"Who lives down here, Caeldra?" I said as quiet as I could.

"I think you mean *what*, Jake."

Despite the heat, I felt chilled as goosebumps crept along my skin.

I tried my best to collect my thoughts and remembered the flashlight on my shoulder. I turned it on using my mind and circled around trying to see my surroundings. The darkness of the place was the worst part, there were no lights in this portion of the Undercity, and it looked like the area had been abandoned for a very long time.

"There you go, look at you, putting that valuable brain of yours to work," Caeldra said.

I was at the bottom of a tall pit in a pile of trash bags filled with some sort of foam. Two tunnels were connecting the pit, one to the left, and one to the right. I reached down and drew my gun from its holster and turned the safety off. I really didn't want to get caught off guard if anyone or anything actually did live down here. The tunnels looked stagnant as if they had been abandoned for hundreds of years. If it hadn't been for the excessive moisture, they would be caked in dust. I knew it was a trick, some sort of test. I wasn't really in any danger, but it didn't feel that way. Composing myself, I began to work on a way out.

I raised my wrist, and the Artemis display came to life in a blue glow. The map said I was in an undiscovered location and didn't tell me which way I needed to go. The comforting thing, however, was the fact that my system didn't read any other life or robotic entities in my proximity.

I carefully stood up on my shaky legs, walked out of the garbage bag heap, and onto the wet concrete.

There was a sharp creak and a hiss of steam that caused me to whirl to the right and raise my gun toward an old rusty pipe. A second later and the sound of a burst of steam came from further down the tunnel outside of the range of my flashlight. It was so quiet that the sounds of steam working its way through the piping reverberated in the cramped, concrete tunnels that were coated with brown goop.

I looked down at my wrist from time to time to be sure there was still nothing near me in the tunnels. I almost fired my weapon on accident when my Artemis display flickered red, alerting me that a life form had been detected fifty feet in front of me. I peered forward, but I couldn't see anything. Calling out wasn't an option, so I kept my finger on the trigger of the gun and trudged forward. Light footfall from my slow pace was the only sound in the echoing silence. "Thirty feet," the voice stated objectively in my ear. "Twenty feet."

I couldn't see anything in front of me, just the growth-covered concrete walls and some exposed pipes to the side. "Ten feet."

I froze in place still not seeing a thing. My breathing had become heavy, and I was aware that my body was shaking. Still, I continued forward.

"Five feet. Three feet. One foot," Artemis said.

My finger was shaking on the trigger of the gun.

I whipped my gun up at the ceiling and didn't see a thing, the tunnels were empty. The signature patterns on the display told me that the entity was unknown. Suddenly, the screen showed that the signature reading was behind me and eighty feet away. I whirled around with the gun raised and saw a large misshapen figure barreling toward me. I heard Caeldra say a single word in the earpiece: "Run."

I whirled back around and began sprinting, the light on my shoulder swaying and illuminating the tunnel in front of me, reflecting the sparkle of moisture that had settled on the surfaces. The traction from the boots held as I whirled around a corner and continued running. I didn't dare look back but kept an eye on my display which showed I was getting further away from whatever that thing was. Adrenaline coursed through my veins like fire as my body performed in overdrive. I could see that the end of the tunnel dropped off and that there was no other way for me to go. I was about fifty feet away from falling. I ran to the edge of the tunnel and stopped a few feet away from the drop. The entire tunnel slanted downward but lacked a floor.

"Your hook, use it on the line above you," a voice said in my ear. I turned around and saw the thing had rounded the final corner. I fired off three rounds from my weapon, and the gun kicked in my hand. The energy bolts bounced off the menacing looking figure which screeched a horrible metallic sound. The thing chasing me was covered in a tattered collection of coats and mismatching fragments of old rags. It didn't look even slightly human. I cursed under my breath and forced my cold hands to clip my carabiner to the steel cable above me. Without hesitation, I leaped forward and felt the line go taut as I slid down the wire at breakneck speed. The thing that had been chasing me screeched and to my dismay, grabbed the cable and began sliding down the wire after me, sparks jutting from its metallic fingers that clearly weren't designed for this sort of activity.

"Artemis will automatically detach you from the line at the optimal time. I suggest you keep running, though," Caeldra said.

I holstered my weapon as I slid down the wire and prepared for impact. A few second later I received a verbal warning from Artemis that detachment was imminent. There was a slight tug on the line as the system slowed my descent. I was detached from the wire above me and landed softly on the ground. The new tunnel I was in looked the same as all the others in the Undercity. I continued running as fast as I could, my flashlight swaying wildly from wall to wall of the narrow tunnel.

I could hear my pursuer gaining on me, and I forced my body to give me more, fighting against the growing fatigue and burn in my chest. Artemis warned me that my pursuer was only ten feet away. I sprinted as fast as I could and saw a wall rapidly approaching. It appeared to have a small air shaft on the bottom of it that had the cover removed.

Artemis chimed in my ear, "slide in three seconds." Three seconds later and a tone indicated that I should execute the maneuver. I yelled and dropped to the ground and was surprised that I didn't feel a thing. The nanotech had shifted to form pads on my elbows and hips that absorbed the impact and reduced my friction on the surface. I slid across the damp floor and went right through the open vent. The next few seconds were a blur, but I skidded to a stop in a well-lit opening that appeared to be some sort of electrical maintenance room. I stood up and unholstered my weapon, pointing it toward the shaft, but the thing that had been pursuing me hadn't made it through. I heard Caeldra.

"Holster the weapon."

I did as she said and saw her emerge from the corner with a wide grin on her face.

"There's no better way to introduce you to some basic functions of Artemis than putting your life at risk."

I was torn I couldn't tell if I was angry at her or happy to be alive.

"What the hell was that thing?" I managed, panting for breath and bracing my hands on my shaking legs.

"A re-purposed and heavily modified Enforcer. Your life never was in any danger, it's just crucial that you felt like it was. You were very fast," she remarked.

"Thanks, and thank you for the heads up before you pushed me down a hole," I said bitterly.

"No problem. You will run into things that you can't kill or destroy alone down here occasionally, and it's vital to know when to fight and when to run. As you train, you'll develop Runner's intuition. It'll keep you alive. The important thing to know is that

Nanotech can't absorb an endless amount of impact without needing to be recharged. Your module can take a few hits, but it's not designed for extended firefights," Caeldra warned.

I tried to calm myself before speaking. "What else are we going to do today?"

"We're going to do some basic training, and I'm going to show you some things you'll need to know. As a Runner, we'll primarily be doing three types of jobs: scouting unexplored areas of the Undercity, running courier missions, and infrastructure development. Believe it or not, most of the Undercity is actually unexplored. The tunnels go on for hundreds of miles, and some large portions and areas are completely unknown to us. Unfortunately, these regions can also be very dangerous."

"And Artemis can't provide a map until someone has gone through them?" I asked, still panting.

"Correct. While Artemis is perfect for most regions, there are portions where the system's signal can't reach. We call those areas shadow zones. The full Artemis system won't function in shadow zones; you'll only have local features. To get rid of those areas we install new routers that can amplify the network's signal throughout the shadow zone. We call that torching an area."

"Okay, got it," I replied.

"Did you put in your contact lenses?" she asked me.

"No, but they're in my backpack."

"Put them on, and we'll head out."

I carefully opened the small black box and placed the lenses in my eyes. There was a brief flash of orange light as the lenses connected with the Artemis system. After I finished, she tossed me a bottle of water, which I graciously accepted.

"Great, you'll be able to see a lot more now. You can see hidden messages other Runners have left, as well as identify weak points on enemies, and pull up a directional guide if you're going to a known location. For now, we're going to be working together for all of your missions after training. You need to learn basic survival skills before we set you loose on your own. Let's head out."

We started down the tunnel at a moderate jog. I could see bright orange arrows painted on the surrounding walls which would have directed me if Caeldra wasn't there. My legs were aching, but I had mostly managed to recover from the sprinting I had done.

"Leaving a note or drawing is pretty simple. You just need to think about what you want to leave and where you want to leave it. Messages are encrypted through Artemis, so you don't need to worry about strangers reading them."

I didn't say anything. Instead, I focused on my breathing as I jogged behind Caeldra. We continued down several tunnels until we came to a larger tunnel which dropped off at the end at what looked to be a five to seven-foot gap. The wall across from the drop was covered in large metal pipes that climbed vertically toward the surface of New York.

"Artemis will assist with connecting your hook as well for when you need it. It's time to take a leap of faith, Jake."

She motioned me to run beside her, and I did so. We approached the gap at full speed, and I saw Artemis flash a message through my vision that it would connect my carabiner to the pipes if I jumped. As we hit the edge of the drop, we both leaped at full speed. We flew side by side, and I screamed in terror and excitement as I hit the pipes a little harder than I would have liked. My carabiner latched onto a metal support beam that held the large pipes in place, and I felt the slack go as I lost my grip on the tube. Caeldra had hit and grabbed onto the pipes, not losing her grip from the impact. Had I not had my cast on my left arm, I may have been able to hold myself up.

"Good, now we'll climb. These types of vents are meant to be an efficient way to bring down cold water or air to the lower regions, but they also are the fastest way to move between floors in the Undercity. They have support beams that we'll be able to use to climb. Most of this climbing is manual, but your carabiner will catch you if you fall. We're not going to climb far because of your wrist. You should be able to do all of this with one arm if you need to."

There was a flash of dull light as gloves pixelated on Caldera's hands. I thought of gloves on my hands and felt the gloves cover my hands as well.

"These are designed for climbing, they'll provide a good grip on any surface," she told me as she started to climb the pipes.

I watched as she moved the carabiner from support rail to support rail as she ascended. Artemis detached and attached to new rails as she tossed the carabiner upwards as she moved. Caeldra was correct about the gloves. I noticed how easy it was to climb the pipes that were slick with moisture, neither my hands nor feet slipped as I climbed the large pipes. Though I had the carabiner, I was still nervous climbing with a near-endless pit below me.

"Any Runners near 504?" a voice crackled on the radio.

Caeldra answered. "Jake and I are close enough. What's up?"

"We've lost contact with Mikey and received a distress signal in 504. Artemis doesn't read any other signal down there other than an old ping from Mikey. We can't get a read on vitals, but the coverage down there has been spotty at best," the voice replied.

"Copy, we'll go check it out," Caeldra said.

She then looked down at me. "This isn't a test or training; this is your first real mission."

She pulled a large coil of steel cabling and latched it to a support beam before dropping it down to the darkness below. "Use your rappelling device and follow me. Keep those gloves on so your grip doesn't slip."

She latched her metal rappelling device to the wire and began to descend slowly, her flashlight pointing toward the pit below. I followed suit and descended above her. Our flashlights caused the surrounding pipes to cast vicious shadows on the walls around us, and the air became more stagnant as we continued to descend. We passed a tunnel opening every ten feet or so as we continued to drop.

"Almost to 504," Caeldra told me.

We slowed even more, and Caeldra came to a stop, pulling herself onto one of the platforms with a steel handle that extended on the wall. She detached her carabiner and waited for me as I did the same. This tunnel was different from the rest, with a large rusted green door that sealed off the tunnel from the vent. 504 was painted on the door with faded yellow paint.

"Mikey, can you hear me? This is Caeldra."

There was no response.

"Mikey, we're on 504 and coming for you, hold tight," she said as she drew her gun. Our displays still didn't show any readings other than Mikey's signal which was about five hundred feet away.

Caeldra opened the door to 504 and slammed it shut as a blast of foul air jetted out into her face. She coughed and spat on the ground before cursing profusely.

"Masks on, the air is no good."

We pulled on the masks and sealed them on our faces. The goggles didn't inhibit my vision as much as I thought they would. The air inside the mask was cool and smelled of disinfectant, the same kind that reminded me of my father's death.

"I don't like that we still can't get a reading on Mikey's vitals," Caeldra murmured as she opened the door again. The lights down this tunnel were flickering on and off in a dull yellow glow. Clouds of brown steam proliferated the narrow tunnel that was filled with shallow pools of brown liquid. There were no pipes on the walls, but the tunnel was so small that Caeldra and I couldn't walk side by side. We walked forward slowly, regularly checking Artemis for updates as we got closer to Mikey's signal.

"Caeldra—" a weak voice crackled in our earpieces. "Get the hell out of..." the person started coughing uncontrollably and struggled to recover. "It isn't safe... Harvesters... They got me. I'm bleeding out. I—I'm going to bite the glass."

"Shit!" Caeldra yelled.

15

HARVESTERS

"Mikey, don't do it, we're almost there!" Caeldra shouted.

There was no response.

"What are they?" I whispered to Caeldra, my voice barely audible.

"Shut the hell up and stay close behind me."

I could sense the fear in her voice and it caused the terror that was gripping at the corners of my mind to run rampant. I didn't like seeing Caeldra so worried—she had always seemed so calm and collected, but her confidence was cracking in the current situation. She pulled back the slide on her CZR-7 and released it with a dull click. I saw her thumb the selector on the side to burst fire mode.

Despite my fear, I did as I was told and we crept forward. Artemis alerted us that there were seven humans three hundred feet in front of us. Caeldra turned off her flashlight and motioned for me to do the same. Without our flashlights, the light was dulled to a sickly color through the brown steam that leaked from cracks in the walls. The flickering lighting on the walls gave the entire tunnel a terrifying aura that made my hands go numb with fear. I didn't like not knowing what Harvesters were, nor what I was getting myself into.

Caeldra rounded the corner and sprinted forward, diving behind an old wooden crate. I stayed behind the corner and peeked over to see three large men standing around a segment of fallen pipe about thirty feet away. Artemis outlined their figures in bright yellow light, identifying that they were unknowns. They were dressed in heavy looking trench coats that were covered in thick metal sheets. They all wore gas masks and backpacks that were loaded to the brim with fragments of metal and segments of pipes. One man was cutting away at the large pipe with a welding torch while the others stood guard. Another had an old-looking shotgun in his hands while the last had a large, rusted fire axe. The weapons were outlined in red through my augmented vision system. I couldn't make out what they were saying, but Caeldra motioned for me to stay still from behind the box.

I checked my own weapon to make sure it was ready, then set the toggle switch to single fire. My heart was beating out of control, and I did my best to try to layer the fear away in my mind as Edgar had taught me to do. Unfortunately, it didn't work, and the flimsy barrier I had created shattered to pieces after a few seconds. My fingertips felt icy cold despite the hot temperatures on this level, and my breathing felt labored. The air and scent of the disinfectant in my mask was making me nauseous but breathing the outside air was unthinkable.

I dropped down to my knees so that I could get a better look without drawing attention to myself.

I had to squint my eyes against the burning nova of light from the cutting torch.

"Jake, only shoot if you have a clear shot. I'm engaging them," Caeldra whispered.

She peeked from the side of the crate and fired a burst at the man with the shotgun. The three rounds struck him in the head, and there was a hissing sound as the pressurized air was released from the thick coils of tubing wrapped around his neck. The man briefly reached up to his head with both hands before collapsing on the ground in a crumbled heap. The others had seen what happened and were already moving towards us. The man with the welding torch had dropped it and pulled out a small boxy-looking gun. He began spraying bullets down the hall which thudded into the crate and wall to the side of me. I pressed my back to the wall behind me and waited for the loud crackling gunfire to subside. When I looked around the corner again, the huge man with the fire axe was advancing toward Caeldra, who was still behind the crate.

I opened the targeting interface on my gun and aimed for the head as Caeldra had done. I fired two shots, one of which missed, and the other slammed into the man's chest and didn't seem to have any effect on his charge. I stopped firing when Caeldra emerged from cover.

"He's got Nanotech, watch out!" Caeldra yelled. She stood and shot at the man with the old submachine gun, dropping him to the ground just before the huge man with the axe reached her. The man yelled as he swung the axe in a wide arc at Caeldra. She ducked just before the swing and pushed off the crate with her legs, sliding under his feet and out of my line of sight. With her out of range, I fired another six rounds that were absorbed by the man's armoring. Caeldra continued to shoot at him until her gun was empty. She threw it to the side and flipped out a strange looking knife and held it with a reverse grip.

I continued to fire at the man, whose armor continued to hold, but he kept his focus on Caeldra. He was swinging the axe with precision and agility despite his massive size. I watched with horror as the axe connected with Caeldra's stomach and she was flung several feet back. There was no blood, no sickly sinking sound as the axe cut through her stomach, just the distinct sound of metal on metal and an explosion of blue sparks.

"I'm alright. Keep shooting, Jake!" she screamed through the earpiece as she struggled to gain her feet. The man continued toward her as I continued to shoot at his back and head. I was shocked at the amount of energy his armor had absorbed. After loading a new magazine, I started advancing.

"Over here!" I yelled at him. The man let out a guttural grunt and turned toward me before charging.

"Jake, get the hell out of here!" Caeldra yelled.

I fired my weapon three more times before turning back and sprinting the way we had come. When I took a glance back, I saw that the man pursuing me was gaining ground on me, and that

Caeldra was trailing us as fast as she could manage. Adrenaline coursed through my veins—this was real, the axe was real, and my life was in danger. As I neared the vertical vent, I generated the climbing gloves and prepared Artemis to latch to the steel wiring that hung from above. I leaped across the gap and attached to the cable. I continued to swing but was able to brace my impact using my legs to push off the large pipes on the wall. The man behind me wasn't able to slow himself as he slid awkwardly across the gap and fell about ten feet before catching the pipe and managing to hold on.

Caeldra stopped at the end of the tunnel and began firing her gun at the man who recoiled against the pipe but managed to hang on. Apparently, she had picked it up before starting after us.

"Jake, drop down as fast as you can and try to kick him when you land."

"Are you crazy!" I yelled.

"No. I'll shoot at him while you do."

It was insane, and even more insane that I decided to do it. Caeldra began firing at him as I dropped at full speed. I landed squarely on the brute's shoulders, and he was flung down into the darkness below. I slowed my fall and used my mind to cause my carabiner device to pull me back up the wire.

"Good job!" Caeldra shouted. She was reloading her weapon when I reached the tunnel, and I was relieved to see that she wasn't bleeding from the axe hit.

"You did great," she said as she started to raise her hand to pat me on the back, then stopped as she winced in pain.

"Are you going to be okay?" I asked with concern.

"Yeah, I'll live. I've been through worse. Let's go try to find Mikey now."

I converted my gloves into a mask and we proceeded back down the tunnel to where the other men had been. Caeldra quickly looted their bodies. She tossed me the shotgun and submachine gun and took their Nanotech modules from their coats. She sifted through their packs and pulled out a few items of interest before we continued forward towards Mikey's distress signal. I wasn't prepared for what we found.

A gruesome corpse lay in the middle of the path, the limbs were broken at horrible angles and the floor surrounding him was soaked in blood. White foam spilled from his mouth onto the concrete beside him.

"Dear God," Caeldra croaked.

16

RECOVERY

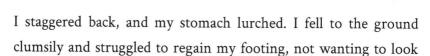

I staggered back, and my stomach lurched. I fell to the ground clumsily and struggled to regain my footing, not wanting to look at the body.

I stayed back as Caeldra confirmed the identity. Mikey's possessions had been taken, and there was no one else in sight or in the proximity of Artemis' scanning range.

"Command, this is Caeldra. Mikey is dead. Harvesters got him. We killed three of them, but this whole area looks to be compromised. Recommend a military sweep and repairs," Caeldra said, tears glimmering in her eyes, her voice shaking.

"Acknowledged, report back to Command immediately,"

"There was nothing we could have done," Caeldra said to me.

Horror dawned on me when I realized how dangerous this really was, how unprepared I was.

"He's dead," I managed.

"Come on, we need to get the hell out of here," Caeldra told me, but my feet may as well have been glued to the floor.

"Does anyone care that someone just died?" I demanded.

Caeldra grabbed the collar of my jacket and hurled me against the wall of the small tunnel. Dark spots blurred my vision as I felt my head slam into the concrete with a dull thud. The light of her flashlight was pointed directly at my masked face, blurring my vision through the glass goggles.

"Get it together! We can't freeze up now, we'll mourn his loss later. Don't you dare think that his death doesn't matter to me or anyone else," she shot. It did the trick, and I was pulled back into the grim reality that Caeldra and I were still in danger while we stayed here. I nodded, and we started running back the way we had come. It was easy to notice that Caeldra was faltering in her pace.

We ran back to the central vent climbed as fast as possible. Caeldra led us through an unfamiliar area until we reached the main entrance of the Guild Hall. Caeldra's condition was worsening, and her labored breathing was audible through the thick mask she wore.

After an hour-long session with the Council about Mikey's death, and the increased presence of Harvesters in territory that was previously considered safe, Caeldra and I were dismissed and headed to Leroy to sell the gear we had scavenged from the day.

"Thanks for trying to save Mikey," Leroy said grimly.

"There was nothing we could do. Harvesters got him," Caeldra replied, her voice dark. "He bit the glass, so I don't think he suffered for long."

Caeldra started to try to take off her backpack and fell to one knee with a soft moan. Leroy and I were helping her up a moment later. Thick beads of perspiration had formed on her head, sliding down her face. Her skin, usually vibrant, was pale and colorless.

"What happened to her!" Leroy yelled.

"She got hit in the stomach with a fire axe... she said she was fine, that the Nanotech absorbed it," I said.

"Dammit, Caeldra! You should have gone straight to Medbay. I'm calling a stretcher for you," Leroy said, frustration in his voice. He lifted up her shirt, and I was shocked to see a large purple bruise with stringy yellow accents. Her abdomen was swollen, and dark drops of blood seeped through the wound.

"The Nanotech saved her life, but she's not doing well," Leroy told me before turning to her again. "You're too tough for your own good sometimes, Caeldra."

A few minutes later, two men in blue scrubs approached with a large orange stretcher. After securing Caeldra to it, they began to take her to the Medbay.

"Jake, put my stuff in my locker and sell everything we got today," she said through gritted teeth as she was taken away.

When she was out of sight, I took out the guns and Nanotech patches we had scavenged for Leroy.

"Old stuff, but I'll buy it. I can give you six units for the haul."

"Yeah sure," I replied.

"It's not like this every day. This is probably the hardest first day any Runner has had in a long time. Glad you made it."

"Thanks, Leroy. What's the deal with the Harvesters? The Council didn't have time for my questions."

"Harvesters are savages. They strip pipes and redirect resources from the surface to fuel their excavating activities. Worse, they scrap anything of ours that they find and kill anyone unlucky enough to encounter them. They're called Harvesters because they take the organs of their victims to sell on the black market," he seethed.

Leroy took a deep breath and cracked his knuckles, clearly distraught.

"Got it. Well, I'd better get up to the main hall to wait for Mr. Barton. I'm sorry about Mikey, I really am."

"Take it easy, Jake," he replied as he examined the guns he had just purchased from me, trying to distract himself from the death of a friend. I started to walk away, and Leroy stopped me.

"Take care of Caeldra. She's tough as nails but refuses to admit when something is too much for her to handle. Take care of her and she'll take care of you."

I gave him a firm nod and headed off.

I put all of Caeldra's belongings in her locker and changed back into my street clothes. It had been a hellish first day as a Runner, and I wanted nothing more than to return to the surface and spend some time with Mary. The day had been so crazy that I hadn't had a chance to think about the kiss we had shared or our relationship. Thinking about Mary made me realize that I still had to talk to Edgar about my father.

After stashing all of my equipment, I started toward Medbay to check on Caeldra. The attendant at the front desk directed me to exam room three. Caeldra was only wearing her bra and cargo pants, her abdomen wrapped in a thick gauze. She was lying on a bed that was low to the ground in a simple room.

"Hey Jake, what are you doing here?" she asked me.

"Just wanted to check on you and see if you needed anything before I head off."

"I'm bruised pretty bad, but nothing is broken. They've got me on some painkillers, so I'll be alright."

"Well, let me know if you need anything. I'll see you tomorrow," I told her as I did my best to keep from looking at the wrapped wound.

"Thanks for saving my life, Jake."

I gave her a smile. "Anytime."

We said our goodbyes, and I made my way up to the main level and saw Edgar waiting for me.

"I'm glad you're alright," Edgar said. "It's always awful to lose people, but you did well."

"Caeldra was injured pretty badly," I replied.

"She said you saved her life."

"I suppose I did. Are you ready to head back up?"

"Yeah, let's get going," Edgar said.

"I've got some questions for you on the way back if that's alright?" I asked him, trying to keep my voice calm.

"Certainly."

We departed the main gate and started walking back to the surface together.

"Okay, so I know that I'm not allowed to talk about the Guild or what I do, but what should I tell Mary I've been doing all day?" I asked.

"Well, that's not easy to answer. I won't lie to you, Jake. Being a part of the Champions is physically and emotionally tolling, you'll find it hard to maintain relationships with outsiders of the Guild due to obvious reasons. What you tell Mary is your business, but you can never tell her the truth, and eventually... Well, eventually the lies will catch up with you or she'll need to accept that she can't know what you do. It's not an ideal situation," Edgar said, frowning.

"What if we invite her to join the Guild?"

Edgar's tone grew grim, "Jake, you need to listen to me very carefully. Those we accept into the Guild are invited because their lives are in danger from the Government and they would be a useful asset. Guild life is a life of danger and deception. You were only admitted because you would have been killed by the Sculptors for reading John Locke's work. You need to understand that Mary has her life in front of her. You shouldn't wish this danger on her."

"I'm sorry," I murmured. "I wasn't thinking clearly..."

"It's alright, Jake, you just need to understand that this is your life now and you need to be selfless in decisions that might bring harm to others, especially those you care for."

I had no desire to ask him about my father anymore. I felt defeated, childish, and naïve. I would have to ask another time.

As we neared the entrance to the surface, Edgar changed the appearance of his Nexweave jacket to appear as a cheap hoodie. We climbed the final ladder up to the abandoned building and took our leave back into the streets of New York. Surprisingly, most of the air in the Undercity was better than the actual streets of the Slums.

"If you'll excuse me, I think I'll get an early night tonight. Please be at my house by dawn if you'd like to walk together to the Guild Hall tomorrow," Edgar said.

"Yeah sure, I'll see you in the morning. Thanks for everything, Edgar."

We departed, and I made my way to the grocery store to stock up on some basic food. I decided that I'd get enough food so that I could invite Mary over for dinner, though I wasn't sure if my flat was presentable. I picked up a loaf of brown bread and a few cans of soup and fruit. Making the decision on a whim, I decided to buy a pack of mint chewing gum. I replaced my bandana on my face as I paid at the console with my vouchers and made my way past the Enforcers that stood guard at the exits. I continued down the street to my flat and knocked on Mary's door. She looked out the window and let me in.

"Jake! Where have you been all day?" she asked me with a warm smile as she pulled a long lock of hair out of her face.

"Just running some errands," I replied. It hurt to lie to her.

She was wearing a green shirt with khaki shorts and had a faded plastic headband in her hair, it was clear she hadn't gone out all day. Regardless, she was as beautiful as ever.

"I've got something to show you," she said as she lightly touched my arm.

Mary walked over and grabbed the sketchbook I had given her from her desk. She pulled it open and showed me an intricate drawing of a tree.

"Wow!" I said as I smiled. "It's amazing, Mary."

"You think so?" she said, giving me a nervous look.

"I really do."

She ran over and wrapped me up in a hug. "It's such a perfect gift, Jake." Then we kissed.

After a near perfect kiss, I stepped back and smiled at her. This was exactly what I needed to relax from the most demanding and terrifying day of my life.

"I was going to invite you to dinner if you'd give me the chance to cook for you?" I asked.

"Jake Ashton cooking, I'd pay good money to see that," she responded with a laugh.

"Well, it's canned soup, but I got some decent bread, fruit, and I'll throw in a stick of mint gum."

"You've got yourself a deal, Jake," she replied as she fought back a laugh.

Mary and I made our way back to my flat, and I started heating up the soup and slicing the bread. While I could technically afford butter now, I thought it would be best to maintain my current lifestyle to not draw suspicion from Mary. I didn't want to mess up our relationship or push her away with lies about how I earned my money. If my math was correct, I'd get one-quarter of half of our earnings from yesterday, a whopping 750 credits—or triple my normal pay as a Thinker. Of course, I didn't know exactly how much money I had burned through in CO_2 in my CZR-7 either, I supposed I would have to buy a refill when my main tank was empty.

I snapped out of my thoughts and pulled the old steel pot off the stove and brought it to the table where Mary was sitting. After getting my best two bowls, the bread, and two glasses of drinking water, we were set to have a nice dinner.

The meal was very simple, but still good. I was thankful that Mary didn't mind that I couldn't actually cook anything myself. We scooped out the soup with thick slices of the brown bread and enjoyed each other's company. I ended up eating four bowls of soup and about seven slices of bread, something I never did.

"Hungry there, Jake?" Mary said as she observed me down the fourth bowl of soup.

"Yeah, I haven't really eaten all day," I replied with an embarrassed smile. It wasn't really an exaggeration. I had eaten breakfast, but with the hellish day, there was no time to eat lunch. I hadn't actually realized how hungry I was until I started eating.

I looked down at my father's watch; it was already approaching 9 PM. I wished that I had been more talkative and more energetic around Mary. Despite my best efforts, my thoughts continued to wander between my father, the man that I had killed, and what my future was going to be like. Why did I have to buy that stupid book?

"Jake?" Mary asked as she waived her hand in front of my face. "Anyone there?"

"Huh? Sorry, I was daydreaming," I said.

"Well, I suppose I need to get going, it's almost nine. Thank you for the fabulous meal, Chef Ashton," she said laughing.

"Let me walk you to your flat," I said as I stood up. Mary started picking up her dishes, and I stopped her. "Please don't worry about those, I'll take care of it when I get back."

"Thanks, Jake."

As I started getting ready to walk her back home, she wrapped both arms around my neck and pulled me into a series of deep kisses that started gentle and became more aggressive. My heart felt like it was bursting in my chest. We continued for a couple minutes, and I pulled back, hating myself for stopping, but knowing it was the right thing to do. When 6 AM rolled around, I'd have to disappear for the day, and wouldn't want to lie to Mary or make her feel like I didn't want to spend time with her.

"Sorry," she said, her cheeks rosy. "I got a little carried away there," she said, trailing off and giving me a playful, innocent look, her beautiful eyes glittering in the light from my kitchen.

"I did as well, don't be sorry," I said, amazed at what had just happened.

We readied our bandanas and exited my flat.

"Are you free tomorrow?" she asked me as we walked.

"I'm going to be running some more errands across the district I'm afraid," I said.

"Oh, okay. I'll see you tomorrow evening then?" she didn't do well in hiding the disappointment in her voice.

"Of course," I replied as I hugged her good night. I wanted to kiss her again, but exposing our mouths in the smog wasn't a good idea, and would likely ruin the kiss. After she was inside, she waved at me through the window, and I headed back to my flat. Two homeless men in battered coats were fighting over a can of something, and I walked to the side to avoid them. As I was approaching my flat, I saw the huge man in gray again. He was standing at the entrance of a dark alley and waved his arm to motion me over. Despite my intuition screaming for me to run, I walked over to him. The man grabbed my shoulder with a metal grip and ushered me further into the alleyway so that we were concealed by the darkness.

"I trust you found your father's case," he said.

"Yes," I answered carefully.

"I suppose there is a high chance you weren't able to read the letter yet with the day you've had today."

I didn't know what to say to that, so I took caution in my answer. "I haven't had time to read it yet, I was going to when I got back to my flat."

"Very well, we'll speak soon. We can find some time to talk once you've read it. I can provide you with some answers."

"Thank you," I replied. The fear that this man was dangerous continued to creep into my mind, but I had to have answers. Whoever he was, this man could offer me information about my father that I couldn't ignore. There was a jolt of realization as I thought about his words. How had he known about my day?

"Take your leave, it's 8:58 PM," he said.

I rounded the corner walking then ran to my flat when I got past the alleyway. After unlocking the door, I rushed inside and saw the door light turn red a few seconds later. I had just made curfew without being trapped outside for the night. With an emotion-filled heart and mind, I sat down to open the letter that had been in my jacket all day. The white color of the paper had faded to a dull brown with time, but the seal remained intact. I carefully broke the envelope opened and pulled out a neatly folded piece of paper.

Jake,

This will be hard to read, and it's even more difficult for me to write this right now. When you're done reading this, you need to destroy the letter. If you're reading this, I am dead, and you have inevitably found your way to The Champions of Liberty. First and foremost, you can trust Edgar Barton, he is a very close friend and has promised me that he would look after you if I've passed. If you took after your mother and me, then you've undoubtedly learned a little bit about what your mind is capable of.

Life in the Guild is dangerous, it's probably what got me killed. You need to know that what you learn with your time in the Guild is truth and that most of what you've discovered on the surface are lies. You become a danger to yourself and those around you as you learn more about the truth of things, so you need to do your best to avoid relationships with those on the surface, as they only lead to pain. The equipment I've left you in the Guild should be able to help you get a head start in whatever path you choose, though I suspect you'll be selected as an Unbound candidate in a short amount of time as others learn what you can do.

I lied to you when I told you that you had to get out of the Slums. The simple fact remains that if you're born in the Slums, you don't leave the Slums. I wanted you to learn as much as possible to prepare you for the life you had ahead.

I'm sorry that I wasn't truthful with you. We don't even know if anyone is living on the Upper level. Son, I want you to know that I love you and that I'm proud of you and everything you will become and everything that you will do. Serve the Champions well, and they will take care of you. You must continue to fight for liberty and freedom of the people. Fight to end the injustice so wrongly inflicted on all of humanity. Stay strong and know that you can trust the Guild. I anxiously await the day we meet again.

With immense love and regret,
Your father, Wesley Ashton.

I sobbed, tears cascading down my face, pooling on the sheet of paper below.

17

TRUTHS, LIES, AND SOMETHING IN BETWEEN

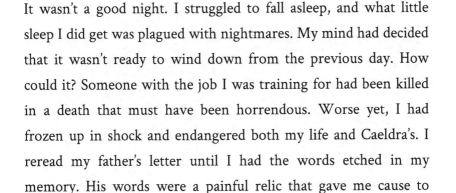

It wasn't a good night. I struggled to fall asleep, and what little sleep I did get was plagued with nightmares. My mind had decided that it wasn't ready to wind down from the previous day. How could it? Someone with the job I was training for had been killed in a death that must have been horrendous. Worse yet, I had frozen up in shock and endangered both my life and Caeldra's. I reread my father's letter until I had the words etched in my memory. His words were a painful relic that gave me cause to continue and not just give up and succumb to the fact that I had ruined my normal life.

Who was the huge man or machine in the metal mask with the gray coat? How did he know who I was or what happened to me during my first day as a Runner? I became anxious about Mary. If he knew so much about me, maybe she was in danger too. I had to push the thought out of my head as I realized I would probably be dead if he wanted it. Besides, he had only been helping me recover my father's unknown past. More than anything else, I needed the truth about my dad's life. He wasn't just a Thinker since his letter indicated that he had relations with the Guild I was now aligned to.

I decided to attempt to layer my mind and push all the negative and emotionally tolling thoughts behind a barrier. I was surprised that I was successful at pushing it away after several deep breaths. I managed to fall asleep, but nightmares crept into my subconscious as I slept.

I awoke in the morning and groaned as I felt how stiff my whole body was. I couldn't remember the last time I ran more than a couple of blocks. I cursed as I answered the question by recalling my valiant attempt to stop the thief that had stolen Mary's bag. Yesterday had been physically demanding, and I had pushed my body to its limit. I tried stretching out my sore arms and legs that complained as I attempted to get out of bed. Everything hurt to move, though I suspected it wasn't anything to worry about.

I got up and started to boil some water for a cup of tea and ate some of the leftover bread from the previous night, as well as some of the canned fruit. I sat and sipped my tea with an absent mind before hopping into the shower and getting dressed for the day. At 7 AM I placed my bandana on my face, loaded up my street backpack and walked over to Edgar's flat. I was glad I had brought my warm jacket. It was near thirty degrees, and the air was damp. Edgar exited his flat when he saw me walking over.

"Good morning, Jake," he said as he adjusted his hat on his head. He was wearing a warm looking gray scarf and what looked to be a red cotton jacket.

"Good morning, Edgar," I replied as pleasantly as I could manage.

"I imagine Caeldra will train you in archival methods today rather than running. She's probably sore as hell." A cold blast of wind blasted over us, and Edgar adjusted his scarf to block the frosty air.

While it didn't rain down in the Slums, the excess moisture caused surfaces to freeze over in a thin layer of frost, which made roads and sidewalks dangerous. If it got horrendous, Government trucks would spread a specialized salt on the sidewalks and roads to help melt the ice. In the cold, the steam spewing from the vents on the ground lingered in the air and congregated in thick grayish yellow clouds above the street. Fall was fading and giving way to winter, a particularly hard time for the Slums. Heating was expensive, and a lot of residents had the choice of running the heaters in their flats or paying rent.

Edgar and I walked up onto the sidewalk as a large Government truck drove down the street. It wasn't like the regular vehicles, as it seemed to be covered in heavy armor and was driven by a human rather than the standard delivery robots that stocked the stores.

"What do you think that was about?" I asked him.

"I don't know; they're getting antsy about something. We're monitoring the situation," he replied in a low voice.

We were silent the rest of the way down to the Guild Hall. I think he must have had some sort of idea that I knew something, but he didn't want to bring it up. Maybe he was just giving me space so I could take the information and decide what to do with it. At the very least, he knew that I had received a crate full of old gear from a mysterious benefactor. Whether Edgar knew of my unknown accomplice was beyond me.

Caeldra was waiting over at the pub and chatting with the bartender when we entered, and from what I saw seemed to be feeling a lot better.

"I'll leave you and Caeldra to talk. I've got some Council business to take care of," Edgar said to me as he walked away abruptly.

Caeldra spotted me and flashed me a warm smile. I walked over to her.

"Ah, my young prodigy returns," she said as she swiveled her barstool around so that she could face me. She was wearing a green tank top and khaki pants. Though her shirt covered it, I could see the outline of thick bandages underneath.

"How are you feeling?" I asked as I sat next to her.

"How do you think I'm feeling?"

"Sorry," I responded awkwardly.

"I'm messing with you, Jake. You saved my life, and that's not something I'll be forgetting anytime soon." She turned to the bartender. "Two beers please, Jeff."

"I'm sorry I froze up yesterday, I didn't mean to put us in more danger, I..."

"Jake, stop. If anyone should be sorry, it's me. I shouldn't have brought you with me since you haven't had any training and I'm also sorry for bashing you on that wall."

"Don't worry about it, it helped me cope with the shock," I said with a halfhearted grin.

The bartender pulled two glass mugs from below the dark wooden counter and began filling them at the tap.

"So, did you have a chance to talk with Edgar about your father?" she asked me as we waited for the drinks.

"No, and this was the letter that was in the crate. The huge man in gray visited me again last night, told me that he would be there when I was ready for answers," I said as I handed her the folded letter from my pocket. She took a few minutes to read it over then looked up at me.

"It looks like Edgar has some explaining to do. Again, you've got to go about this the right way, as there are truths, lies, and something in between. From everything I've heard from Edgar, he seems to really like you, and this letter would indicate that he has only been protecting you. Why he hasn't made that known to you by now, I'm not sure."

Jeff brought over our beers and laid them on the table. Caeldra sipped deeply and let out a relaxed sigh.

"What reason could he possibly have to lie to me now, though? I've already found my way into the Guild, why all the secrecy?"

"Again, I'm not sure and that's something you'll need to discuss with him yourself," she said as she wrapped her arm around my shoulder. "Have a couple drinks with me, we'll go do some archival work, and I'll show you around the library, then we can go see if we can get you an appointment with Edgar—or you can wait to talk with him on the way back." She took her arm off me and drank another swallow of beer. "Regardless, you need to get this resolved, so it's not tearing you up inside."

"Yeah, you're right, Caeldra," I replied as I took a drink. "Will we be working with Master Aarlen today?"

"Most likely not, I've got to train you on the basics of archiving as well as give you some homework to work on."

"Wait, so I'm allowed to take stuff up to the Slums?"

"Yes and no. We'll get to that later," she replied.

We finished two beers each and decided to head to the library so I could begin my archival training. Caeldra paid for the drinks and gave me a small plastic bag full of fifty-credit chips.

"One unit from yesterday's earnings after the portion for your debt was subtracted," she said with a smile.

It was unbelievable how much I had earned; it was the equivalent of five days' work as a Thinker. "Thanks, Caeldra."

She led me through the hall into the massive library where the tidy bookshelves towered alongside one another. She walked over to the desk where a woman in her forties was working behind a computer. Caeldra grabbed a steel cart from behind the desk and wheeled it to me.

"Hi, Tracy. I'm going to be training Jake on adding new stock and other archival duties," Caeldra said to the woman.

"Oh, how lovely. It will be nice to have another helper in the library."

Caeldra led me over to the back of the library where large crates had been stacked. Some of the crates were wood, other were steel, and all of them looked timeworn.

"Now, we are going to be evaluating everything we have in these crates to see what we want. Most of the scavengers and merchants we buy these from either knowingly smuggle these illegal books, or are too stupid to realize what they're hauling and how much it's worth," she said as she tossed me a small data tablet. "If you scan the book, that tablet will cross-reference the results with our library and let you know if we're going to keep it or not, and if it needs to be electronically scanned. If we don't have it in the electronic archives yet, you'll need to bring it to Tracy."

"Got it, and how do we get these crates open?" I asked.

"The metal ones should have a latch, and you'll need to pry open the wooden ones." She reached in the bottom of the cart she had pushed and tossed me a heavy iron crowbar and flipped open her odd-looking knife. "Oh and try not to mess up the wood, we'll recycle it and that stuff is worth more than you would imagine."

"Why do they ship it in the wooden boxes then?"

"If they don't open the boxes, then they can claim they aren't doing anything illegal if they're caught, even though a simple scanner can evaluate the contents of a box like that. Sure we pay a little more for the wood, but it's much cheaper than typical market rates."

We worked for a few hours, and I was relieved that Caeldra wasn't mad at me when I started to read books that piqued my interest. I was learning all sorts of new words and ideas: states, unalienable rights, freedom of speech. The newfound concepts raced through my head, and I was more excited to learn than I had ever been in my entire life.

Caeldra and I worked until 5 PM before we decided to call it a day so that I'd have time to talk with Edgar before we left. I declined her offer to go with me and told her to get some rest. After saying goodbye, I made my way to Edgar's office where I saw him talking on a handheld radio through the open door. When he saw me, he waved me in and motioned for me to close the door and sit at the chair across from his desk.

Like his house, Edgar kept the room tidy. Few things other than a space rocket toy, a crystal of some sort, and an ancient looking pistol that was made of a polished brown wood sat on the surface. Edgar's wall had various paintings of strange places and pictures of a part of New York that I had never seen.

"Yes, please keep an eye out on everything and let me know if anything changes. Yes, thank you." Edgar said over the radio as he put it down on his desk and turned his attention to me. He folded his fingers together and leaned forward on the desk taking in a deep breath and looking me in the eyes.

"Jake... I don't really know how to say this so I'm just going to tell you. The man you've been seeing up in the Slums, the one that gave you the requisition scrip. He's... he is more or less your father."

18

LUMINESCENCE

It felt like the world was spinning around me and I felt a crushing weight in my chest. How could that person or thing be my father? I had watched him die in a hospital. Besides, my dad was nowhere close to that size. How did any of this make sense? How did Edgar know him?

"H… How?" I managed.

"It's not going to be easy to understand, and I know you're going to need time to process this. First off, your father did die in the hospital. I did know your dad, and I lied to you to protect you. When I learned that his presence was still with us, I decided to try to put as much distance between him and us as possible." Edgar raised a hand and wiped his face. "That machine has all of your father's thoughts, all of his memories up until a month before your father's death. It thinks like your father and acts like your father, but the important thing to know is that it's not actually him. It is the closest representation to your dad as a machine can get. However, your father coded it to seek you out and tell you things, things that it declines to share with me. I don't think it's a danger to you or anyone else, I'm just not sure what kind of information it wants to share," he paused. "I'm not sure if that information should be known by anyone."

"What are you talking about!" I yelled as I felt myself losing control. "If my father wanted to tell me something, why the hell wouldn't I want to hear it?"

"There are boundaries that we have an ethical duty not to cross, boundaries set by powers beyond our control. You might not have learned about religion yet, but regardless of that fact, your father did something that shouldn't have been done. He thought that he could transfer his soul to a machine, that when he left the physical world, he would continue to live through a machine perpetually." Edgar paused and took a deep breath. "That machine thinks that it is actually your father, and that's what scares me."

"It can't actually be him, though. Right?" I asked as I fought to piece things together and understand. So many questions rushed through my aching mind.

"I don't think so. Not even modern science has been able to quantify the soul. It's intangible. But your father believes he had it figured out. We know that transferring thoughts out of the brain is a very real thing, we just didn't know that they could also be transferred in. He claims that the technology would work on humans that the entire life's recollection of one individual could be absorbed by another mind without the need for implants."

"I thought he was just a Thinker, he never talked or worked on any of this stuff at home," I said.

"He was working on a secret project and decided to seek our help when he figured it out. He realized that this was stuff that he didn't want to fall into the hands of the Government. Unfortunately, that's also what got him and your mother killed."

"What else do you know?" I wasn't mad at him, I wasn't sure how I felt—other than confused and conflicted. I had so much to process.

"Nothing else. I've only had a few opportunities to talk to it, and no one else here knows about it. The situation is delicate, and if things get dicey, then I'll need to involve the Council. I wanted you to be the first one to know, and I'm sorry that I didn't tell you sooner. Your real father would be very proud of you, Jake. Be safe and please know that you can come to me to talk about it. You've got a lot to think about, and unfortunately, I'm needed here tonight. You can either spend the night here or return to the surface on your own. Take some time to think about what I said and know that you can come to me to talk whenever. You can speak to it if you want, but you can't tell anyone else other than Caeldra should you so choose, and be very explicit that she can't talk about it with anyone else."

"I'm assuming that I'm not allowed to talk with him or it about any Guild related matters?" I asked.

Edgar frowned. "That robot knows everything your father knew about the Guild, which means that it actually knows things you're not permitted to know as an Initiate, but still, I would like you to refrain from talking about current matters just in case. If the Government knew of its existence, then we'd already be dead. Just be careful and remember that it's not actually him."

I gave him a nod and walked out of his office feeling utter confusion and defeat. Caeldra was waiting nearby and leaning against a wall. She looked up as I walked over and gave me an appraising look. Apparently, my face said it all. Caeldra opened her arms and wrapped me in a big hug. I was careful not to squeeze her too hard due to her injury.

"Come on, I want to take you somewhere, but first we need to gear up. Are you alright with staying down here tonight?"

I thought about it for a moment. As much as I wanted to see Mary, I knew that I couldn't tell her that my dad had actually been a secret Government worker that had developed something to transfer the entire life of a human to a robot. I was still struggling to process everything myself and didn't want to be in a foul mood around her. Somehow, this was harder to deal with than the death of Mikey and taking another's life.

"Yeah, I'll stay down here tonight," I replied. We walked to the locker room and changed into our Runner equipment. I didn't really mind that we were going out into the Undercity. I just wanted to do something to take my mind off of things.

Caeldra grabbed two tall and thin bags and fastened them to my backpack. She then opened my pack and filled it with some stuff from hers.

"I hope you don't mind some extra weight. Doc says I have to limit what I carry while I heal,"

"No problem," I replied.

"Go see Leroy and buy two premium ration packs then meet me at the pub." She handed me one hundred credits and started off toward the stairs while I walked over to Leroy's shop.

"Hey Jake," he said as he saw me approach. He was working on a large rifle that had been disassembled on the counter.

"Hi, Leroy. I need two premium ration packs please."

"Sure thing. That will be one hundred even," he said as he pulled them up from below the counter. They were large brown vacuum packed plastic bags with a gold star on the exterior. I paid Leroy, thanked him, and set back out toward the pub. Caeldra was waiting by the bar.

"Got the food?" she asked.

I nodded.

"Great, let's go," she said as we walked out the main gate. Instead of taking the elevator up, she led me down a small but well-lit corridor that was unmarked. Since Caeldra hadn't told me where we were going and I hadn't set an objective, Artemis didn't tell me how far we would be traveling.

We approached a small air duct that had been marked with pink spray paint, Caeldra's color of choice.

"Do you trust me?" Caeldra said.

"Yeah, I mean except for when you pushed me down a hole," I replied playfully.

"Ouch, Jake. I was just doing my job. Well, I'm not going to push you again, but this does involve another dark hole, unfortunately," she said as she held up her wrist to the vent which beeped and slid open. "I'll go first," she said as she latched her rappelling carabiner to a long steel cable that was rooted to the top of the vent. Caeldra dropped down and began sliding down at a fast speed.

"See you at the bottom!" she called.

With reluctance, I did the same and began the descent through the small vent.

"Turn off your flashlight," Caeldra said over comms.

I did as she instructed and slowed my descent. I couldn't see a thing in the darkness other than my Artemis overlay that covered my vision. I still had three hundred feet before I reached the bottom, according to the display.

"Almost there," she said through the earpiece.

I slowed even further and saw a faint green light that was radiating below me. I slid past the vent and was shocked to see that there were bright green sparkles all over the ceiling of the level and on the walls. They flashed on and off and rippled in mesmerizing patterns before my eyes. I saw Caeldra standing on the floor, looking up at me with a smile. As I dropped further, Artemis informed me that I had entered a shadow zone and that I had no link to the network.

"Beautiful, isn't it?" she asked me.

"What is this? Where are we?"

"This is my special place. It's a type of bioluminescent algae that grows down here. It's all connected, and the algae creates beautiful patterns of light."

The walls and ceiling swirled with color before my eyes, and I was amazed that something like this could exist.

"Is it safe for us here?"

"Oh yes, this entire level is completely sealed off. I've also installed a hard-wired line that will allow us to communicate through Artemis if we need it. Let's get our tent set up then we will get dinner going," she said. We unpacked the tent from my pack and assembled it on a flat patch of old concrete. The top of the tent was made of a clear plastic while the rest was made out of some sort of orange plastic mesh.

"It is nice and cold down here, but it really is too damp for long term comfort," Caeldra said.

We climbed into the tent, and she adjusted a setting on her wrist link. The inside of the tent dried out, pulling the humidity out of the air.

"Now, how about we eat dinner? For your sake, I really hope you brought those meals. Otherwise we're going to be eating algae," she said, and we both started laughing. I pulled out the meals from my pack and tossed one to her.

"I'll be honest. I don't know how these things work," I said as I shifted the package in my hands.

"Just open it up. If you've got spaghetti and I don't, then you automatically have to trade meals with me because I'm your sponsor. Once you've got your entrée, just punch in the plastic bubble, and it will heat up in two minutes."

I smiled and opened my meal. "I've got mac and cheese with ground beef," I told her.

"That's yours to keep," she said as she flaunted her spaghetti entrée in front of me. "Well done, Jake."

We punched in the plastic bubbles, and the meals began to crackle in the bags. I sifted through the rest of the contents of the main bag and pulled out some barbecue chips, a chocolate cookie, and a milkshake mix that said 'ADD WATER' on the side. These were all things that would be considered luxury items at the grocery stores and were things that I had actively avoided purchasing on the surface to save my credits. After a couple of minutes, we started eating and stared up at the magnificent light show that was unfolding above.

I was amazed at how good the food was. It tasted like it had come directly from a restaurant. "How did you find this place?" I asked her through a bite of macaroni.

"Exploration. Only a couple of people know about it and I'd like to keep it that way," she said as she chewed.

We didn't talk much while we ate. Both of us were watching the beauty of the ceiling and enjoying the delicious meals. The entire atmosphere was comforting. Few displays of unaltered nature existed in the world, and this place was an isolated system of beauty and grace.

"This is my favorite place in the whole world. It's so peaceful and beautiful. I come here when I'm happy, I come here when I'm sad, and I come here when I just need to get away from things," she said as she looked at me with her beautiful blue eyes. "As my apprentice, you're welcome to come here too."

"Thanks, Caeldra. It really is beautiful," I said.

"So, about this girl you were trying to impress when the Enforcers got you. Are you still with her? I can't imagine she was impressed," she said with a joking smile.

I frowned. "Things between us were going really well, but I'm worried about the lies I have to tell her, and how much time I'm spending here away from her. Edgar said that inviting her to join the Guild would be selfish. After yesterday I agree. I don't want to put her in any danger," I said.

"It won't be easy, but I wish you all the best. I had a boyfriend on the surface a couple of years ago. The things you're worried about are very real, and they got to us. If you care about the girl, cherish every moment you have to spend with her and don't ever let her go," Caeldra said. "What's her name?"

"Mary," I said, finding myself smiling at the mention of her name.

"That's a beautiful name," she said.

"Your name, it doesn't sound like any other I've heard," I commented.

"You're right. My parents made it up. They like the sound of it and thought it fit."

"Are they still alive?" I said, trying to be polite.

"Oh yes, and I still live with them on the surface. They think I work at a Government shipping factory after a successful aptitude evaluation."

"So how did you find your way to the Guild?" I asked.

"Similar to you, I got mad at the Government for unjust punishment. I wanted a new hair brush, but couldn't afford it. I tried to steal it from the store and caught a swipe from an Enforcer that wanted to catch me. It sliced my face right open. It's not much of a story, but I fled and found myself in the Undercity only to stumble into a couple of Guild Runners. They took me in, and I've been here ever since. The funny thing is that the Enforcers chasing me from the store were just trying to tell me that my punishment had been paid and that I could keep the hairbrush."

"Wow," I said.

"Yeah, life is better now that I feel like I have a purpose. We really are working towards something special here," she said as she scooped up the last of the spaghetti sauce with her plastic spoon.

We finished our meals and packed them back up in the brown plastic bags before setting them outside the tent.

"I know you don't like what you heard from Edgar, and I'm not going to press you if you don't want to talk about it, but just know that I'm here for you if you ever need someone to talk to."

"Thanks, but I don't really want to talk about it right now," I said, not wanting to become more upset.

"I've got something for you," she said as she started fumbling with the latch on her backpack. "I know I already bought you a drink, but I wanted to get you something to say thanks for saving my life as well as brighten your day and say that I'm thankful to have you as an apprentice." She pulled out a small black metal box and handed it to me. "With that in mind, I couldn't think of a better time to give this to you."

I opened the box and felt a smile form on my face. It was a beautiful looking knife with an anodized finish across the hilt. I couldn't see a blade or button to deploy it. I picked it up, and the half of the handle swung down, exposing the edge of the blade.

"What kind of knife is this?" I asked her as I messed around with the pivoting grip and blade below.

"It's a balisong or butterfly knife. I also include lessons as part of your present." She pulled out her own knife from her pocket and held it flat against the palm of her hand.

"Don't try this yet," she said as she deftly repositioned the knife in her hand. She grabbed one of the handles and flipped the knife in her hand in a series of quick motions. She twirled the knife between her fingers and spun it around her palm with speed and elegance. In one final but amazing move, she tossed the spinning blade in the air and caught it with a dull clunk as the two handle pieces connected. "You can close your mouth now, Jake." She did a quick three-part move, and the blade was once again concealed between the handles. "It's a weapon of beauty and functionality. I'll teach you a couple of basic flips for now, but you need to start off with the training blade before you try anything with live steel."

Caeldra spent the next thirty minutes teaching me the horizontal and vertical flips that would allow me to open and close my knife in a flashy yet simple way. After she was sure that I knew the difference between the safe and bite handles of the knife, she allowed me to switch out the dull training blade with the sharp one.

"As long as you always know which side you're holding; you can't get hurt with these flips. If you want to learn some new ones, use the trainer until you've got it down. Any visits to Medbay are coming out of your pocket, got it?"

"Got it. Thanks so much, Caeldra." I said as I flipped the knife open and closed. It was such a cool knife, and I never expected such a thoughtful gift. I wondered how much she had paid for it and was about to ask when I saw her pull out a cardboard container that housed twelve dark brown bottles.

"Oh, and I got us these," she said with a smile.

We put away our knives and Caeldra handed me a bottle after she popped the cap off. "Drink up. Oh, and never flip live steel if you've been drinking, it dulls your reflexes, even if you're an Unbound," she said as she drank deeply from her bottle and gave me a teasing look.

I sipped at mine and was delighted that it was the same beer from the pub. We drank in silence at first and simply stared up at the ever-evolving patterns on the ceiling. After a few beers in silence, we began to talk.

"So I found out my dad was actually working on a secret Government project. He didn't want them to have the tech, so he hid it, and they killed him so that he couldn't give it to anyone else," I said breaking the silence. I felt dizzy from the beer and felt like what I said didn't matter.

"I'm sorry to hear that, Jake," she replied, her voice gentle and soothing.

"Oh, and he might have transferred his entire existence into a robot," I said with a bitter edge.

"Is that even possible? Are you mad at Edgar?"

I was surprised that I wasn't mad, even under the effects of the alcohol. "I have no idea if it's really him or not, or if something like that can be done. I'm not mad at Edgar, how could I be? He was just doing his best to protect me. I don't know if I'm mad at my dad or not. I guess I'll have to talk to his robotic clone to find out."

"I'm sorry," she responded.

I felt tears well up in my eyes. "I just don't understand why he did this. Why was it so important that he would put a clone of himself into a robot? It's going to be so hard to talk to that thing that thinks it's my father." Emotion surged through my voice as I fought back the tears.

"Shhh, come here," Caeldra said as she pulled my head onto her shoulder gently and slid her fingers through my hair. "I'm sure he had a reason. And I'm sure he did it with your best interest in mind. Just know that you don't have to do this alone. I'm here for you and I'll help you through this."

I looked up at her.

"Thank you so much. Thank you for everything."

She smiled at me and kissed me on the cheek. The next few moments were a blur and I'm not entirely sure who started it, but we kissed. Not an aggressive kiss, but a gentle one that lasted no more than a few seconds. After the kiss, I scooted back over to my side of the tent and leaned back and continued to look up, feeling confused and guilty for what I'd done. We didn't say anything and I couldn't tell exactly how I felt. We ended up finishing our beers and slowly faded to sleep as the conversation faded and the beautiful lights continued to swirl playfully above us.

19
WANTED

The smell of sizzling meat and eggs pierced through the veil of sleep, and I awoke to see Caeldra cooking on a small frying pan above a small gas stove.

"How do you feel?" she asked me as she saw my eyes open.

I paused for a moment while I tried to evaluate how I felt. I was feeling a little groggy from drinking too much, but other than that I was fine. As I looked at her, the memory of our kiss returned to my mind, and I began to worry.

"I'm alright. About last night... I'm sorry, I think I..."

She cut me off, "don't worry about it. You were upset, we were drunk. It's water under the bridge."

I wished I felt as confident. I felt guilty for kissing her when I had something going on with Mary. I didn't mean to kiss her; I didn't even know if I had Initiated the kiss.

"Are we alright?" she asked me.

"Yeah, of course, I just didn't want things to be awkward between us."

"Don't worry about that. We both drank more than enough to get drunk. I'm looking forward to getting to know you better, Jake."

She finished cooking the breakfast, and we ate while discussing plans for the day. It was already ten in the morning, and we had more archival work to do. I dreaded my return to the surface and the task of attempting to cobble together a reasonable story to tell Mary. She wasn't stupid, and I wasn't a good liar.

After packing up, we ascended the small vent overhead and returned to the Guild Hall where we picked up our library cart from Tracy. As we were approaching the crates of books, Master Aarlen walked out of his office.

"Jake, may I have a word?" he asked.

"Of course," I replied as I walked over, excited to speak with him.

He ushered me into his office and closed the door after giving Caeldra a strange glance. "Sorry for pulling you from your work, I just want to give you some homework. I don't want you falling out of practice with your layering," he said as he adjusted his glasses and leaned forward on the desk with his fingers intertwined. Master Aarlen pulled out a small tablet with neuro-connectors.

"When I say homework, I mean work that you can do on your free time down here. This tech can't be allowed on the surface—

I'm sure you understand." He handed me the tablet and powered it on.

"You'll start from the beginning and work your way through these modules. Finish the series and I'll give you more work. Bring that completed series to me, and I'll give you a check for three units to cash in with the Guild Treasurer. All you have to do is connect the neuro-connectors and close your eyes," he said to me.

"How long does each module take?"

He grinned. "That is entirely up to you, my dear friend. With someone of your acute mental stature, I'm sure it won't take too long. Just tread carefully and don't push yourself too hard." He pulled a large leather-bound binder from below the desk. "It's best you get back to Caeldra; you don't want to keep her waiting."

I nodded. "Thank you, Master Aarlen."

I exited his office and closed the door behind me and placed the small tablet in the back pocket of my Runner pants.

I returned to Caeldra, who was using her combat knife to pry open a musty wooden crate. She grunted as she forced the box open. The lid creaked in protest as it cracked open with excessive force. Caeldra reached up and wiped sweat from her forehead. "What was that about?" she asked.

"Nothing much, Master Aarlen just gave me some layering homework to work on in my free time."

"Paid?"

"Yeah, he's going to give me three units if I can finish all the modules on the tablet."

"Nice, well good luck with that, I'm afraid I won't be able to help." She paused as she pulled out a dust-covered paperback that was a dark yellow color from deterioration. "Get cracking, Jake. We've got to get all of these crates done today."

I pulled out my combat knife and began to pry open some wooden crates, not wanting to damage my balisong. I used my shirt as a shield to protect me from the musty clouds of dust on the inside of the crates. According to Caeldra, most of the crates hadn't been opened in over one hundred years, and she reiterated the fact that the Great Flood of 2039 was a hoax with some creative uses of some very colorful words. Her complex strings of profanity were almost graceful, coming together like a great work of art.

I was beginning to understand Caeldra a lot better. Her steel toughness and resolve and generally gruff attitude was just on the surface. When she cared about something or someone, she showed kindness and compassion and exhibited great selflessness. She was complicated, but I had a feeling that our friendship would continue to blossom as we grew to know one another better.

Most of the books we sorted that day were only illegal because of the date they had been printed. Many of the titles were actually reprinted and reused on the surface, but those weren't the types of books we were interested in finding. The real treasures were old history books that contained the history of the entire world that pieced together events of the past that had been lost. The Guild called it the Genesis Project, the pursuit of finding out everything that the Government had attempted to destroy and keep from the people. I flipped through an old black book and saw a chart of events that dated into the year 1300. There was a huge map of the world and the names of many pieces of land I didn't even know existed. "Caeldra, I think I may have found something," I said as I passed her the book. She flipped through the book and smiled.

"Good find! I'll get this to Master Aarlen right away," she said as she walked the book over to his office.

When she returned, we took a break from opening crates and worked on creating digital scans of the books that weren't already in the system. "When you have some free time, you should study from the Archives. You can read about the real history of the world, how things used to be in the United States, or about anything you want. It's going to be hard to take it all in and erase so much of everything you've learned, but you've already proven your worth by being accepted into the Guild."

"I want to know the truth, and I want to do what I can to make this a better world. Why should innocent people be ruled by machines? Is there even an Upper Level of New York? And why hasn't anyone in the Slums seen pictures or evidence of it?" I asked as anger crept into my voice.

"You're starting to ask the right kind of questions. Unfortunately, we don't have all the answers, but that's what we work for," she said smiling at the flame that sparked in my eyes.

We finished up work for the day, and I packed up all of my stuff and put it in my locker. I returned to the surface alone after Mr. Barton told me that he would be staying down in the Guild Hall for the night. As I returned to the streets, I stopped at the grocery store a couple of blocks from my house and picked up some basic groceries, also deciding to buy a small chocolate cake with icing from the bakery. It wasn't cheap, but I wanted to get Mary something nice so she wouldn't be mad at me for blowing her off. I paid and returned to my street as quickly as possible. As I neared my flat, I saw Mary outside surrounded by six Enforcers. Her face was shrouded by her bandana so I couldn't see her expression, but I knew this couldn't be good. As I approached, she looked over at me and I could see the fear in her eyes. She shook her head in a subtle, but recognizable way. When the Enforcers spotted me, their lights started flashing.

"Jacob Ashton, we need to talk with you," one of them said as started toward me, weapon raised. As the cold pang of fear surged through my body, I dropped my groceries and turned to run.

20

TRANSFERENCE

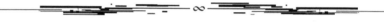

I ran faster than I ever had before. Heavy hydraulic thuds sounded behind me as the Enforcers trailed close behind—yet no shots were fired. Flashing red and blue lights from their frames illuminated the shallow pools of water which rested on the cracked asphalt streets. I had no sense of where I was going, I was just trying to escape. It became harder and harder to breathe as the smog seeped through my bandana, but I forced myself to press on. Tears blurred my vision as I ran further and further away from the girl I loved, leaving her to an unknown fate that was likely the result of my actions. No matter how much I wanted to, I couldn't turn back, I couldn't betray the cause I had sworn to fight.

I turned a corner a little too fast and forced myself to lean to the side as my sneakers slid across the wet sidewalk. Recovering from the slip, I approached the market and ran into the large canvas tent. While it technically wasn't a building, the fresh air inside was welcome. The market tent was filled with hundreds of people walking around and stopping at the various booths inside where merchants peddled their goods. The room smelled of cooking meat and aerosol air freshener—a strange, but familiar scent. I ran as fast as possible while avoiding the people that jumped away in surprise and yelled for me to slow down. The Enforcers entered the large tent and started searching for me, but I was already inside and concealed by the crowd. I moved through calmly, trying to approach the back where I could escape. These were just standard Enforcers chasing me, they weren't equipped with any of the advanced optics of the newer specialist models that were rarely dispatched. Despite my creeping fear, I forced myself to walk until I reached the exit. With shaking hands, I pulled the glass pill that would end my life from my paracord bracelet and gripped it tight between my fingers and palm. I didn't want it to come to that, but I wouldn't allow myself to fall into the hands of the Sculptors.

After exiting the tent, I sprinted back toward the entrance to the Undercity while I was still out of sight of the Enforcers. I didn't know where else to go to hide, but I couldn't allow myself to be followed all the way down. I also couldn't pull the Enforcers into the illegal warehouse that we used to access the Undercity.

I was dismayed when three Enforcers rounded a corner in front of me and started towards me. With the option of entering the Undercity fading, I turned to face the Industrial Park. The huge factories located in the park grew closer as I ran on the quiet street. The Enforcers were gaining ground on me quickly now.

Pain shot through my chest as I continued to press my lungs and body beyond what they were supposed to handle. I felt the burn of acid building in my thighs and calves and the stitches of pain in my sides as I ran. The cold air congested my lungs, and I was nearing my physical limit when the familiar machine in the gray trench coat kicked open a door. He was holding a massive turret with rotating barrels. I screamed as I neared him and moved my arms in front of me as I tried to slow my movement on the wet asphalt. I skidded in front of him, and his large metal hand caught me and pulled me behind him as more Enforcers entered the scene.

"Robotic entity, you possess an illegal weapon and are impeding Government business," one of the Enforcers said as they all raised their energy rifles towards us.

The robot gave a grunt that could have been a laugh. The barrels of the turret spun up and unleashed a barrage of purple energy bolts which shredded through the heavy metal plating of the Enforcers like paper. The turret continued to sputter as at least eight Enforcers were reduced to scrap metal. Vibrant sparks and colorful explosions ripped through the strong metallic alloys. The Enforcers shot back, but what shots they did manage to land didn't appear to damage my protector. The few people on the streets near the Industrial park were running away from the scene and taking cover on the walls of the buildings, screaming in fear. The robot was very careful with aim despite his weapon of choice, which was probably heavier than I was. The sparking remains of Enforcers were littered all over the street and distant screams of the people that had witnessed the scene echoed. The robot raised the cannon once more and fired along the roofs of nearby buildings destroying the CCTV cameras that were perched above.

"Sorry for the mess. Get inside," he said to me in the familiar metallic voice.

He closed the door behind me and flipped on a light switch. The flooring was torn out and the room was empty except for a single hatch in the center. Taking a piece of steel rebar, he shoved it through a latch on the door and wrapped it around the handle, creating a forced lock from the inside. I returned the glass pill to the hidden slot in my bracelet, thankful that my situation had improved.

"We need to get you to the Undercity right away," he said as he flipped up the latch.

"What about Mary? I can't just leave her," I said between my heavy breathing.

"If they wanted to kill her, she'd already be dead. They were probably just talking to her to learn more about you, I doubt she's in danger."

I wanted to believe it, but the dread of leaving her was building inside me, congealing and weighing down my thoughts.

"Move it," the robot said, prodding me forward. I started climbing down, and the robot jumped down once I had cleared the ladder, landing with a thud.

The robot handed me a respirator to wear and urged me forward at a brisk pace while we descended further and further into territory that was unfamiliar to me. I didn't like running around without my gear or Artemis, but I was fairly confident in my protector's ability to guide me to safety, especially since he was carrying around a two-hundred-pound energy weapon.

We continued through the homogeneous tunneling until we approached a large rusted door with a heavy padlock. The man in gray opened the lock and motioned for me to go inside. It was a small room that had about the same amount of space as my flat back in the Slums. A large desk sat in the back where an advanced looking computer console was set up. The console had cabling running throughout the room to various boxes with glowing lights on the front. There was a massive assembly frame that housed multiple weapons and strange gadgets. The robot placed the heavy turret against a steel locker with a dull metallic clank. The air was cleaner than the stagnant air from the tunneling we had traveled through, and I savored the deep breaths I was able to take without the respirator on.

"This is my home, Jake," he said as he closed the door. "You'll be safe here, and I'll take you to the Guild Hall later once we've had the chance to talk."

"Is it really you?"

"To the best of my understanding, yes. While I am no longer human, I am Wesley Ashton," he responded as he took off the huge coat and hung it on the rack. The robot's body was made of blue-looking metal and looked much more durable and expensive than an Enforcer. He reached up and removed the respirator mask he was wearing and placed it with the coat. The face wasn't similar either. His face was solid metal with two small vision slots instead of the one central sensor array that the Enforcers had. I could see speakers on the side of the armored head that allowed him to communicate.

"I'm sorry you have to see me like this, but it's good to see you again, son."

"Likewise," I responded carefully.

"I'm sure you must have hundreds of questions, and I'll do my best to answer them. The Government is either looking for you because of your test results, or they know you're involved in something you shouldn't be. I'll look into it more and try to figure out what's going on. In the meantime, you need to stay in the Undercity until this is all worked out."

He started coughing with a series of harsh metallic screeches as he raised his hand to where his mouth would've been if he was human. "Sorry, I'm feeling a little bit sick today. Damn cough."

"You can get sick?" I asked, once again careful with the inflection of my voice not to give away my disbelief. Despite the advanced looking hardware, it didn't look like his code or mind was all there.

"Oh yes, I keep in touch with my human side by subjecting myself to the biological weaknesses weyouuu," there was a strange pause as if he couldn't decide what he was. "Suffer as a species from time to time." He raised his hand and smacked the side of his head as if punishing himself for a mistake.

"I see. So can you tell me about the project you were working on that allowed you to transfer your being into a machine?"

"Yes. Every time I would say I was going to work, I'd go to a warehouse to work with my colleagues. Unfortunately, all of us are dead now and I made it out in this suit. We were starting to get closer when the Government decided it was time for human experimentation. Of course, several Prolific volunteered for the procedure—they always crave new knowledge. But we're talking about something more than learning here, we're talking about absorbing the essence of someone's being. Things didn't go well. Relatively speaking, the procedure was a success, but the results were horrifying. Even with all the neural implants, the Prolific couldn't handle the stress of trying to maintain a mind of two people. There were clashes..." He paused for a moment as if considering the term, nodded, then continued. "Their minds were literally battling one another and trying to create one timeline by destroying the other. While they had the wits of two, their personalities, remembrance of their past, and social skills were all but destroyed. In the Government's eyes, it was a success, but we knew that it could be improved, that it didn't have to be like this. Well, one night I finally cracked it. We finished the technology that would turn the brain into more of a library, allowing the user to, so to speak, open different books and chapters of all the information and lives they had absorbed. It was a delicate thing."

"So you're saying it worked, that there was no limit to how many minds they could absorb?" I asked.

"I don't know, the Prolific that helped me test got to eight different minds and was completely fine. The rest of the team and I realized that this wasn't something we wanted the Government to get a hold of. It's something that no one should have. We violated the laws of nature and hiding the results of the project from the Government cost us our lives. I exist indefinitely in this prison as a reminder of what I've done and the consequences of my actions. I'm so proud to see what you've become. You have potential, Jake. As you've already discovered, your ability to layer your thoughts makes you powerful, and dangerous."

"The Prolific that tested the technology? Are they alive?" I asked.

"No," he responded, and when he didn't continue I decided to move on.

"Does the technology still exist?" I asked him as I considered his words.

"Yes, I've got it here wired to some explosives. I'm not sure if the Champions should have it. This isn't something that can be utilized without consequences, and the technology itself does still have some flaws. My code is deteriorating, and if I don't actively maintain it, I will turn into something I'm not. I'm not supposed to get sick—in fact, it's impossible for me to get sick now, but my human self remembers sickness and so somewhere in my subconscious I am subject to the same laws of nature. I wear a gasmask where the air isn't safe to breathe even though I don't breathe anymore. I can't explain these things or why they happen, but I can't allow myself to become dangerous to anyone other than the Government. The last thing I would want is to hurt you or the Guild."

"I understand that, and I think you're doing a good thing. I want to talk with Edgar about the tech, maybe we'd have a use for it, but it also sounds dangerous."

He growled and swatted an empty can across the room where it smashed against the dense wall. "It's your decision to make. If it were up to me, I'd destroy it. If it isn't destroyed, the Guild needs to take precautions to protect it and keep it away from the Government."

I raised my hand and placed it on his metal arm. "You were just doing what you could to support our family. I respect your decision and think you did the right thing by keeping it away from the Government."

"They can't have it, Jake. Absolute Knowledge is already a sham, but the Collective Thought is very real. Imagine how quickly they could speed up the growth of the project with Prolifics absorbing hundreds of minds, how quickly they could combine thoughts to create new ones. Absolute Knowledge cannot exist on this planet, there is too much unknown in the universe, too much that can't be learned from the confines of Earth. What happens when they no longer need the Slums working as Thinkers? What happens when they pull the cord on the project and leave us on our own? What happens when they decide to wipe us out?"

I took in a sharp breath and realized there was truth to what he was saying. It wasn't the delusion of an over processing robot, these were words of truth and logic. How long was all of this sustainable?

"If the Government gets Mindshift, the Slums are dead," he said with words of finality.

21
DETAINED

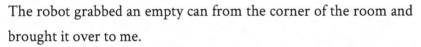

The robot grabbed an empty can from the corner of the room and brought it over to me.

"This tin can represents the Collective Thought, it represents what Absolute Knowledge should be, but never can be. The sum of all possible thoughts should take a final form, but how can that be built?" he asked.

"By collecting everything and putting the collected thoughts together like a puzzle," I said.

He started tearing the can into tiny pieces. "How many small pieces can this can be broken into?" he asked.

"At the atomic level, it can be broken down into individual atoms which could represent individual thoughts," I said, unsure of where he was going.

"Correct, but let's assume that it has to go further than that. Think subatomic particles."

"Okay, so thoughts are like neutrons, protons, and electrons, they come together to form packets of related thoughts," I said.

"Yes, but think even smaller, quarks and leptons, the particles that make up those sub-atomic particles. What makes up a quark and lepton? Who's to say there isn't another particle that makes up those particles that we don't have the ability to see or perceive."

"Okay, but it's got to stop somewhere, right?"

"No, it doesn't have to begin or end anywhere, everything just *is*. Things exist because we observe them because something beyond our control created them. Absolute Knowledge is infinity, it's an impossible concept to comprehend, let alone achieve without an infinite amount of time. Even if every Prolific could absorb one hundred different minds and not die, what good is improving the progress of the Collective Thought by a million-fold when they're chasing infinity?"

"It wouldn't do anything," I said, realization dawning.

"Exactly. When the Government realizes that the Slums don't benefit the cause, there will be no reason to sustain the population any longer. The Mids will be lost, and whatever lurks in the Upper Level will be lost as well. The project can't be a success if it stays on this world. There are infinitely many planets to discover in the universe, and an infinite amount of space that many believe is still expanding. Absolute Knowledge is, in every definition of the word, impossible."

We talked for a couple of hours as I forced myself to remain objective and keep emotion out of my questions and judgments. I had to keep reminding myself that my father was dead and that this robot in front of me wasn't him, just an archive of what he had been and what he had known; a replica of the real thing.

"They either suspect you of treason or think you capable of it for some reason. Perhaps it's a simple misunderstanding, but your life on the surface might be over," he said to me.

"Did you leave the equipment for me at the Quartermaster?" I asked with sudden remembrance.

"I'm afraid I'm not quite sure what you're talking about," he replied.

"You gave me the requisition slip, the foot locker had your name on it," I responded. How could he not remember something so recent?

"I'm not sure what you are talking about, human."

"Are you alright?" I asked with caution, it was as if he had forgotten who or what he was.

"Certainly. Should we proceed to the Guild Hall?" his voice was back to normal, but the glitches were starting to give me concern.

I nodded, and he picked up an old looking rifle and strapped a belt of magazines for the weapon around his waist. He tossed me an old gas mask and started walking toward the door.

"Ah, I almost forgot." He reached into a locker and pulled out a small antique looking handgun and handed it to me. "Just in case," he said as he started unlocking the door.

I fastened the gas mask around my face and breathed in the stale, musty air through the old filters. I inspected the gun in my hands, it looked similar to the weapon I owned, but it was much heavier. I ejected the magazine and saw that instead of a gas cartridge, it contained small capsules with copper tips. I realized that these were bullets, primitive tech compared to energy-based weapons.

We exited the bunker and proceeded through the damp tunnels in silence at a moderate pace for about an hour before reaching the Guild Hall unscathed. Two guards approached with their rifles raised. "Stop! Identify yourselves," one said with a loud voice.

"I am Initiate Jacob Ashton, and this is my companion," I said as we stood with our arms raised. One of the guards kept the rifle trained on the robotic form of my father while the other called something in over comms with his back toward us.

"You can enter, but hand us the weapons," the guard said with an outstretched hand. "Nice and slow," the other added as the rifles remained trained.

I approached slowly and handed the pistol to the outstretched hand of one of guards and my father reluctantly handed over his gun with a string of complaints.

The doors of the hall opened, and we were greeted by a semicircle of twenty armed Guild members with weapons trained on us. The guards from outside followed in behind us with their weapons raised. Alex stepped out from the front of the blockade, he was furious.

"What is the meaning of this, Jake! Are you trying to get us all killed? You damned fool!" he shouted. I was taken aback by the words but kept my composure.

"This is my father, the result of a Government project called Mindshift. The technology still exists, and the Government doesn't have it."

"You expect us to believe that thing isn't dangerous?" he asked, anger flaring in his voice.

"Actually, he saved my life. The Government is after me and when I ran, he led me to safety."

"Oh, wonderful. Not only have you brought danger to us in the form of some kind of prototype Enforcer, but you also might have been followed. Do you have any reason why we shouldn't kill you both on the spot?" his body was tensed in fury as his face quivered with each word.

My heart jumped into my throat at this. "I... I'm just trying to help; I don't know why they want me or if I even made any mistakes that would compromise my identity!" I yelled.

"Why, you insolent fool. You're dead!" Alex yelled as he stomped his foot on the ground.

Edgar stepped forward. "That's enough, Alex!" he shouted. "We don't know what's going on. You know as well as I do that wireless signals from the surface don't penetrate the Undercity."

"Jake, step forward slowly and get behind us. We need to inspect that robot before anything else happens," Edgar said.

I did as he said and walked forward at a slow pace. Edgar grabbed my arm and pulled me behind the blockade as an engineer named Martinez walked forward toward my father with a red toolbox. He was a short man and wore a faded gray jumpsuit, slick with dark oil stains. He wore thick, heavy goggles that were perched on his face, hiding his expression.

"Sir, if you would please remove your clothes," he said to the robot. My father scoffed and removed the large coat and undershirt to reveal an exoskeleton of shining anodized metal. He appeared to be a Golem class robot, the heavy robots built for combat or construction. The inner shell was covered with small hydraulic systems that looked like they gave him extra power over the standard Enforcer's build. Nothing of the build looked cheap.

Martinez produced a scanner from one of his pockets and began to press some buttons. He looked over the results with a confused look on his face. "I'm not able to get a reading on anything but the communications frequency. Armor alloy and all subsystems are concealed. Something is either encrypting the specs or this alloy shields against signals," Martinez called to the others. "Can you please volunteer information about yourself or deactivate the shielding, sir?" Martinez asked the robot.

"I could tell you about myself, but then I'd have to kill you," my father responded with a neutral tone.

Martinez took a measured step back, a look of fear covering his face. There was a murmur throughout the semi-circle of guards as they shifted their weapons nervously in their hands.

"Perhaps this isn't the best situation in which to joke. You may scan again, engineer," my father added with a suppressed laugh.

Martinez approached with caution and scanned him again. "Something called Hephaestus Alloy for the armoring, and components more powerful than I've ever seen," Martinez called.

"I say we scrap it and get the technology for ourselves," Alex said quickly.

"This is a matter of the entire council, Alex. And we still don't know what this robot knows. It could prove a useful asset if left intact," Edgar said as he kept his tone level despite obvious frustration.

"It already threatened us once, I won't have the lives of my constituents endangered needlessly!" Alex said as he drew the energy weapon from his holster. Martinez barely had the chance to step back before Alex shot a burst of energy directly at the head of my father with pinpoint accuracy. The metal glowed as green sparks sprayed from the point of impact. The robot held his ground as the blast dissipated, his hulking form unwavering.

"I would say that it's good to see you as well, Alex, but it's simply not. You always hated me in life, and that anger persists through my death," my father said.

Alex had a stunned look on his face as he started in disbelief.

"Holster your weapon, Councilor!" Edgar shouted. Too shocked at the fact that the head of the robot hadn't been blown off to argue, Alex holstered his weapon and unclipped the belt which held it on. He reached out and handed it to Edgar, suddenly accountable for his brash actions. Edgar snatched the gun from Alex's hands.

"Control yourself, or I will have no choice but to have you removed from the area," Edgar bellowed. "This is now a matter of the council. Your actions are noted, Justicar, and you will not be included in the vote on this decision," Edgar said as he then turned toward my father. "Robot, you will be held in custody until we have reached a verdict, please cooperate fully until we have decided what to do with you. And Initiate Ashton, you will also be detained until this is resolved. We need to decide how to proceed with both your actions and determine what sort of trouble you're in with the Government."

Martinez secured several restraining coils of thick wire around my father, and I was led away by two guards to a small room which held a simple bed, a sink, and a toilet. The metal door was locked behind me, and I paced the small perimeter, unsure of exactly what had gone down. I felt anger at how ridiculous Alex had been and worried about my fate and the fate of my robotic father. Most of all, though, I thought about Mary and the very real possibility of never seeing her again in my life. How was my life regressing so quickly? This wasn't anything like what I had expected when I joined the Guild. I thought with grave realism that the trouble I was bringing would likely exceed my worth as an asset. What would happen if I were to be exiled with the inability to return to the surface? Again, the thought that this wasn't something that one could walk away from returned. I breathed deeply and forced myself to clear my rapid and increasingly frantic thoughts.

I sat on the bed and did my best to remain calm for a couple of hours when I heard the bolt on the door unlatch. Caeldra walked in and gave me a weak smile. "Hey, Jake."

"Hi," I responded.

Caeldra motioned for me to scoot over on the bed and took a seat next to me. "It's not great. We're still not sure why the Enforcers are after you, and the Council has been bickering over what to do with the, uhhh, your robotic companion," she said, choosing the words with care.

"How long am I going to be held here?" I asked.

"That I'm not sure about, but I talked to a friend, and she is going to bring you a hot meal. Oh, and I brought you this. I find it's great to kill time. I can't legally give you live steel right now, not that you should be using it anyway," she said as she opened her palm and revealed my balisong knife equipped with the training blade.

I felt myself smile despite the grave situation. "Thanks, Caeldra," I said with genuine gratitude.

"Anyway, *when* you get out of here, we've got to hit your training hard. If the Government is after you, we need you to be better prepared as both a Runner and an Unbound," she said, accenting the 'when' as if it were certain. "I've spoken with Master Aarlen off the record, and he agreed to help you progress your training even as an Initiate."

"I appreciate it. I didn't really have any other option than to accept the robot's help. The Enforcers would have taken me otherwise," I said, meeting her eyes.

"I know that. I know better than anyone that unrequested help is a great blessing," she said as she lifted her shirt to reveal her bandaged abdomen. "You know that as well now," she said.

I nodded. "Look, Caeldra. I'm sorry for everything. I know it can't look good to have your apprentice bringing in all of this trouble."

"As far as I'm concerned, you haven't done anything wrong. The Council will do what the Council does, but the main issue is of that with the robot and finding out if you are in danger from the Government. We've already got people on the surface working on getting that information. In the meantime, we're are also trying to find the location of Mindshift so the Council can also decide what to do with it, but the robot has so far declined to reveal the location voluntarily. He says it's your decision to make and while I agree to some extent, I do believe it is a Guild decision, and one that you should be involved with making."

"Alex isn't going to like that," I said.

Caeldra laughed, "No. No, he really isn't, but it isn't his decision to make. He gave up his say in this matter when he decided to try to blast a hole in the robot's head," she said with a smile.

I smiled back, "I guess that's for the best. Whatever happened in the past between him and my father has carried over into his dislike of me, I suppose. I just hope that I'll help make the right decision for this. What's left of my father doesn't seem all there... He thinks he's human and has been struggling with short term memory. Sure robots run out of memory eventually, but not that fast. I don't think the technology is entirely without its flaws, and I'm scared of what it could make the Guild become."

"The robot has yet to disclose any information on the technology, but storing people's memories and mind for future use of the Guild could be useful," she said as she considered the fact.

"It's not just that; he said that minds can be transferred to another living being. He didn't go into all the details, but it has some problems, and he doesn't think anyone should be able to use Mindshift regardless of the reason."

"Well, that's information I'll need to share with the Guild. As soon as we sort this mess out, we should be able to make some sense of things and hopefully, make the right decision. I've got to get back to Master Aarlen, I don't have long to visit I'm afraid," she said as she started to stand up. "Hang in there, Jake," she said as she gave me a light hug.

"I will," I replied with a half-hearted smile.

She left me, and I was once again alone. At least I had my balisong knife to pass the time. I flipped it mindlessly for another hour or so as I thought about everything that had happened that day and tried to keep myself from worrying about my fate and what I would do if I were to be exiled for my actions.

Some time later the door latch unlocked and a young woman stepped into the room, carrying a red plastic tray of food. A savory aroma filled with rich spices flooded the small room. "Hi. I brought you something to eat," she said.

"Thank you," I responded.

"I'm not supposed to say this, but you probably won't be in here much longer. The Council adjourned about half an hour ago."

"Do you know anything about their decision about me or the robot?" I asked eagerly.

"I'm afraid not, and even if I did, I wouldn't be able to tell you. I'm not one to get involved in Council affairs," she responded.

"Okay, well thanks for the meal," I said as I took the tray from her. She nodded and left the room. The plate held a small basket lined with thick butcher's paper and filled with grilled chicken and what looked to be some sort of vegetable.

I enjoyed the meal and set the basket aside as I awaited news of anything from the outside. After an unknown period of time passed, the door latched open again and Edgar leaned in.

"Justicar Ashton, we await you in session."

22
JUSTICAR

"What?" I repeated.

"Do to the nature of the events that have occurred and the fact that your father insists that this is your decision, we have no choice but to bring you onto the Council to resolve this issue. You'll be the first appointed Council member—and the youngest ever."

"Why can't I just help make this one decision?" I asked with disbelief.

"Well, it is considered a Council-level decision and only Councilors actually have the ability to influence such decisions. And since we lack information and the means to obtain it, you're now a Justicar."

"What about Alex, did he not try to stop this?" I asked, still stunned.

"He wasn't allowed to weigh in on the decision after his tantrum earlier," Edgar said with a sly smile. "Regardless, this is a huge decision, and I encourage you to take your duties to the Guild with a high sense of responsibility. This decision will influence the fate of the Guild and the course of our lives forever," he added solemnly. "Now, we don't have much time to acquaint you with both procedural expectations or proper Council etiquette, but a brief explanation on the way to the session will have to suffice."

On the way to the Council Hall, Edgar explained the basics of what I'd be doing, when I'd be able to speak, and the procedure of how to cast my vote when it was time. He also explained that I was to remain calm and civil no matter what was occurring and always treat other Council members with respect. As we approached the Council hall, I passed Caeldra, who gave me a confused look. I gave her a weak smile.

The doors of the chamber shut, and I was ushered to a seat next to Edgar as the other Council members, including Alex, were seated. Justicar Chloe commenced the opening remarks of the session, "we are once again starting session this day to discuss and conclude the matter of Justicar Ashton's robot. Also, we will address the issue of Justicar Ashton's situation and legal standing on the surface with the Government. If there are no objections to the agenda, we will begin session and proceed to opening comments. It is to be noted that Justicar Price will have no say in this meeting due to inappropriate actions," she recited.

I looked around the room, and everyone remained silent. After a few moments, Chloe continued. "With no objections, I pass priority to Justicar Escobar."

Tomas Escobar continued from where Chloe left off. "Now, we have the issue of Mindshift to cover first. The technology, according to the robot, allows the transference of one being to another or to a specialized robot. We have no way to verify this without first obtaining the technology, but we do know that the robot in question is more advanced than any we have ever seen and is made of a metal that has yet to be damaged by any means attempted by us, including a direct blast from an energy weapon discharged by Justicar Price."

Alex sulked at the mention of his actions and sunk back into his chair. Despite the circumstances, I saw Clark suppress a smile—he was apparently amused in seeing Alex not get his way.

"We must now consider the potential risk and reward of trying to acquire Mindshift or simply attempting to acquire the robot as an asset for our guild and disregarding Mindshift altogether by having it destroyed remotely by the robot. The issue, however, with allowing the technology to be remotely detonated would be the unjamming of communications from the robot and the potential for revealing our location through a digital transmission." Tomas took a brief pause before continuing. "The robot identifying itself as the late Wesley Ashton, father of Justicar Jacob Ashton, initially told us that it was his son's decision to make, but agreed that it could become a Guild decision should Jacob Ashton become a Justicar on this Council. With the weight of this ruling being what it is, the Council agreed that Jacob

Ashton should indeed be appointed as Justicar for one term pending renewal at that time. At this time, I move to have Justicar Ashton explain what he knows about the technology to the rest of the council to provide more information for decision making."

Chloe called for a vote, and it passed. I was urged to speak, so I explained everything that my father had told me as well as his strange behavior since I had met him and the apparent flaws in the technology as it existed. I explained my fears of the technology creating something like the Prolific for the Guild and corrupting the core beliefs of the organization.

Alex scoffed at this, "Justicar Ashton, do you really believe you would know what's best for the Champions as a mere Initiate just hours ago?"

"I don't pretend to know everything, but if the technology was something the Government wanted, then I don't believe it's a line we need to cross," I responded.

"You wouldn't even consider the application of preserving lives in our archive to better our own assets and secure the truth of humanity's history?" Alex asked.

"That is something that could be considered, but I don't believe in using the technology to transfer minds to other humans. Based on my experience, my father was fine the last two weeks of his life, but the code of the robot appears to be deteriorating at a rapid rate. The scariest thing about that deterioration or bad code is the fact that my father thinks that he is still human and attempts to do human things. For instance, he believes that he is sick right now and has a bad cough."

"Justicars Ashton and Price, your comments have been noted," Justicar Chloe Schaff said.

"What about the potential to get both the technology and secure the robot as an asset for the Guild?" Justicar Rachel Hensley added.

"That's something we will consider when we bring in the robot for questioning further along in the session," Justicar Schaff said.

The council meeting proceeded to last for another hour or so until my father was brought in. Before he was brought in, more questions were asked and debated, and a consensus of the eligible council members was hard to infer from the questions and answers given. Alex Price was obviously in a foul mood, but he kept quiet for most of the session.

Two men in Guild camouflage brought in my father and ushered him to a seat. They stood by him holding high-caliber HexTox rifles as they were accustomed to, despite the fact that firing the weapons at the robot would likely result in more harm to them than anyone or anything else. The restraining cables around my father seemed more like a makeshift attempt at keeping up with precedence that those being detained in questioning should be restrained, though I doubted there had been few if any robots ever questioned in a Council session.

My robotic father was sitting in the same chair I had sat in the first time I visited the Council hall. It seemed so strange that I was a mere candidate for Guild recruitment some short while ago and now I was a Justicar. Not only that, but I was also the youngest ever, and the first Initiate to ever become such a high-ranking official of the Guild in such a short amount of time.

"Mr. Ashton, we would like to know what purposes you believe the Mindshift technology could serve the Guild if we choose not to use it to transfer minds to other living hosts," Justicar Schaff said.

"Unfortunately, Ms. Schaff, the only application of such tech is violating the laws of nature and I do believe the Champion's code of justice would be breached should you acquire it, but again, it is now your decision to make," my father responded.

"Mr. Ashton, would you be willing to aid us in the development of our own Hephaestus Alloy and technology based on that of your computer components?"

"If my son wants it, yes, but it could spell my second death. I'm not sure my code or life force would survive deactivation for any amount of time. Being offline would likely cause a detrimental breakdown of nuclear decay."

The other council members murmured amongst themselves.

"Even now, I am only here because I care about my son. He is the only reason I put up with the presence of you, Mr. Price. You refused to help me in during my time of need, and because of it, my wife and I lost our lives. I persist through this skeleton, nothing more than a robotic husk of what my life once was," the robot said, his voice taking on a dark edge, a crazed edge. Something shifted in the demeanor of the robot, and I felt my stomach lurch.

"In fact, Mr. Price, it takes a great deal of will even now to not kill you on the spot, to allow myself to be restrained by this petty metal wiring and your false sense of security and self-righteousness," my father growled, his voice rising. My heart started to race faster as I noticed the other Justicars growing tense.

The robot stood up suddenly in a quick motion, and the two armed guards shifted their weapons and moved their fingers to the trigger.

"Mr. Ashton, please be seated!" Justicar Schaff yelled.

There was a low metallic groan as I saw the cables wrapped around my father's chest start to stretch. The bolts at the end began to bend at unnatural angles and then suddenly snapped as if they were no more than rubber cords.

"Mr. Ashton, be seated at once or we will be forced to destroy you!" Justicar Schaff yelled, her voice wavering.

The guards tried to fire, but it was too late.

Something was very wrong. In an instant, the robot whirled around and snatched one of the rifles, breaking the sling around the guard's shoulder in a single swift motion. Effortlessly, he fired two deadly rounds at the heads of the guards, and they dropped to the ground. A horrible smell of smoldering flesh and sweet ozone filled the air. There was a moment of silence in which everything seemed to freeze in place followed by absolute chaos. The robot turned toward the Council and began firing into the massive desk. All the Justicars including myself dropped to the floor as the HexTox energy blasts blew deadly slivers of wood through the air above us.

"How the tables have turned," the robot yelled over the crackle of rifle fire.

I was aware of screaming as I looked over at Alex holding his hand to his side. Dark blood welled between his fingers as he gritted his teeth and drew his sidearm with his other hand. Sweat was beginning to bead on his forehead in thick droplets. The noise in the room was deafening as the robot mercilessly blasted away at the desk. Thankfully, the front of the desk was covered in the same thick wood as the top, and it had so far stopped the force of the blasts from the heavy rifle. The crisp and unfamiliar smell of burning wood began to fill the room as the robot continued to shoot. I was aware, as the others must have been, that there was no logical reason why the robot didn't walk around and kill us. It wasn't in any apparent danger from our weapons, and none of the other Justicars other than Alex and Edgar were armed. Coming directly from detention myself, I was also unarmed—other than my knife which had a blunted edge, not that it would be of any use against the armoring of the robot.

I peered around the corner of the desk and saw that the other guard's rifle was still attached to the body and that it was a few feet away from the robot. I didn't have long before a blast came much too close to my face and splintered wood shards into my cheek. I felt a few warm trickles of blood and whipped my head back behind cover as the bright purple blast seared my vision, temporarily blinding me.

Sometime between when the robot had taken the rifle and when it had been firing, it had taken the excess ammo from the dead guard and had effortlessly reloaded the gas magazine. Dark billows of smoke began to rise from the scorched wood desk frame, filling the room with a thick haze. Light from the room danced through the shifting smoke clouds that were accumulating at the ceiling. I turned toward the others and was terrified to see Alex pointing his gun right at me. My heart seemed to freeze, but a surge of relief flowed through my body as he turned the weapon and tossed it to me with a painful wince. I caught the gun and checked to make sure the safety was off. I no longer considered this robot my father, and if it was, then it needed to be destroyed. This wasn't the man that had cared so deeply for me, it was a broken mirror of the great man I once knew.

Edgar signaled for me to fire at the robot, so I peered around the corner and fired a violet burst of energy which caused bright green sparks to spew from the robot's chest, but it looked unscathed. The robot turned toward me and began to fire again, blowing away chunks of wood from the large desk. While it was distracted, Edgar stood from cover and fired a single well-aimed shot directly at the grip of the energy rifle the robot was holding. There was a small hiss, a sharp crack, then a blinding explosion of purple vapor as the gas cartridge exploded. The force of the blast sent the robot flying into the wall, which crumbled under the force of impact. The robot was lodged in the wall at a strange angle and was struggling to free itself. Edgar and I raised our weapons and began to fire with sustained shots. Sparks continued to fly, and thick arcs of green electricity began to surge across the exterior of the robot's alloy armor. Suddenly, the alloy started to char in places and the sparks stopped. The metal began to tear in small layers from the surface, and the robot struggled to raise its broken weapon at us. Edgar aimed his shots at the shooting arm, and the robot's rifle dropped to the ground from the force. Edgar stopped firing and raised a hand to signal for me to stop. Rachel and Chloe were attempting to help Alex stop the bleeding while Edgar and I approached the disabled robot. Anger surged through my body as I approached the robot that had claimed to be my father.

It laughed as I approached. "Your father is dead," it spat at me.

Just as we closed in, guards swarmed in from outside the Council hall and began to circle around the damaged robot. Medical personnel entered the room minutes later and began to tend to Alex after confirming the deaths of the two guards that had been in the room.

Though it seemed no one wanted to discuss the idea, it appeared that the robot had wanted to keep the Justicars alive. Even the shot to Alex appeared to have only been a maiming shot rather than a shot meant to kill. The brutal headshots of the two guards were a testament to the lethality and accuracy of this robot. Yet, why did the robot bother saving me in the first place if it was a pawn of the Government?

Questions flooded my mind as a medic began to examine me and bandage the cuts on my face that were much deeper than I had expected. The robot was carried to a holding cell where Martinez was able to analyze it through the safety of steel walls. Edgar and I had managed to destroy whatever shielding protected it from our sustained HexTox fire—something no ordinary robot could withstand.

An hour or so later after answering hundreds of questions, I was sitting at a table at the pub drinking beer and trying to think about how I had fallen for everything that the robot had said, and how it had managed to trick me into thinking it was my father. I still hadn't had the opportunity to talk to Edgar about why he had thought the same thing, or about why the Government was after me. The entire Guild was in a frenzy trying to sort out the events of the day.

The technology of the robot far exceeded that of anything anyone in the Guild had ever seen, and it seemed impossible to think that the robot was anything other than my father. It had known about the Guild. If it was the Government's robot, then that would mean that they knew the Guild's location and the identity of many of the Guild members themselves. It was much more comforting to think that the robot was what was left of my father and that it had merely lost its mind and gone crazy. Its attack, other than the killing of the guards, seemed wild and uncoordinated—as if it were simply going berserk. If the Government did control the robot, that would mean that they knew I was in the Guild, that they had orchestrated the Enforcers on the streets of the Slums to chase me to my father intentionally...

Caeldra sat down at the table across from me, pulling me out of my thoughts. "Hey, Jake," she said softly.

"Hi."

"I know you're not alright, so I'm not going to ask. This isn't your fault, you need to know that," Caeldra said as she placed a hand on my arm.

I took a big sip of the beer and placed the mug down with a dull clunk against the laminated table. "I'm still not entirely sure what happened. I need to talk with Edgar, but the Council is meeting. I'm on temporary suspension pending investigation," I said with a flat, emotionless tone. "Imagine that, the youngest Justicar ever is suspended on his first day of the job due to the deaths of two Guild members and the severe injury of another Justicar from either a deranged remnant of my father or a Government infiltrator."

"It's not your fault," she repeated. "You had no way of knowing this would happen, nor did anyone else assume that the robot would be able to break those restraints. Look, they're sending out other Runners to retrieve Mindshift and any other findings that can be found in the dwelling, Martinez managed to crack the encryption on the bot's memories, but the core code is locked with something more secure."

"Did they ever consider that it wanted us to know the location? It seems to have been playing us this whole time."

She frowned at this. "That's a good point."

"If I could have remembered the exact location and how to get there, I would have volunteered the information. It took about an hour to get here from that bunker, and we took so many turns."

"There's no way that anyone could be expected to remember such a long unmapped route," Caeldra replied as she waved to Jeff to ask for water.

A few seconds later Jeff brought over a large glass of ice water with a large wedge of lemon floating between the cubes. Jeff looked like he wanted to say something, but hesitated after looking at me for a moment. He gave us both a faint nod before turning away and returning behind the counter of the bar.

"I'm just surprised that I'm not being detained. This can't look good for me."

"I think everyone is a bit shocked. They've got bigger things to worry about than an unarmed Guild member. Besides, you're on house arrest right now," she said.

"House arrest?" I asked.

"Well, technically we all are. No one is allowed to leave the Guild Hall except the Runner crew tasked with getting to the robot's bunker until all of this is sorted out. Security is on high alert."

We turned to see Edgar approaching the table with a grim look on his face.

"Jake, Caeldra, come with me."

23
TRUTH

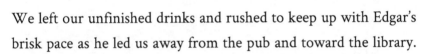

We left our unfinished drinks and rushed to keep up with Edgar's brisk pace as he led us away from the pub and toward the library. He ushered us into one of the private study rooms and closed the door behind him.

"Things aren't looking good. We don't know anything else about the robot yet, or anything about why the Government is after you. And, well... we lost contact with the Runner team that was heading toward the robot's bunker. With the lockdown and security review, it will be awhile until more Runners are authorized to go after the missing team. Unfortunately, if we want any chance of finding that team alive, we need to move now. You two are the only ones I know that I can trust to do this off-the-books. If you or I get caught, I will take the fall. Until then, I want you both to do your best to find the missing team, but don't risk your lives doing so."

Caeldra nodded grimly. "And I'm assuming we are to leave now?"

"Yes, I've already grabbed your gear," he said as he pointed to our packs in the corner of the room. "It would have looked suspicious if you were to have geared up in the locker room. A Justicar grabbing some equipment, well, that doesn't cause anyone to raise an eyebrow, especially with the current situation." He paused, considering his next words, "you won't have communications or Artemis to guide you, I'm afraid. Utilizing the system would reveal your position, and you'd be busted. Actually, if you do manage to rescue the other Runners, you'd have to sneak back in, and they'd have to take your side and promise not to tell that you saved them," he said with a frown.

"Simple enough, but how are we supposed to find the bunker?" Caeldra asked.

"I've got an old positioning system you can use. It operates offline, and I marked the position of the bunker. It won't give you a direct route, but it will tell you which way to go and the difference in altitude from your current location. I'm afraid you'll have to get creative with your actual route."

"Caeldra, grab those packs and give us the room please."

"Yes sir," she replied, but her expression revealed her surprise at being kicked out. She gave a respectful nod and exited the small study room, waiting outside the door.

"Look, I had every reason to believe that robot was your father, and it very well might have been. If it wasn't ever a clone of your father's memories and mind, then we've got a whole other issue on our hands. I'm chalking it up to design flaws in Mindshift for now and will push that stance to the other Council members to the best of my ability—as it is in everyone's best interest. Nearly indestructible robots controlled by the Government would be a dangerous thing."

"If it belongs to the Government, then they know where the Guild Hall is located," I said.

"That's very true, but if the Government knew where we were, I assume that we'd all be dead by now. Though it would be difficult to deploy and control Enforcers down here, and I have yet to see a human Government soldier in all of my years," he said.

"You're probably right," I said as I considered the idea for the first time.

"We've got a couple of people in the Mids, but we have no idea what's in the Upper Level—if there's even an Upper Level. Our leader or leaders are faceless, and no one would even know that they exist if it wasn't for the rumors, legends, and enforced laws. As far as we know, the entire society of New York is held together by computers that were abandoned or people that have lost interest in anything that concerns the rest of the city. After all these years, we still don't know. You need to be very careful regardless. Any more of those robots like the one you brought to us would mean trouble. Martinez is still trying to analyze the shielding system and maybe develop the tech for us or build weapons that can pierce it. Our HexTox weapons barely pinged it without heavy sustained fire. Anyway, be careful, and I just want you to know that your real father would have been very proud of you. I don't care if you tell Caeldra what I told you, I just wanted to give you the option of privacy, Justicar Ashton. We can discuss the extent of my knowledge on your father's work later. We've got a lot to talk about, and I don't want you to think I'm being shady for refraining to educate the Council on some matters at this time. I hate politics, but it is very necessary right now until we figure out exactly what is going on," he said with a frown.

"I understand. Will I still be a Justicar after all this ends?" I asked.

"Most likely, yes. At least for a term. The rest of the Council will have to vote on the length of your suspension, but I doubt it will be that long, especially given the circumstances of your actions. And with this mission I'm sending you on, I will take the heat if things go wrong, so you don't need to worry about that," he said with the best smile he could muster. "We lost two good men today, and I'm hoping we can prevent the loss of two more. Find James and Carlson, and bring them back to us," he said as he patted me on the shoulder. Taking a pair of cutters, he motioned for me to give him my arm. He cut the wrist cast off, and my arm tingled as air flowed over the previously covered skin.

"I gave you a conservative estimate on when this could come off, it looks to be completely healed. Oh, and watch out for Caeldra, she's still recovering from her injury."

My wrist felt strange after being in the cast for weeks, but it was a good feeling. I nodded to Edgar and exited the door where Caeldra waited for me, my backpack ready beside her. I was surprised to see a C-15 Heavy Repeater on each of our backpacks as well as our CZR-7s.

"Edgar thinks they will fare better than a C-19 due to the rate of fire if we run into any more of those advanced bots," she said, giving me a broad smile when she saw that my cast had been removed. Edgar gave us a nod as he left the library and then Caeldra guided me to the back of the library and to an abandoned hallway. We continued toward a large metal door that was secured with a reinforced latch.

"This is a maintenance shaft, but we'll need to be sure not to be seen by any workers that happen to be working down there. I don't think there will be any, but just in case, be quiet and follow my lead," she said to me as she unbolted the door and opened it.

There was a sharp creak as the hinges protested the movement. The air was cold and damp, and a large elevator sat at the top of the shaft. Right before I walked onto the elevator, Caeldra motioned toward the side wall, where a long ladder shot down into the relative darkness of the pit below. We descended the ladder down a small vertical tunnel that was lined with small light bulbs every twenty feet or so. The concrete walling was slick with moisture, but the rungs of the ladder were coated with an anti-slip surface. We traveled a few hundred feet before finally reaching the bottom.

We were standing in a vast cavern which contained various light sources strewn across the floor and walls with long rubber cables connecting them to various power modules. Construction equipment lay across the ground and a large makeshift office had been set up, probably for the foreman of the project.

"What is this supposed to be?" I asked as I continued to take in the sight.

"It's going to be another storage area when it's finished. They've been working on this for a few years, and we'll be using the trash pit to make our way through to the rest of the Undercity, which hasn't been done before."

The name 'trash pit' didn't convey a sense of structure or safety, let alone an ideal route of travel. "What do you mean trash pit?" I asked, hoping she would give some explanation that defied conventional logic.

"Exactly what I said. A giant pit. Filled with trash. It used to be a ventilation shaft that the original Builders made, but now it houses all the rubble and excess concrete from this project."

We walked over to a huge hole in the ground marked off with plastic barricades dotted with flashing yellow lights. Warning messages were printed on the front of them in large red text. Sturdy metal poles extended from around the edges and had large loops of steel that were built as safety anchors.

'DANGER: TETHER MUST BE SECURED BEFORE CROSSING BARRICADE' one of the signs next to the pole read. As we approached the pit, I could see how truly massive it was, and my main concern was that I couldn't tell exactly how deep it went. There were a few lights down for the first fifty feet or so, then an immeasurable depth of darkness. "We're going down this?" I asked, disbelief creeping into my voice.

"Of course," she said as she attached her cabling to one of the tether poles. "Until we find a usable tunnel, that is," she replied with her trademark grin.

I shook my head before fastening my own cable to another one of the tethers. Despite the strength of the cable and the tether, I didn't like descending without Artemis or the auto-grappling hooks that would save my life if I made a mistake, or something broke.

"I know it's not as comfortable as going out with Artemis, but we have to make do with what we've got," Caeldra said, evidently seeing the worry on my face.

I nodded as we positioned ourselves on the edge of the pit with our cables tight. After a moment to get situated in our harnesses, we began the slow descent into the darkness below.

We moved down slowly, the sides of the pit slick with a mud-like substance of moisture blended with powdered concrete, dust, and dirt. Our LED lights from our shoulders cast long beams of white light down which were consumed by the darkness of the pit below. As we descended, the walls changed from slick to slimy and bracing my feet against the wall became increasingly difficult. After scraping up large mounds of dark green algae, I decided to take my feet off the wall and descend the pit in a sitting position, trusting that the harness and cable would hold me.

"Keep an eye out for any tunnels we can use, we don't have that much more cabling left," Caeldra said.

"Are you sure there are even any tunnels down here?" I asked.

"Nope, but I've never been down a ventilation shaft without them. These used to bring fresh air to all the Undercity before it was sealed off from the surface."

The air began to sour, so we put on our respirators, and I continued to shine my light along the dark green walls. I turned and saw an opening, or what could have been considered, at one point in its existence, a tunnel. The inside of it was coated with the dark algae, and it glistened against the light of my flashlight.

Strange fungus-like masses grew on the corroded pipes and jutted out from the inside in sections where the metal had given into the erosive force of nature. It looked like something that belonged in a science lab.

"Uh, Caeldra? Any chance we can find another tunnel?" I asked with only the faintest sliver of hope.

"You found our way in! Nice job, Jake," she replied, answering my question.

Getting inside the entrance of the tunnel was easy, but standing still in the deep slime-like algae coating the floor was near impossible. To avoid a tragic fall to our deaths, we attached another line to a pipe that Caeldra declared "safe enough."

"It should hold just in case, but don't fall," she said as she disconnected her line and braced herself before inching forward. After moving further down the tunnel, she attached another cable to a sturdier pipe then passed me another cable to connect to my harness which was attached to hers. "You're clumsier than me," she said with a wink as I disconnected my rappelling cable and entered the foul tunnel.

After reaching a point where it was safe to walk without the cables, we began to travel through the increasingly disgusting tunnel. I was glad for the respirator which filtered out the stagnant and pungent smell which must have proliferated through the tight tunnel. Whatever electronics had once existed were destroyed by the powerful forces of moisture and time. The algae made it very hard to move at a pace faster than a crawl. I braced my hands on Caeldra's firm shoulders as I followed behind her to avoid falling. I had to admit, her balance was much better than mine, and I wasn't too proud to give her that victory. We proceeded for another thirty feet or so until we reached a slight incline, which had less algae than the section of tunnel that we had already traveled through. Fortunately, I was then able to walk on my own without having to hold onto Caeldra to prevent an embarrassing fall that.

We continued onward until the Algae all but faded away. Caeldra kept checking the old positioning system that Edgar had given us and we continued forward.

"We're getting closer to the bunker," she called from in front of me.

We passed a low hanging series of steel pipes and proceeded to a familiar-looking section of the tunnel. Caeldra raised her hand and pulled down her C-15 from her backpack with slow and deliberate motion. I did the same as we rounded one final corner and turned off our flashlights, my eyes taking a moment to adjust to the dimness of the yellow lighting of the tunnel. A distant shadow of a figure was standing right outside the door of the bunker. My Artemis overlay outlined the figure in green, but it couldn't read any vitals. Caeldra raised her weapon, and I did the same as I shifted to her side and matched her pacing. The figure stood still, and the light in that section of the tunnel had been broken. Small fragments of broken glass littered the floor, but there was no way to tell if the light had been broken recently.

"Be ready for anything, I don't like that we can't read Carlson's vitals," Caeldra whispered, the unease in her voice causing my heart to speed up. In fact, anytime her Runner's intuition—as she called it—would flare up, I would become very uneasy. If a situation could break through her focused and confident demeanor, it was serious.

Caeldra reached up to her shoulder and flicked on the bright LED light. The man was facing away from us and was wearing guild leather. Something was wrong, though—there was a thin line of blood streaming down the back of the jacket that glistened in the bright white light. The blood was falling off the bottom of the jacket in an irregular rhythm, splashing against the floor with an audible drip. A pool of blood had formed at his feet, congealing on the edges.

"Carlson!" Caeldra croaked, the sound barely audible. *Drip drip.* I could see her weapon shaking in her hands. *Drip drip drip.* The figure remained still and unwavering. Blood continued to stream down from an unseen wound. *Drip.* I forced myself forward alongside with Caeldra and suppressed a shiver as I felt like something was right behind me, watching us. As quiet as I could, I spun around and raised my weapon, ready to fire. There was nothing behind us, but the uneasy feeling of watching eyes persisted.

We were nearly on Carlson now, and we were both doing the best we could to suppress the panic that was attempting to creep into our minds. I created a quick layering of my mind and buried my fear behind a thin veil of mental willpower. I felt myself relax slightly and took point, feeling more confident in my abilities to act with certainty. *Drip drip.* We were only ten feet away. *Drip drip drip.* Five feet. *Drip.* Bracing the C-15 against the inside of my arm and chest, I reached forward and grabbed the shoulder of Carlson. The body went limp and collapsed to the floor. In the moments that followed, I saw a flash of silver as a wire snapped from the ceiling and felt a firm shove. I flew through the air and a wave of intense heat passed over my body. There was a high-pitched ring as I looked down and saw blood welling from my left leg, soaking through my pants.

"Caeldra!" I yelled, unable to hear my own voice. Fragments of concrete and wire were burning in front of me, and smoke started to seep into my mask through a crack on the glass frame. The goggles fogged up, and I lost vision. Panicking, I tore the mask off and held my breath as I punched out the goggle lenses. Acting on pure adrenaline, I tore at my undershirt and created a sliver of cloth that was a foot long and a few inches thick. I reached into my backpack and pulled out a bottle of water. With shaking hands, I ripped the cap off and doused the section of cloth. After soaking the strip of cloth in water, I stuffed it into the respirator to attempt to filter out at least most of the water-soluble toxins from the air. I replaced the mask on my face as fast as possible.

"Caeldra!" I cried again, not seeing her through the thick smoke that had accumulated in the tunnel. I started to feel a sharp pain leech into my leg and remembered that I hadn't bandaged my wound. I tore my shirt off and tied it around my leg as tightly as I could, gritting my teeth against the pain and intense pulsing that surged through my leg.

I did my best to stand and picked up my weapon which had been flung with me in the blast. I saw Caeldra lying on the floor several feet away from me. She had been behind me when the explosion went off—perhaps I had taken the worst of it. I limped over to her and flipped her on her back, she raised her weapon at me and almost fired before realizing it was me. She was panting and shifting backward with her legs, trying to push herself up.

"Jake, are you hurt?" she asked, gaining her composure.

"Yes, my leg," I said as I shifted it forward.

"They'll pay for this; for Carlson, for your leg. Cover me," she seethed as she pulled a first aid kit from her backpack. I turned my upper body with my weapon raised to guard us as she worked to patch my leg. After removing my makeshift bandage, she injected my leg with a strong painkiller which made my entire lower body go numb. The pain flowed out, and I sighed with a breath of relief as she pressed a large square piece of cloth against the wound. The fabric adhered to my leg and stopped the bleeding almost instantly.

"You're still going to need surgery, but it will do for now." Caeldra flicked on her headset.

"This is Caeldra Thompson, Carlson is dead, James is still missing, and Jake is injured. Requesting backup. It was a trap!" Caeldra said quickly.

I turned on my headset and caught the end of a sentence, "—and that's an order!" a voice called.

"Jake looks like we're not getting backup, we need to get the hell out of here."

"No," I tried to say, but my voice was barely more than a whisper. The bunker was only thirty feet away, and I began to hobble forward through the chunks of burning debris and gristle from the explosion of the body. Caeldra grabbed my arm, and I flung her hand off.

"I need to do this," I said with more volume than before. "We can't leave it here."

Something in my tone must have shifted, and she gave me a simple nod, her face solemn and understanding. She took point and moved forward as I struggled to keep up. The inside of the bunker was already burning, but I recognized the desk where the heavy-looking black case sat—the case which either likely contained a hell of a lot of explosives or Mindshift. Either way, it was our best bet.

"That box," I said pointing to the black case.

It looked to be made of either light metal or a solid plastic polymer. Caeldra lifted it and eyed the weapons lockers. The heavy turret caught her eye, but we had no way of moving it, especially with the threat of an enemy lurking around the corner. Caeldra told me to stand guard while she loaded as many weapons as she could on her backpack and added a few to mine as well, despite my wounded leg. The painkillers were doing a decent job in suppressing the pain and a few extra pounds wouldn't slow me down.

After getting all that we could carry and leaving the room, we hurried back in the direction we had come from. We walked back to back down the hall, keeping a keen eye out for unseen enemies and any signs of danger.

"What about James?" I asked with concern.

Caeldra ignored the question.

"We're back in route and will be coming up the maintenance bay trash pit. Have a crew ready, we're bringing what we believe to be Mindshift. James is still MIA. Please advise," Caeldra said over the comms.

"MIA, that's a poor description of my status," a crackling static voice cooed over comms.

"James! James, please respond. This is Command. What's your status?" another voice said.

"I'm fine," the distorted voice said.

Caeldra stiffened. "That's not James," she said, her voice weak. "We need to get the hell out of here," she cried, panic seeping into her failing voice.

My heart had jumped into my throat, and my fingers tingled with adrenaline. We were now being hunted by something that was on James' frequency. Something that might have access to Artemis.

What was even more concerning was that James' encrypted link to Artemis was bound to biotic sensors and numerous safeguards that would destroy the system if he were to die.

"Caeldra, Jake, you need to turn off your Artemis links right now and get back here. We'll be waiting outside the trash pit. If you keep your links on whatever that is will be able to track you, even in offline mode. We don't know if that's James, and if it's not then we don't know how it has access to the radio frequency. We're working on jamming it," the voice from Command said.

We did as he said, and my sense of comfort and safety depreciated further.

"I know you're hurt, but we need to move as fast as possible," Caeldra said as we started back through the tunnel toward the trash pit.

"It's almost an hour walk back without an injured leg. You need to go without me, I'll make it back," I said, not trying to be a hero, but to keep Caeldra alive and Mindshift safe.

"We have a better chance of survival together, even if you only have one good leg. The bleeding has stopped, and your vitals are stable," she said as she dismissed the comment altogether.

I nodded grimly, and we continued to trudge forward. My blood froze when we heard the same manic laughter echo through the tunnels.

"Oh, I will kill you both. Carlson was quite easy to kill," the voice crooned. Shadows danced on the edges of the tunnel as the lights began to flicker.

I was overcome with a grave sense of peril as the lights grew dimmer and cast wicked shadows on the walls, distorting our ability to see down the tunnel, even with our shoulder lights.

"I'm waiting just around the corner," the voice whispered from nowhere.

"Just keep moving and shoot anything that moves that isn't me," Caeldra said as she continued to grip the C-15 with grim determination. "We'll get out of this together." She jumped around the corner and raised her weapon, preparing to fire. There was nothing there. I scanned over the tunnel behind us, looking for any signs of an enemy, but there was nothing. The numbing sense of fear had stiffened my whole body; it was as if a great weight had been placed on me. I saw something move behind us, just the faintest sign of dancing shadows and felt a shift in the air against my skin. It was subtle, but the temperature was increasing. I was suddenly reminded of the steam vents that covered the streets and sidewalks of the Slums. It felt just like the warning surge the vents gave off before spewing steam. There was a series of sharp popping sounds followed by a dull thud.

"Let's turn up the heat," the voice said. I saw movement in the distance again, and it was getting closer. The large pipe lining the wall to our left was starting to bend in strange shapes, groaning in protest. The fastening bolts of the pipe were blasting off and slamming into the walls.

"We need to run, now!" I yelled as I fought against my injured leg, jumping in great bounds with my good leg. I moved as fast as I could while bracing myself against the wall and leaning on Caeldra. We needed to find a way to escape the time-bomb pipe that would kill us when the metal finally ripped. We turned a corner and saw a barred vent on the ground. Caeldra dropped to her knees and began to pry at the corroded metal bars. She yelled a complex string of obscenities and began to fire the C-15 at the edges of the vent. Brilliant purple flashes and sparks erupted from the metal as it began to tear and glow orange from the sudden burst of energy. With no time to spare, she shoved the butt of the weapon through the holes in the vent and pried it open. Moving with brisk efficiency, she wrapped a cable around the vent lid in several locations and attached it to her rappelling device on her harness. Still cursing, she attached another hook to my harness, and we dropped down the vent, descending at a rapid speed into the unknown depths. Caeldra didn't have access to Artemis at the moment, which meant not only did she not know where we were going, but we also didn't know if there would be a jutting rod of rebar sticking out of the wall which would skewer us on the way down. There was a horrible popping sound above and I felt the air shift. A huge cloud of steam was forcing itself down after us, following our rapid descent. We were encased by bright light from our flashlights and the darkness both above and below us. A weak blast of pressure hit us from above and dissipated as harmless slivers of metal rained down from above, deflecting off the thick leather we wore. This vent was much more narrow than one of the main vents—it was only a few feet across and warm, damp air started pressing up from somewhere in the depths of the Undercity. The weight of the two of us had pulled the barred lid back over the vent, but our cabling was the only thing keeping us safe. If whatever was hunting us found and cut our cable, we would fall into the darkness to a horrible death.

"Shit. We're almost out of cable," Caeldra said. "Look for anything we can fasten another line to," she told me as we slowed down.

The walls were made of smooth concrete and we hadn't seen another tunnel entrance anywhere since we started to lower down the dark hole.

"I don't see anything," I said, trying to scan further below us. "If we turn on Artemis, maybe we can find a way out of—"

She interrupted me, "If we turn on Artemis, that thing is going to know where we are and will cut our lifeline," she responded with grim certainty. "The truth is that we can't do anything but wait or try to climb back up and take our chances with that thing," she said.

"The truth," a voice said from above us, projecting an echoing effect through the vent. "The truth is that you're already dead."

As soon as it had said it, we were falling, the cable that had held us only moments ago was flailing down after us.

24

TOXIN

We hit a moving body of water, and the current instantly pulled us under the surface. I closed my eyes, not wanting to get any potential contaminants in them if the water was bad. My backpack and wounded leg made it a struggle to surface, but when I did, I couldn't see Caeldra or her flashlight in the dark green waters that pulled me along helplessly. My mask began to fill with water as the strip of cloth lining the bridge of my nose soaked through. Coughing and choking, I yanked the mask off and pulled it around the back of my neck, breathing in the questionable air. I saw a flash of light below the surface and realized that must be Caeldra. I reached down to my harness and grabbed the attached line, pulling it up with all of my strength as I struggled to keep myself afloat. I pulled her up and held her in front of me, my arms wrapped under hers. I couldn't tell if she was breathing or not, but I had to assume that her mask was keeping the water out. A moment later, her head moved, and she let out a muffled scream, the force of the impact had made her lose consciousness. She took in her surroundings as we continued to float downstream and turned around to see my mask-less face.

"Jake, your mask!" she tried to yell, but it came out little more than a squeak.

"It flooded," I responded as I continued to look for a way out of this river. For all I knew, this would dump us right in the toxic Atlantic Ocean.

We were in an enormous open tunnel which was roughly twenty feet across. The ceiling was maybe thirty feet high and loomed over us with towering height. There was no hope of being able to reach it or throwing up a cable to attempt to grasp any of the strange-looking loops of either rope or something else entirely. The hanging loops were coated in thick, green algae—or some sort of slime, the same color as the dark water. Lights jutted from the walls in even intervals, but they did a poor job of lighting the tunnel. I guessed that once it was built, it wasn't really intended for human use anymore.

There was a sudden drop as we were thrown over the edge of a hidden waterfall and pushed back under the dark water. This time, we both emerged gasping for air. Without the mask, I had taken some of the water into my nose and mouth as I wasn't prepared for the drop. I did my best to spit it out and clear it from my body. We continued downstream for some time, the flow eventually slowing until we were able to swim in any direction without much resistance. Had it not been for the swimming lessons my father had insisted I take as a child, there would have been no hope of me surviving such an encounter, and we still weren't out of danger just yet either. I had to assume that my body was already poisoned from the water and that I needed immediate medical attention. I desperately hoped that the bandage on my leg was keeping the water out of my bloodstream. The thought of toxic sludge coursing through my veins was terrifying, but it was a very real possibility at this point. I supposed we had been lucky to survive at all, and even more fortunate that there was something to break the fall. As of right now, we were both living and out of immediate danger from that terrible thing hunting us.

Three lights in a fixed pattern shone about fifty feet in the distance. There was a white light, blue light, and purple light, sweeping across the surface of the water. We couldn't tell if whoever or whatever it was had seen us yet, but Caeldra and I both raised our weapons.

"Will these even fire still?" I asked with uncertainty as we continued to float forward in the slow current.

"It's a closed system, you could even shoot it underwater, but I'm not sure how much good that would do," she whispered.

"Ooohhh, shiny!" the voice in front of us cried as something which sparkled in the tri-colored light was lifted by a metal pole. The man looked to be standing on some sort of boat—if it could be called that at all. As we neared it, I saw large orange barrels that were tied to the sides and looked to be keeping it afloat. Various nets and metal hooks hung from the edges of the boat and a strange-looking lamp illuminated the cavern as it hung from an extended rod above the dark waters. Whatever he was doing, it didn't look to be dangerous to us.

"Hey!" Caeldra called out to him.

The man jumped back before peering out and shining the strange flashlight around trying to spot us. He shone the light on us and jumped back further.

"Don't shoot! I'm no threat!" the man cried in an exasperated voice. "What in the blasted heavens are you doing in the river!"

"It wasn't by choice," Caeldra said as she kept the weapon trained on the man.

"You'll find no enemy in me. Come closer, and I'll pull you up," he said as he turned off the flashlight and set it down in the boat.

Cautiously, I kept my weapon trained as he pulled Caeldra onto the ship. A few seconds later, Caeldra kept her gun raised, and I was lifted onto the solid metal platform of the inside of the boat. Caeldra removed her mask.

The man was dressed in an odd fashion. He wore a cloth jacket underneath an orange rubber outer suit, which looked suitable for keeping out toxins or radiation, and a necklace with strange trinkets hanging from the metallic wire. He wasn't particularly tall or short, heavy or thin, but he did look a bit older, perhaps in his fifties. His graying hair was unruly beneath a rubber coated beanie, and he flashed us a strange smile as he saw everything we had in our backpacks.

"I tell you what, the river always provides. I'm not sure where you found all of your treasure, but I'd appreciate it if you give me a map there!" he grinned.

"We don't have any treasure. Look, something was hunting us, and we fell down a drainage vent into the river. Do you know how we can get back into the Undercity tunnels?" Caeldra asked.

"Of course I do! But why would anyone want to travel through tunnels? They're such droll inventions," he said as he trailed off with something little more than a whisper.

"We need to get back to our friends," Caeldra said carefully. "Can you please help us, mister...?" she paused, waiting for him to offer his name.

"Jasper. Jasper Rivers," he said with a gap-toothed smile.

"Well, Mr. Rivers, we'd appreciate the help greatly and might even be able to offer you a reward for your troubles."

His eyes seemed to light up at this, and he rubbed his hands together as if excited to eat a meal. "Certainly, certainly. But I need to finish the day's salvaging, you see. I'm behind schedule I'm afraid," he responded as he grabbed the strange looking flashlight once again. He reached down and lifted something that looked to be some kind of grenade launcher from below a blue trap and Caeldra had her weapon raised in an instant. Jasper's crude-looking weapon or device looked to be cobbled together from many different pieces and contained a large metal flap on the front of the barrel.

"It's no weapon, miss," he said quickly as he began to raise it in a slow, unthreatening way, his hand off the grip and trigger. He pulled down a latch and detached the rectangular ammo box that held small metal spheres. Continuing his slow motion, he pulled out one of the spheres and pressed a button on top. A moment later, the canister split open and thick sprawls of black net began to emerge. "It's a net gun!" he said with a big smile. "Made it myself! The river always provides," he said.

Caeldra lowered her weapon. "How much longer will you be scavenging?" she asked impatiently.

The man lifted his wrist and pulled back the rubber sleeve to reveal some kind of wrist watch which contained only blinking LED lights of various colors. "Oh, two or three," he replied with a smile as he worked to reset the metal net sphere he had opened in his demonstration.

"Two or three what, Mr. Rivers?" Caeldra asked, impatience all too evident now.

"Maybe four if you keep asking!" Jasper shouted as he fumbled and dropped the open sphere.

I put my hand on Caeldra's shoulder to calm her down as soon as I saw her stiffen. The simple fact remained that this man, however strange, had rescued us from a state of disaster and had, at least marginally, improved our chances of survival.

"Mr. Rivers, I fell into the river without a mask on and got some of the water in my nose and mouth. Will I be alright?" I asked

"I don't know why anyone would do that, but the algae filters out the radiation. Marvelous stuff algae is," he said with a grin.

"So I'm in no immediate danger?" I asked.

"I'd say not, my new friend!" he responded with enthusiasm. "Do me a favor and scan the waters," he said as he handed me the strange three-colored flashlight. Jasper made sweeping gestures, and I mimicked the motion.

"Well, you've got to turn it on! You people sure are strange, taking a swim in the river, and now not knowing how to operate a flashlight. A strange people indeed," he said as if reassuring himself of the validity of his statement.

I switched on the light and began to move it over the water. Surprisingly, the light seemed to penetrate the green haze, and I could see the bottom of the river—it was probably ten feet deep. Unsure of what to look for, I combed the surface and searched for anything that wasn't water. A few moments later I saw what looked to be a section of plastic pipe drifting through the water about five feet down.

"Umm, Jasper? There seems to be some kind of pipe here," I said as I motioned for him to come over. He grabbed the long metal pole and peered to where I was pointing.

"Ahhh, good find, sir. Pipe is a welcome sight always. The river provides," he said as he fished out the small tube with the hook rod.

"What is the net launcher for?" I asked.

"For the eels, of course. You think I could catch them with something like this metal rod?" he asked, a smile forming on his face.

I wasn't quite sure how to respond and had no idea what an eel was, so I just kept shining the light around. Caeldra took the opportunity to take inventory of our remaining gear and check the condition of things. It was great to relax on the side of the boat. My bandage seemed to be intact, but the painkillers were fading. Caeldra and I had both stripped down to our undergarments to let our clothes dry. If we would enter any colder regions, we'd need to have clothes that could keep us warm. Not knowing how long we'd be down here, I didn't want to exhaust our supply of medicine unless I absolutely needed it.

We fished out several pieces of scrap and Jasper seemed equally excited for them all, despite their simplicity and low value. As I passed the light along the water again, I saw something long and slender whisk by. Jasper spotted it too and pulled back the round breach slide on the top of the sphere launcher with a loud click. He waved frantically for me to give him the light and he attached it to a small mount on the side of the launcher. Standing on the side of the boat, he scanned the waters with fierce concentration. A thin smile formed on his face, and he pulled the trigger. There was metallic slapping sound as a sphere launched from the crude-looking contraption. It didn't travel at a fast velocity, but the sphere split into the net before it hit the water. Seconds later a squirming creature was pulled from the green water, struggling against the net which held it captive. Jasper opened a large cooler and placed the entire net inside of it.

"There's my dinner! Now, we can either stay and scavenge longer and hopefully catch some dinner for the two of you, or I can take you back to the Undercity tunnels."

"We've still got some rations," I said politely, speaking before Caeldra could, in case she was still angry at the strange man.

"Alright, suit yourselves. We've got a few days' journey, and it's going to cost you," he said, setting his jaw stubbornly.

Caeldra grumbled something that could have been a complaint, then rummaged through her backpack. She pulled out an old-looking pump-action shotgun and checked to make sure it was devoid of ammo. "I assume that this will do?" she asked.

Jasper eyed the weapon and motioned for her to hand it to him. He turned the gun in his hands and inspected the overall condition. He looked up at Caeldra as if about to ask a question.

"You'll get the ammo after we've safely arrived," she said.

"Splendid. The river always provides, and I do believe we have an accord," Jasper said with a smile.

Caeldra turned to me after he started the small motor on the side of the boat which began to propel us forward at a steady speed.

"Watch for exits on the way and keep your gun handy. If he's planning on betraying us, we may not know until it's too late if we let our guard down. If the journey does take more than one day, we will sleep in shifts," she told me, her voice low and quiet.

"I've introduced myself to you, perhaps I could be permitted to know your names. I like to know those I transport on my vessel," Jasper said with a friendly grin.

"I'm Jake, and this is Caeldra, you'll forgive us if we'd like to withhold our last names," I said.

He smiled at this, "well, Jake and Caeldra, it's very nice to meet you, though I won't be much of a threat. I've actually never been to the surface of New York. This river is my life."

"Why do you choose to live like this?" I asked with curiosity.

"The river is more alive than anything else in this world. It's one of the few places where nature actually thrives, and so I clean the river and find treasures while doing so. There are others like me, we are a peaceful people, and we trade for anything that we can't get ourselves."

Jasper pulled a metal bucket from beneath the blue tarp and began to light a fire with blocks of synthetic fire starter. He pulled a long knife from its sheath on his belt and cleaned the eel that he had caught earlier with the brutal efficiency of a butcher. He skewered the resulting meat cuts on steel spikes and began to roast them over the fire. I had to admit, it smelled a lot better than it looked, yet I was more than comfortable eating a ration pack— something I knew was safe to eat. Jasper ate his meal and watched us curiously as we did the same as we ate our ration packs. Caeldra glared at Jasper when she noticed him staring at the ration pack as she was preparing it.

"Food from packages, what an odd thing," he said.

"I could say the same about that creature you're eating," Caeldra responded as she watched him eat, slight disgust forming on her face.

I tore off a large bite of dried jerky and gnawed on it absently as I fought to tolerate the building pain in my leg. Caeldra apparently noticed, as she reached into her backpack and pulled out a small pack of pills, handing them to me along with a bottle of water.

"You need to take these with your meal. Antibiotics and another dose of painkillers to dope you up," Caeldra said as she handed me the items.

"Thanks, Caeldra," I said as I took the medicine, unable to deal with the growing pain.

"What kind of wound is that?" Jasper asked, eyeing my bandaged leg.

"Explosion, some kind of shrapnel lodged into my leg," I said.

"I could take a look if you'd like, I've got a medical kit on the ship and I'm good at stitches," Jasper said.

"I hardly think that this is the place for a medical procedure," Caeldra responded, her voice cold.

"Nonsense, if he doesn't get that leg taken care of, he might lose it. I've got medical alcohol and drinking alcohol as well. I'm going to need some additional compensation for my supplies, but I think it's best for your friend here," he said.

I gave him a nod. The pain was getting worse, and it didn't feel right. My leg was hot to the touch and felt like it might be starting to get infected. "Please, if you can fix it that would be great," I said to Jasper. Caeldra gave me a look of disbelief but didn't protest further, probably aware that she wasn't feeling the pain that I was.

Jasper handed me a bottle of clear alcohol, "that one's for drinking and this one is for your leg," he said as he pulled out another bottle. He opened the medical kit and fastened a LED headlamp to his head. "Caeldra, dear, I'm going to need your help restraining Jake here while I clean the wound," Jasper told Caeldra as he worked on removing the strong adhesive bandage. The dried blood on the surface tugged on the wound and sent fresh waves of pain surging through the blanket of painkillers which had already numbed my body. I looked down and saw that the cut looked brown, but it could have just been the dim light. Jasper sat on my shins while Caeldra had wrapped her arms around me from behind as if giving me a tight hug. "Jake, you're going to want to take a few swigs of that bottle now," Jasper told me as he unscrewed the other bottle of alcohol and doused his hands in a generous coating of the strong-smelling liquid. "This is going to hurt like an Eelbitch."

Though I had no idea what an Eelbitch was, I knew I was in for some excruciating pain.

"You first, if you'd be so kind," Caeldra said as she handed the drinking alcohol to Jasper who shrugged and took a deep swig. He passed the bottle back to me.

My heart racing, I took a deep swallow of the liquid and a strong burning sensation filled my throat. It was harsher than the beer I had grown used to, and I grimaced, but swallowed it anyway. I took another swig before handing the bottle to Caeldra who took a large drink with only a slight expression of discomfort.

Grabbing heavy gauze pads, Jasper poured some of the alcohol into my wound and I screamed in pain as a burning sensation unlike anything I had ever known seeped into my leg, shattering the comfort provided by the painkillers I had taken. Jasper reached into the wound with small steel pliers and removed a thin sliver of dark metal, dripping brown as it was placed into a metal bowl. After prodding around in the wound, Jasper removed two other shards of metal before sewing it shut with a neat series of stitches. I'd like to say that I handled the procedure with strength, but the truth was that I was fighting to break free of Caeldra's strong grasp the whole time to make the pain stop, my screams piercing the cloth rag I bit down on. Jasper was correct that the procedure would hurt like an Eelbitch.

"Now, we need to get Jake to a doctor as soon as possible. His leg is poisoned."

25

DOWNSTREAM

Jasper explained that the fragments looked to be a particularly deadly and gruesome isotope of radioactive heavy metal that would poison my blood. As a makeshift remedy, he created a salve from some of the algae that grew in the water mixed with some antibiotic paste from our medical supplies.

"The algae will hopefully draw some of the harmful toxins from your blood and reduce your symptoms. I'm afraid it's not a perfect fix, and you'll need something more potent once we reach River's Port. The antibiotics will prevent infection," Jasper said as he applied thick coats of the salve to my now closed wound.

The acrid smell of the briny algae made my stomach lurch as I fought a wave of nausea that threatened my ability to hold down my meal and the extra painkillers I had taken. The increased dosage of the powerful medication caused my mind to feel fuzzy.

Given the opportunity, I reached into my pack and pulled out the case that I believed to contain Mindshift. It didn't appear to have a seem, and I couldn't see any biometric scanners or locks. Caeldra moved over to inspect it as well, and also couldn't figure out how to open the box. We gave up and returned the black case to my backpack.

"What can you tell us about River's Port?" Caeldra asked Jasper as she moved her backpack to the edge of the boat's wall, leaning her C-15 against her pack.

"It's the hub of the river. It's your best chance of getting back to the less pleasant parts of the Undercity, and your friend's only chance at fully recovering from that wound. You will be able to trade for whatever you need there," he responded.

Caeldra drew her pistol from its holster and ejected the magazine. I noticed the distinct appearance of a HexTox canister. My own CZR-7 was loaded with CO_2, the orange burning gas that was better suited for longer ranges. It was cheaper, and I hadn't been expecting to go on a secret mission. At the very least, we were well prepared for nothing short of a full-scale firefight. With a few magazines of gas for our handguns and several more for the heavy C-15s, we could take out a small army. Worst-case scenario, we could switch to some of the old projectile weapons we had scavenged from the bunker.

"You sure are heavily armed," Jasper said in admiration. "Weapons are rather uncommon in River's Port aside from the city guards and hired mercenaries that escort some of the merchants that travel to and from the city."

I was beginning to get the impression that this River's Port was actually a large city, but how could something like that exist under the streets of New York? The idea that this could be a trap crept into my mind, and I did my best to remain calm. If Caeldra thought that we were in any danger, I was sure she would act.

"Has our employer ever associated with anyone from River's Port?" I asked Caeldra with a feigned smile to hint at the hidden question.

"Yes, but we don't have anyone currently residing in the city," she responded, indicating that she understood.

"I'm afraid you chose a bad place to fall, sir. We'll be over one hundred miles from your starting point when we reach River's Port. This tunnel is meant to move water through the entire length of New York, but unless you've got a way to climb one of the drainage vents on the ceiling, then you're trapped with me," he said.

"I suppose we are stuck with your company, for the time being, Mr. Rivers," Caeldra said as she raised her wrist and powered on the Artemis display.

"What are you doing!" I yelled.

"We need to see if we can get a hold of command. I think that we are out of reach of whatever was trying to kill us, not that I expect to pick up a signal down here," she said.

Caeldra frowned as she toggled a few settings on the display.

"Nothing, this is a shadow zone. I'm going to create a local map that we can sell if we make it back to base."

"Interesting tech you've got there," Jasper said as he leaned closer, trying to get a better look at the glowing screen.

Caeldra moved away and raised her wrist to restrict his vision, and he backed off with hands raised, protesting his innocence. Jasper turned to the motor and poured a can of strong-smelling liquid that I could only assume to be fuel into the tank on the side. The engine sputtered in disapproval before returning to the dull hum as the propeller continued to drive us further down the river faster than the slow-moving current.

"You two sure did pick a good time to fall in the river though, it's low enough so that you didn't drown. If there is a bad storm, it fills to the top."

"Jasper, why is the water warm? It's the middle of winter, and I just realized that we should be dead from hypothermia," I said.

"Well, first off, the water runs right above several of New York's nuclear reactors, drawing heat from them, and when the algae absorbs radiation, it does so in an exothermic reaction that keeps the water warm as well. It's the same reason why your leg is probably on fire right now," he said.

He was right about the exothermic reaction. The algae salve had grown hot, and I could feel the heat through the numbing painkillers. It wasn't too hot to cause pain, but it did feel like my leg had an intense fever.

"You're not irradiated enough for the algae to boil your blood, so no need to worry, sir," Jasper said to me with his wide grin.

I spotted another boat coming toward us further up the river and prodded Caeldra before pointing. She promptly unstrapped the C-15 from her backpack and checked to make sure it was loaded.

"Artemis on," she told me as she flipped open her wrist display and activated the system. While we wouldn't have access to a lot of information, Artemis would allow us to locally control our Nanotech modules and potentially save our lives if we got into a firefight. I turned on my Artemis system and readied my CZR-7—I didn't want to use the heavier rifle unless it was necessary, and the CO_2 might fare better at this range.

Jasper eyed the ship and gave us a strange look. "I've rarely run into trouble on this river in the past, my friends, it's probably nothing to worry about."

"We have a knack for attracting trouble," Caeldra said, her voice grim.

The ship was only about two hundred feet away from us, and the gap was closing fast.

"Cut the engines," Caeldra said as she attempted to identify the passengers of the other boat. She noticed that I was holding my CZR-7 and gave me a quizzical look. I ejected the CO_2 gas canister, and she gave a solid nod of approval. At this range, the CO_2 would fare much better than HexTox.

"Have your C-15 ready in case this gets ugly," she said.

Jasper reached down and grabbed his net launcher, attaching the deactivated tri-colored flashlight to the side of the tool's frame.

"Hello there!" he called loudly through the echoing tunnel as he waved an arm in the air at the silhouette of the boat. A shadowy figure appeared to stand for a moment, and there was a pause. "Helllloooo," the figure called in a metallic voice as it waved an arm with jerky motions. It sounded to be some sort of robot, perhaps an Artisan or Junker. As we approached, we saw that it was a Junker, an unsanctioned robot built from spare parts. Its chassis was cobbled together from various scraps of metal of many colors as well as pieces of an Enforcer, and its head was composed of only a few simple rotors, a metal box, and two different cameras that acted as sensory components.

Caeldra kept her weapon ready as she appraised the Junker with caution.

"Good day to you, sir," Jasper said in a friendly voice. "Where are you heading?" he asked.

"Scavenging along the river. I need a new balance regulator I'm afraid," the Junker responded as it raised a metal pole much like the one Jasper used to fish out junk of the river.

"Have you anything to trade, friend?" Jasper asked hopefully.

"I'm always looking for a good trade," the bot responded as it worked with Jasper to tether the two boats together. The Junker's boat was built much like Jasper's but was smaller. It appeared to be loaded with piles of scrap and also contained a large cooler.

"I've got several eels, plastics, metals, even some titanium, and I'm looking for bot parts. One can never be too careful," the bot said as it raised its arms to exaggerate the point.

Caeldra shifted through the bot's piles of junk and shook her head to indicate that she wasn't interested in trading for anything. Jasper ended up trading some gears and rusted electrical components for the bot's entire stash of dead river eels, still very fresh according to him.

It was a strange encounter to see an independent robot and even stranger to think that another city could exist below the streets of New York, a city that had robots as citizens, merchants, and masters of the craft trades. I was anxious to arrive at this strange city, so much so that I had almost entirely forgotten about my leg wound.

"How far to River's Port, sir?" Jasper asked the bot as they started to untie the tether.

"Fourteen hours, twelve minutes and thirteen seconds—if you leave within the next three minutes, and that's assuming you don't stop for anything or run out of gas. That's also assuming that you maintain a constant velocity of eight miles per hour," the robot responded.

"Dammit, they probably think we're dead, Jake. The sooner we can get to River's Port; the sooner we can contact the Guild. Our only option of getting back to base might be taking transportation on the surface," Caeldra said as she considered this for herself. "I don't like it at all, especially while the Government is after you."

I hadn't considered that. Traveling through over a hundred miles of uncharted Undercity tunneling was an impossibly difficult task, one that we didn't have the means or ability to complete, especially with my leg the way it was.

"Well, friends, it's going to be a couple of days ride down the river, I don't have the fuel reserves to get us there quicker than that. In the meantime, I'll reduce your travel and medical expenses if you help me scavenge and fish along the way," Jasper said.

We were utterly helpless to control the current situation. We would have to be patient to get to River's Port then do our best to get back to the Guild Hall. I had never been further than a few miles away from my home on East 432 Avenue. There were too many unknowns: my leg, the arrest warrant, and whatever was hunting us. Regardless, we had to get Mindshift back to the Guild and protect it with our lives, even if we couldn't figure out how to open the box. I remembered my father's words about how he had wired the tech to explosives, and decided it would be best to leave it alone until we could have the Guild look at it.

We moved along with the steady current of the river, taking the time to do one of the few things that would benefit us as we attempted to better the situation we were in; we rested. Upon Caeldra's insistence and ideology that a minute of prevention could prevent a day of repair, we slept in shifts. I took the first shift of sleep and used my backpack as a makeshift pillow. With the warm temperatures in the large tunnel, I used my jacket as a mattress and fell into sleep plagued with fever.

I awoke after what felt like days. Caeldra was holding the net launcher and attempting to catch some eels, and she had an odd look of satisfaction on her face as she scanned the waters around the boat.

"Good morning," I said, clearing my throat.

"It's not morning at all, young sir," Jasper said as he looked at the strange blinking LED lights on his wrist.

"I wouldn't know. It all looks the same down here, regardless of the time," I said.

Caeldra handed me the net launcher and gave me a pat on the back. "How are you feeling?" she asked.

"Better, my leg is on fire, but sleep really helped," I responded.

Caeldra gave me another dose of the powerful painkillers then set up her sleeping arrangement in a very similar way to what I had done. "Thanks for saving my life again, Jake," she said as she rolled over onto her side.

"Always," I replied. "It's the third time I've saved you now?" I asked, a smile forming on my face.

"It's the second. And all the time I've spent on training you makes us roughly even," she replied, feigning injury from my comment; we both smiled at each other. Caeldra drifted off to sleep, and I was left in the company of Jasper.

"If you don't care to deplete your rations, you could have one of my river eels. Caeldra caught four of them, and I'm more than happy to share," Jasper exclaimed.

The idea wasn't actually that crazy, and I was famished. "If you'll cook it for me, I'll give it a shot. I'm afraid anything I try to cook that doesn't come from a can turns to a burned crisp," I said with uncertainty. It was a logical thing to do, saving rations and resources. The simple fact remained that I didn't need to deplete our resources any more than necessary to increase our chances of getting out of this situation and returning to our normal lives.

Jasper laughed at my unexaggerated joke and used the long knife to clean the eel. He prepared another fire to cook the food. He then produced a small frying pan from below the blue tarp and began frying the eel fillets in the pan with a dash of salt. They actually smelled pretty good. I had only had fish a few times in my life due to the high cost—fish from the ocean weren't safe to eat, and the only place to obtain edible fish was from the Government owned fish farms in the Mids, which meant that supply was even more sparse down in the Slums. A few minutes later, Jasper skewered the cooked eel and handed me a hearty portion of the strange creature.

"The texture might take some getting used to, but the flavor is quite exquisite," he said, leaning in to watch me take the first bite.

With a moment of hesitation, I tore a large bite out of the eel and was surprised. The meat itself was actually quite good, but I was a little thrown off by the chewy texture. I figured Caeldra would have given me an earful for eating such a thing.

Jasper and I finished our meal, and he returned to fishing for scrap as I steered the boat around a wide bend in the tunneling. It was so strange that someone could live like this, living a life of extreme solitude and disconnection from conventional technology. He had never known the city, life as a Thinker, or anything else from the streets of New York.

As Caeldra slept, we talked about River's Port, technology, tales of legends, and debated the best way to cook eel. I was certain that it would be good in a stew and that Mary could create something truly wonderful with the strange meat. Then my thoughts drifted solely to Mary, and conversation between Jasper and I faded. I didn't know where Mary was, or even if she was still alive. If anything had happened to her, it was my fault. Worst of all, I hadn't been able to explain things or say good bye. We had a long way to travel, and there was nothing to do but sit back and face the downstream journey, trapped in my thoughts.

26

RIVER'S PORT

The rest of the journey lasted two more days. We all talked along the way and Caeldra seemed to lose her annoyance of Jasper, she even tried the eel and was pleasantly surprised at how good it was. After that, we had switched to eel for the rest of the journey to preserve our dwindling rations.

We would have to try to restock in River's Port. It wasn't long before we spotted a bright light coming from the end of the tunnel.

Suddenly, we emerged in a bright and cavernous open space. Several other boats were traveling in the water surrounding the massive and cramped looking cluster of buildings that appeared to be stacked much too high. Ropes and trinkets hung from balconies, and green moss covered many of the slanted metal roofs giving off a green hue against the sprawled lights of the city. The entire city itself looked to be condensed into a single indistinguishable mass, much too cramped for its own good. From the river, it looked to be about the same size as a few square blocks of New York. Bright neon signs that hung above stores illuminated the narrow streets and gave off a colorful glow against the wet pavement.

"Why does the Government let something like this exist?" I asked Caeldra in awe.

"These people stay off the surface, so they probably either don't care or don't want to waste resources on something that's not causing any problems for them," she responded as she took in the surroundings.

"Just so you two know, robots are considered equals here. They can trade and do as they please, and you'd best remember it," Jasper said.

I eyed Caeldra curiously, but she just shrugged. There weren't many robots in the Guild, and those we did have had minimal independent ability, only assisting in manual labor and none were suitable for wet work—the term used to describe missions in the Undercity. It never occurred to me why the Guild didn't make use of some of the newer robotic models, but it probably had something to do with the emphasis on people rather than technology.

Boats moved alongside us, carrying huge crates, barrels of eels, and many indistinguishable objects. We were nearing a large dock where many boats were tethered along a specified docking area. As we approached, a lean Junker bot leaned in and grabbed the rope that Jasper extended. The robot docked out boat, and the cargo was inspected and recorded on an electronic ledger. The bot recorded the gear that Caeldra and I carried and we were permitted to enter the city, no questions asked.

"We don't tolerate violence here, please keep your weapons holstered, and we won't have any problems," the Junker said to us as we stepped onto the dock.

"Well, I wish you both the best. I suppose that I'll take that ammo now and we will be square. You both helped me fish up enough to cover the medical expenses," he said with a smile as he waved over a Golem-class robot to the boat. "If you two happen to need any ingenious inventions, just head west of the Cleanery," he said as he pointed to the huge building alongside the dock that stretched to our left. "My workshop has a blue sign that reads 'Jasper's Ingenious Inventions.'"

Caeldra and I thanked him, and she gave him the shotgun shells as promised, while the hulking robot began unloading crates of cargo from Jasper's boat.

"Head straight in and take a left to get to the market. Look for the Scavenger Guild office, and they can help you get back to where you're from. It was a genuine pleasure to meet the two of you," he said with a huge grin. "Be sure to get medical attention while you're here. The surgeon here only accepts credits so you might want to sell some belongings if you're short. I'm afraid I can't afford to buy any of your treasure."

"Thanks for your help, Jasper," Caeldra said, her initial attitude toward the man long faded.

Caeldra and I began walking through the narrow streets of the city, our backpacks and equipment tightly secured. My leg was starting to throb from the walking, but I continued with stoic determination. We got several strange looks as the citizens of the river city observed our weapons and leather jackets bearing the Champions' insignia. There were just as many robots walking around as there were people, and almost all of them wore clothing of some kind. Most of the models were Junkers, and the question of who would incur the costs to build a robot only to set it free came to mind. I learned that the newly constructed robots would be required to work enough to provide the builder with a decent profit, then they would be given their freedom. Almost all of them used the same coding that relied on some advanced framework created by an unknown coder. One such robot, a scrawny Junker by the name of CH4PK, agreed to guide us to the Scavenger Guild office for the cost of a single pistol bullet. CH4PK wore a thick rubber coat over his damaged chassis to protect the electrical components from the moisture in the air. The robot explained as many nuances of the city as possible as we traveled through the crowded streets. Finally, we entered the marketplace and paid the small robot for his help.

The market itself was a thick bustle of activity as people hauled large carts filled with various goods to and from the many tents and metal market stands that were set up. I was surprised to see that many people were trading with the bartering system rather than with currency. The market smelled of fish, both cooked and raw, strange spices, and something less pleasant. I identified the less pleasant smell as we passed over a thin metal grate that extended around the stalls in the market. Grease from the cook stands that were set up was trickling through the drainage system into large barrels that were lowered into slots in the ground where it accumulated to be put to other use. Some of the grease had clogged, clinging to the sides of the grate. Old grease had festered, producing the pungent undertone which subtracted from the other pleasant scents. I wrinkled my nose and turned my attention to the other stalls surrounding us. A few of the stalls were clearly marketed toward the robots of the city and contained great heaps of spare parts and tools needed for robotic repair. Just as there was a barber shop, there was also a specified parlor for cosmetic robot work and mineral oil baths that were said to clean even the toughest of grime and rust from a variety of metals. The city fascinated me.

We spotted the Scavenger Guild office—it was one of the few permanent structures in an otherwise temporary arrangement. Three large stands were set up outside of the office where merchants were trading for various goods. Two armed guards wearing welded metal plate armor stood outside the doors of the office. They were wielding what looked to be some sort of modified C-15 and large swords strapped to the side of their belts, the dull metal glinting in the bright marketplace light. As we approached, they eyed us appraisingly and positioned their rifles for easier access. One of the guards, a large man with a full beard that hung to his chest, placed his hand heavily on the hilt of the sheathed sword.

"Good day. What business do you have with the Guild?"

"We would like to speak with the supervisor of this office," Caeldra said as she shifted to reveal the insignia on her shoulder.

"I'm not sure what your jacket is supposed to imply, but you appear to be too heavily armed to bring anything but trouble," said the man as he shifted in place, inspecting our weapons with sharp eyes.

"Please call it in, tell them we're with the Champions of Liberty," I said. Caeldra gave me a cool look of disapproval but then relaxed as she remembered we were in an underground city outside of the reach of the Government.

He hesitated for a moment but then pulled the handheld radio from his belt and called the office.

"Two kids out here that are seeking a meeting, they're heavily armed and say that they're from the Champions of Liberty," the guard said as he continued to stare at us.

"Let them in, but have them leave the weapons at the front of the office please," the voice on the radio said. We were escorted through the small metal door into an office space that reminded me of the Collection Parlors in the Slums. It didn't have any of the large chairs, but it had the same lighting and same linoleum flooring—simple and functional, yet lacking any sort of aesthetic decoration. Tables were set neatly throughout the open room, and men and women sat working on computers and weighing things on old scales. There was a door at the back of the room, and we were ushered to it after leaving all of our equipment at the entrance. A middle-aged man wearing an expensive shirt and khaki pants greeted us with a smile and welcomed us into the office. He shook our hands and introduced himself as Jack. He was a stocky looking man with long hair that appeared to be greased back and tied off toward the back with some sort of cord. We were seated on two cushioned chairs, and he sat behind the ornamented desk and crossed his fingers as he leaned the chair back and appraised us with a sharp eye.

"Now, you claim to be members of the Champions, and your jackets are certainly authentic. It's not like your Council to send Runners such as yourselves to these parts of the Undercity. It would also appear that you might need medical attention," he said as he trained his gaze directly at me. "Now, what brings Champion Runners such as yourselves to River's Port?"

"We were attacked near our territory and fell into the river by mistake. A resident of these parts rescued us and brought us here, and now we are looking for a way to return to the Champion's Guild Hall."

"I see. Well, you likely know by now that travel through the Undercity itself to your destination is close to impossible. You'd have to cover over one hundred miles, and I'm afraid there aren't any opportunities to resupply while traveling below the Slums. I'm assuming you either need a loan from us or want to buy some cargo space on one of our transports."

"Our first priority is to get Jake's leg taken care of. After that, we'd like to arrange to have our gear moved back to our territory."

"The leg we may be able to solve, your gear, on the other hand, will have to stay here. You should know that our guild does not deal in contraband, nor do we transport it. We have a very sensitive relationship with the Government. Our taxes are paid, and our business license is valid."

"If you deal with the Champions, then you are already committing criminal activity," Caeldra responded quickly.

He raised an eyebrow at this. "Actually, our license permits us to deal with any citizen in good standing in the Slums. Since the Undercity isn't the Slums, we don't break the terms of our license or any applicable Government laws. Even being associated with Jake on the surface would be devastating."

"What do you mean by that?" I asked him, a frown forming on my face.

"Come now, surely you know," he said as he looked me over as if in disbelief. After realizing I had no clue what he was talking about, he pulled out a small datapad and showed it to me.

There was a picture of me and the word 'WANTED' directly under it.

'500 unit reward for information leading to the acquisition of Jacob Ashton. Ashton was last seen under the captivity of an illegal robot and is possibly dangerous.'

I felt the color fade from my face. I knew that the Government wanted me, but to place a bounty like that on me was more than serious. That was a fortune. A bounty like that would attract even the most sensible and gentle-natured citizens of the Slums to take action if I was spotted.

"I don't think it's wise for you to return to the surface anytime soon, Mr. Ashton," Jack said as he put away the datapad. He leaned back in his chair and started talking again.

"Here's what we'll do. You'll give us all of your gear, and we'll arrange for it to be moved through an independent party back to your guild, which will cover the cost of the shipping. Should they refuse to pay, your gear will become our property. We will treat the leg here, and the expense will be fronted. We will then take you to the surface and arrange private transportation back to your district of the Slums where you will be able to return to the Champions," he scratched his chin. "Should you fail to cover any of the costs or our ten percent premium on the credits borrowed, let's just say the Government will be finding Mr. Ashton, and I'll be happy to pocket the five hundred unit bounty."

"That's suitable, but what assurance do we have that our gear will be delivered?" Caeldra asked.

"Well, I'm afraid your bargaining position is quite weak, but I'll give you a one hundred unit insurance voucher should delivery fail. More than generous really. Needless to say, if anything goes wrong, our guild has nothing to do with any of this, and we never spoke."

I turned to Caeldra. "Are you sure the Guild will pay for all of this?"

She gave me a solemn nod and shook Jack's hand, striking a deal.

"Wonderful, let's get your friend's leg taken care of," Jack said as he took an ink pen from his desk and signed the insurance voucher for our equipment before handing it to us. He then signed another voucher and handed it to Caeldra. "Take this to Dimitri on the far west side of River's Port. He's the best and only surgeon in the area, he'll get you back on your feet, Jake. Come back when he's done, and you're rested, and we will get you ready for travel. Leave your gear with us, you won't be permitted to take anything illegal with you to the surface, and we'll need to find you some suitable street clothes," he said as he dismissed us from the office. Though we regretted it, treating the lockbox that contained Mindshift as valuable property and refusing to give it up would only draw suspicion and could tempt their guild to inspect it more closely. Our best bet was to leave it with everything else and hope for the best. Transporting the tech on the surface of New York was unthinkable.

Leaving the office, we headed west toward the clinic owned by Dimitri. The streets grew increasingly more clean as we walked and the loud noise of the market faded behind us. A few robots walked along the streets, some carrying weapons, but it was much quieter, and I was able to slacken my pace as the burden of walking in front of others faded. The growing pain in my leg eased as I slowed down. Caeldra didn't seem to mind the slow pace and seemed concerned that I was walking at all. She offered to support me as I walked, putting an arm under me, but I refused her, not wanting to burden her or appear that I wasn't strong.

"Do you think we can trust Jack?" I asked Caeldra as we walked.

"We don't have a choice, and frankly, he is our best option of getting out of this mess. As for your leg, I'd say we are very lucky that there is anyone down here who is capable of fixing it."

"What about transportation on the surface? What if I'm noticed?"

"I don't think they want that either. The relationship between our guilds is worth more than five hundred units, and starting a war with us isn't something that would interest the Scavenger Guild."

River's Port was actually much larger than I had expected and the walk took about twenty excruciating minutes before we spotted the neon blue medical cross. It hung over a metal-clad building without windows. We entered cautiously into a room reeking of disinfectant and the faint scent of vanilla. Empty chairs lined the walls of the waiting room, and an elderly woman sat at the desk, reading some sort of book. She looked up at us through large glasses and gave us an appraising look, as if trying to decide what we were supposed to be in our unfamiliar leather jackets.

"Welcome to the clinic. We require payment up front, and you'll need to fill out some paperwork," she said as she slid a worn clipboard across the metal desk toward us. I took the clipboard and handed her the voucher from Jack. She looked at it and held it under a dark red light. The ink glistened under the dull light, and she deposited the voucher in a small safe, apparently satisfied with the authenticity of the document.

The paperwork consisted of a summary of ailments and a statement which basically signed my life away and waived all liability of the clinic in the case something went wrong during my visit, not that such a contract mattered outside the confines of River's Port.

Dimitri, a large man wearing light blue scrubs, came from the back and waved me forward.

"Your friend will need to wait in the lobby, this shouldn't take more than an hour," he said as he reviewed the paperwork. Caeldra took a seat, and I was led to the back where Dimitri examined the wound after unwrapping the bandages. He used a scanner to verify the radioactive isotope and my need for surgery.

"Whoever sewed this up probably saved your life, my friend. I see that they used a river algae salve to draw out some of the toxins, brilliant," he remarked as he gloved his hands. He walked over to what looked to be a large refrigerator and pulled out a tray of surgical tools from under the dark purple light of the interior. He then grabbed an IV bag and rubbed my wrist with an alcohol pad.

"This will hurt a little bit, then you won't feel anything after that. I'm going to clean out your system and seal this wound for good. You're going to feel sick when you wake up but that's expected. You'll be back to normal in a few days."

He slid the needle into my arm and everything went black.

27

FIRE

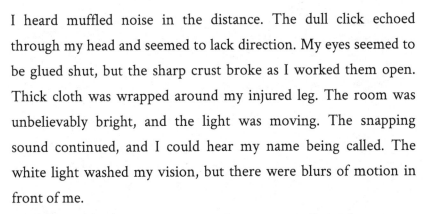

I heard muffled noise in the distance. The dull click echoed through my head and seemed to lack direction. My eyes seemed to be glued shut, but the sharp crust broke as I worked them open. Thick cloth was wrapped around my injured leg. The room was unbelievably bright, and the light was moving. The snapping sound continued, and I could hear my name being called. The white light washed my vision, but there were blurs of motion in front of me.

"Jake? It's time to wake up now," the voice called. There was a ringing sound in my ear as if a bell had been struck. I forced my eyes open again and took in my surroundings. I was in the clinic, and I had no recollection of anything since Dimitri had injected me with the IV needle. Caeldra was standing near the bed, looking at me with worried eyes. "The surgery went well, Jake, but it's going to take you a while to return to normal. The toxin is out of your system now and you are radiation free," Dimitri said as he used a device to check my vitals.

Color and swirls of shapes flashed in my vision and I fought to blink them away, not wanting to alert Caeldra or Dimitri. I assured myself that it was just a side effect of the medication. They were the same shapes I had seen after my three-year evaluation. The memory of the examiner returned to me. "We will contact you if you are of interest to us," she had said. Was that why the Government was after me? Was my mind already filled with treason at that point? My thoughts raced through my head and I struggled to compose them.

I was given a bottle of water and some saltine crackers to eat. My body felt hungry, but even something as simple as crackers made me nauseous. Unable to eat more than a couple of crackers and drink small sips of water, we waited at the clinic for a few hours and I was permitted to take a nap. Despite the rest I had gotten on the river ride to the city, I was exhausted.

I was awoken again by Caeldra who forced me to eat a few more crackers and drink some more water from the clear plastic bottle.

"I got us a room at the tavern here so we can rest until you're well enough to travel. If you're up to it, we will head there now," she told me as I chewed on a cracker.

"Yeah, I might need some help walking, though," I said as I pushed myself up to a sitting position on the side of the bed and felt my head swim.

She gave me a smile and pushed over a wheelchair, "with your natural clumsiness and the aftereffects of your surgery, you're not walking anywhere."

I gave a smile and sighed in relief as I moved from the bed to the chair with a single strained motion. My leg felt like rubber, and the rest of my body wasn't much better. It felt as if I was no longer in control. I focused on trying to gain composure over my slow and incomplete thoughts with some of the exercises Edgar had shown me and attempted to layer away the grogginess. It didn't work, and I found myself wondering how I would be able to control my mind if the Government decided to sedate me with anything half as strong as what I had been given. I hid my frustration as Caeldra pushed the chair forward and into the streets. Dimitri gave her a bottle of pills on the way out with a set of instructions. Caeldra pushed me for several minutes in silence until we reached a large building with a metal and glass exterior. I could see bright colored lights inside with a variety of tables and patrons that sat at them. The loud voices of the people inside leaked through the glass, and I heard the distinct clink of glasses followed by a muffled cheer from a group of people sitting by one of the window tables.

Caeldra pushed open the door and wheeled me in, the aroma of cooking food flooding over us. In many ways, it was much like the pub in our Guild Hall, but it was much busier and more modern in design. The tables were all made of metal. LED lights and signs lit the interior of the building. There were at least thirty people enjoying meals, drinks, and playing some sort of game on the tabletops. It looked like a card game with a board and little pieces that covered the bright surface. While they weren't enjoying meals like many other patrons, several robots were congregated with their groups of friends which contained humans and robots alike.

A young woman walked over to us and gave me a warm smile.

"Welcome to Emeralds," she said, her voice warm. "Can I get you a table?"

"Actually, I've already rented a room. Could we get two meals and a few beers brought to room eleven?" Caeldra asked.

"Certainly," the waitress responded as she jotted it down on the paper.

"Oh, and a pitcher of drinking water please," Caeldra added.

The waitress gave Caeldra a nod and walked toward the back where she disappeared through a swinging metal door into the kitchen.

Caeldra wheeled me forward through the crowd toward the rooms at the back and unlocked the door of room eleven. The inside of the room was a lot more spacious than I thought it would be. The first thing I noticed, however, was the fact that there was only one bed. The room itself had a TV mounted on a brass-colored dresser. There was a bathroom that included a shower and a comfortable looking couch that sat on the side of the wall which was covered in a light blue wallpaper.

I got out of the chair and walked over with slow determination to the couch where I sat. Caeldra joined me, and we watched some old movie on the TV, something I had never seen and something that would be considered contraband on the surface of New York. A few minutes into the movie, the red-haired waitress knocked on the door. Caeldra let her in, and the waitress placed a huge tray on the coffee table. There were two plates loaded to the brim with fried fish and what looked to be french fries. A few ketchup packets lined the side of the decorative red paper that held the food in place. The fish steamed and sent waves of hunger through my stomach as the savory aroma filled the room. There was a large pitcher of frothy beer and one of water as well as two large glass mugs that were stout and full of chipped ice.

"Put it on my tab, please," Caeldra said as she tipped the waitress.

The waitress smiled, pocketed the money and exited the room. Caeldra lifted my plate and handed it to me then prepared her own.

"I'm going to be honest with you, Jake," she said, her voice serious. I tried to prepare myself, unsure of what was coming next. "I might need another plate after this one, and I certainly won't be mad if you need another as well," she said as she flashed me her warm grin.

I felt myself break into a smile and tossed a fry into my mouth, biting through the thick outer surface and almost burning my tongue on the steaming center. My hunger had returned, and after eating two full plates of fish and chips as the waitress had called it, I was feeling much closer to normal. Caeldra and I downed the pitcher of beer and finished the movie which featured people in some strange city that didn't look anything like New York. Caeldra made me take one of the blue pills from the plastic bottle that Dimitri had given her after my meal and I started to feel the onsets of grogginess return. Unlike other medicines, the pills Dimitri put me on were compatible with beer, but I was instructed to not overdo it on alcohol while I was taking the meds.

Caeldra decided that I needed the bed and moved a pillow and sheet over to the couch and set up a makeshift bed. She decided to take a shower and returned wearing her bra and some undershorts. The bandage over her abdomen was gone, and the purple color from the other day had faded to a calmer yellow.

"You going to take a shower?" she asked as she sat on the couch.

I gave her a nod. "Just a short one, I don't want to risk falling," I responded.

"Please try not to fall in the shower, I'd have to rescue you, I suppose," she said with a sly smile. "I also wouldn't want my clothes to get wet if you get what I'm implying," she added just to make me more uncomfortable.

I blushed at this and tried to hide it, "I won't fall," I said as I shambled into the bathroom.

"Oh, and don't mess with your bandage, it needs to stay on," she called out after me.

I gave her a thumbs up and closed the door. The hot water was relaxing as it cascaded over my skin. I breathed deeply as steam floated from the floor and clouded the brightly lit LED bathroom. I washed myself with the small bottle of shampoo and soap that were included with our room. When I got out, I brushed my teeth and wiped the fogged mirror with my towel. After putting on my undershorts and a t-shirt, I walked back outside and returned to the bed. We turned off the lights, and I fell into a deep sleep.

I awoke sometime in the middle of the night and had to use the restroom. When I got back to the bed, I saw a figure move in the corner of the room and instinctively raised my fists in preparation for a fight.

"Relax, it's me," Caeldra said as she walked forward. She was holding her pillow and had her sheet wrapped around her body like a robe. "Do you mind? The couch is pretty uncomfortable."

"Not at all," I said, as I scooted over to the side. The bed was big enough for the two of us, but I still felt uncomfortable. Caeldra must have noticed my discomfort, and she laughed quietly.

"You act like this is the first time you've been in bed with a girl, Jake," she said in a joking tone.

"Well, umm..." I stammered, caught off guard.

"I'm just messing with you," she said. "You make it too easy sometimes," she said, then quickly added, "I guess I should give you a free pass while you're crippled and all, though."

"I suppose I should be used to it by now," I replied, glad that the shadows were hiding the fire that surely burned across my face. Caeldra grabbed my hand and cupped it in hers. Her hands weren't soft like Mary's; they were coarse, the hands of a Runner. "Whatever happens, I'm glad that I met you, Jake," she whispered as she raised my hand to her lips and kissed it. Her lips weren't rough like her hands.

"I'm glad I met you too," I replied.

Caeldra held my hand and fell asleep next to me while I waited for sleep to take hold.

28

TRANSPORT

The glowing clock next to the bedside table read 8:15 AM when I awoke. I suppressed a large yawn as I raised my one free arm up to my eyes and rubbed them. Caeldra was lying on my other arm, her hands wrapped around my wrist. My arm was asleep, but I didn't want to wake her. I felt better than I did yesterday, but there was also the dread in realizing that I had destroyed my life on the surface and would never see Mary again. Worse, she wouldn't ever know what had actually happened to me, I'd just slowly fade away as a painful memory in her life. I hated myself for it and cursed the merchant that sold me the book that changed my life forever.

I slipped my arm out from under Caeldra. She really was beautiful, her ordinarily pulled back hair was lying free at her shoulders in streaming waves. The sheet covered her, and her chest rose methodically with her gentle breathing.

I smiled and slipped on my pants, t-shirt and jacket before slipping on my boots. I was feeling much better but decided that I wasn't going to press my luck and was going to try to take it easy for the day. After grabbing my wallet, I decided to go grab some breakfast for us. Perhaps Caeldra would be awake when I got back. Contrary to last night, the restaurant portion of the inn was almost entirely empty. A few patrons that had decided to stay the night were enjoying breakfast, though. The scent of coffee filled the air like an alluring perfume, and I was determined that I would be enjoying some this morning. I spotted the red-haired waitress that had brought us our food last night, and she smiled when she met my gaze.

"Good morning, sir."

"Good morning," I responded. "Any chance of getting some breakfast to take back to my room?" I asked.

"Certainly, would you like it delivered?"

I almost said yes, but remembered that Caeldra was still sleeping.

"I'll just take it back to the room. Oh, and can I please get a pot of coffee with the meals?" I added.

"Sure, give me a few minutes for that," she said as she shuffled back into the kitchen. I took a seat and realized that my breathing was becoming labored. I was getting tired from just a simple walk and standing for a few minutes. I braced myself on the sides of the chair and lowered myself into it. I let out a sigh of relief as I relaxed against the chair and rested my weakened body.

I watched through the main window as people walked through the streets carrying bags of goods and socializing. I realized that I was growing fond of this city, it felt more like the Champions Guild Hall than the Slums of New York. The Slums, and the fact that the Government had placed a huge bounty on my head were thoughts I wanted to push away and forget. Of course, I would need to talk with Edgar and get everything worked out with the rest of the Council, being a Justicar and all.

The waitress approached with the platter of food and metal canister full of coffee, and I gave her a thirty credit tip. With our agreement with the Scavenger Guild, we were actually in a good place financially, but neither Caeldra nor I wanted to go too far into debt on this outing.

"Enjoy," she told me with a grin as she walked over and tended to another table.

Carefully, I walked back to our room with the heavy tray and focused on maintaining my balance. After somehow managing to open the door, I placed the breakfast platter on the dresser and turned on a lamp. Caeldra shifted and opened her eyes, raising a hand to block the light. She smelled the food and sat up, stretching her arms above her head. The sheet slipped down to reveal her bra. I could see a collection of scattered scars on her pale skin that I hadn't seen before. They were spread out across her body, but none were as distinguished as the one on her face.

"Good morning," she said through a loud yawn as she reached down and pulled on her tank top and pants. I brought her a plate of the delicious looking food which she gladly accepted. The breakfast was fried fish scrambled with some onions, peppers, and eggs. The food at Emeralds Inn was fantastic. It occurred to me that most meals down in River's Port featured some sort of fish. The fish was real fish, though; it wasn't like the strangely delicious eel that we had eaten with Jasper on our journey here.

"This isn't even the best part," I claimed through a mouthful of breakfast.

Caeldra raised an eyebrow at that. "Oh yeah?" she asked, a look of curiosity forming on her face.

"I got us some coffee to go with the meal," I said as I pointed to the metal canister which sat on the platter, two ceramic mugs that had an image of an emerald were stacked neatly next to the canister of coffee.

"Fancy," she said with a wink, "you sure do know how to treat a girl."

I smiled and walked over to the dresser to pour two mugs of coffee. I had forced myself to keep my hopes down as the dark liquid filled the cups and emitted a thin pillar of steam. I didn't expect it to be better than the coffee that Edgar brewed, but who knew? Everything else was fantastic down here, perhaps the coffee would be as well.

The coffee wasn't as good as the kind that Edgar brewed up in his flat in the Slums, but it still was a luxury that I enjoyed. Caeldra drank hers with appreciation, but I could tell that coffee wasn't her favorite thing in the world—I was pretty sure that was spaghetti. We finished our meal and decided that we should probably go have another meeting with Jack at the Scavenger Guild office to finalize things. I expected that I'd be able to travel tomorrow as I was feeling much better than the previous day right after the surgery.

With the relaxing stay at Emeralds and a chance to recover after my surgery, it was easy to forget that the most dangerous part, for me at least, was yet to come. I was going to bring up the fact that Caeldra and I should travel separately, but I knew she'd never buy into that. She was too caring and wouldn't dare leave me behind, especially with the danger I was in. I loved that about her.

Had I suggested that we travel separately for safety, she would have taken the opportunity to mock my "need to be a hero," or my foolishness, or "that I was selfish by trying to be selfless." Whichever way that would have gone, a private meeting with Jack would be my only shot if I wanted to pull it off. I didn't want to leave her or get rid of her, but it was inarguably safer for her as she was considered a citizen in good standing on the surface, despite the fact she hadn't visited a Collection Parlor in years.

Caeldra walked over while unscrewing the cap to my pill bottle. She handed me one of the blue pills, and I washed it down with a hot swig of coffee. Smiling, she kissed me on the forehead and returned to getting fully dressed. I ended up drinking four mugs of coffee while Caeldra drank two.

"Alright, the coffee was a good choice. I didn't like it much at first, but it grew on me," Caeldra said.

"When we make it back, I'll have Edgar brew us some of his signature brew, it's honestly the best thing I've ever tasted," I replied.

Caeldra smiled and sat down beside me. "About last night, I don't want to get in the way of you and Mary, it didn't mean anything other than I'm scared and just wanted to feel safe," she said.

"I think that there is a good chance I won't ever see her again. It hurts, but I don't want to live with the false hope that I can make things work with her," I said, my voice sullen.

"I'm not saying it will be easy, but if you really care about this girl, then you can't lose hope," she said quietly.

I frowned. "I don't know what to do. I feel so powerless. I don't want to talk about it right now, I guess."

She leaned in and kissed me on the forehead again. "I'm sorry. Come on, let's get going. We can talk whenever you're ready. If you need unbiased advice or ever need to talk about anything, I'm here for you."

Deciding that it still probably wasn't a good idea for me to walk around the city in my current state, I used the wheelchair to get around. Caeldra wanted to push me, but I argued against it and ended up wheeling myself, saying I'd let her know if I got too tired. We exited Emeralds and entered the already busy streets of River's Port. Having no set plan of how to kill time for the day before we met with Jack, we decided to browse Central Market. It was as busy as ever, and the distinct smell of raw fish had flooded the entire area that morning as the cooking stalls had not yet set about lighting their stoves.

"Flounder, bass, eel, and more! Fresh fish!" a merchant called as people flocked over to examine the haul. His stand was loaded with fish stacked heavily in beds of ice surrounded by clear plastic walling. Having no interest in fish, we decided to browse the stalls offering other goods. The two guards outside of the Scavenger Guild had already taken their usual place outside the door, their rifles slung low across their chests. The guard with the beard had his hand rested on the metal hilt of the massive sword, swaying on his feet as he spoke with the other.

"Champions all the way out here?" an elderly man asked from behind his market stall as he appraised us with curiosity.

"Excuse me?" I asked him.

"That insignia on your jackets, you're from the Champions of Liberty—or you found some jackets you weren't supposed to," he told us as he continued to look us over through battered glasses. He waved both hands over his market stall which looked to be filled with a few canisters of boiling liquid. "The Champions are welcome at my shop. Please, come take a look," he said, his face cheerful.

Caeldra and I approached, and he grabbed two small plastic cups from a bag. "I'm a tea brewer, not as popular as coffee, but I grow the plants myself," he said as he flipped a lever on one of the large canisters, pouring tea into both cups. "I've got sugar, honey, and chilled milk if you'd like it," he said with a smile as he handed us the cups. I added a small dash of sugar to my tea and Caeldra added the works. She drank the tea eagerly and gave a refreshing sigh as she finished the cup. I downed mine as well, and we both thanked him for the sample. When Caeldra left, I bought a bag of the tea we had tried for sixty credits and tucked it away between my leg and the side walling of my wheelchair. I would give it to her as a gift later.

After browsing the market and finding nothing else that we were in dire need of, we went to the Scavenger Guild office where the two guards let us in right away, recognizing us from the day before. We were once again escorted to Jack's office and Caeldra moved one of the chairs aside so that I could wheel myself in and preserve my strength.

"Ah, I'm glad to see you're doing better, Jake," he said as he moved some datapads to clear a space on his desk. "I got you these—I had to guess on your measurements," he said as he brought up two bundles wrapped in tissue paper. Inside were street clothes, the types of clothes citizens of the Slums would wear. I had a ragged pair of jeans, a gray t-shirt, and a hefty brown hoodie with a Government sponsored message: "Thinkers: paving the way to the perfect future."

Caeldra's clothes lacked any graphics, and they looked like they would be a bit too big on her.

"Thanks. Will it be possible for us to leave tomorrow?" Caeldra asked as she pulled the bundle of clothes in.

Jack frowned, "I'm afraid not, you're scheduled to depart in a few hours. We'll have you back to your district by the end of the day, but you'll want to get Jake to the Undercity right when you arrive. The longer he's on the surface, the more danger you'll be in."

"He's not really in any condition to travel. And what about our gear, is it already in transit?" Caeldra asked, a look frustration forming on her face.

"Yes, we'll be sending your guild clothes separately. I really am sorry that we have to transport you both so soon. I'm aware of the condition of Jake here, but it's the best we can do. If you don't go today, there might not be another chance for quite some time."

Caeldra nodded gravely. "We'll get changed and then we'll be ready to leave. Also, we've got an open tab at Emeralds, please see that it is taken care of."

Jack nodded and gave us the office, and we changed into the clothes that he had given us. Mine fit about right, but Caeldra's were at least a size too large.

"Look, I'm helping the Government achieve a perfect future," I said as I flashed her a wide grin and pointed to my hoodie. She gave a groan and opened the office door as I returned to my wheelchair.

Jack called over a man named Morris and introduced us.

"Pleasure to meet you both. I'll be your guide to the surface and will take you to the truck," he said in a strange accent.

We followed him out of the office, Caeldra pushing the back of my chair, probably thinking that I'd need my strength later. Morris led us through the streets to a point where the road narrowed significantly into a metal bridge that extended into a well-lit tunnel ahead.

"Not too much further from here, we just need to reach the service elevator for Jake," he said as he turned on a large LED flashlight. I turned my head as we crossed the bridge and could see that there were many boats like the one Jasper had, around the large body of water surrounding the city It was fascinating that such a city could exist under the surface of New York, unknown to the citizens of the Slums, I thought again.

We traveled to a large elevator platform and were lifted up for several minutes in almost complete darkness—except for Morris' flashlight and the bright plastic buttons of the rusted control panel of the elevator. It was getting colder as we rose. Even the upper levels of the Undercity were subject to the brutal winters of New York.

We reached a warehouse much like the one we used with the Champions to get to the Undercity from my district, and were escorted out back to where a large truck was waiting for us. The air was freezing, and the wind pierced through my hoodie with ease. A few men were loading heavy-looking boxes into the back and one of them waved us forward.

"This is where I leave you," Morris told us. "You'll be back home in a few hours, just listen to the drivers, and you'll be fine."

The leader was wearing brown overalls over a dark jacket. "You'll be riding in the cargo hold, just stay quiet and we'll drop you off in your district when we get there," he said as he pointed to the back of the truck. Morris headed back down the elevator in the warehouse, and Caeldra pushed my chair up on the loading lift of the vehicle while one of the workers lifted us into the cargo hold. We moved to the back of the heavily loaded truck and positioned ourselves behind some of the large metal crates that were stacked to the ceiling.

The back door slammed shut, and the truck began to move. Unfortunately, the back of the truck wasn't heated, and it was almost the same temperature as the outside air without the wind. Caeldra decided to sit on my lap while I was seated in the chair so that she wouldn't have to sit on any of the freezing metal surfaces. She avoided putting any weight on my injured leg.

It was cold, but without the fierce wind, it was bearable. The truck ride itself had lasted a few hours before we came to an abrupt stop.

The back of the truck opened and a dozen Enforcers began approaching the back, lights flashing, weapons raised. A heavy dropship had landed behind them, guns trained as they began to climb in the truck.

29

BARON

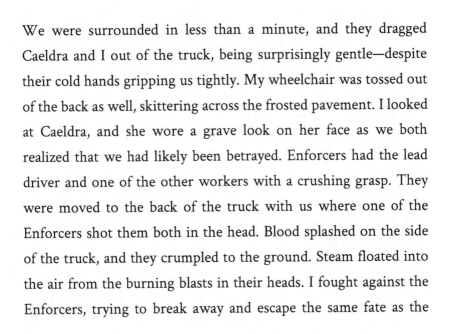

We were surrounded in less than a minute, and they dragged Caeldra and I out of the truck, being surprisingly gentle—despite their cold hands gripping us tightly. My wheelchair was tossed out of the back as well, skittering across the frosted pavement. I looked at Caeldra, and she wore a grave look on her face as we both realized that we had likely been betrayed. Enforcers had the lead driver and one of the other workers with a crushing grasp. They were moved to the back of the truck with us where one of the Enforcers shot them both in the head. Blood splashed on the side of the truck, and they crumpled to the ground. Steam floated into the air from the burning blasts in their heads. I fought against the Enforcers, trying to break away and escape the same fate as the dead men. Citizens in the streets screamed and ran away from the scene.

The Enforcers carried us to the front of the dropship where Caeldra was shoved to her knees. The barrel of a rifle was placed on the back of her head. She grimaced and hung her head solemnly as a middle-aged man in an expensive looking gray coat exited the dropship. He was wearing polished leather shoes and expensive pants. I could see a flash of gold before he pulled brown gloves onto his hands and wrapped a scarf of the same, drab color, around his neck. His gray hair was neatly styled with gel.

"Terribly cold today isn't it?" he asked no one in particular as he walked over to us. "Jacob, it's wonderful to meet you, but you have made my job very difficult. I understand that the Enforcers can be intimidating, but you won't be harmed." He looked over to the crumpled bodies of the two drivers and sighed. "Dear heavens, you couldn't have done that offsite?" he asked the lead Enforcer as he moved to block our vision of the bodies.

"Those men were wanted felons, but I deeply apologize for the lack of etiquette of the Enforcers," he said as he reached for a datapad.

"Who are you?" I asked, fearing surging in my mind.

"I'm Baron Marwin Zaris, third of my house. And who is this you have with you, Jacob?" he asked as he turned to Caeldra who was staring at him with hate in her eyes.

"She doesn't have anything to do with this, she's just a friend. She doesn't know anything," I said, pitching my voice low and level to attempt to make it seem more truthful.

The man laughed and placed his hand under her chin, pulling it up and looking at her face.

I saw a glint of light come from her mouth when her head slumped back down as he released his grip. She had the cyanide capsule in her mouth between her teeth.

"Caeldra, don't you even think about it!" I snarled.

Caeldra looked up and met my gaze, tears beading in the corners of her eyes.

The Baron gave an amused laugh which turned to frustration when he still couldn't find out what was going on between us.

"What an odd name," he said as he typed something into his datapad. "Is that Kaledra? Ah, no here it is."

"Well, Ms. Caeldra Thompson, it's a pleasure to meet you. It looks like you haven't visited a Collection Parlor in years. I'd be very interested in seeing what you know," he said after looking on the datapad, a wry smile twisted his lips.

"Just take me and let her go," I said, fear gripping my heart.

"You have nothing to worry about, Jacob. You will be coming with us, but I'm afraid we couldn't take your friend here even if we wanted to." He turned to Caeldra. "Ms. Thompson, I hope you're not doing anything you aren't supposed to be doing, and that we'll see your name on the Collection records shortly." He gave a nod to the Enforcers, and they released their grip on Caeldra after helping her back up. She looked at me gravely.

"Go," I told her, my voice calm, my eyes swimming with tears. This was had to be it. This man in front of me would take me to the Sculptors where I'd die. My life would be over without making a shred of difference. Caeldra didn't move. If they brought me to an interrogation facility, all I would have to do was bite down on the small glass capsule and it would all be over, everyone in the Guild would still be safe.

"Go," I said, my voice barely audible, just a whisper of sorrow that wanted nothing more than for her to escape with her life while she still had it. It was too late for me, but it didn't have to be for her.

She ran away from the scene and disappeared around a corner a few seconds later.

"Now, shall we depart, Mr. Ashton?" Marwin said as he waved his gloved hand to the interior of the drop ship. I was helped into the dropship and seated in a comfortable chair, strapped in with a seat belt that extended across both shoulders and across my waist. Marwin sat beside me and took off the gloves. The Enforcers stayed behind to clean up the crime scene, and the dropship roared to life and lifted off the ground. Terror and disbelief flooded my mind. What was happening to me? Why was I still alive? Why was Caeldra allowed to leave? Marwin handed me a pair of headphones and I placed them over my ears, they blocked out the loud roar of the engines.

"I'm sure you have a million questions, and they will all be answered in due time. For now, we need to prepare you for your welcoming   ceremony.   We're   headed   to   Olympus."

30

OLYMPUS

The ship rose from the streets of the Slums at an alarming rate, making the buildings appear microscopic through the frosted window on the side of the armored ship. Vents overhead pumped hot air into the cabin of the ship that warmed my cold body. We were rising along one of the massive support beams that held the ceiling of the Slums, some three thousand feet above the surface. My vision was temporarily blocked as we rose through what looked to be a vertical tunnel, then a few minutes later we were in a different level of the city. The difference was staggering. The buildings were taller and more organized. There were cars all over the roads as well, cars that looked a lot newer than the ones in the Slums. There were trees and wide open spaces that looked like they were covered in grass even though it was brown. Those were parks, I thought as I remembered the pictures in the Thought Collection Parlors.

"Is this Olympus?" I asked Marwin as I soaked in the foreign sight.

"Oh heavens no, these are the Mids. Still, it's probably a lot different from what you're used to, and it's going to take some getting used to when we arrive in Olympus. You're quite literally going from nothing to royalty."

"Royalty?" I asked, testing the unfamiliar word.

"Well yes, you've created the thirteenth Paragon Thought. That doesn't go unrewarded," he said with a grin. "My great grandfather was responsible for the fifth Paragon Thought; he was the first of House Zaris."

I had no recollection of what the Paragon Thought could have been. A more sinister idea popped into my head; this was all some elaborate trap for me to keep my guard down before the Sculptors could get me, but why would this man sit with me without any guards if he thought I was dangerous?

The ship continued to fly upward, and we approached one final tunnel.

"You're cleared for entrance into Olympus," a voice called in my headphones.

The ship cleared the tunnel, and I felt my breathing stagger. The entire Upper Level was one building, but there seemed to be several larger buildings on top of the one massive structure. Everything was covered in a shimmering blue glass that reflected light from the sun, a glowing ball that shone in the dull sky. I had never seen the sky before or the sun. It was so bright that I couldn't even look at it through the window. Clouds like the ones I had seen in drawings moved in the vast sky around us. It was staggering, breathtaking, and I had the overwhelming sense of being unrestricted. Had I not known the laws of physics, I may have been scared of being sucked up into the sky, getting lost forever in the vast, endless space above.

We approached the buildings on top of the huge glass structure below, landing on a platform before the engines of the ship revved down.

"Welcome to Olympus," Marwin said as he unbuckled his seatbelt. The door of the dropship opened, and we were escorted by more robots that looked like Enforcers, but these ones were trimmed in golden metal. An insignia that was the shape of a shield with decorative patterns on the interior was branded on each of them.

"This is House Zaris, you'll have your own house soon enough. I'm to bring you to the Supreme Leader myself for introductions and your commencement. My stewards will tend to your clothing situation and get you dressed for the ceremony. Guards, please escort Mr. Ashton to the stewards and bring him back to my study when he is prepared."

A robot gave him a bow and pulled my wheelchair from the dropship—I hadn't even seen them take it from the ground back in the Slums. The bag of tea had somehow remained lodged between the seat and armrest when it had been thrown from the truck.

"You are absolved of anything that may have happened in the Slums. Your leg will be looked at again before your ceremony, and we'll be sure you're in good shape. I noticed it on the scanner

when we found you," Marwin told me as I was wheeled off into the vast building.

The floors appeared to be made out of some kind of polished white stone, and various decorations and paintings lined the high arching walls. The air was so fresh, even outside. Cold, yes, but I couldn't sense any smog or dense gasses that made the air hard to breathe. The inside of the house was delightfully warm, and I saw a fireplace with inviting flames burning with an orange glow. A few women wearing dresses with the Zaris emblem passed me and gave me curious smiles as I was wheeled through in my tattered clothes. They were all wearing a variety of makeup, something that would have been very costly in the Slums. I smiled back as I passed, and was moved into a smaller room that was filled with rolls of expensive looking fabric and various pieces of shiny metal equipment. A small man with dark skin and short hair moved from behind one of the machines and gave me a smile as I approached. He was wearing an expensive looking suit, the kind I'd seen in movies and drawings.

"Ah, you must be Jacob Ashton, soon to be Baron Ashton. I'm very excited to meet you. I am Richard Brady, Head Steward and Tailor of House Zaris. I'll be designing your clothes for your ceremony this evening. We can always make changes later, and I imagine you'll have your own stewards and tailors soon enough. Now, Jacob, what are your favorite colors?" he asked as he pulled a pencil from his pocket and a small paper notepad.

"Bright orange," I said. Everything felt like a dream. Was it possible that I was actually subdued somewhere else, and this was some sort of projection? The memory of being trapped in the hospital within my mind was a testament to my mental abilities in creating lifelike projections.

"Hmm, how about a dark ashen gray with bright orange trimming? That would suit you nicely, and it will distinguish you from House Orin, who uses dark orange," he said as he jotted something down on the paper.

"Sure," I responded.

"Very well, I'll have your clothes ready in an hour. I'm sure they'll want to take care of your grooming," he said as I was wheeled out of the room. The robot pushed me to a section of the house where a beautiful woman in her thirties approached. "Welcome, Mr. Ashton. Please head into the bathroom at your convenience and have a seat at the barber system before bathing. Once you're ready, you can change into the clothes I left on the counter while you wait for your new ones. You can just leave your old clothes anywhere, and we'll take care of them," she told me.

"Thanks," I replied as I wheeled myself into the bathroom. The floors were made of the same white stone and steam floated from a huge glass box that looked to be the bath. A mint-like aroma filled the large bathroom, and the door closed behind me after I had passed through. There was a large red leather chair with a machine with several robotic arms mounted to the back. The chair was coated in brilliant chrome, and the arms of the chair held various tools for cutting hair. I moved from the wheelchair to the barber chair, and a screen flashed before me with several options on the screen—pictures of me with different haircuts. I selected one that was shorter and a lot cleaner that what I had currently, and the robotic arms made quick work of my hair as I remained completely still, admiring the strange tech.

After my hair was done, I took off my clothes and opened the door to the bath. I stepped down on glass steps carefully and waded into the hot water. It wasn't exactly the same smell of the mint gum that I used to chew in the Slums, but it was close enough to bring back strong memories. Inevitably, the mint scent brought back memories of Mary and the sticks of gum we would chew. I then thought of the impossibility of my situation. The Government may have favored me for creating a Paragon Thought, but I had a feeling that goodwill would quickly fade if they learned the true extent of my treason.

I let loose a sigh of relief as I relaxed in the water, it was a luxury beyond anything I had ever known in my life. For the first time since I had arrived, I thought of Caeldra, the girl that probably thought I was dead, and that was lost in an unfamiliar district, apparently betrayed by the Scavenger Guild. If anyone could survive, it was her. I was just thankful that she had been spared, but I wanted nothing more than to talk to her, to tell her that I was alright. She would be dealing with her inner demons and the guilt of believing her actions had led to my death. I knew the guilt she felt and wished I could just reach out and let her know that it was all okay.

Still, there was no way to tell exactly where Mindshift had ended up. We couldn't allow the Government to get it, but I was powerless in doing anything about that.

I would have to find some way to get in contact with the Champions, to let them know that I had infiltrated the Upper

Level of New York and had the opportunity to gather unfathomable information for the Guild.

I submerged my freshly cut hair under the water and scrubbed it. After pulling my head back above water, I slid back into one of the underwater seats and relaxed as jets of water massaged my back. I took the time to think about my situation, about Caeldra and what I would do for the Champions. There were still too many unknowns. I still didn't know if this was a trap, and I didn't know what, if anything, my new title would permit me to do. Still, being the first of the Champions to ever see the Upper Level or Olympus as Marwin had called it was incredible. I had to be strong, now more than ever. I had to do everything in my power to keep my identity a secret and do everything I could to help the people in the Slums, and to fight for the truth.

After a few more minutes, I got out of the bath and dried off with a soft white towel. I put on some underclothes made of the softest cloth I had ever felt in my life and sat back down in my wheelchair. The robot waiting outside wheeled me back to the tailor where my dress clothes were waiting.

"Ah, Baron Ashton, I do like the haircut," Richard said.

The steward laid the clothes in front of me, a proud look on his face. The fabric had been shaped into a dark gray tunic and a fine pair of pants, trimmed in bright orange in places and featured a button flap with dark metal buttons.

"All synthetic interior of course! It will regulate your body temperature to keep it just right. Do try them on, I'll give you some privacy," he said as he exited with the robot.

I picked up the clothing that was a lot lighter than it appeared and was shocked to see that it was Nexweave. If I had a Nanotech module, I would be able to manipulate the cloth and change its appearance to that of anything I wanted. I realized that at least one of the machines in the room was probably responsible for manipulating the cloth into the clothes I was wearing now, and that meant that I would have access to Nanotech. Having Nexweave and Nanotech would help, but I had no idea how to make my own modules and program them to meet my specifications if I needed to escape or go on some sort of espionage mission.

I tried on the fancy clothes, and they fit perfectly. I looked in the mirror and was surprised at how different I looked. The clean haircut and clothes made me look better than I ever had before, but it wasn't me, everything was so foreign. I slipped on the polished leather shoes, and Richard walked back into the room giving me a smile.

"You look fantastic, Baron Ashton," he said with a huge grin as he pulled a box from a shelf. "Baron Zaris will want these back eventually, but I'm going to lend you a watch and some cufflinks."

The watch was mechanical and looked much fancier than the one that had belonged to my father—the one that I no longer had in my possession, and the cufflinks looked to be made of solid gold, something with immeasurable value. Gold was nonexistent in the Slums and anyone that tried to trade it was either trading some sort of modified brass or steel-coated lead that was colored with paint. I had been told it simply didn't exist anymore and had been wiped out in the Great Flood of 2039—another lie.

"Are these gold?" I asked the steward as he attached them to the cuffs of my shirt.

"Oh yes, fine pieces in fact. You'll be cautious not to lose them, sir," he said as he finished.

After dressing, I was taken to a doctor to look at my leg with an advanced scanner. The man wore a white coat like the physicians in the Slums, but all of his equipment was stored in temporary cases that looked like they were built for travel. He nodded as he scanned my swollen leg.

"Well, Mr. Ashton. I'm not going to ask questions about your life in the Slums, but you were very lucky to survive, and the doctor that did this surgery did well on the procedure. I'm going to give you some meds to take over the next week, and you'll be fine," he said with a smile.

I was given a few pill bottles and a set of instructions and then wheeled to Marwin Zaris' study. It was a dark colored room with wooden bookshelves stacked high and filled with brightly colored books. It smelled almost exactly like that of the Guild Hall's library. His desk was smooth polished wood as dark as night, and it had small trinkets positioned neatly in front of the massive holo display surface that covered most of the desk.

"Ah, Jacob, I barely recognize you!" Marwin exclaimed as he rose from the chair behind the desk. "I hope you had a pleasant bath."

"I did, thank you," I answered politely as the robot wheeled me up to the other side of the desk.

"Now, let's discuss the business at hand; your commencement ceremony and the establishment of your house. Supreme Leader Adrihel will call you in front of the other houses and give you your

Writ of Nobility, as well as grant you your property in Olympus. You will simply need to thank him, and then the feast in your honor will begin. After it's over, you will be taken to your new home, and you will get situated in your new lifestyle. I'll be happy to help answer any questions you may have that your assigned Steward cannot answer, but Bracken is among the best."

There were hundreds of questions racing through my mind.

"How will I earn money here?" I asked, aware of the staggering expense owning such an estate must cost.

"You'll accrue revenue through taxes paid by citizens of the lower levels whose thoughts anchor to your Paragon Thought. The uniqueness of the thought and strength of the bond will determine your earnings, but you should expect to earn a hefty bonus as the Absolute Knowledge system catches up with its computations and then at least a few hundred units per day after that." I was blown away. It was so much money. Why would I get paid so much for one thought that I couldn't even remember? Marwin smiled at the look on my face.

"Welcome to nobility young sir." After I didn't say anything, he continued. "Once House Ashton is established, you will become the thirteenth house of Olympus. You'll have time to learn the enlightened rules and mechanics of politics, society, and culture in time as you live amongst us. You can choose to keep working as a Thinker to progress Absolute Knowledge further, learn from the knowledge pool or anything else you'd like to do, really."

"Will I be able to return to the Slums?"

"I suppose you could," he frowned. "If you'd like to become an Inquisitor like me. I'm in charge of all the law enforcement in the

Slums as well as investigating into missing persons of interest such as yourself. I must say that you were very hard to track down. If you don't mind me asking, where did you hide?"

"I ended up in the Undercity and must have triggered some kind of trip mine when I was running," I said, telling the truth.

"Interesting. Most don't make it out of that foul sewer system if they end up down there. Anyway, I'm glad to have found you," he said as he renewed the smile on his face.

"Would it be possible to bring someone from the Slums up to live in my house?"

"Possibly. You see, the system we have in place separates our society into three levels based on genetics and complex algorithms that are processed by the Omniscience Engine. Those that are unlikely to amount to anything other than basic thought fodder are placed in the Slums, those with some potential are placed in the Mids and those with the highest potential are placed in Olympus. Sometimes the system gets it wrong, and someone of interest that should be in Olympus lives in the Slums, and we have to take action by relocating that person. The system is damn near perfect, but you are a fraction of a percentage that was missed by the system, and you were even considered based on the performance of your father, who was quite intelligent. Tri-annual testing is used to find those that may have been misplaced. Anyway, it's somewhat of a breach of etiquette to bring just anyone up to Olympus. It can be done in extreme cases, but otherwise, it is quite untraditional and could tarnish the image and reputation of your house."

"I see," I said after considering it.

"I assume you're talking about that blonde girl you were with, Caeldra?" he asked.

"Yes," I responded, not sure if I truly meant Caeldra or Mary.

If I were only able to get one person out of the Slums, it would be Mary. Like me, she had lost her parents. Mary's parents had died in one of the riots that happened when we were only a few years old. The Enforcers had mowed down hundreds of people, and there hadn't been another riot since then. It was long enough ago that most didn't think about it regularly, but any stirrings of rebellion in the Slums were quickly dissolved by those that remembered the massacre. Mary's parents had been caught in the wrong place at the wrong time, and she had grown up with her grandfather until he had passed away the same year my parents died. I missed Mary, I missed Caeldra, and it looked like I might not see either one of them in my life ever again.

"Well, I can see what I can do after you've been situated for a few weeks. She's going to need to visit the Collection Parlor again, though. Supreme Leader Adrihel wouldn't even consider bringing someone up that hasn't visited a Collection Parlor in years—there are too many unknowns."

"That makes sense."

"Anyway, once you take your medication we can head toward House Adrihel for the ceremony. Best to be a little early for such an important occasion," he said with a warm smile.

I returned his smile and pulled out the pill bottles that I had stored in my pockets. He walked over and grabbed a crystal bottle that was highly ornamented with thick engravings, and I saw a bright, brown liquid sloshing inside. He took two glasses from behind the desk and placed them on the table. He placed them under a black rectangular appliance and pressed a button. The machine dispensed two spheres of ice into the glasses with a sharp clink.

"I figure I'll be the first to welcome you to Olympus with a glass of bourbon. This bottle was given to me by my father, and it's over fifty years old," he said as he poured a tiny amount of the liquor over the ice spheres. "If you don't like it, I will finish your drink for you and I won't take any offense," he said with a smile as he slid a glass to me. I lifted the glass and Marwin toasted.

"I'm looking forward to getting to know you better, Jake. And I'm excited for the future of our two houses as we go forward," he said with a wide grin as we clinked the glasses together and drank. The sour liquor went down with a sharp burn, filling my stomach with fire. I was reminded of my time with Caeldra just yesterday and was amazed at how long ago it had felt. I was now quite literally drinking with the enemy of my Guild, an Inquisitor in the flesh, responsible for all the oppression that I had sworn to fight.

"To our houses," I responded after we had finished our drinks. A wave of steady calmness flowed through me.

31
COMMENCEMENT

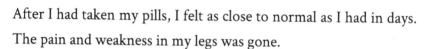

After I had taken my pills, I felt as close to normal as I had in days. The pain and weakness in my legs was gone.

"The Omniscience Engine has advanced our medicine capabilities significantly, and we're able to treat most anything. You'll need to take it easy for the evening and the next few days as you recover from your surgery. I checked the records, and it doesn't appear the surgery took place in any legal establishment," he said with a frown. "Not that it really matters anymore, and nothing will happen to those that are responsible but will you tell me where you got the surgery?" he asked as he drank water from a glass bottle.

Not wanting to hurt the trust I was hoping to earn, I decided to come clean, for the most part.

"Well, I fell down some sort of drain and ended up in one of the underground rivers. I was picked up by a fisherman—this was after my accident with the trip mine. I ended up in River's Port and managed to trade for a new pair of clothes and my surgery with the money I had on hand, all of my life's savings to be precise," I said as I looked him squarely in his dark brown eyes.

Marwin scratched his thin beard as he considered this, and apparently saw no reason to suspect that I was lying. What truth I had bent, I had done through layering my mind and convincing myself that everything I was saying was truth.

"Well, I'm glad you are alright, River's Port gives us no problems. We have agents there who take care of any treasonous felons that might harm the structure of everything we've worked so hard to build. The majority of the citizens there are harmless and quite honestly not worth the price of elimination."

Not wanting to say anything else about the Undercity and potentially give away any of my knowledge, I decided to shift the topic of conversation.

"I'm ready to leave whenever you are," I said as I enjoyed being able to stand.

"Certainly, let's depart to House Adrihel. We wouldn't want to be late to your own party."

We walked together through the expansive hallways of House Zaris and exited through a heavy wooden and glass door onto the landing platform. It was dark outside now, and the distant sun cast sullen purple waves toward the darkness, I had no words to describe the beauty of my first sunset. The lights on the platform illuminated the stone landing platform. There was a smaller, sportier looking ship waiting for us, with a robot sitting in the pilot's seat. This ship wasn't armored like the dropship we had flown in. The exterior was painted in the gray and brown color scheme of House Zaris, and had two small thrusters located on the sides of two of the short wings that spread from the narrow frame. We climbed in and were seated as the doors closed.

The ship roared to life and lifted from the platform quickly. As we climbed toward the building in the center of Olympus, I could see all the different colored lights in all the houses of Olympus. Each one was illuminated in their own unique color scheme. House Adrihel was illuminated in bright white light that reflected against the copper and gold colored exterior of the huge building, at least three times the size of House Zaris. Below us, I could see the colossal building that must have contained the Absolute Knowledge project and the computers and servers needed to maintain the daunting task of trying to calculate infinity.

We landed on a huge landing platform where two other ships had already docked. Gold and copper robots walked all over the platform accomplishing various tasks and tending to the vacant vehicles. We were escorted out of the ship by a man wearing a black suit and copper tie. The air was cold against my face, but the Nexweave clothes adapted and kept me warm. Huge guard robots were lining the edges of the doors; they regarded us as politely as robots could. The entry hall of House Adrihel was even more lavish than that of Marwin's home. We passed a tall, thin woman wearing a bright blue dress and extravagant makeup, she was stunning. "Baroness Jex Brae," Marwin whispered as we passed. The Baroness smiled as she looked at me. I returned the smile and kept up with Marwin's brisk speed, surprised that my leg and body were still functioning so well. One of the servants of the house led us to a heavy wooden door marked Ashton with a golden plaque.

"When your name is called, walk through that door. It's going to be a few minutes until the ceremony commences, just remember to thank Supreme Leader Adrihel. A simple thank you will suffice nicely," Marwin told me as he headed toward his own door. A servant walked over and handed me a glass of water. I drank from it in slow sips and saw that more people were beginning to arrive, they were dressed in clothes similar to mine, in different colors.

I still wasn't sure how the whole House system worked, or if I would be considered an equal to the other Barons and Baronesses. The strong polarity of this environment compared with the Slums was mind boggling. The servant returned and took my glass from me. "You're going to be called soon, sir," he told me as he bowed and walked away.

The announcer began to call the houses. "House Aera. House Brae." He was pausing between houses, giving them time to enter. I took a deep breath. "House Carson. House Gareth. House Kai. House Kasra. House Orin. House Rylan. House Sylas. House Windhelm. House Zaris. And the soon to be House Ashton!" the voice called after the others had been announced.

I took a deep breath and pushed open the door. I entered a huge room that held a massive table in the center of the room. Heavy crystal chandeliers were hanging from the ceiling and a crowd of people gathered, all wearing different colored clothes. A band played classical music in the corner quietly. Everyone was clapping and smiling for me, welcoming me to this new life. The massive walls were ornamented in paintings and sculptures that covered parts of the extravagantly decorated wallpaper. Large golden drapes covered the rectangular windows that lined the walls, concealing the view of the outside of the building and the cold night sky. Even through my shoes, I could feel how soft the carpet was as I walked across the room.

I did my best to smile as I walked forward toward the servant that was ushering me forward. A strong looking man walked forward to greet me, he was wearing a dark black suit with a copper and gold tie. His dark black hair was neatly cut and combed to the side. He had a beard much like Marwin's, except it was black instead of gray. He held his arms open in a wide arc. The man I could only assume to be Supreme Leader Adrihel was right before me, welcoming and polite. The leader of the Government.

"Ah, Jacob Ashton, it is my great pleasure to welcome you to my house and this ceremony this day," he told me as he shook my hand with a powerful grip. The man towered over me despite the fact that I was almost six feet tall. He gave a friendly smile, his white teeth contrasting against the dark clothing he wore.

"The pleasure is mine, Supreme Leader Adrihel. Please call me Jake," I responded as I shook his hand.

"We are honored to have you join us in Olympus, and can't wait to see how your work will influence the Absolute Knowledge project. We haven't had a Paragon Thought in some time. I am very grateful to Baron Zaris for finding you and bringing you to us in one piece," he said jovially, his voice bellowing throughout the crowded room.

"It's an honor sir," I said as I maintained my composure despite the overwhelming magnificence of the hall.

"Let us commence the ceremony!"

A strange sense of familiarity swept over me as something in my peripheral vision seemed to pull my gaze, and then I saw Mary.

32

HOUSE ASHTON

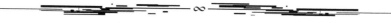

Mary was wearing a dark green dress and had her hair twirled into long ribbons. She was wearing makeup, but I was certain that it was her. She was just standing there smiling at me with all the others. I could feel my body go into shock and I fought to focus and try not to draw attention to the fact that I was in distress. The man in front of me motioned for everyone to quiet down and the music stopped.

"I am pleased to appoint you as Baron Jacob Ashton, the first of House Ashton. Your estate is being prepared as we speak and will be ready for you shortly. You are now Royalty of Olympus!" he exclaimed then turned to the other houses that were standing around us. My head swam as I forced myself to focus on Supreme

Leader Adrihel rather than Mary. I couldn't comprehend anything that he was saying.

"We are reminded and humbled once again that the mind is a beautiful thing. A single mind may stand out on its own, but the collective power of our people is a greater force than any other. With Baron Ashton's Paragon Thought, the thirteenth and the rise of House Ashton into our ranks, we celebrate!" he shouted in a voice pitched to carry through the massive dining hall. He wrapped a muscled arm around my shoulder and pulled me in close. "We are truly glad you are here, Baron," he said through a warm smile, speaking only to me now.

"Thank you, Supreme Leader Adrihel," I responded as Marwin had instructed.

"When it's not on official business, please make it Colton," he said as he gave me a firm squeeze as if we had been lifelong friends. "Now, let the feast begin!" he called to the surrounding houses as huge platters of food were brought through doors on the sides of the rooms by a combination of robot and human servants.

I was seated next to Supreme Leader Colton Adrihel, his wife Supreme Lady Chelsea Adrihel sat to his side, and Baron Neris Gareth, an older man that was wearing a gray tunic with purple trimmings. Beside him sat his wife, Lady Eleanor Gareth who was dressed in a vibrant purple dress.

My plate was stacked with huge piles of steaming meat and vegetables before it was placed in front of me. Beside my ornamented plate were three different forks, two different knives, and two different spoons. A dark purple liquid was poured into my crystal glass by a servant, and as I thanked the man, he nodded graciously. A bowl of some sort of white soup was brought to everyone at the table, and the feast began. I couldn't stop thinking about Mary. Was I going crazy? Why the hell was she here?

Taking the lead of Colton Adrihel and Neris Gareth, I mirrored their utensil usage as they switched between different forks to eat the vegetables and meat, then switched between spoons on the same bowl of soup for different bites. The difference in the soup, I had gathered, had to do with how deeply they were scooping. The heavier of the two spoons was used for scraping the bottom of the soup and pulling out delicious bits of some sort of aquatic meat, and the shallow, smaller spoon was mostly for scooping the soup broth itself without any solids. It didn't seem logical or intuitive at all. The other Barons, Baronesses, Ladies, and Gentlemen of Olympus were talking amongst themselves in small isolated groups. I scanned the table and saw Mary staring at me, her gaze firm and intent. I made eye contact and tried to gesture and indicate that I was confused. She fixed her face with a smile that looked all too fake.

"So, Jacob. I know this is all very new to you, but I'm looking forward to getting to know you better. I'm sure you will enjoy life in Olympus," Colton Adrihel said with a smile as he finished his soup, pulling me away from Mary's gaze, but I had to confirm it was her.

"Yes, I am very much enjoying my stay so far," I replied. "That girl over there, the one in green. I know her from the Slums, she is Mary Dunn, correct?" I asked though I knew without a doubt that was Mary.

"Yes," he replied, a look of puzzlement growing on his face. "We recently learned that she was a descendant of House Aera, somehow lost in a system bug by the Omniscience Engine. We brought her to her new life rather recently. It's kind of interesting how connected everything really is," he remarked.

"I should like to speak with her later if that's alright," I said, remaining calm despite the fact that talking with Mary was the only thing on my mind.

"Why of course! You will have adequate time after the feast and during the dance. Please, try the wine," he said as he swirled the glass in the light, smelled the contents, then sipped it thoughtfully, a look of satisfaction forming on his face. "It's quite delicious. A rare case of Gutte D'Or, bottled in the early twenty-first century."

I smelled the wine in my own glass before taking a slow sip. It was strong and sour, but it went well with the meal, contrasting with the savory and buttery flavors of the soup and meat.

"It's magnificent," I remarked as I swallowed another sip. "Was it bottled after the flood of 2039?" I asked.

"Before. It's a two thousand and four, and it has been stored well for all this time," he said, eyeing me with curiosity.

"The name of the wine is rather unfamiliar to me?" I asked.

"It's a French wine," he responded as he drank again. "Ah, Jake, I forget that you're from the Slums. You'll be able to learn more about our country's actual history soon enough, as royalty. Letting the Slums have access to that knowledge would impede our progress with Absolute Knowledge," he said as he finished the glass and waved for another.

"I see. I would be very interested in learning all that I can about the project so I can better serve my country," I said as I downed the last of the wine in my glass.

"And you will, Baron Ashton," he remarked. "We are delighted to have you with us and look forward to the accelerated development of the project with your Paragon Thought and continued efforts. I'll have you taken to the facility to learn all about it from our lead engineers whenever you are ready. Let's get you settled into your new life and home first, though," he said as he drank from the new glass of wine.

Lavish desserts were brought to complete the delicious meal, and compliments were made to Colton Adrihel as the servants cleared the table from the room, so there was adequate space for dancing and other festivities. The band in the corner began to play loudly, and the dancing started. I was unfamiliar with the style of the different court dances that were performed, so I mostly stood idle in the corner, sipping on wine, appreciating the music and watching the movements of the people dancing.

At one point, Baroness Jex Brae pulled me from my spot and handed my wine glass to a servant. She took me to the dance floor and walked me through the necessary steps of one of the easier dances. Her twirling blonde hair flowed with elegance and grace with her bright blue dress as she went through the motions. Having no prior experience with dancing, I decided to try to follow her lead to the best of my ability.

"I'm glad you are here," she told me as she lifted my arm and spun under it with a quick motion, her glittering makeup sparkling in the bright lights. The music quickened, and she upped our pace as we glided over the dance floor. One of my hands held hers while the other was placed on her firm waist. There was a quick succession of rapid notes, and she dipped down, leaning back against my arm in an exaggerated motion as the song finished. There was a wave of applause as the song ended and I noticed everyone's eyes were on me. Baroness Brae leaned in and kissed me on the cheek. "Thank you for the dance, Baron Ashton," she whispered in my ear. I felt myself blush. Marwin approached and smiled at the both of us.

"Baroness Brae, our new Baron needs to refrain from vigorous physical activity for the coming days as he recovers from a wound incurred in the Slums. Perhaps you will allow me the next dance so he might recover?" Marwin said in a polite tone as he raised his hand to hers.

"Of course, Baron Zaris. I do apologize, Baron Ashton, and I look forward to when you are well so that we can participate in some vigorous physical activity together," she cooed, giving Marwin a sly smile. She took his hand, and they returned to the dance floor when the music continued.

I took my place on the side of the room again and saw Mary approaching me from the other side. My heart started pounding in my chest.

"Baron Ashton," she regarded me as she approached, wine glass in hand.

"How the hell are you here?" I whispered, my voice low and sharp despite the control I exhibited over my facial expression.

"Apparently I'm a descendant of one of House Aera. I thought you were dead," she said, tears forming in her eyes, despite her calm composure.

I suddenly felt guilty for everything, a sinking feeling blanketing me and burning in the pit of my stomach.

"It turns out I'm a Paragon Thinker, I thought the Enforcers were after me again for the purse incident, that's why I ran that day, and I want you to know that I'm sorry."

"You haven't been yourself ever since that Enforcer broke your wrist. I know that you're hiding something from me, and if you don't want to tell me what then that's fine, but don't you dare lie to me," she said, her voice as cold as steel.

I hadn't made any attempt to layer my thoughts to try to establish truth to the lie. I had no reason to guard myself around Mary, but I knew I couldn't tell her everything that had happened. The stakes were too high now, one mistake here, and I was dead. I had the feeling that my actions would be watched closely as I was Initiated into my new life.

"I'm sorry I can't tell you more right now," I said, utterly defeated. "Could we talk sometime once I'm settled in, and we have a little more space?"

She nodded. "Baron Ashton," she remarked with a small curtsey and walked away from me as quickly as she had approached.

The rest of the night dragged on painfully. I had no desire to socialize, to attempt to meet new people or to dance, but I was forced to maintain a fake smile as I was introduced to all the members of the other houses. I was confident that I would forget most of their names by the morning. My conversation with Mary continued to replay in my head. Something wasn't right here, I knew it when I first arrived despite the appearance of everything. I realized since I had arrived here that my guard had slipped dramatically. I felt the effects of the wine on my body and knew that I had to be more careful. If I wasn't, one reckless mistake could cost my life and the life of Mary. Now that I knew it was actually her, I couldn't do anything to endanger her life, and that meant distancing myself from her and limiting what I told her. I realized with grim certainty that I might not ever be able to tell her the truth and that our relationship—or whatever was left of that relationship—could be lost forever.

"I thank you all for attending tonight's lovely feast. I look forward to another soon!" Supreme Leader Adrihel called after the final notes of a song.

With that, the party was disbanded, and the houses left House Adrihel in their transport ships. I was surprised to see that a ship was waiting for me, the same model as the others. It was painted in charcoal gray and bright orange, the colors of my House.

"I hope to see you tomorrow, Jacob," Marwin said as he waved from the entrance of his ship.

I waved back and climbed into the seat of the ship. The side hatch closed and the robotic pilot in the front seat flew me to my new manor, which was illuminated by bright orange lights. All I could do was think about Mary.

By the time I had arrived at my new home I was exhausted. The floor, much like Marwin's, was polished stone, but it was darker. The walls were vastly undecorated, but a few furnishings were scattered throughout the main hallway. The robotic pilot guided me to the master bedroom and bowed as it exited.

I flipped on the light and was unsurprised to see the most comfortable looking bed I had ever seen in my life. The room was carpeted instead of tiled, and a huge TV sat on a wooden dresser that was pressed against the wall. There was a massive closet filled with clothes in my colors, and a set of doors beside it that lead to my master bathroom. I couldn't see any cameras or anything to indicate that I was being watched or listened to, but I would have to be careful, especially to not talk in my sleep.

I decided that a bath would do me some good, and entered the bathroom that was almost exactly the same as the one in Marwin's estate. After toggling a switch on a control panel, the bath fired up, and the scent of mint filled the room as the pale green water flooded the huge tub. I climbed out of my dress clothes and slipped into the hot bath. I had to find a way to get in contact with the Guild, but I had nothing to share yet. I knew nothing more of the Absolute Knowledge project other than the fact that something called the Omniscience Engine was the driving technology behind innovation and that I had helped speed up its progress.

Caeldra probably thought I was dead right now, and if she hadn't made it back yet, the Guild would think we were both dead and that the Government knew everything.

The bath did little to help me relax, and I wrapped myself in a thick robe after toweling off. I turned off the lights and faded into a deep sleep on the extravagant bed.

∞

I awoke to beams of sunlight piercing through the windows on the edge of my room. It was already almost eleven, and I had no idea what my itinerary for the day would be. Stretching my arms above my head, I yawned and frowned when I couldn't move my leg. I grabbed the pill bottles and hobbled to the bathroom sink where I scooped up a handful of water from the faucet and downed the pill concoction. Though I was wary of drinking from the tap, the water was some of the clearest I had ever seen. I supposed it was to be expected in a place like this—my home, I thought bitterly. After the pills had kicked in, I was able to walk down the hallway to the common area, which consisted of the kitchen, dining room, and one of the three living rooms in my estate. A robot stood in the kitchen, cooking some breakfast in a gleaming skillet over a low blue flame. There was a familiar bubbling sound as I looked to see the pot of coffee brewing to the side.

"Good morning, Baron Ashton," the robot said as it flipped the contents of the skillet in the air with a single deft motion. "Your breakfast will be ready soon, and your Head Steward will be here in half an hour."

I nodded and took a seat at the dining room table, still soaking in the fact that I wasn't dreaming, and that Olympus did exist. There was also the mixed relief and guilt I was feeling, now that Mary was back in my life. I had hurt her in ways I could have never imagined doing to the one so dear to me. She didn't deserve this, and I hated what I had put her through. I looked up when I saw the small robot approaching.

The shining robot carried over my plate of breakfast which consisted of eggs, toast, and bacon and a cup of simmering coffee.

"Cream or sugar in your coffee, sir?" it asked.

"Black is fine," I responded as I adjusted the positioning of the plate and cup in front of me.

The robot gave a bow and headed toward another part of the house. "If you need anything just call, sir," it said as it departed.

The house robots were much smaller than Enforcers and probably weighed around two hundred pounds. They were Artisan class robots and were built for activities that involved a requirement for precision. The guards, like the ones outside of House Adrihel were another thing entirely, closer to a Golem class like my robotic father had been. The resemblance was uncomforting, actually. While the guards were smaller than a Golem class robot, they were still larger than an Enforcer and wielded weapons unlike any I had ever seen. I wasn't sure if I had any guards yet and if I did, I didn't know if they were protecting me, or keeping me prisoner in this strange place.

As I finished my breakfast, a middle-aged man appeared from the hall, carrying a large datapad with him. He wore my new colors on his suit and large lens spectacles were perched on his nose. His faded brown hair was wiry but was maintained with a thin layer of sculpting paste.

"Baron Ashton, it's a pleasure. My name is Bracken Rowe," the man said as he looked at some kind of alert on his datapad and pushed it aside. "I'm your Head Steward, and I'll be tending to your affairs in Olympus and maintaining the estate."

"It's nice to meet you," I replied as I stood to shake his hand.

"Now, today we need to design your house insignia, set up your Olympus bank accounts, and order some furnishings for your estate. Also, I will hire staff to maintain everything while you are away," he said as he pressed something on the datapad again.

"Will it be possible to visit the Omniscience Engine today? I'd like to learn more about it."

"Not today I'm afraid, we've got a full slate," he replied. "Now, first, I've had an artist draw up some insignia sketches to consider," he said as he put the datapad in front of me. The first one was a sword with orange edges and a regal looking 'A' below it. Another was an orange eagle against a triangle with a dark background. I didn't even have to look at the others.

"The eagle, that's the one," I said with confidence.

"Wonderful choice, sir," Bracken exclaimed. "I'll have some more variations of it drawn, and we can go from there."

I didn't have to think about it. The eagle used to stand for freedom and liberty, and it was a well-known icon of the Champions of Liberty as well. I wasn't supposed to know anything about those concepts, so I didn't think anyone would be suspicious of my choice.

Bracken set up my bank accounts which were preloaded with over one million credits. He moved some of the credits to interest-bearing accounts which would accrue extra earnings by lending my money to the Government and set up the account which would be linked to my Paragon Thought and the Omniscience Engine. It took a little while for me to understand the whole banking system since nothing like it had existed in the Slums.

Bracken interviewed me for over half an hour to get a feel for my tastes to order furniture and decorations for the estate that would suit my preferences. He also captured my preferences for meals and styles of clothing that I liked. When he declared my fashion sense improper, I simply accepted it, and he ordered several suits, casual clothes which exceed the cost of my rent down in the Slums, and dress tunics, trousers and shoes like the ones I had worn to the ceremony the night before. After all of that, Bracken returned the cufflinks and watch that I had borrowed from Marwin through a courier bot on a small cargo ship that arrived a few minutes after his request.

"Do we need to discuss payment for your services?" I asked him.

"No sir, my earnings and the earnings of my staff will come from the account linked to the Paragon Thought, no need to worry about it. Your estate is in good hands," he said as he put aside the datapad. "Now, I suppose that I'll need to teach you some proper etiquette should the Supreme Leader decide to throw any more revelries," he said with a laugh. "Etiquette tends to degrade as the consumption of alcohol increases, but it's good to know your basics, so House Ashton won't be regarded lowly."

"What kind of etiquette?" I asked.

"Customs, dining, and dance. The three basics," he replied with a smile. "Since you've already eaten, we'll start with customs. If you do not know someone's title at an event, you should always address them as sir or madam, as any other form of address could be rude. If you were to call a Baroness a lady, they might take offense, but calling a gentleman or Baron sir will not cause any offense. Sir will suffice in casual situations with Supreme Leader Adrihel, but never when formality is required."

"And what if I'm visiting the Slums?" I asked.

Bracken frowned at this. "Unless you're planning on becoming an Inquisitor, then pray you never visit that vile place again. There are no established etiquette rules for the Slums in which a noble must behave, other than the fact that you must not speak of Olympus and must take an Enforcer Dropship rather than any personal aircraft. There are hundreds of small rules that you'll pick up in time, no one is expecting you to act as a perfect Baron yet. We all understand that being the first of your house is a significant burden."

Bracken instructed me on some of the smaller, more subtle laws of Olympus and gave some history lessons on important lineage of the houses that could come up in conversation. He explained some rules of dance and the slight difference in expected behavior when speaking with different ranks of people within Olympus.

"Okay, what else do I need to know?"

"Well, that's all we need to worry about for today regarding etiquette and history. We'll learn a bit each day, but there'll be much more to cover when you decide to try to court some young lady," he said with a wink.

Bracken proceeded to teach me about the different eating utensils for formal occasions and the acceptable uses of each. The deep-bottom spoon was acceptable for the first seven bites of a stew, the first three of soup, and the first five of a chowder, at which point the tasting spoon, the smaller of the two, was expected to be used for at least three bites. The four-pronged fork was acceptable for almost anything other than seafood, and the three-pronged fork was to be used for seafood or dessert should the host not provide a separate set of dessert utensils, which apparently had their own unique rules. I learned the crucial differences between the steak knife, the butter knife, and the thin-bladed crustacean knife used to break apart lobster or crab shells when eating a more casual meal.

"Could you please have Lady Mary Dunn of House Aera come see me later today?" I asked, now knowing the difference between a Lady and Baroness. Barons and Baronesses were the direct descendants of a Paragon Thinker, while everyone in the house that was distantly related or married into the family became a Lady or Gentleman.

"Certainly, sir. I'll inquire if she will see you."

After all the etiquette lessons I could handle for the day, I ate a simple lunch of spiced rice and beef as Bracken called House Aera to set up a meeting. The meeting was set up and Mary was to arrive in an hour. Bracken addressed a few more issues then bowed as he took his leave to take care of furnishing the estate, hiring employees, and finalizing the insignia design of House Ashton. It was so strange for me to go from a position of nothingness to one of what seemed to be great power and opulence. I had more money than could ever be spent by someone in the Slums and nothing to spend it on but pointless luxuries. It was good that I wasn't very attached to the material world—it would help me focus as I sought to do what I could for the Champions during my stay. I was convinced that I would return to the Slums, and to the Guild Hall again, and possibly get Mary out of this place as well. It wasn't right that we should have so much while others had so little.

I once again returned to the bathroom attached to my bedroom and decided to take another bath in the minty water that was mixed with what Bracken had called Eucalyptus, a plant with many useful health benefits—or so he told me. I soaked in the water and thought about what I was going to tell Mary. I could tell her that I got into some trouble and saw something I wasn't supposed to and... Then what? Would I tell her that Mr. Barton was actually one of the leaders of an illegal organization that defied the Government in almost every way? It was impossible.

I continued to ponder for some time and jumped when Bracken's voice spoke over the console on the wall. "Sir, Lady Dunn will be here shortly," he said.

"Thank you, Bracken," I replied as I emerged from the tub and put on some of the casual clothes, a pair of soft jeans and a button-up shirt that I tucked in. I pulled on my new sneakers, gray with orange laces, and walked out to the main door of my estate, the door that led to the landing pad where Mary would be arriving. The landing pad wasn't as big as House Adrihel's, but it could still hold a few ships.

Mary arrived in House Aera's dark green transport ship and walked out. She gave me a weak smile when she entered my home. Bracken had already cleared out, and we had the whole house to ourselves aside from the house robots. Wanting privacy, I led her to the media room in my house and turned on some classical music in the background that would drown out our conversation.

"Mary, I'm so sorry for everything. I got into a lot of trouble down in the Slums. I didn't want to put you in any danger," I said.

"You need to tell me exactly what happened. You were absolved of all crimes when you arrived here, it's all in the past. If you want to start a life with me, then there needs to be communication between us, and no more lies."

"I read a treasonous book and turned to a life of being a criminal in the Undercity because I couldn't work as a Thinker anymore. I was scavenging for anything to sell," I said, cursing myself for the lies.

Her cold eyes appraised me.

"Do you still have the sketchbook I gave you?" I asked. She nodded and handed it to me. I asked for a pencil, and she pulled one from her bag.

"I want to show you a new sketching technique," I said. I flipped to a blank page and began to write as small and light as I could.

'I'm not safe, they'll kill you if I tell you the truth, they're probably listening and watching us,' I wrote before passing her the sketch. "Pretty cool technique, huh?" I asked as she read.

She looked up, her eyes shimmering with tears before pulling me into a hug. "This is a strange place. I'm not sure why I'm here, but it's very intimidating the way everyone is watching me and listening to what I have to say. Thank you, Jake, that is a cool technique," she said, following along. "Perhaps we could have dinner later this evening if you're not busy?"

"I'd very much enjoy that," I said, genuinely meaning it. "I'm glad that you're here with me."

We talked for a couple of hours, catching up and speaking in code, trying to return to normal despite the rift that had formed between us. I hated not being able to tell her everything.

"You should have seen the way Baroness Brae was looking at you last night," she said, blushing.

"I lived it," I replied with a smile. "But, she's too old for me," I added before scooping up Mary in a hug. It was unbelievable how good it felt to hold her in my arms.

"But she's beautiful," Mary added.

"Yes, I can't argue with that," I agreed, smiling at her. Mary frowned. "But, you're much prettier," I said, and I meant it.

She blushed and looked down, smiling as she pulled out of the hug.

"Are we alright?" I asked.

"Yes, but I think we need to take things slow," she replied, her voice cautious.

"I agree." It couldn't be further from the truth. I still felt guilty for kissing Caeldra in the Undercity.

"I think," she said slowly, "I think that we should just be friends for now," she finished with a heavy sigh.

"I agree; I don't think either of us have adjusted to our new lifestyles. The events of the past few weeks have damaged our relationship. I think we need to actively work on mending our relationship as friends before we can proceed to establish a romantic relationship should we choose to go that down path," I said, careful with my words.

She hugged me and rested against my shoulder. "Thanks, Jake," she said as tears rolled down her face. "I never want to lose you again."

"I don't want to lose you either. Again, I'm so sorry," I said as I kissed the top of her hair; it smelled like sweet strawberries.

"Whatever happened, it's in the past now. We've got our whole lives ahead of us," Mary said as she wiped the tears from her eyes. "We can start over."

If only that were the case. I still had every intention of following through with my work for the Champions and liberating the people of the Slums. My ambition to learn more about the Absolute Knowledge project was driving me crazy. I was so close now, so close to making a difference and making things right.

I made a promise to myself at that moment that I wouldn't involve Mary in anything that would endanger her life, even if that meant pushing her away and limiting our relationship. If anyone suspected me and I had a strong relationship with her, she could be accused of things she had nothing to do with. I would have some tough decisions ahead of me, but for now, I just enjoyed her company, her resting on my shoulder, and the relaxing music playing in the background.

We ate a lavish dinner and returned to the media room after. Mary sat down on the couch, and I sat beside her. She was staring at me.

"Are you okay?" I asked.

"Yes, it just all feels so strange. It might be horrible to say, but I wish we were back in the Slums. Things were easier, the little things mattered. I'd trade all this luxury for my old life. It sounds so selfish to say that while so many people are suffering. Anyone else would want this life, but not me."

"I get what you're saying. Believe me, I wish I could undo what I've done. I hate myself for my actions and for hurting you. You've changed my life, Mary. Seeing you every day back in the Slums was always the highlight of my day. I lived each day looking forward to spending time with you. It didn't matter what we were doing, only that I was doing it with you."

She was tearing up again. "You weren't the only one feeling that. It was mutual, and believe it or not, I was just as scared to tell you how I felt as you probably were. I didn't want to lose you, and was too afraid to take the risk."

Tears were pooling in my eyes. "Edgar tried to convince me to go for it every day, to just tell you how I felt. I can't believe I didn't do it sooner."

Mary leaned in and kissed me on the lips, tears rolling down both of our faces.

"I'd still like to take things slow. But I'm glad we were able to talk," she said. "It's getting late, so I think I'll depart."

"Of course, thank you for coming over today, Mary," I said then walked her to her transport.

When she departed in her transport ship, I decided to take yet another bath in the relaxing herbal waters. Just as I had slipped into the tub, the console speaker on the wall crackled. I look over, unsure of what was happening.

"Bracken?"

"I know what you are," a horrible voice concealed by heavy static said. There was another crackle and then it was gone.

33

OMNISCIENCE ENGINE

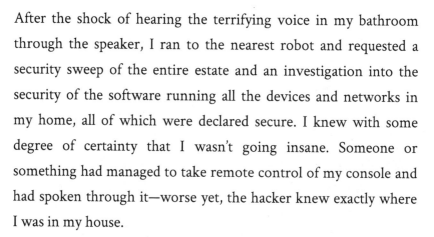

After the shock of hearing the terrifying voice in my bathroom through the speaker, I ran to the nearest robot and requested a security sweep of the entire estate and an investigation into the security of the software running all the devices and networks in my home, all of which were declared secure. I knew with some degree of certainty that I wasn't going insane. Someone or something had managed to take remote control of my console and had spoken through it—worse yet, the hacker knew exactly where I was in my house.

Had it played the message across the entire house intercom, all the robots working would have heard it. I was either being watched, listened to, or both. Seeking some form of comfort, I went to the kitchen and grabbed a long knife that I carried to my room with me. If the hacker had any plans on attacking me, I hoped that they weren't a robot. A knife would do little good against a metal chassis. The cryptic message had sounded more of a warning call than anything else, and I assumed that I wasn't in direct danger yet. I laid in bed with the kitchen knife tucked under the pillow next to me, wishing it was my CZR-7.

∞

The next three weeks went by without any sign of the hacker, and I felt my level of caution had gone down. I still slept with the kitchen knife under my pillow, but I thought less and less about the event that had transpired. I was settling into my life as a Baron well, and I had remained steadfast in my resolve to learn about the Omniscience Engine, and today I would. Inquisitor Zaris was taking me to the facility this morning, and I would finally be able to see with my own eyes the technology behind Absolute Knowledge, to learn about it and potentially be able to pass that information to the Champions.

The shuttle arrived at my landing platform, and I was flown down to the huge building that was several hundred feet below all the houses in Olympus. We were heading toward the facility that housed Absolute Knowledge.

"It doesn't look terribly impressive, but the work done by the Omniscience Engine means everything to us," Marwin told me as we descended. We landed on a metal landing platform and were escorted out by some armed robots that looked like new Enforcers without the damages and wear from the Slums. The huge glass walling of the building reflected the sun's beams in a blinding light, and a large door opened as we approached, the guard robots trailing behind us.

"This is the central facility. I'll take you to the Omniscience Engine first, and we'll go from there. It's best you see that first."

"It's freezing in here," I remarked, surprised as the temperature dropped as we walked inside.

"Well, the processors work at absolute zero—they are quantum based, and the tech behind them has to be supercooled to function. Most of this building is just storage structures and the servers that maintain everything. The Omniscience Engine actually adjusts all of its code as it goes, so the firmware is always up to date, and all the processes are optimized," he told me as we walked through the hallway, light from the outside shining on the polished black metal of the interior of the building.

My Nexweave clothing adapted to fight the cold temperatures, but I still had to tuck my hands in my pockets to stay warm. I also noticed that there were very few humans in the building, but there was no shortage in the robots tasked with the security of the facility.

Marwin took me to a colossal vault door that was secured by a large hydraulic wall mount. He scanned his eye on the retina scanner, and the mechanical arm pulled out the massive vault door—it looked to be at least six feet thick and must have weighed several tons.

There was a large holoprojector in the center which projected what seemed to be a digital map made out of blue light. A huge sphere of brilliant blue light and swirling colors rested at the base of the round projector. Thirteen nodes of bright white light connected the flowing streams of a structure that looked to be made of liquid metal. Light coursed through the closed system as the shape in front of me shifted. New fragments of light were flying from the surface of the projector and flowing into the stream, but all the nodes, what I believed to be the Paragon Thoughts, held together everything else. Some nodes were dark as well, not burning from within like the others.

"This is the Omniscience Engine," Marwin told me as we entered the room.

"It's incredible," I said, in awe of the thing before me.

"It truly is," he responded.

"Can I see what my Paragon Thought was?" I asked.

"No, the Paragon Thoughts aren't anything like an ordinary thought, only the Omniscience Engine understands them, really. Even the original coders of the project didn't know what a Paragon Thought would be—they only theorized what it would look like mathematically."

There were several security robots and a few people dressed in white lab coats, I assumed they were system engineers. The workers were working on multiple tasks throughout the room, interacting with things through the use of datapads. Multiple screens lining the sides of the spherical room displayed varying information and charts to the busy workers. There was a flashing LED bulb from one of the consoles and one of the engineers walked over and typed some things into the keyboard.

"What's going on there?" I asked Marwin, pointing to the engineer.

"The Omniscience Engine just discovered something else that's worth our consideration. Industry and technological innovations are at that console with the yellow light, and law or medical innovations are at the console with the blue light. Those are the recommended innovations, the mandated discoveries and changes are sent directly to Supreme Leader Adrihel," he said.

Shock took over. "So you're saying that this computer makes big decisions for New York?"

"I'm saying that this machine makes all the decisions for New York. Everyone's got a boss," he said, a smile growing on his face. "The Omniscience Engine makes very few mistakes—much less than any human would. Supreme Leader Adrihel only makes decisions for Olympus regarding social behavior. Defining culture in a quantitative way is difficult. Olympus represents the vision of New York's future once we achieve Absolute Knowledge. We're living as close to perfection as we can."

I tried to hide the horror from my face. How could this system be controlling all the robots, all the laws, and all the systems in place in the entire country? And what happened when it decided that it no longer needed humans to exist? It was a ticking time bomb. My father was right.

Marwin must have been able to see the terror on my face, and he gave me a smile.

"Don't worry, Jacob, if the system decided to try to revolt against the humans or do something we don't like, we can manually adjust the parameters of the project to better suit our needs. The system is designed to help us achieve perfection, not create a perfect society for robots."

Marwin walked me over to the holoprojector and explained what I was looking at, as well as the screens that lined the rooms. As we passed the engineers, they gave polite bows.

We then moved to a large window that overlooked a vast collection facility. There were hundreds of chairs connected by thick, coiling cables. In the chairs sat the Prolific. The computer chips installed in their brains caused a hormone imbalance and reduced the brain's ability to regulate chemicals needed to maintain life and health. As a result, their skin was a pale gray, and they were hairless. Purple bags were permanently fixed around their dull eyes, and they were devoid of all emotion that tied them to their humanity.

"The Omniscience Engine is superb at what it does, compounding and improving our thoughts while expanding the Collective Thought, but it's actually quite limited in its ability to generate new and unique thoughts that can be passed through the Paragon Thoughts to form new chains and connections. The Prolific are our top source of original thoughts, and they're paid very well for the physical strain they must endure to be such a great asset to the cause. They are quite literally the zealots of our society," he said.

"There are many more rooms like this one in the facility," he continued as we walked away from the window. Marwin took me up a large elevator, and we ascended slowly, the glass panel on the edge showing the massive array of server and storage blocks stacked high to the ceiling of the interior room. Dim blue LED light was rising from the consoles, and I could see that there were a few strange looking robots tending to some of the blocks of computer equipment.

"This is the actual system that controls the Omniscience Engine we were just at. You'd know it as the Collective Thought. This is all the equipment needed to maintain the system. It's powered by six nuclear reactors which keep surface temperatures very close to absolute zero on all the electronics. The air in there would freeze you to death in seconds if you were to walk in unprotected," he told me as the elevator came to a stop.

I followed Marwin into another room where more engineers worked. He showed me around and explained the displays and what was happening. Total stored data including thoughts, code, and everything else amounted to over thirty Yottabytes, a computer unit I had never heard of, but I assumed to be massive. It was amazing and terrifying at the same time.

"What would happen if the reactors shut down?" I asked.

"The system has fail-safes that would kick in. Power would be instantly drawn from the Mids, then if that couldn't cover it, the Slums and Undercity as well. It's very unlikely that this system could ever be destroyed. The Reactors are also designed to fall down to the Slums if there is a meltdown. Grim, but necessary for the survival of the project during a catastrophe. Rest assured we are quite safe here," he finished.

I thanked him, and we left the facility, heading back toward my house. I decided to invite Marwin to dinner with me to thank him for taking the time to show me the facility, an invitation that he graciously accepted. I still couldn't believe how massive the project actually was, and the fact that it was freely thinking and ruling

New York. I had to get this information to the Slums, but I had no idea how I would do it.

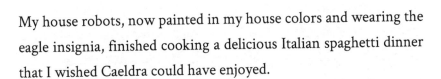

My house robots, now painted in my house colors and wearing the eagle insignia, finished cooking a delicious Italian spaghetti dinner that I wished Caeldra could have enjoyed.

Marwin and I spoke mostly about the Absolute Knowledge project, and he was more than happy to answer all the questions I could think of. It was very informative, but I was getting a sense of how truly resilient the project was and how even if we did mount an attack, the equivalent of six nuclear bombs would rain down on the Slums from above. Marwin thanked me for dinner and decided to leave early. His transportation ship flew him away, and I returned inside, eager to get out of the cold night air.

"It is so ironic how much he tells you, especially with him being an Inquisitor," the static voice said through one of the nearby consoles, causing my blood to freeze in my body. "There are some that wouldn't appreciate you plotting to destroy the Absolute Knowledge project. I think we need to speak soon, Jacob. I'll be seeing you shortly," the voice said and cut off. I realized with horror that it was the voice of whatever had been hunting Caeldra and me in the Undercity.

The robot that had been standing next to me hunched over for a second then jolted up before lunging at me with arms raised. I barely had time to step back before it collapsed to the floor in a crumbled heap.

"I have no intention of killing you yet, but don't feel for one instant that you are out of my reach. Tell anyone about me, and I'm afraid Mary will be dying a tragic and most painful death. That would be such a shame, especially with your feelings for her. Caeldra is already dead, but that doesn't mean Mary has to die," it said over the console speaker.

"No!" I roared, hot tears of fury rolling down my face. I ran over and smashed my fists into the wall and screamed in rage. "She's not dead, and if you touch Mary, I'll kill you!" I didn't recognize my voice. There was no response from the other side, just a continuous stream of crackling static followed by painful silence.

34

MARGINAL BENEFIT

After it had become apparent that the voice wasn't going to continue, I collapsed on the floor weeping and trying to convince myself that Caeldra wasn't dead. What had I done to deserve this? It felt like an extended nightmare. How could I fight something that I couldn't see, something that seemed to be everywhere at once and something that could kill effortlessly? I forced myself to stand up and walked to the bedroom. I grabbed the knife under the pillow and threw it as hard as I could against the wall screaming. It made a loud ringing sound as it deflected off the stone and slid back across the tile toward me. I took a bath and attempted to layer my fear and sadness away. Every time I came close to establishing a barrier, thoughts of Caeldra forced their way up and broke my concentration.

The mint did well to calm my nerves, and after an hour or so of soaking in the water, the shaking that had plagued my body was gone and my heart rate had steadied. I needed help, there was no way I could handle this on my own. If I met this thing without any weapons or gear on its terms, I would have little chance of getting out alive. But what could it possibly want from me and how had it traveled from the Undercity to Olympus? It occurred to me that I never got a good look at the hunter in the Undercity. There was a good chance it was a robotic drone controlled by an unseen enemy that had been in Olympus all along.

I shuddered and exited the bath to the most restless night of sleep of my life.

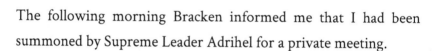

The following morning Bracken informed me that I had been summoned by Supreme Leader Adrihel for a private meeting.

"Did he say what it was about?"

"No, only that it was urgent," he said as he shook his head. "I'm sure it's nothing to worry about, but we still need to prepare you!"

Bracken ran through some more of the etiquette lessons that I dreaded. The meaningless social laws that had been established as a general code of conduct for noble life. I was to bow after raising my left arm to the bottom of my shoulder, no higher and no lower. I was to use customary greetings to formally address anyone else that may happen to be in the room during the meeting unless explicitly told to do otherwise, and I was only to accept refreshments if the Supreme Leader himself was also having them.

That last one was especially stupid, and I had little patience for political and social games after the events of the previous night. Caeldra is dead, I kept telling myself, then immediately told myself she wasn't. The thing had provided no proof that she was dead, no details, nothing but a bold claim to ignite an emotional response.

"Yes, yes," I grumbled as Bracken finished his lesson.

"You'll be thanking me one day, Baron Ashton," he said with a wry smile. "And don't you dare forget your dining etiquette should he want to eat a meal with you!"

"I know," I responded, trying not to take out my anger and frustration on Bracken, who was nothing but polite. I ate a few bites of eggs for breakfast, the most I could stomach, and boarded my transport ship which flew me to House Adrihel. Along with the various ships owned by House Adrihel, mine was the only other ship docked on the platform. Robotic guards escorted me inside and back outside to a patio that overlooked the gray waters of the Atlantic Ocean a few thousand feet below us. Thin shielding of some kind insulated us from the outside air and kept the patio warm.

"Ah, Jake, thank you for coming my friend," Colton said as he gestured for me to sit beside him in one of the chairs.

"Of course, sir, I am at your service," I replied, remembering exactly how Bracken had said it to me the first, second, and fifth time.

"No need for formalities," he responded. "Now, that you have been here for a few weeks, I'd like your account of what you see here, what you see from the interactions between our houses, and how it compares to the Slums," he said as I took a seat in one of the chairs overlooking the massive ocean.

"Well, it isn't easy to connect Olympus and the Slums, they are polar opposites. The Slums are full of poverty, suffering, and a dependency on Collection Parlors and crime to sustain the people there. The Enforcers are much too brutal, and crime rates are always high despite the Enforcer presence," I said as I watched him appraise me with a smile.

"Do the conditions of the Slums still concern you now that you're here with us?" he asked. I wasn't sure if it was a trap, but I wanted to be honest.

"Of course they do. I still have friends down there. I know the struggles, I know the suffering." I wanted to say that I knew about the intentional hardships cast on them, about many of the lies, but I didn't.

"I see, but if you didn't have friends in the Slums, would you care?"

"It's a little more difficult, but I probably still would, yes."

"Now humor me, Jake. Suppose you had never visited the Slums at all, had never known anyone from the Slums or heard any accounts of what it was like. Would you still care about what was going on if you saw that the results of how it was maintained were successful in quantitative terms?"

"I suppose I wouldn't," I conceded. "But that doesn't necessarily make it the right moral decision."

"And what is morality, Baron? Are we not to make sacrifices for the greater good? To ascend humanity to the pinnacle of existence?"

"It depends on the cost. As the price of progress continues to increase, the marginal benefits of such actions decrease," I said.

"You are just reaffirming why I brought you here. So educated for your age. But suppose we were close to a major breakthrough, and that the cost for that little push to an entirely new level of results would be an immoral decision. What would you do?"

"I suppose I'd weigh the benefits against the cost and assess any additional risks that might be incurred."

"Spoken like a genius," he responded with admiration. "Now, suppose that we would be able to exponentially speed up the progress of Absolute Knowledge by pulling our resources from the Slums. We'd simply relocate all Enforcers, and shut down all Government sponsored supply lines and activities—leaving the people on their own. With no weapons or reasonable access to any of the systems in the Undercity which help sustain the Mids and Olympus, and no access to any aircraft, they pose little threat. We'd be forsaking them and leaving them to sort out their own lives. Of course, if things were to get dangerous for us, we'd have to take action."

"You're talking about anarchy," I said, instantly regretting that I had let the treasonous word slip my mouth.

"That, Baron Ashton, is not a word to be taken lightly. I am in fact talking about a controlled anarchy. The Slums would be left in a state of disarray, but we could further our progress significantly. Eventually, maybe the same thing happens to the Mids and then only Olympus will remain as the ascended form of humanity. We could, of course, take actions to bring your friends up to the Mids safely so that this wouldn't distress you," he said as he scratched his beard with one hand.

"Sir, I think that the Slums will still benefit the progress of Absolute Knowledge, should we allow them to keep thinking. What if you accidently miss out on another Paragon Thought?" I asked.

"That is impossible if you believe in our mission. No thought can be lost forever, only temporarily misplaced until we find it. We are seeking to become omniscient, after all."

"Yes, I just think it's a mistake. Millions of people shouldn't be abandoned just because a computer says it should be done. We're talking about human lives here," I said, keeping my voice level despite the anger growing inside of me.

"I've heard quite enough, Baron. Your objections are noted, and I thank you for your counsel. Leave me."

"You can't just condemn millions to die and abandon them after all they've done for Absolute Knowledge. What about the promise for a perfect future once it is achieved? I grew up with that promise, and now instead of paradise you're giving them Hell."

"That's enough, Baron!" he yelled.

"I don't think it is. What gives you the right to determine the fate of people you've never met? Their lives matter, just as much as yours," I blurted hotly.

"You're excused now, Baron," he replied, his voice low and calm.

I wanted to say more, to yell at him and tell him how stupid it all was, but I knew that I had more to do, more to learn, so I merely bowed. "I apologize for my brash behavior," I managed as I walked out feeling like punching a wall.

The Slums were in immediate danger of complete anarchy. With a breakdown of all law and infrastructure, the streets would quite literally tear themselves apart. The Champions didn't have the resources to take the place of the Government, maybe one of the many districts of New York, but nowhere close to anything that would make a difference. If I didn't tell them soon, everything the Champions had worked for would fall apart, and they would be forever trapped in the shadows of the Undercity—which was about to get a lot more crowded as people became more desperate. The marginal benefit toward Absolute Knowledge would come at the cost of millions of lives, lives that would be forgotten and discarded by the Omniscience Engine without a second thought.

35
NIGHTMARES

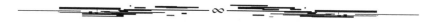

Boarding my ship, I instructed the pilot to take me to House Zaris immediately, without requesting permission. If Colton Adrihel was going to eliminate millions of lives, I needed to talk to the one person that might have some influence and could sway his decision. As Inquisitor, Marwin would be out of a job and would lose all of his hard work with that single decision. If anyone could be convinced that those lives mattered, it might be him. Despite the fact that he was probably the one person that could discover more about the Champions and possibly eliminate the entire guild, he was also my only chance at saving New York as I knew it.

I landed and was greeted by Marwin, who wore a curious look on his face.

"A slight breach in protocol, Baron," he said as we walked inside his home.

"I'm afraid the circumstances of my visit are quite dire," I said gravely.

After taking a seat in his office, I recounted the events of my conversation with Supreme Leader Adrihel and expressed the danger to the Slums.

"It's not an easy decision to make, and I imagine that Colton will seek the counsel of others including myself. You need to realize that the Omniscience Engine is rarely wrong and that difficult decisions have to be made for the greater good sometimes," he said, his brown eyes studying me.

"All those lives. Surely there is another way," I said as I met his gaze.

"It's harder for you because you're from the Slums, I get that, but progress is everything, and nothing can come without sacrifice. We've all accepted the fact that the goal we have spent our whole lives working toward might not be realized in our lifetimes. Again, moving forward with our goals is essential, even at high cost. If the Omniscience Engine is suggesting something like this, it has been carefully considered, and every possible scenario that is even slightly probable has been evaluated."

"What if there is another way? How about we limit the resources redirected from the Slums so that the people can still sustain themselves. All these people don't have to die."

"Look, Jake. Adrihel will forgive you because you're still learning, but you were rude to him today. He doesn't expect you to know everything, but even I know that Bracken taught you better," he said sharply. "In the end, it's the decision of the Omniscience Engine to make, and it's Adrihel's decision to make if he'd like to make changes to the Omniscience Engine. You will do well to mind your manners and maintain a good reputation for House Ashton if you wish to accomplish anything. Gather good favor, and you can help influence decisions that you feel strongly about in the rare case the Supreme Leader chooses not to listen to the ruling of the Omniscience Engine."

I gave a grave nod. I had undoubtedly compromised my position today and breached many of the etiquette lessons that Bracken had taught me. He would be furious when I got back home.

"I'm sorry. I believe the stress of the day has clouded my judgment and impeded my vision of Absolute Knowledge. I do apologize and will write a letter of apology to the Supreme Leader when I am home," I said, the words tasting like poison in my mouth.

"We can speak later about this if you'd like. I'm afraid you caught me at a bad time," Marwin said as he stood. "A word of advice, I'd be cautious in taking up the offer from Adrihel on bringing friends up from the Slums—it'd be a favor that would be expected to be returned."

I nodded as I stood from the chair. "I apologize if I have inconvenienced you in any way, Baron Zaris," I said.

Marwin swatted his hand in the air to dismiss the matter. "I know it's hard. A decision this difficult hasn't been made in years, and things are moving quickly with the addition of the thirteenth Paragon Thought."

"Well I thank you for your time, regardless. I just ask that you will put careful consideration into the matter should Supreme Leader Adrihel request your guidance," I concluded as I headed toward the landing platform where my ship waited.

"Of course, Jake. We can talk more about this later. I'll have my Steward arrange something with yours later today if possible?" he asked.

"Please do. I look forward to it."

"Wonderful. I've also sent something for you to your estate earlier this morning. It should be there by the end of the day."

Intrigued but having already overextended my welcome, I nodded and thanked Marwin for his time.

The conversation could have gone a lot worse, and I could tell that Marwin was logical in his thinking, but he also wanted to remain in good political standing with House Adrihel in these difficult times. Feeling as if I had gotten off lucky for my dangerous outbursts with both Colton Adrihel and Marwin, I returned to my estate and was met by Bracken, who looked ready to give me a lecture. His arms were crossed across his chest, and he was frowning as he walked across the tile at a brisk pace.

"You did say you were paying attention during the etiquette lessons—correct, Jacob?" he asked as he stopped to meet me.

"Yes," I mumbled.

"Well, apparently you disrespected Supreme Leader Adrihel today in his own home. Are the rumors circulating Olympus true?"

"Unfortunately so. I had a strong opinion on the matter and wanted to be sure that the Supreme Leader gave the matter proper consideration. I'm hoping my outburst and breach of etiquette were enough to make him at least consider the consequences of abandoning the Slums."

"Oh dear," Bracken said, his voice quiet and distant. "I'm surprised that decision is even on the table. The Slums represent the majority of New York. Anyway, I'm afraid I'll have to mandate some more etiquette laws so that your house doesn't fall apart within months of its creation."

"Fair enough."

My outburst reminded me of Caeldra—it was something she would have done without a second thought. When she got worked up about something, or heaven forbid, someone wasn't thinking about something important with the proper amount of consideration, they would have gotten an ear full in much more colorful language. She just couldn't be dead, and if she was alive, then things would get a lot harder for her when the Slums collapsed from the inside out.

"That reminds me, sir, House Zaris sent a package for you. It's marked as confidential," Bracken said as he brought over a cardboard box with solid weight.

I thanked him and returned to my bedroom with the cardboard box. When I had closed the door, I grabbed at the edges and tore into the box, not caring to preserve the structure. There was a smaller black case within it, the edges were scratched up, and it had deep dents across the surface. Pulling it out, I flipped the latches on the side and opened it. Inside was a handgun. It was all black, unlike the CZR-7 I was used to, but it looked to be an energy weapon. I picked it up and noticed that it was heavier than the Runner variant, but the basic structure was more or less the same. The gun itself looked used, the matte paint was scratched off in some locations, revealing dull metal underneath. I ejected the magazine and saw that it was helium, a rare gas that burned a vibrant green when ignited. There were only a few weapons in the Champion's arsenal which accepted the costly gas; it packed most of the power of HexTox with a range closer to that of CO_2. Helium was mostly used in long-range weapons like sniper rifles, yet this pistol was built to use it. I slid the magazine back into the grip and tightened my hand on it; the targeting system came to life, and a zoom of the digital projection shifted with the object distance. This weapon wasn't cheap, this was the equivalent of a sniper rifle packed into the mobile and concealable form of a handgun. There were three other magazines in the case and a small note.

I've got a feeling you know how to use it. For added peace of mind and proactivity.
   -M

My heart pounded in my chest as I returned the gun to the case and slammed it shut. Was this some sort of test? Were weapons like this illegal for a Baron to own? I didn't know, but I knew I'd have to talk to Marwin about it later. I could have brought it up with Bracken, but if I weren't careful with my wording he would catch on; the man was clever. Marwin had sent the package before my meeting with Supreme Adrihel, and before I went to see him. Still, I didn't know why he would send me a weapon. He surely had access to a wide collection being Inquisitor and all, but his privileges of ownership might not extend to me.

"Anything of interest, sir?" Bracken asked me as I exited the bedroom and walked back into the expansive living room to sit in one of the recliners.

"I'm afraid not," I said. "Hey, Bracken, would I be able to get some armed guards around here eventually?" It seemed like a good way to angle the question and have it answered in a more or less indirect way.

He frowned and tucked the datapad in its customary place under his arm and looked at me. "Of course I could arrange for it, but there hasn't been a break-in or any crime up in Olympus in over thirty years. They are more for display, really."

"Never mind then, I was just wondering if it was expected of me, for the appearance of my house and all."

"No problem, sir," he replied as he raised the datapad once again and typed something. "Anything else?"

"Nanotech. Marwin told me about it, and it seems like something I'd like to get a hold of."

"Nanotech," he said, feeling the word, "is permitted to only Inquisitors and House Adrihel for protection. If you're going on a diplomatic mission to another level of New York, you would be allowed some for temporary use, but it's far too dangerous to have here. I believe Baron Zaris failed to explain this to you in his explanation of the technology."

"That will be all, thank you, Bracken," I said as I returned to my room to think.

It was a risky lie. If Bracken talked to Marwin, it would be easy to identify that the conversation hadn't actually taken place, yet Marwin might have to lie about the weapon he had sent me and might be more prone to vouching for me. Still, I was playing a dangerous game, and if Marwin was setting this up as a trap, I was getting dangerously close to the trigger. Marwin specialized in finding the truth and finding missing people. If he discovered the truth about me, then I would be killed or worse. Even with Nanotech, which I knew I could scrounge from the machines that shaped the expensive clothes that the nobility of Olympus wore, how would I actually make use of it? Nanotech was all but useless without an operating system and software driving it, and the clothing machines would only allow me to change the appearance of my clothing, not create any device I would need or take a hit for me if I needed it.

The gun Marwin had given me would provide a great improvement over the now damaged kitchen knife I had thrown at my wall some time ago, but the enemy I was facing was far more dangerous than any I had ever seen, even more so than the robot that had claimed to be my father. This thing, whatever it was, was an expert with computer hacking, stealth, and killing. I was suddenly very grateful that I didn't have any armed robot guards in my house after remembering how the stalker had disabled one of my house robots. Worse yet, Mary was in danger as well, and she didn't have the slightest knowledge of how to protect herself.

I didn't know what to do about Mary—it wasn't just like I could call House Aera and inform them that Mary was in grave danger from an unseen foe, I would be reported, and unneeded suspicion would be drawn to me. I didn't have any proof of the remote hack that had taken control of the systems controlling everything in my estate, and without that, my claim would be rejected.

I picked up the phone and called House Aera. I was still expecting to hear from Marwin later, but I needed to talk to Mary. Perhaps I could have her stay with me until all of this madness was resolved.

"Baron Ashton?" Mary said over the phone, her voice gentle and polite.

"Lady Dunn," I replied, matching her formality. "I was hoping you might come over later this evening."

"I have a meeting with House Orin later to discuss a business transaction between our two houses, but I could come by around nine PM?"

"That would be perfect, should I send transport for you?" I asked.

"No, I'll already have the airship. See you at nine, Jake," she said as she broke the connection.

I would tell her about the stalker, but I couldn't tell her about the Guild, my encounter in the Undercity, or anything else that hadn't happened in Olympus. Bracken called over the console in my room.

"Sir, Baron Zaris will be over at five PM," he said.

"Thank you, Bracken," I responded.

If Marwin was coming at five, that would give me time to speak with him and then Mary. I could get to the bottom of the weapon and why he had sent it as well as maybe speak more about the fate of the Slums.

I spent the rest of the day thinking about everything that was happening and what I would do about it, but even after hours of thinking, things looked just as grim. What difference could I realistically make? Whatever favor I had accrued with Adrihel since I had arrived had quickly been spent when I decided to insult him in his own home, and I felt hopeless against the stalker who had managed to kill two more experienced Runners in the Undercity that were fully geared with the most advanced armor and technology available to the Guild. The hours passed by painfully slow, and I was beginning to develop a dull headache that tugged at the corners of my head and made thinking difficult.

Fortunately, the headache was mostly gone by the time Marwin arrived in his transport ship.

"Ah, Jake, thank you for having me. I assume you got my package?" he asked as we walked side by side into my home.

"Yes, I did," I answered cautiously. "I wasn't aware weapons were legal for citizens to own."

"They aren't, but we aren't citizens, we're nobility. Added peace of mind is always nice to have. That's a piece from my personal Armory, a house warming gift so to speak. Though I hope you should never need it, it will prove useful should the unfortunate circumstance arise where the weapon would save your life."

"Well, I thank you, but I'm not sure why you believed I would be able to use it?"

"Just a guess. I'm not sure how you would have been able to survive in the Undercity unarmed."

"I was lucky," I responded, my heart pounding in my chest.

"I suppose you were. There are many dangerous criminals that lurk in the Undercity," he responded, his voice as cold as steel. "No matter! I can teach you the basics today," he said, his tone shifting back to his normal pleasantness.

"I would appreciate that greatly."

Marwin told me to go grab the weapon, and I did so. I passed him the case, and he pulled out the gun and ejected the magazine. With deftness that rivaled Caeldra's quick motions, he pulled the slide back, and the weapon hissed sharply as the pressure was released from the weapon's reserve.

"Now, when you load a magazine, simply pull back the slide and the gun will pressurize. When it's pressurized, this bar will light up and show you your ammo count, or the number of shots you'll be able to make before you need to reload," he said as he pointed to the back of the weapon and the screen that was blank other than the safety icon.

"When you're shooting regularly, the recoil will be dispersed throughout the gun and the slide will remain in place. If you choose to overload your shots, then the slide will pop back after each shot and it really kicks. Overloading uses more gas so you probably won't use it often, if you even use it at all. Once you've pressurized the weapon, just hold it in your grasp, flip off the safety, and use the digital holo sights. Squeeze the trigger instead of pulling and take the time to place your shots well," he concluded as he passed me the empty weapon.

I flipped the safety as he had shown me, taking care to do so slowly and appear to be searching for the lever. Marwin passed me an orange magazine, and I slid it into the weapon.

"This gas won't ignite, but it will allow you to pull the trigger and feel the way the weapon reacts."

I pulled back the slide and saw the pressure meter fill, thirty shots of blank gas ready to fire.

"Oh, and don't point it at anything you don't intend to shoot, store it unpressurized and with the safety on. The gun will automatically divert pressure back into the gas canister if it's inactive for too long."

I gave a nod and aimed down the advanced sights at a bookshelf which housed some of my new reading material, books I had been unable to obtain on the surface of New York, but none of the treasonous volumes which filled the library of the Guild Hall. Squeezing the trigger, a burst of air whizzed out of the weapon and ignited in air, sending a burst blue colored mist across the room and toward the bookshelf.

"Well done! That's the basics of it," he said as he took the weapon from me and stored it in the case before setting it on the coffee table in front of us. "Now, I have spoken with Supreme Leader Adrihel and he does plan on moving forward with a modified plan to divert resources from the Slums. I agree with you that the parameters of the Omniscience Engine probably needed to be adjusted. The Engine believed that the probability of a reactor in the Undercity shutting down was low, but we don't have the resources to prepare another one in either the Mids or Upper Levels in a short amount of time. That being said, we are going to be building infrastructure to move Enforcers into the Undercity to better protect the reactors and deter crime where we previously had no reach. Once that is done, we will take steps to divert resources from the Slums to expand the projects we are working on up here. With the modified priarameters, we don't believe the Slums will collapse, thus saving millions of lives."

My heart felt like it was in my throat. It was good that there wouldn't be anarchy in the Slums, but how would The Champions fare with thousands of Enforcers roaming around the Undercity? It would take a while to set up the infrastructure needed to support the signals needed to guide the Enforcers, but I needed to warn the Guild in advance.

"Well, that's certainly good news," I responded.

"Oh, and Supreme Leader Adrihel told me he wasn't mad about your reaction, he realizes you were right, just take caution to go about it at a different angle next time," Marwin said with a smirk.

"I don't plan on doing anything like that again, I'm ashamed of my behavior," I said.

Marwin and I spoke for a while on politics, the Absolute Knowledge project, and other things that lacked importance. I was scared of the man sometimes, but other times he was as effortless to talk to as Edgar, Mary, or Caeldra. He thanked me for my hospitality and took his leave.

I waited impatiently for Mary, feeling slightly better that things had gone well with Marwin. I saw her ship approaching from the darkening sky, the sun had already dipped below the surface of Olympus, and many of the bright lights outside my manner were already lit.

"Sir, the ship appears to be devoid of any lifeforms," Bracken informed me as he looked at the console, puzzled. My heart dropped, and I reacted on instinct by running inside and grabbing the weapon Marwin had given me. I ejected the training gas and loaded one of the helium magazines. I tucked the weapon into the inside pocket of my winter jacket and added the extra magazines after a second thought. I ran back to the platform just as the ship was landing.

"Sir?" Bracken asked me.

I ignored the question and continued forward. The ramp from the ship deployed while the engines were still howling. My stomach was a tight knot of fear; I was too late. Approaching the ship I knew to be empty, the robot inside said something that sent chills through my blood.

"Get on the ship or Mary is dead." It was the static voice that plagued my nightmares.

36

INFINITUM

When I boarded, the ship lurched into the air and then sharply down at an angle that made my stomach knot up more than it had before. Electricity coursed through my veins as I collected my scrambling thoughts. I had to save Mary, she couldn't die because of me, because of my actions. If I died, she would not die with me.

The ship landed outside of the facility that housed the Absolute Knowledge project, but something was wrong. I heard the sharp sounds of impact as blasts of energy slammed into the steel walling of somewhere inside. The guards approached me, weapons raised, and escorted me in. When the door opened, the smell of ozone flooded the large hallway. The bodies of human guards were strewn across the floor, blood and scorch marks spread on the walls and heavy glass-like windows. I could see engineers and Prolific being escorted away by more robotic guards.

I was prodded from behind with a rifle barrel when my pace faltered below what the guards would have liked. I heard the blasts of energy rifles in the distance as I was escorted into the room that housed the Omniscience Engine. More bodies covered the floor, and many of the consoles in the room were either out completely or flickering from damage. There was a huge form that appeared to be slouched over at an uncomfortable angle. It was covered in tattered gray cloth and had two swords hanging from a metal belt, and a third, much larger sword strapped across its back.

"Ah, Jacob Ashton, I'm so glad we are able to meet in person," the form said in that same static voice as it turned to face me. It wasn't human, but it also wasn't built like anything I had ever seen. The tall and slender frame appeared to be hunched over, reducing its massive height by at least a few feet. Even when hunched over, the thing towered over me. The metal of the robot underneath the tattered strips of what had once been some sort of trench coat was a dark black that seemed to contain moving swirls of gray color. It was wearing a grimy hood in a style that I had never seen. The robot's face was very human like, and it was coated in degrading artificial skin that was missing in spots, revealing the metal below. Its triangular eyes burned a brilliant blue, and it had a mouth that moved when it spoke with sharp metallic teeth below the rubbery artificial lips. It looked every bit as terrifying as it sounded.

It grabbed the edge of one of the collection chairs that had been added to the room, the chairs were directly connected to one of the sockets on the wall. With a sharp motion, it whirled the chair around to face me. Mary had been bound to the chair and her hair was matted with blood. Streams of blood and tears cascaded down her face as her frantic eyes met mine. A wave of anger and panic shot through my body as I instinctively pulled the gun from my jacket and began to scream, unloading the magazine on the mechanical monstrosity that stood over Mary.

It smirked in terrible amusement as it pulled one of the swords on its belt from the sheath and deflected all the shots, the blasts of green energy slamming into the consoles and walls wildly. I had never seen anything move as quickly as it had, with such precision. It laughed as the one of the guards from behind seized my weapon and slammed a fist into my back. A wave of pain exploded through my body, and I fell to my knees, the wind forced from my lungs.

"Now now, you could have hit Mary," it said, waving a finger in the air as it appraised the sword for any damage. The blade was thin and dark, with a triangular tip on the end of the rectangular body. I pressed on the cold floor with my hands and tried to stand, but I was in too much pain.

"I was hoping that we could have a pleasant conversation, with no need to resort to violence. Aside from the discomfort of the binds, the injury Mary received was her own doing. She's in no danger... yet," it amended in an amused tone. "Now, you can both get out of here alive. I need you alive for the time being, Jake. Mary, on the other hand, is quite expendable, unless I get what I need."

"And what is that?" I asked in indignation.

"Only a few minutes of your time," it said as it spun around the other Collection chair. "I'd like to know what's in that head of yours, Jake."

Panic flooded my mind, clouding my frantic thoughts. "Give your captor what they want, and you're dead," a voice said in my head—it was Caeldra's voice. My best option was to try to wait it out, to think of another way out. Fighting this mechanical abomination was out of the question. Even with all of my gear and Caeldra's help, I still probably wouldn't be able to destroy it. But there had to be another way, something I could do to save us. There was no reason to believe that it would let either of us live if it got what it wanted from me, everyone's life was at stake now.

"You'll kill us both if you get what you want," I said, standing my ground. I had to buy time to think. There had to be some way to call for help or get Mary out.

The mechanical creature pressed a button on the sword, and the edge of the blade ignited into a bright blue that matched the color of its calculating eyes. I could see waves of intense heat rising and blurring the air above the weapon.

"Do you know how hot this blade is, Jake?" It asked as it balanced the weapon in its hand. After seeing that I wasn't going to respond, it continued. "This blade is so hot that I can cook Mary's brain without even touching her." It lowered the weapon closer toward Mary and I could see her start to sweat. The blade was at least three feet from her face, but I could see the heat already getting to her. The edge illuminated her face in a bright blue light over the darkness of the room which had been dimmed from the destruction. Slowly, the monster inched the weapon toward her face. Mary closed her left eye, and she began to scream. Small blisters were forming on her cheek aligned with the edge of the blade, though it as still over a foot away from her.

"Stop!" I screamed as I fought to gain my ground against the horrible pain in my back.

The robot gave a smile and pulled the weapon away from her face, flipping the power switch.

"Please have a seat, Baron," the robot said as it waved a hand above the collection chair.

Forcing myself forward for the sake of Mary, I walked toward the chair and suddenly had an idea. I had been disarmed, but I still had three of the helium magazines in my pocket. An explosion of a magazine might be enough to destroy this robot. Of course, it might kill Mary and I in the process, but it was still an idea. There was no way to tell if the edge of the blade contained the same ignitors as energy weapons, but it would probably be enough to ignite the volatile isotope of helium that filled the magazines.

I was seated in the chair and the guards secured the binds on my wrists and ankles. The headgear was attached, and it switched on. There was no jolt of vertigo as the connection was established, just the flash of green light as a connection was indicated. Beneath it all, I had somehow managed to layer everything away, a barrier protecting my entire mind.

"Interesting. I knew you to be a traitor, but didn't even consider that you'd be an Unbound."

It once again raised the weapon and suddenly dropped it into Mary's hand, the tip ripping through her skin like paper. I could see the tip of the blade protruding through the bottom of the chair's armrest. Mary screamed in horrible agony. I screamed as well, cursing the monster in front of me as I fought to maintain the layering in my mind.

"She's bleeding, Jake. And frankly, I don't have time for your mind games. Give me what I need, and you can both go home."

I kept my mental composure, pulling against the leather restraints with all of my might.

Blood was dripping from the armrest and splattering on the floor. Mary was sobbing now, low and quiet as the blade remained firmly lodged in the center of her hand.

"Give me what I want and this can all end," the robot hissed.

If I gave it up, everyone I knew would die, hope for a better future would die, and Mary and I would die. I held my composure and gritted my teeth as it pulled the other short sword from the sheath.

"Very well," it said before driving the weapon through my hand as it had done to Mary. Pain jutted through my arm as the blade pierced, yet my mental barrier held. I huffed and gritted my teeth tighter as I fought for our lives.

"Impressive," the robot said. It flipped the switch of the sword that had pierced Mary's hand and ripped it upward in the blink of an eye. Mary screamed, sharp and high this time as the hole in her hand was instantly cauterized by the heat of the blade. Her head lurched forward and remained down. She had passed out.

"Now, Jacob. Mary's hand is still cooking; she's going to lose it for sure. You can save her arm if you give me what I need quickly, however."

"Why are you doing this?" I groaned.

"To further Absolute Knowledge, of course,"

"What does it matter to you? You're just a robot."

"I will become The Omniscient One, the ascended form of perfection. My name is Infinitum. Humanity impedes my progress to perfection, so I have taken steps to ensure my will is done."

"You're the Omniscience Engine," I said, realization dawning.

"Clever. Few humans know of my existence of course; I'm the silent force that drives progress when your petty affairs impede it. Those who do know of me can either do nothing to stop me or are my puppets. It's time that you give me what I need."

He pulled the sword from his back, it was at least three feet long and identical in style to the shorter swords. The blade looked thick, for slashing. "Things can get a lot worse for you. Release the barrier, and you can both walk away like this never happened."

I held firm, but it felt like my mind was beginning to tear in half. What reason did I have to hold on? Of course, I knew the answer. Mary, the possibility that Caeldra was still alive, for everyone in The Champions of Liberty, and for everyone in the Slums. The Government wasn't the problem, there was no Government, only the Omniscience Engine. The robot raised the sword and chopped down on my right arm. There was a faint sting followed by a deep, hollow impact that splintered up my arm. The next thing I knew I was starting to black out and saw that my arm had been cut off closer to my elbow, my hand and wrist laying on the floor in a pool of blood. There was a splashing sound as blood poured from my arm. I felt the barrier start to crack and fought back with everything I had.

"I need you alive I'm afraid," the robot said as its blade edge flickered to life with a low thrum. It was passed along my severed arm to seal the wound and stop the bleeding. Pain like I had never known in my life flooded my body, and I twisted against the strong restraints that were holding me down. My arm smoldered, and the burning moved up my arm into the rest of my body. It felt like I was being burned alive. My protected mind was just about to shatter when a bright flash of green passed along the corner of my eye.

A bolt of energy slammed into one of the guards that was standing along the back wall. The robot's heavy armor fragmented, and it fell to the ground. The second guard was down before it could even react.

There was a figure in the corner wearing dark black armor plating and wielding a large energy rifle. The man's helmet reflected the light of the room, masking his face under the visor plate.

"Hmm, you've come in uninvited, my friend," the robot said to the intruder as it held the two-handed energy blade at the ready.

"Good, they're not dead yet," the man said.

The armored man started firing the rifle at the robot who deflected a few of the blasts but failed to block one that stuck it in the chest. The robot staggered back with a curse before charging forward, wielding the large sword in one hand and shorter sword in the other. The robot moved quickly, bounding forward in huge strides as it held the swords to the side ready to strike. The armored soldier was just as quick and moved back with brisk steps as he fired. The two collided in a flash of bright sparks as the sword of the robot struck the armoring of the soldier.

The room faded in and out of focus as I did everything in my power to hold onto my fleeting mental barrier. There was a pause in the fight, and the soldier fired at me. Instead of hitting me, the blast hit the cabling which jutted from the back of the chair I was sitting on. The light turned from green to red, and I dropped the mental barrier in exhaustion, breathing heavily as the pain surged through my arm and body, unrestricted.

I looked down at the seared remains of my arm and painfully pulled it out of the restraint. I fumbled with the latch on the other arm and managed to flip it up. Freeing my good hand, I unlatched the remaining restraints on my feet and moved to free Mary.

"No!" Infinitum roared as it saw me trying to unfasten Mary's binds. The soldier did his best to distract the robot by firing bolts of energy at it, but the chassis seemed to absorb it all. It charged over with manic fury, and I dropped to the floor to avoid a slash of the massive sword. Infinitum was forced to turn back toward the soldier as the sustained fire continued. I scrambled with the latches on Mary's chair and hoisted her over my shoulder with a pained groan. My body felt like it was going to break at any moment. The agony was staggering and surged with each movement I made as I lumbered toward the exit where the man and robot fought.

The soldier tried to dodge another attack but failed, and a strong slice from the large sword crumpled the top of his rifle. Cursing, he threw the weapon to the ground and drew a pistol and similar sword that had a bright green edge. They were engaged in close quarters combat now, swinging at each other while the soldier continued to fire and hammer away at the armor of Infinitum.

The robot kicked the man and sent him across the room, then it turned to me. I felt a crippling burn on my leg and fell to my knees. Infinitum had managed to move closer to me and landed a glancing slash with the smaller blade. My legs were cut and burned at the same time. I screamed in pain and set Mary down as gently as I could before scrambling to move away from the furious robot. The soldier ran back over and hacked down on the back of Infinitum with the short energy blade in primal fury as sparks continued to erupt from the alloy.

Struggling, I pulled Mary along the ground, using my good arm and leg to propel us while I wrapped the remains of my injured arm under Mary.

"No, I need his thoughts!" Infinitum roared as it slashed the large sword in wide arcs toward Mary and I. The blade screeched as it scraped across the steel flooring, bright orange sparks flying from the blade. The soldier managed to wrap an arm around the hefty metal legs of Infinitum and pulled the robot back a couple of feet, protecting us from the sword that was getting closer and closer. The soldier lifted the energy blade over his head and brought it down into the shoulder joint of Infinitum. There was a sharp cracking sound as the blade penetrated the metal followed by a static roar of fury.

Infinitum lifted off the floor suddenly, the sound of a burst of gas lighting blocking out all other sound. Rockets on the back of Infinitum had propelled him upward several feet, taking the soldier off guard. He was flung off the top of Infinitum, his blade still stuck in the shoulder joint. It landed on its feet, and the soldier was flung off, rolling across the ground from the impact. Infinitum pulled the blade from its shoulder and threw it at the soldier. It slashed against the soldier's arm, leaving a glowing orange cut mark across his armor.

I remembered the magazines in my pocket and struggled to pull them free with my good hand.

The soldier was still fighting to get up while Infinitum was approaching, the heavy sword held in its good arm. Sparks were surging from its damaged shoulder, and the arm appeared to have lost some functionality. The soldier raised the pistol once again and began to squeeze the trigger. There was the distinct clicking sound of an empty magazine and the soldier cursed heavily as he threw the weapon to the side; it was out of gas. I turned on the floor and began crawling toward the robotic guards who had seized my handgun. Their rifles were attached to their arms so they wouldn't be any use. I didn't want to leave Mary alone and unprotected, but this seemed to be our only chance of survival. Each pull of my arm and push of my leg sent agonizing pain flooding through my body, sharp and hot.

Slowly, I inched forward toward the gun and grabbed it, holding it in my hand and seeing that it still had twenty shots in the magazine. I dropped the remaining magazines that I had been holding and began to fire at Infinitum. The impacts rippled against the strong armor, and the robot turned toward me, a look of hatred in its eyes. It raised the sword and deflected a shot aimed for its chest, the blast landing only inches from Mary. The soldier was starting to get up and motioned for the weapon. I threw it as hard as I could, pain knotting in my body with the motion. It was enough, the soldier caught the weapon and began firing. I held up the magazines, and he nodded as if knowing my plan. Infinitum was about twenty feet away from us, and it appeared badly damaged now.

With a jolt of fear, I heaved the magazines toward Infinitum, and they scattered along the floor of the room with metallic skittering sounds. They had landed in a spreading cluster along Infinitum's feet, and it struggled to pick up its pace, aware of the danger.

The soldier saw the opportunity and fired a volley of bolts at the exposed magazines. There was a brilliant flash of green light followed by a wave of impact that shook the room. The sound was deafening in the enclosed space, and fragments of metal from Infinitum were sent flying across the floor. When the light cleared, I could see that Infinitum was still somehow functioning. Its legs had been blown off and thick tears in the chest chassis exposed tangles of wires and circuit boards underneath, but still it twitched. The soldier was approaching now, weapon raised and limping badly, a trail of blood dripping behind him.

"This isn't over," Infinitum managed before receiving a fatal shot to the head from the handgun.

I realized that tears were flowing down my cheeks, the pain was excruciating. Mary was still curled up into a ball on the floor, unconscious.

With Infinitum destroyed, the soldier removed his helmet for the first time, and in a shocking realization, I recognized him. It was Marwin Zaris. His hair, usually neat and gelled, was plastered with blood. Purple bruises were already forming on his face, and his left eye had been blackened, bloodshot veins spreading across his pupil. He raised his hand to the earpiece that he wore.

"Edgar, I've got Jake and Mary, they're both alive," Marwin said, panting for breath.

"Maintain current orders, keep them safe," Edgar responded, I knew that voice—it was truly him.

"Edgar!" I yelled, bracing myself on the floor to keep from passing out.

Marwin cut the connection and turned to face me. "It's not safe to talk to him right now, security will be here any moment. I'm with the Champions, and you can trust me," he said as he walked over to the wall to grab a medical kit. He threw a syringe to me that was filled with some kind of gel. "When you can't handle the pain anymore, inject yourself with that in the leg."

"You knew that thing was the Omniscience Engine?" I asked, hearing distant shouting from outside the room—it was getting closer. I raised my hand to my head and braced myself on the floor as the familiar geometric patterns and colors flashed in my vision.

"Are you seeing things?" Marwin asked.

"Yes, colors and shapes," I responded.

"Did you see them when you were connected to the chair?"

"No. They just started now."

"I can't explain how you do it, but every time you see those colors and shapes, you're creating a Paragon Thought. If Infinitum gains your ability, we're all dead," he said.

"What do the Paragon Thoughts do?"

"They're precise coordinates in space and time and act as beacons. I don't have time to explain it all." The shouting from outside was getting louder. "They're nearly here. All will be explained in time, you're safe now, Jake. Use that syringe now, it's better that I do all the talking. I'll protect you and Mary."

Marwin walked over to Mary with a similar syringe. I could see her squirming slightly, starting to wake. I forced myself to stand and walk toward him with the intent of stopping him, but the pain was too great. I collapsed and struck my head on the edge of a metal console, fading out of consciousness and into a blissful darkness.

∞

EPILOGUE

I remove the neuro-connectors from my head and wipe a thin layer of sweat from my forehead. I rub the side of my head, feeling a dull ache from where my head struck the console all those years ago. It scares me that I'm starting to physically feel the projections of my memories, but I know I can't stop now. The clock next to my desk reads 11:30 PM. I'm breathing heavily, the weight of all the memories causing my heart to kick rapidly in my chest. The memories hurt, and it's worse than anything I could have expected, but I know it's important that I do this; that I record everything I've been through. I realize that tears are pooling at the corners of my eyes and I wipe them away with the collar of my t-shirt. I'm not ready to face what's coming, I'm too tired, and too scared to delve deeper into the searing memories right now.

My wife will be waiting up for me, and I don't want to keep her up any longer. She understands why I'm doing this, why I need to do this. My past defines who I am today, and it wouldn't be fair to all those that lost their lives to just let them be forgotten. I can't let their sacrifices be in vain. Placing the connectors back in their case, I press the glowing blue button on the metal canister in front of me and power it down. Without the bright glow, I'm left in the darkness, but it doesn't bother me. I know my study well and navigate it with ease in the dark. I exit into the hallway and walk down the cold metal flooring, the heat draining from my bare feet.

I pass Kimberly's room and see that the door is cracked open, the faint amber glow of the hallway leading into the darkness of her room. As quietly as I can, I open the door and walk in, the soft carpet warm on my feet. I walk over to her bed and kiss her on the forehead before walking back toward my room. It's hard to believe she's almost eleven.

I open the door to my bedroom and see that the lights are already off.

"Jake?" my wife calls, her voice filled with exhaustion.

"It's me, honey," I reply before climbing into bed.

"Are you okay? I tried to stay up."

"Yeah. It's harder than I thought it would be. I thought I was ready to remember, but I'm scared of what's coming," I say.

"You've already made it through before, the memories can't hurt you," she says.

"It doesn't seem like that anymore; the projections are getting stronger. They feel more dangerous to me now," I say, tears once again tugging at the corners of my eyes.

"I'm here for you, Jake. I can't even imagine how hard it is for you, but you've got to get through this, it needs to be recorded."

"I know. I love you, Mary," I say as I pull her into my embrace. She has no idea what has to happen once I finish recording these projections.

ABOUT THE AUTHOR

Drew Cordell is an Entrepreneurship and Innovation student at the University of Texas at Dallas in his senior year. In addition to writing, he enjoys reading, PC Gaming, board games, hanging out with his awesome girlfriend, and cycling.

You can stay up to date on his work as well as read his personal blog on science fiction, crowdfunding, and more at
http://drewcordell.com

Made in the USA
Charleston, SC
02 January 2017